2018-228

The Other La Bohème

Yorker Keith

The Autor of *Remembrance of Blue Roses*

OVERTURE

Begin your song, oh Muses.
Let me join the zesty tune.
My heart needs no more sorrow,
Neither discord nor despair.
Induce me to embrace love,
Peace, and hope in harmony.
Lift, lift me up, oh Muses.
Let us sing a song of joy.

ACT I

Scene 1

*M*uses were singing in glory in the fine October sky—
the image Henry saw in the clouds as he strolled along
Broadway near 72nd Street, several blocks from the Metropolitan
Opera House. He even recognized the Muses' sweet song. His chest
swelled in anticipation as he continued a few blocks to the Café
Momus, where his friend Stephanie was working as a waitress. The
restaurant attracted a loyal clientele among connoisseurs of opera
and classical music, who appreciated the authentic French cuisine
at reasonable prices, especially before or after a performance at one
of the many nearby theaters. Henry paused outside the window
and peered in. Since it was not yet five o'clock, patrons occupied
fewer than half of the thirty-odd tables. Stephanie stood before the
bar in her black uniform, casually watching the customers. Henry
fished a digital pitch-maker from his pocket and found C-sharp. He

cleared his throat and inhaled, assuming the role of Marcello. Then he burst through the door and began singing, extending his hand toward Stephanie.

"*O Musette, o gioconda sorridente!*" ("Oh Musette, oh radiant smile!")

Stephanie broke into just such a smile as Henry continued his serenade in his burning tenor voice, praising her charms. His rich tones reverberated in the intimate restaurant. Stephanie immediately replied to his aria in her coloratura mezzo-soprano, wagging her right index finger.

"*Badate! I miei difetti non nascondo.*" ("Mind you! I don't hide my defects.")

She cautioned Marcello that she was a capricious vagrant, living day to day. When she completed her aria, both joined in a duet: Marcello, adoring her, and Musette, warning him. The music entwined to a dramatic climax with a soaring high A, then descended slowly, ending with their simultaneous murmur: "*Musette!*"…"*Badate!*"

"Bravo!" Waiters and waitresses shouted their kudos while the patrons applauded. Henry bowed and Stephanie curtsied. As they rose, they met each other's eyes and laughed.

Henry took a table amid the traditional mahogany furnishings. Sepia photographs of mid-nineteenth-century Paris in Art Nouveau frames, lit by Belle-Époque crystal lamps, accented the walls: le Quartier Latin, Montmartre, l'Opéra de Paris, la Comédie Française, and le Pont Neuf. Henry nodded to the proprietor of the café—a portly, cultivated Frenchman in his sixties with gray curly hair and a dapper mustache who seemed to date from the same period. Legend had it that in his youth he had wanted to be an actor.

His wish had not materialized, and fate instead had bestowed upon him his restaurant. He had named it the Café Momus in honor of the café in his beloved opera *La Bohème*. His sympathies remained with singers and actors, who endured challenging lives in Manhattan while pursuing their dreams, and he generously hired them as waiters and waitresses. So his employees and patrons alike affectionately called him Père Momus.

As Stephanie appeared next to Henry, waiting to take his order, Père Momus bustled over, grinning with approval.

"*Très bien*, Henry," he said. "This duet is new to me. *Qu'est-ce que c'est?*"

"It's Leoncavallo's *La Bohème*," Henry answered, beaming with pride. "Stephanie and I are studying it now. We'll be performing it next March."

Père Momus raised his bushy eyebrows. "Leoncavallo? Not Puccini?"

"That's right. Puccini's is famous. But Leoncavallo, too, composed *La Bohème*. You must come and hear it. It's as good as Puccini's, and not many people know about it. Besides, all four of us from our group Dolci Quattro are in it—including Stephanie."

Père Momus gave a Gallic shrug. "Such riches! I won't miss it." He turned to Stephanie. "Why don't you take a break, my diva, and chat with your co-star?"

Stephanie broke into Musette's smile again and withdrew to the kitchen. From there came sounds of clapping and whistles. Her laughter, too. Père Momus sat next to Henry.

"Your voice always makes me happy," the older man said, patting Henry's shoulder. "Whenever I see you, I fancy you're an actor. You know, I always wanted to specialize in Racine's tragedies."

Henry knew the legend, but this was the first time he had heard Père Momus mention Racine. The comment intrigued him, because some of Racine's plays, like *Andromaque* and *Iphigénie*, had been adapted into operas. He imagined Père Momus performing these on the stage. In his more slender days, he must have looked Hollywood handsome.

"You would have made a fine actor," Henry said.

The old man narrowed his eyes as though trying to visualize his early years. "*C'est vrai.* The world has missed out on a great talent." He clasped Henry's shoulder once again. "Youth is a gift. Enjoy it while you can." He stood. "*Bon,* carry on, *mon ami.* I want you to be a great opera singer."

"*Merci beaucoup, monsieur,*" Henry said. "You're too kind."

As Père Momus headed for the kitchen, Henry surveyed the waiters and waitresses who were attending customers. They were all singers and actors. In the early years of his singing career, he, too, had worked here for extra money. He would always feel grateful to Père Momus. Now Henry no longer needed to do this kind of work because he had a job as a web developer for a mutual fund company near Wall Street. One of the fringe benefits was the flexible working hours. He could come to his office earlier and leave earlier when he had lessons and rehearsals. The salary was adequate to pay his rent and fees for lessons. In all, he felt content as far as his financial situation was concerned—but if only he could make a living by singing alone. He checked his iPhone for messages, then visited his web pages on the Internet, something he was required to do every hour or so in order to address any emergency or malfunction on the website. Today was a peaceful Saturday. He patted his gadget.

Stephanie returned with a big teapot, two cups, and two generous slices of fruit tart. She announced that dessert and tea were presents from Père Momus. Henry rubbed his palms and grinned. She sat down next to him and served them both. Admiring her short brunette hair, hazel eyes, and gently upward-curved nose, he thought she looked twenty-five instead of thirty-three.

"I just came from a coaching session with Mr. Carré," he told her. "I made it all the way through Act I." He pointed to the thick music score on the table. "I can do it."

"That's great. A few days ago I worked on the same part with my coach. I must have sung this phrase ten times."

She flipped through several pages of the score and showed him the passage she had rehearsed the most. Nodding sympathetically, he put the score safely on a chair beside him, then speared a piece of cake and savored the sweet taste. The hot tea felt soothing after the singing. He glanced toward the door to see an attractive blonde woman and a sturdy man enter the café, both carrying thick scores.

"Hey, it's Jennifer and John," he said. "How perfect!"

After enthusiastic hugging, kissing, and handshaking, the four friends ceremoniously presented their right hands forward, their palms stacked one on top of the other.

"Sing on!" they shouted, then burst into a belly laugh.

As they took chairs at the same table, other patrons turned their heads, frowning as if to say, "Those singers; that's enough. Let us eat in peace, will you?" Henry saw Père Momus reappear from the kitchen. He shook a warning finger at the clamor, but his eyes twinkled. He soon came back with tart slices and tea for Jennifer and John.

"Dessert for Dolci Quattro!" he announced. "The Sweet Four!"

The four singers chorused their thanks and dug in.

Jennifer nibbled the final crumbs from her fork. "I just finished with my coach," she said in her coloratura soprano, her green eyes sparkling. "I'm almost through with Act I. I'm making good progress, so I thought I should treat myself to a pastry. And then I ran into John."

"Me too," chimed in John in his sonorous baritone. "I rehearsed Act I with my coach just now." He swiped his olive-toned forehead. "Whew! But I'm getting there."

On his friends' faces, Henry saw the same excitement he felt. How long it seemed since they had finished their master's degrees at the Manhattan School of Music together. Reluctant to separate, they had formed Dolci Quattro, pledging to support one another as they ventured into the world of professional opera.

"Do you remember our graduation performance of Puccini's *La Bohème*?" he said. "We were great, right?" He met his friends' eyes, one by one. "I still can't believe we've now got the same principal roles in Leoncavallo's version. It's challenging. I can sing Puccini's Rodolfo from memory, but I have to learn Leoncavallo's Marcello from scratch, because he is the tenor. And John has to switch roles too, because Rodolfo is a baritone here. Jennifer is still Mimi, but for Stephanie, the mezzo is named Musette, not Musetta. It's confusing."

"It is," Jennifer said. "But no excuses. We have to sing well, and we have less than five months to prepare."

Stephanie shook her hands in the air. "It's so exciting! Since Leoncavallo's *Bohème* is rarely performed, this will be our big chance to get attention."

"Absolutely," John affirmed. "I feel like we're just one step before the Met."

"We've come a long way since graduation," Henry said. "Even though our group hasn't sung at any first-tier opera companies yet, at least we've been living as professional opera singers. I couldn't have survived without you guys." He saw his friends nodding.

"Yes, it's not easy," said Stephanie. "But our creed seems to be working well for us. Remember? *Absolutely no hanky-panky between us.* I swear I haven't slept with Henry or John." She giggled.

"I'm engaged to Richard," Jennifer declared, showing her ring.

"I'm married to Michelle," said John, also displaying his ring.

"And I haven't slept with Jennifer or Stephanie!" Henry pressed his palm against his heart.

They laughed. Henry thought they were all feeling the same gratitude that they had kept their pledge. They turned to another subject, the casting. Arthur DeSoto, their artistic director, had a reputation for picking the best singers available to him. He had given Schaunard, an important role, to Mike Walton. According to John, Mike was a tall, polite black man with a big smooth baritone voice— the kind of guy they could get along with well.

"We should arrange a rehearsal with him as soon as possible," Henry suggested.

"What about the understudies?" Stephanie asked.

"It's amazing," Henry replied. "Irene is Jennifer's understudy, and Bruce is mine."

At the thought of Irene, Henry felt a familiar heartache. He remembered their early days together: their long walks in the park, candlelit dinners, and snuggles in bed. But over the past summer, Irene had left him for Bruce, complaining that Henry was dull. Bruce's adventurous nature excited her, she'd said, licking her lips. *Go to hell, slut*, he felt for the hundredth time. If she thought it cool to ride with Bruce in his Porsche, so be it. Henry did not need that kind of flashy life. He wanted to sing at the Met; all else was trivial. *No more girls for a while*, he had decided. He needed to concentrate on the new opera.

"An understudy is no threat," Jennifer told him. "Just don't get sick."

"I know that." Henry dropped his voice. "But Jennifer, I must warn you about Irene. She won't just sit and wait for you to get sick. She can be nasty. She might stab you in the back to take Mimi away from you."

Jennifer's eyes widened. "Thanks, I'll remember that."

"Do I see a conspiracy here, Stephanie?" John chuckled at her. "Bruce is Henry's understudy, and Glenn is Mike's. Aren't you dating both?"

"I didn't influence Arthur to choose them, if that's what you're implying," Stephanie said with a grin. "Besides, they're just friends."

"Right. Sure." John drummed the table with his fingers. "I knew you'd say that."

"It's outrageous." Henry rolled his eyes. "Stephanie is juggling between Bruce and Glenn, and at the same time Bruce is juggling between Irene and Stephanie. You'd better be careful, Musette, or you might get hurt."

"It is a little messy right now," Stephanie said lightly. "But I'll sort it out."

Suddenly Henry was deluged with somber admissions from his friends about their personal difficulties. Jennifer divulged that she had not seen her fiancé for several days. Since the coaching session had gone well, she was going to visit Richard's apartment after this. John confided that Michelle was frustrated because he was out too often, between lessons, rehearsals, church singing, and his job at Music Universe, a big digital media store where he worked as a sales clerk in the classical music department.

"Whoa!" said Henry, holding up his hands. "I'm sure this'll all work out. But remember that Michelle asked Stephanie to organize the entertainment at the opening of her group show on the first Saturday of November." He turned to John. "We'll all be there singing, so maybe it'll be a good opportunity to talk to Michelle about the life of opera singers."

"Maybe." John sighed. "It's worth a try."

❮❮◉ ◉❯❯

Henry left the Café Momus with Jennifer and John, while Stephanie stayed on to finish her shift. Outside it had grown dark. People were hurriedly walking home from shopping or work. The wind gently blew brown leaves onto the street. Jennifer hailed a taxi to go to the East Side to see Richard. She threw a smile at Henry and John, then slipped into the car, sputtering the address to the driver as if she could no longer wait. Watching the disappearing taxi, John muttered, "Happy love bird." Henry sensed some envy in John's voice. Instead of going back to Music Universe, John decided to go home to Washington Heights and called the store on his cell phone. They walked north along Broadway. John would take a subway at the 79th Street station, and Henry would walk home.

"Tomorrow morning I have to be at my church at nine o'clock for the rehearsal before the ten-thirty service," John said. "Small odd jobs here and there. It never ends."

"Yes, but you're tough enough," Henry said, patting John's shoulder.

A group of children came toward them. While making way for them, Henry saw a young woman walking with a tall man on the other side of Broadway. Although he was not certain, he thought that the woman was Michelle. He pretended he saw nothing. But John froze, looking in the same direction. A moment later John composed himself with obvious effort and told Henry that he would go back to Music Universe after all. Without waiting for Henry's response, John turned and hurried away toward the south. *What was that all about?* Henry wondered.

The air was crisp. Heading north to his apartment near Broadway in the nineties, Henry practiced the lyrics of the duet. At the café he had sung it well, but he had been insecure with the words. A few times he had had to fudge them, which he hoped nobody had noticed. He needed to memorize them perfectly. He spoke with clear diction. "*O Musette, o gioconda sorridente! O giovinezza ardente, riso perenne e canto spensierato, tinnulo, cristallino;…*" ("Oh Musette, oh radiant smile! Oh ardent young woman, everlasting laughter and lighthearted, tinkling, crystalline song;…") Sometimes he stumbled and had to refer to his score.

"Hey, wake up. You're going to walk into that light post."

At the crystal soprano voice, he looked up to see Irene with Bruce. Had he known they were coming, he would have avoided them; but it was too late. He greeted them awkwardly. Irene seemed embarrassed, disguising it with a benign smile in which he sensed hostility. Bruce seemed carefree.

"Congrats for Marcello's role," Bruce said, tilting his face to flaunt his best look.

"Thanks. I saw you're my cover," Henry replied with the same politeness.

"And I'm ready," Bruce said. "If you can't sing for whatever the reason, I'll perform Marcello perfectly with one minute's notice."

"Well, don't be disappointed if your opportunity never arrives."

Bruce shrugged. "We'll see."

"Aren't you going to congratulate me too?" Irene asked. She tossed her fine red hair, showing off her exotic cheekbones like a *prima donna.*

"Yes, congratulations," Henry said. "A lot of work to be Mimi. I hope you can handle it."

"Don't worry. I'll manage," she replied, sticking her nose up. "Tell Jennifer I'm all set."

"I'm sure she'll sing beautifully."

Irene forced a smile, but her eyes flashed ice. Bruce held Irene's waist as she nestled closer to him. Their heads high, they passed by Henry and kept walking south. A few steps away, Henry saw Bruce thrusting his thumb down and Irene cracking up. Their naked rivalry shocked him. This was unusual. Normally the understudies were no issue at all. They were thrilled to have a learning opportunity. Plus, there was always the possibility of performance if something unexpected happened to their primary, no matter how slim the chance. On many occasions in the past, Henry had never seen his understudy at all. This time, however, he and the other Dolci Quattro would have to endure the antics of blatant competitors. Henry hastened his pace. He wanted to reach home quickly. He had to master Marcello entirely as soon as possible. *I can't fail.*

Scene 2

*J*ennifer arrived at a large, red-brick building on Park Avenue in the nineties. Darkness had descended. She juggled her purse, thick music score, and a large paper bag containing lamb chops, a bottle of wine, and a bunch of roses, which she had bought at nearby stores. A uniformed doorman greeted her courteously by name and ushered her into the bright, chandelier-lit lobby. She paused to adjust her burdens on a side table, which held a huge vase of fresh chrysanthemums. She thought of announcing her visit to Richard at the concierge desk, but decided against it. This would be a surprise. The doorman pushed the elevator button for her.

Richard, already a manager in the foreign exchange department at a major bank, owned a co-op apartment here. In his spare time he wrote fiction. When he completed a story, he showed it to Jennifer. She was delighted to read his creations and felt he had a gift for storytelling. She complimented the parts beautifully written and offered suggestions for improvement, encouraging him to continue. In turn, he wrote her passionate love poems and read them aloud to her. He enjoyed listening to her singing and faithfully attended her opera performances, presenting her a lush bouquet at the end. She gazed at the engagement ring he had given her over a year before. He wanted to wait to schedule their wedding until he achieved a senior position at the bank. Although she respected his wish, she wanted to get married. Lately, while they had spoken over the phone several times, he had always sounded preoccupied with something. When had she slept with him last? Today, definitely, she would stay overnight.

She got out of the elevator on the fifteenth floor and checked her reflection in a corridor mirror. Usually for coaching sessions she wore jeans and a shirt. She was glad that today she had dressed in a black velvet jacket, striped blouse, long brown skirt, and black boots. She applied lipstick on her flowery lips, rearranged her fine blonde hair, and straightened her dress. She pressed the doorbell. There was no response. *Gee.* She should have checked to see if he was home. She pressed it again. She heard footsteps approaching. The door opened. Richard was a handsome man in his mid-thirties with a tall masculine body. His short, dark-brown hair was neatly combed. He wore a dark-blue blazer jacket, clean white shirt, silver-gray trousers, and a pair of brown suede shoes: a perfect gentleman at a Park Avenue apartment on a Saturday evening. The only casual signs were a pencil resting on his right ear and no necktie. Seeing her, his eyebrows shot up on his high forehead. He opened his mouth, but no words came out. She cheerfully greeted him and stepped into his apartment. He immediately composed himself.

"S…sorry," he stammered. "I thought it was the food delivery I was expecting."

"You guessed right," she said. With a big smile, she held up the paper bag.

As she headed for the kitchen, he abruptly intercepted her. "I didn't know you were coming," he mumbled. "Actually I'm in the middle of something." He removed the pencil from his ear and slid it into the chest pocket of his blazer. "Can you come back some other time?"

She apologized for not having called him earlier, and told him about her excellent coaching session. "I missed you, honey." She hugged and kissed him. "I know you're busy. I'll make you a nice dinner. I'm worried you eat too much junk food. A healthy diet is essential for a young executive like you. I brought lamb chops, your favorite. Beaujolais, too. It'll be a small feast. Just you and me." She winked.

"Thanks. But…" A frown of annoyance crossed his white face. Instantly he covered it with a neutral expression. "Don't you under-stand? Not tonight. I've got some important work to do." He tried to guide her back to the door.

"I know, poor baby." She shook off his arms in a familiar ges-ture. "Whenever you're too busy, you become so stiff. Relax, Richard." She pulled the bunch of roses from the paper bag. "I'll put these in a vase. Aren't they beautiful?" She brought the red, pink, yellow, and white blooms closer to her face, inhaling deeply. "It's been a long time. Did you miss me, sweetie?"

"Of course I missed you." He tapped the pencil in his pocket. "But I have to get back."

"Stubborn as usual. I need to learn how to deal with your stubbornness. A good wife should be able to handle that, don't you agree?"

"Forget it." He nudged her toward the door. "It's not important."

"All right. I've forgotten it already. Now, I want a kiss." She stuck out her lips, her eyes closed. "Show me you love me."

He pecked her on her lips.

"You call that a kiss?" She opened her eyes. "You feel like a dead fish. Can't you be more passionate?" She sighed, her spirits sinking. "I'm really disappointed, but I give in. I shouldn't pester you too much. I suppose this is my fate for being engaged to a busy bank manager. See? You have a very understanding fiancée."

"Now you're making sense." He appeared relieved. "I'll take care of the roses. Don't forget your purse and the music." He took the flowers and tried to usher her to the door again, this time with force. "I'll talk to you later."

"Don't push me." She shrugged him off and spun to face him. "You're acting strange. Are you hiding something?"

"No, of course not. Just, uh, today is no good." His face trembled.

Suddenly a feeble swirl of perfume wafted from the far edge of the spacious living room adjoining the foyer, followed by a woman's voice. "Aaah, sooo refreshing. Richard, I left the hot water running. Why don't you take a shower? I can join you there if you want. I looove sex in the shower. I feel horny already. Are you ready for another?"

Jennifer gaped in the direction of the voice. A woman stood there, her face down, drying her long, red-gold hair with a towel, otherwise completely naked. She was tall and shapely, her body ripe with pinkish white skin. Her plump breasts bounced as she moved her hands over her head. Her nipples were deep red. Her navel was pierced with a gleaming pearl. Her pubic hair was trimmed to a thin, feathery line. Hearing no response from Richard, the woman peered between the edges of the towel and saw Jennifer. She let out a few inaudible words and disappeared hurriedly, covering her body with the towel.

Jennifer stood frozen, too stunned to utter a word. Richard gave her a bewildered look, completely speechless. She stared back at him, the betrayal rising. Her cheeks quavered. Flushing, her fiancé clutched the roses to shrink from her gaze. The chill silence persisted. She felt her heart pounding. Her eyes welled up. She thought she might be sick.

"How could you?" she managed, lurching for the door.

◖◗

Crossing Central Park in a taxi, Jennifer barely managed to keep her composure. When she reached her building on West End Avenue in the eighties, she staggered into her apartment and broke down with a loud wail. She gulped, almost choking. Hot tears poured down her cheeks. Her mind burned with the image of that naked woman, humiliating and undeniable. She seethed with mounting rage. She fell flat on the sofa.

You cheater! You dirty creep! You bastard! I hate you! No wonder you've been avoiding me. How long have you been sleeping with her? How serious are you with her? When did you meet her? How couldn't I have known? Stupid of me. What shall I do?

Jennifer worked as a secretary at a law firm. It allowed her flexible hours so she could maintain her career as an opera singer. She lived in a studio co-op apartment that legally belonged to her wealthy aunt, Maggie, a childless widow retired in Florida. Aunt Maggie paid the maintenance for the apartment and let Jennifer live there. Whenever Aunt Maggie wanted to visit New York, she stayed with Jennifer. Aunt Maggie was happy with this arrangement because she could give discreet support to her niece's opera career. In this way, Jennifer was able to spend her modest salary on her music lessons, clothes, and food, free from the heavy housing expenses of Manhattan. The interior of the apartment, dominated by an upright piano, was decorated simply. Here she had always felt secure. At this time in her life, the most important thing was to successfully sing her role in the new opera. She needed to muster the courage. But how was she supposed to concentrate with that naked woman foremost in her mind? And her future, her engagement, in ruins? *Focus*, she told herself. *Focus on music.*

She breathed steadily. Her tears ebbed. She found a box of tissues, wiped her eyes, and blew her nose. On the side table stood a few framed photos of her and Richard, both happily smiling. She knocked them over and dumped them into the drawer. She removed her engagement ring and threw that in, too. She slammed the drawer and sighed. She wanted to be strong but felt forlorn. She needed something to divert her mind. She was not hungry, but went to the kitchen to make salad and tea for supper. She brought these with a glass of orange juice to the dining table in the living room. She couldn't eat even half of it.

She sat at her piano and opened the score of Leoncavallo's *La Bohème*. She tried to study but the notes on the pages just bounced emptily, then blurred. She swiped her tears away and attempted to vocalize, but her voice wouldn't come out either. This was a dangerous sign. She knew that whenever a singer experienced an emotional disturbance, it would hit the vocal cords. This was the last thing she needed. She had spent the whole past summer rigidly disciplined, building up her voice to its best shape ever. Now the best she could muster was a froglike croak. As her spirits sank, she realized that in spite of her anger, she missed Richard. *This is stupid*, she said to herself.

She sat in a lotus position on the rug and tried to meditate. With her eyes closed and her palms clasped on her lap, she took a deep breath and exhaled slowly. She repeated it. Her breathing was steady. Bouncing breasts…red nipples. *No!* She banished the image. She went to the bookcase and took out Willa Cather's *The Song of the Lark*, her favorite novel. Sitting at the dining table, she tried to read. In the past, the courageous life of an opera singer, Thea Kronborg, had always inspired her. But tonight she found herself reading the same two sentences over and over. She went back to the sofa, feeling exhausted. Her life had been shattered. No fiancé, no voice, no will. She thought she should go to bed. After a long sleep, she should feel better. *Get this devastating night over with. Just tonight. Let me get through. Tomorrow I'll be strong, I promise. I'll be like Thea.*

She changed into her nightgown then went into the bathroom, where she found a bottle of sleeping pills in the medicine chest. She swallowed two pills, washing them down with water. Two more. Then, one by one, the rest. She returned to the living room and crept into the bed. She turned off the lights. The room was quiet. She closed her eyes. Richard's image appeared. She remembered how happy she had been with him for the past year. Gradually his image became nebulous and was replaced with a drizzling silver mist. The mist diminished into twilight. Finally all disappeared, a darkness pervading. She felt a peaceful tranquility. No more anguish, no more misery, no more suffering. *Come, sleep; take me away.*

⊰⊱

The clanging telephone jarred Henry awake. He fumbled for the receiver as he peered at the digital clock on the bedside table. A familiar voice burst out in frenzy of incomprehensible words. He reminded Stephanie that it was two o'clock in the morning.

"I know, but it's an emergency," she said, more controlled. "Jennifer took an overdose of sleeping pills. I'm at her apartment now. Can you come help?"

"What? What happened?" He threw back the covers and switched the light on.

Stephanie hurriedly explained that Jennifer had caught Richard with a lover. She was so depressed that she took the pills. Luckily her stomach couldn't take it, and she threw them up. She had gotten scared and called Stephanie.

"Now she's lying on the bed. She's conscious but totally sick," Stephanie said. "She insists it was an accident and she didn't mean to kill herself. She begged me not to call 911. She doesn't want to get involved with an ambulance and the police. I don't know what to do."

Henry asked her to make a big pot of tea. Then he hurriedly dressed in the jeans and sweater he had taken off just hours before and rushed out of his apartment. Never mind a taxi. It was only fifteen blocks. He ran with his full energy. In less than ten minutes he arrived at Jennifer's apartment, panting but wide-awake. Stephanie opened the door. She had no makeup on. Her short dark hair looked spiky. She wore blue jeans and a cardigan over a cotton shirt, clumsily creased with wet stains. He peered over her shoulder. Jennifer lay curled up on the bed.

"What exactly did she take?" he whispered.

Stephanie showed him a medium-size bottle of over-the-counter sleeping pills. "She said the bottle was about a third full," she added.

If Jennifer had taken only the pills from this bottle, it wouldn't have been sufficient to kill her, Henry thought. Besides, if she had thrown it up, some of the drugs should already be out of her stomach. "Did she take anything else?" he asked. Seeing Stephanie shaking her head, he relaxed. His brother was a doctor, practicing in Ohio. Although his brother's specialty was cardiology, Henry had heard from his brother about numerous cases of attempted suicide and how the doctors had treated them. Jennifer's case did not appear life threatening. Complying with her wish, he decided that it would be best to assuage her pain instead of calling for an ambulance.

Stephanie brought him to the bed in the corner. Jennifer lay in a ball, wrapped in her bathrobe. Her face was cadaverous, her hair stringy, and her lips swollen. She was moaning with her eyes closed. He called her. She opened her eyes slightly and nodded to him.

"Henry…sorry…I made…such…a mess," she said with difficulty. Her voice was hoarse and hardly audible. "I'm so scared."

"Don't worry," he answered, inclining his head. "First we need to know how many pills you've taken. Were they only from this bottle? It's important. Tell us."

"That's…all," she managed. "I swear. But I threw up. My stomach is burning."

He asked Stephanie to bring the teapot and a cup. He supported Jennifer's shoulders and helped her sit up. "Jennifer, this is tea. You have to drink it, lots of it."

"I…can't. I'll throw up again."

"That's exactly the point. You have to throw up everything from your stomach. The tea is not too hot. Drink. You can do it. Open your mouth."

He brought the cup to her lips. Encouraged by her friends, Jennifer slowly started sipping the tea. First cup, second cup. Jennifer gagged. He brought her to the bathroom. Third cup, fourth cup. She threw up into the toilet. He asked her to drink more. She blubbered she couldn't. He pressed her to do it. Fifth cup, sixth cup. Again, she threw up. To finish off, he put his fingers into her mouth and pushed her tongue down. With a loud groan, she vomited further. Then she collapsed on the floor. He cleaned up her face and carried her back to her bed.

"The amount of pills doesn't seem dangerous," he told Stephanie softly. "She threw up most of it. Now we have to keep talking to her and keep her moving until the drug has mostly worn off. We can't let her sleep. This is another reason why I asked you to make tea."

"Do you think her voice is damaged?" Stephanie was crying.

"I don't know." He shook his head. "I hope not."

"What about our opera?"

"We'll worry about that later." He anchored Jennifer's hand on his shoulder with one hand and held her waist with his other hand. Then he started slowly walking. Stephanie supported Jennifer from the other side.

"I…can't…walk," Jennifer protested.

"You have to," he said sternly. "Let's walk together, OK? One, two, three…"

"Jennifer," Stephanie chimed in, "walk. It's important. C'mon."

As they slowly shuffled around the living room, Henry peppered Jennifer with questions to keep her awake, like her favorite songs and what she had eaten for lunch and dinner. Urged by him, she talked, although her speech was garbled.

Attended by Henry and Stephanie, Jennifer spent over an hour drinking tea, walking, talking, and vomiting. By four o'clock in the morning, convinced that she was out of danger, Henry lay Jennifer on her bed and covered her with the blanket. No sooner had she lain down than she was lost in a deep sleep. Henry and Stephanie collapsed on the chairs at the dining table. They had done their job for now. But there was no question of leaving Jennifer alone in this state. Stephanie slept on the sofa, wrapped in an afghan. Henry lay down on the rug near the piano.

When Henry woke up, it was nearly eleven o'clock. He felt stiff from sleeping on the floor. Luckily this was Sunday. None of them had to worry about work. He made sure that Jennifer was sleeping soundly and that Stephanie was all right. Then he went out to a nearby market to buy things for breakfast. Returning to Jennifer's apartment, he woke Stephanie.

Before awakening Jennifer, Henry and Stephanie agreed that they should keep the incident to themselves. As far as they were concerned, this was an unfortunate personal accident and nothing more. He would inform John discretely about the incident, as it was understood that the Dolci Quattro would share the burdens of life together. Next, they discussed what to do about Richard. He would have to be informed, they concluded. Henry would come up with the best way to tell Richard and would do so. Further, they decided that since Jennifer should not be left alone, after breakfast Stephanie would go back to her apartment, tidy up and organize herself, then come back to spend the night with Jennifer again. Henry would stay and watch Jennifer until Stephanie returned. As to the post-trauma treatment, they decided that at a proper time, Stephanie would insist Jennifer see a therapist.

Stephanie prepared breakfast while Henry made tea. It did not take long before the meal was ready. At Stephanie's signal, he gently shook Jennifer. She moaned and opened her eyes. He told her that breakfast was served. She shook her head. He persuaded her and helped her to the dining table. She walked unsteadily, but she managed to reach the table and sat.

"How are you feeling?" Stephanie asked.

"Awful…ah…terrible headache!" Jennifer replied, rubbing her forehead with her both hands. "I'm sorry for all the trouble." Her pallid face contorted.

"Don't worry," Stephanie said. "I'm so glad you called me last night. Now you have to recover your strength. You may not have too much of an appetite, but here, try."

Jennifer listened calmly and nodded. She unfolded a napkin and daintily placed it on her lap. Slowly she drank orange juice and ate cereal, yogurt, banana, and apple, all in tiny amounts. She sipped tea with honey. Henry and Stephanie also ate their breakfast, watching with relief. Even though Jennifer's speech was still slurred, at least she was mentally coherent and emotionally composed. Most of all, she was willing and able to take some food. These were all positive signs, which convinced them that she was going to be all right.

Abundant sunshine flooded the apartment through the raised blinds on the windows. Yellow and red foliage brightened the air. Birds were warbling. Inside the apartment, however, an awkward silence arose. Henry and Stephanie patiently gave Jennifer time to recoup herself. They did not turn on the TV, nor rush into too much hasty conversation. Instead, from time to time, they spoke quietly about the pleasant weather and the fresh foods.

After breakfast Jennifer wanted to lie down. While Stephanie cleared the table and washed dishes, Henry reclined on the couch and closed his eyes to catch some more sleep. Stephanie finished the dishes and came back to the chair.

A peaceful stillness permeated the living room. The room was warm and bright. From the windows came distant sounds of children playing on the street. Dogs barked, chasing the children. Pigeons cooed on the sills. Someone played the piano a few stories above. A Chopin étude wafted in the air. Henry and Stephanie listened until they were caught by the sound of sobbing from the bed. They gazed at each other and turned their attention to Jennifer. She was talking to herself, half asleep, pausing and resuming in varying intervals.

"Richard," she murmured. "You traitor!" She coughed. "I'll never forgive you."

The pigeons flapped away from the sills. Sparrows alit and took over their places.

"Stupid of me." She exhaled. "How couldn't I know?"

The girls on the street shrieked, laughing. The Chopin ended.

"But why? Why would he do this to me?" She punched her pillow.

The shadows of branches danced on the windows, responding to the autumn breeze. Birds twittered. Sunlight deluged the room. The noise outside subsided. Henry heard a soprano voice beginning to sing, feeble and hoarse.

> *Verranno a te sull'aure i miei sospiri ardenti,*
> *Udrai nel mar che mormora l'eco de' miei lamenti.*

> (Born on the gentle breeze, my ardent sighs will
>   waft to you.
> Hear the murmurs of the sea that echo my laments.)

Henry recognized the soprano part of a duet in Act I of Donizetti's *Lucia di Lammermoor,* in which Lucia and Edgardo sing of their dismay at their separation while pledging their everlasting love to each other. It was one of the most fervent love duets in all opera. Jennifer was singing it with difficulty, yet with all her ingenuousness. Henry shuddered. The opera was famous for Lucia's mad scene near the end. She had been forced to marry a nobleman she did not love. In her despair, she seized upon an illusion that she was marrying her beloved Edgardo. She lost her sanity, which would ultimately lead to her death. Was Jennifer singing the duet as a subconscious foreshadowing of her doom? Henry saw Stephanie shaking her head. She mouthed quietly, *I know what you're thinking.*

Scene 3

"So who was the guy I saw you with earlier today as I was leaving the Café Momus?" John asked Michelle, trying to sound casual rather than accusatory. Apparently he had failed. Their talk soon escalated into one of the heated arguments that had grown more frequent between them over the past few months. Her defense was that since he neglected her, she needed to enjoy herself without him. She had started seeing other men for movies, drinks, or dinner, but no sex. She didn't think it was improper. "But you are married to me," he shouted, pounding the dining room table. "What?" she yelled back. "You claim you're married? Stop that crap. You're never here!" As usual, the argument ended up with her tearful babble, "I want a divorce."

He'd always considered her statements an impulse from the frenzy and did not take her seriously. Indeed, in the past she had never seemed to mean it, as she had soon resumed casual conversation with him. He had grown used to these intermittent domestic quarrels, which he thought were part of married life. But this evening something was different. She said that she had been talking to a lawyer about their marriage. Surely this, too, was a result of another paroxysm, he thought. She was just trying to balance her frustrated mental state.

The next morning, she asked him to come home early so they could discuss their marriage. "It's important," she said. This being Sunday, he'd had to sing at his church, as usual. After that he went to work at Music Universe. Business happened to be unusually brisk for a Sunday, and his boss had asked him to work extra hours. He was so exhausted that he forgot his wife's request. He came home late. Michelle had already gone to bed.

Early on Monday, Henry called him to tell him about Jennifer's *accident*, as she called it. John was glad she had already begun resuming her normal life. But it seemed to him that the personal lives of the Dolci Quattro were all in disarray. He sighed. *What's happening to us?* Then, that very afternoon, while he was working at Music Universe, a messenger arrived with an envelope and requested he sign a receipt. After the messenger left, he opened it. Inside he found a letter of summons for divorce from Michelle's lawyer. Hot blood shot up to his head. His heart pounded. His chest swelled and contracted rapidly. His hands and legs trembled. He had to sit down. He had absolutely no idea what to do. None of other Dolci Quattro were married or divorced, so he couldn't seek advice from them. He needed time to think of the best course of action. That evening, therefore, he resolved not to discuss the issue with her. He avoided eye contact with her. She searched his face but otherwise kept silent.

Next morning, he called in sick and checked the Yellow Pages for a divorce lawyer. He had a free consultation with the attorney, who explained how divorce cases were handled in New York. There were two types of divorces: consented and contested. In the latter, which Michelle had chosen, there had to be a legal reason: adultery, cruelty, or abandonment. After the consultation, John pondered. He had never had affairs with other women. That would rule out adultery. Although he and she had argued sometimes, he had never abused her or used violence. So it couldn't be cruelty.

That left abandonment. He often came home late, as lessons, rehearsals, and performances sometimes went well into the evenings. He had two regular jobs: one at Music Universe and the other at his church. He also took ad-hoc singing jobs for weddings and birthdays. This was the life of a professional opera singer. Partly he loved it, but partly it was necessary because he had to pay the bills. Could this be grounds for divorce? He didn't think so. According to the lawyer, abandonment in a divorce case usually meant that a husband had left his wife, or vice versa, or that a husband refused to have sex with his wife, or vice versa. He was still living with her in the same apartment, and their love life had been pretty good, he thought. So what was her legal reason to file for divorce? He slammed his fist on his thigh. Suddenly it occurred to him that when she had repeatedly said, "I want a divorce," she truly meant it. *Why couldn't you have realized it before she began the legal action? You idiot!*

⦅◎ ◎⦆

In the late afternoon, John decided to visit his parents to lift his spirits. The Bertucci family lived in a two-story house in a middle-class neighborhood close to Prospect Park in Brooklyn. He was their only child, born and raised here. Displayed on the wall in the living room were John's diplomas from his schools. Several framed photographs of him stood on side tables: the church boys' choir, his first prize in a singing contest at the elementary school, and his debut as an opera character. His bedroom was kept as he had left it. On a pillar in the kitchen wall, he could still see the hand-carved marks of his height on his birthday for each year of his childhood.

At the dining table near the kitchen, his father served drinks. His mother happily busied herself preparing dinner for her men. They told him all the news about themselves and their neighbors. In turn, they were eager to hear how his singing was coming along for the new opera. He told them that he was making steady progress learning the new role and sang a few bars. They cried out with delight, clapping their hands. Naturally they asked how Michelle was doing. He described his married life, like walks at the Cloisters, dining out, and parties with their friends. His parents' faces lit up with joy. It pained him that he didn't have the courage to tell them the truth. What a horrible disappointment a divorce would be to them. Someday he would have to confess to his troubles, but not today. Dinner warmed his heart as well as his stomach. He felt at home and secure. He remembered all the tender care he had received from his parents while he was growing up here. He forced himself to be talkative.

"Ma, your pasta and veal chops are the best in the world."

"Don't flatter me, John. I'm just glad to have you here." His mother waved her hand, but he knew she was pleased with his compliments. Her round face, set off by wisps of gray hair, looked like a smiling moon. "How's Michelle's cooking?"

"She's a good cook, too, but she's still young. You're much more experienced."

"You should bring her over so I can cook with her. I want to pass on several of my secret recipes. That would be exciting."

John promised her that he would bring Michelle more often. In spite of his efforts to be cheerful, he was saddened by his impossible promise. The word *divorce* stabbed his heart. He tried to coerce a smile without success. His father caught it.

"Son, are you in trouble?" he said with a sharp look.

"No, I'm all right," John replied in haste. "Today I got a day off because I worked last Saturday and Sunday. So I thought I'd stop by and have dinner with you. I missed Ma's cooking."

Not convinced, his father pointed to an old photograph in an oval frame next to John's diplomas, a portrait of a middle-aged man in a formal suit with a tie, proudly displaying a medal on his upper left chest. "I've told you this many times, but let me repeat it," his father said with a ceremonious air.

"Again?" John protested. "I've heard it a million times." He caught his mother waving her forefinger, covertly asking him to hush. This was his family legacy his father was fond of telling. "OK, Pa, go ahead."

His father straightened his posture and began in all solemnity. "Your grandfather came to America from Italy after World War I, right before the Great Depression. All he brought with him was one suitcase, his good health, and his determination. Back in Napoli, he had been a voice instructor, teaching opera. Here he couldn't find any job in opera. So he had to work as a baker. He never made money, but he settled and raised his family. His only indulgence was to listen to records of operas. Imagine, a baker listening to operas. That was him. You could smell the aromas and hear the arias all the way down the block."

They all laughed at this key point in the story.

Though in his late sixties, John's father was still vigorous, physically and mentally. Both men shared the same stocky build, dark good looks, and a deep baritone voice. His father looked down at his hands, which were rough and wrinkled. "I never made money either, and I retired as a mere subway engineer. I never regretted it, though, because your mother and I are happy to have you, our first college grad. We're proud you earned scholarships and graduated with honors and a master's degree. Look at you, my boy. An opera singer! Your grandfather would have been honored." His father gazed at the portrait and the diplomas. His mother followed. Then they looked back at John with affection. "Son, sing…sing. If you want to make your mother and me happy, sing out. We don't care if you make money. We don't care if you become famous either. But sing. Verdi's operas, Puccini's, Rossini's, Donizetti's. Sing like Caruso and Gigli. Sing the glory of Italian opera. Remember, opera is in your blood."

John felt his family heritage swell deep inside him. He resolved to fight back against the problem he was facing now. "Thanks, Pa." He pushed back from the table to return to Manhattan.

John and Michelle lived near the Cloisters, close to 200th Street in Manhattan. From their apartment they could see the George Washington Bridge, the Hudson River, and the cliffs of New Jersey, which featured beautiful seasonal changes as the months went by. Michelle's parents were wealthy. They wanted their daughter to have comfortable living quarters, as well as a practical studio for painting. They had bought the spacious two-bedroom co-op apartment and given it to her as a wedding gift. She used the second bedroom as her studio. Since the studio faced north, it had steady light during the day, which was perfect for her oil painting. For him, the studio served as his practice room because it was large enough to hold his piano as well as her easels. They had been living there since their marriage two years before.

Michelle held an MFA degree in painting from the Parsons School of Design. She worked as an art teacher at the Rudolf Steiner School off Fifth Avenue near Carnegie Hill. The school emphasized the students' individual creativity through art and music—so her job was as high as an art teacher could go, except for teaching at a college or an art school. Since the school had seasonal breaks, she had sufficient time for her own pursuits: traditional Impressionist landscapes, still lifes, and figures. She had formed a group with two other female artists from Parsons: Helen, an abstract painter; and Sarah, a watercolor painter. Each of them had a contract with the same art gallery on Madison Avenue in the seventies. Michelle had named the group the Graces, honoring the three Greek goddesses of beauty and creativity. This was the group that was to have their show in a few weeks.

John remembered his first blind date with her. As they were both of Italian descent, they discovered a mutual zeal for opera and art. Right away, they hit it off. They went together to museums and opera performances often. He even sat for her as a model, supposedly a renowned opera singer in a singing pose. She came to every opera he performed. It didn't take long for them to become inseparable. They went to Italy on vacation. In front of La Scala in Milan, he proposed, kneeling and singing, and she accepted, breaking into happy laughter and tears. Soon after, they wed at St. Patrick's Cathedral on Fifth Avenue. Henry served as his best man, while Helen and Sarah were her maids of honor. Jennifer and Stephanie sang wedding songs. For their honeymoon they went back to Italy, visiting Venice, Milan, Florence, Rome, and Naples. They ate all kinds of Italian cuisine, drank wine, and made love every morning, afternoon, and evening.

What had happened to those happy days? he wondered. He recognized that as he needed to earn more money after their marriage, he had spent less and less time with her. Exhausted from work, he had grown forgetful in caring about her. At this stage, could he make up with her? Would she accept him again? He would find out this evening. One thing he promised himself was not to lose his temper. The most important thing was that they talk about the problem rationally. He knew their Italian temperaments. If he lost his cool, she would match him and shout even louder. Then they could never have a constructive discussion.

By the time John arrived home, it was after ten. Usually Michelle went to bed about this time to get up at six for work. This evening she was still at the dining table, reading a book. Normally she would have been painting, but she still wore her work clothes from school, a comfortable wool skirt, and a cashmere sweater. Her paint-stained working jeans and shirt lay untouched on one of the chairs. Had she been sitting there all night waiting for him? He sat opposite her, gazing at his attractive wife, memorizing her fine light complexion, dark hair, and rich brown eyes. She seemed somber and introspective, not the lighthearted wife he had come to take for granted. He asked her if they could talk. She nodded. The apartment was quiet. He heard the ticking of a clock.

He took a deep breath and began. "Yesterday I received the letter from your attorney. I was so upset, I couldn't discuss it with you. Today I had a consultation with a lawyer. He explained how things are handled in these cases." He avoided the word *divorce*. "Michelle, I'm sorry to say, but I don't understand. We've been married for two years. I've been happy with you. I thought you were happy, too. I know I'm not a perfect husband. I often come home late because my lessons and rehearsals run long. This is my life. Otherwise, I think I'm a good husband. What don't you like in our marriage? Yesterday and today, I spent a lot of time reflecting. But honestly, I couldn't find any answer. So tell me. What's wrong?" What he had just said was not entirely true, as he knew he had been insensitive to her. But he wanted to hear it directly from her.

"I've told you, John. At least I've tried." Her voice was tight. "Do you remember three weeks ago, when I asked you call in sick to Music Universe so we could have dinner at home together? That I wanted to talk to you about something?"

"I remember," he said, embarrassed. "I said I couldn't do it because I needed the money."

"You have paid sick days," she said. "You just didn't think talking to me was important enough to use one. And do you remember the week after that, when we had made a date to have lunch together on a Sunday?"

"Yes, sorry." He flushed. "I went out with some singers from the choir after church and came home late. You were already gone."

"I waited for you at the restaurant, but you called on the cell to tell me you had a last minute rehearsal come up. Then there was that voice lesson that had to be rescheduled, and last week you took an extra shift at Music Universe, and—"

"OK, you made the point," he interrupted. She had been trying to reach him for the past few weeks. Yet he had simply ignored her. How inconsiderate he had been.

"And last Sunday—"

"I apologize. I forgot," he interrupted again.

"Forgot, you say?" She widened her eyes and raised her voice. "What kind of answer is that? I told you I had been talking to a lawyer. I wanted to discuss our marriage before taking action. Didn't I say it was important? You missed your last chance to come to friendly terms."

He nodded in despair. He wanted to say he was sorry but couldn't, as his throat ached with defeat. He saw her eyes welling up.

"So I said to my lawyer, go ahead," she continued. "I'm sorry, John. This didn't happen overnight. I've been thinking about it for a long time."

She seemed to contemplate her discomfiture of the past few months. He knew now how she had felt driven to take action. He was the one to blame. It took a long time for him to muster the courage to speak again.

"I know I've neglected you," he finally said. "I've been blind. I'm sorry. But now that we've talked about it, I swear I'll try to do better." He crossed his heart with a big swing of his hand. "We can fix things."

"I don't think so." Michelle frowned. "When you're unhappy with your marriage, you have only two choices: endure it and be unhappy for the rest of your life, or bite the bullet, end the marriage, and start a new life. I chose the latter."

"But you haven't given me a chance. It's normal to have bumps in a marriage. So why else are you unhappy?"

She did not respond immediately, appearing to gather her thoughts. "To you," she said, "I may be just a spoiled kid, crying for a sugar cookie. But I'm tired of life with a name-only husband. I want to cook for my husband and eat dinner together. Stroll in parks and along streets with my husband. I want to go shopping with my husband, go on vacations with my husband. I'm not asking too much. All I want is an ordinary life with my husband." She burst into tears. He waited for her to let out whatever she held piled up in her mind. She gradually controlled her sobs. "But what do we have here?" she resumed. "Early in the morning, I leave for work while you're still sleeping. You come home late after I've gone to bed. Even on weekends and holidays, you're gone. We have no time to enjoy ourselves together. We're still newlyweds, John. These should be our best years. Think about it. When did we last have a decent conversation? When did we last have dinner together? Go out walking or gallery hopping? When did we last visit our friends together? Visit your parents or mine? Invite our friends for dinner? When is the last time we took a vacation together? Have we ever celebrated our birthdays and anniversaries together? Think. We haven't done any of these things. I don't want this kind of marriage."

She spoke rapidly, in a tone that was full of grief but not accusatory. She exhaled and wiped her tears with her handkerchief. As he listened, her words hit his body like a swift succession of bullets from a machine gun, jolting him with pain. She was right. She must have told him these things a hundred times before. He had had a hundred chances. It took him some time to regain his rational mind. He needed to clarify one thing.

"Michelle, are you sure this is your real problem? You don't think I'm having affairs or I've been abusing you, do you?"

She waved off his concerns with her handkerchief. "I'd be happier," she said, "if you were having an affair or abusing me. In that case, I could divorce you without a moment's hesitation. Do you think it's easy for me to take action against you like this?"

Somehow he felt relieved because she wasn't accusing him falsely. Her reasoning was understandable. Sadly, he had to concede that what she had said was just. "I understand what you mean," he said. "You grew up in a wealthy family. You never had any financial difficulty. I wish I could make more money with my singing. Then I'd have more time to be with you. We could take vacations in Europe together. Go to good restaurants, concerts, museums. If I got hired by the Met, it would be different. But I'm not there yet. Someday, I want to make it there. Someday, definitely. But to get there, I have to do what I'm doing now." He exhaled, hoping to find a way toward reconciliation. "If that's your real problem, divorce may not be the solution. I love you and want to stay married. If you don't want me to live here, I'll move out. We can see how it goes. Over time, there may be a change in me, in you, or in our circumstances. Shouldn't we try that first? If our separation doesn't work, then we can consider a divorce."

She seemed to contemplate this. She shook her head. "John, I'm not happy. I'm tired. I do love you. But what good is loving you if I never see you? I want to end this marriage now and start a new life while I'm still young."

He looked around the familiar living room. This was their home. He might lose it soon. The clock was still steadily ticking. The air felt heavy. "I can't change my life quickly as far as my career is concerned," he resumed. "If you're unhappy with me, it's my fault."

In the long stillness, his heavy breathing was audible. He clenched his fists, struggling to control himself. He felt sorry for her. He didn't want her to be unhappy. If he couldn't have an opera singer's career and a married life at the same time, he would have to choose the opera. Not that he didn't love her as much as opera, but opera was his life; without it he wouldn't be the man who fell in love with her. He fought against the pain of losing her. He desperately wanted to find a solution. He had believed that he could have both an opera singer's career and a home life. That seemed unlikely now. He could see no way to salvage their marriage.

"All right, Michelle, I'll tell you what." He swallowed. "If you want to divorce me, and if a divorce will make you happy, I'll consent. All that's required for a consented divorce is a mutual agreement between you and me. I don't need a lawyer for that. I don't need anything from you as a settlement. We'll end our marriage, and you'll be free. Then you can start your new life as you wish. Ask your lawyer to come up with a consent settlement. If that's what you want, I'll sign."

She must not have expected this. She took in a sharp breath. "You're too generous, John," she said. "Your lawyer must have explained to you the principle of equitable distribution. You would get a lot of money out of this divorce if you contested. Why don't you do that?"

"Oh, Michelle," he bristled, almost recanting. He controlled his hurt and anger. "I didn't marry you for your money. I married you because I love you. Can't a painter and an opera singer have a family with a few kids? What's wrong with that?"

His words seemed to have struck her heart. She slumped, burying her head in her arms. "I know what I'm saying is selfish," she finally said. "I know you're simply struggling with your career. Nothing is wrong with you, John. I should be more understanding, more patient, more supportive. I should be willing to sacrifice myself for our future. After all, I've taken a solemn vow to share my life with you 'for better or for worse.' So I'm the one who's breaking the vow. I feel like a miserable failure. But I can't help it." She sobbed again quietly.

John concluded that this was enough. He could see that she had her mind made up. Her mouth was set in that little pout he always used to think was so cute. The die had been cast. "Think about it," he said. "Talk to your lawyer. There's no need to fight each other. I've been happy with you. I love you very much, Michelle. Remember that."

They did not speak for a while. He heard her despondent breathing. As time passed by, he saw her countenance veering into reproach.

"Is that all you want to say?" she asked at last. "Aren't you going to fight to keep our marriage? Am I so dispensable? I'm disappointed. You don't really love me, do you?"

He wanted to blast, *What the hell are you talking about? You're the one who started the divorce action, not me.* Instead, he pursed his lips tight. As his lips quivered, he had to bite them hard. He remembered his promise to himself. If he lost his temper now, he would be the vanquished. Besides, this attested that she, too, was suffering from two contradicting desires. In spite of all the talk about divorce, she was still clinging to a hope for reconciliation. He decided that it was best not to directly respond to her, for now.

"You have your show coming," he said, searching for a more pleasant topic. "You've been looking forward to it so much. Is everything ready? I know you still have to prepare. Stephanie is arranging the entertainment as you requested. Jennifer and Henry will come. I'll be there, too. It'll be a great opening." He felt that he had done as much as he could for today. The rest, time would have to resolve.

He moved to the studio and sat at the piano. On the music stand, the score of Leoncavallo's *La Bohème* stood open. Other opera scores were stacked on the piano case. Beside it, a table held a CD player and dozens of CDs of operas and recitals by famous opera singers. They were all he had. Not much. But that was him, an aspiring baritone. Someday, he promised himself, he would make it into a first-tier opera company. Someday.

He found the score of Verdi's *La Traviata* and opened to the page of Germont's aria *"Di Provinza il mar"* in Act II. In the aria, Germont pleads with his son to come back to his home in Provence by the sea to restore the family honor and allow his daughter to be married. John sang the heart-rending melody in *sotto voce*. From time to time his throat tightened. While singing, he pondered. He knew that he couldn't afford to live in an apartment by himself and still pursue his career. He would have to go back to his parents' home with his meager belongings. If that was what she wanted, he was ready. He had been happy with their marriage for two years. He had no regrets, save that he had failed to make her happy.

As he sang deep in thought, he was not aware that the door of the studio had swung slightly open. When he looked up, he saw her standing in the shadows, watching him and listening to his lament. She was crying.

Scene 4

*A*t half past seven on Monday morning, Stephanie, already in her business suit, cooked scrambled eggs. She brought her plate to the dining table and sat down. The convertible sofa remained open. With her piano, she could hardly move about in the living room. As she was eating, Bruce came in after a morning shower. He wore blue jeans and a sweater.

"Are you really going to kick me out of here this early?" he asked, yawning.

"I have to work," she answered.

He downed a bowl of cereal, then scooped up scrambled eggs with a fork, swallowing them with sips of orange juice. She knew that he loathed her apartment.

She lived in a small studio apartment in the nineties off Columbus Avenue. It was one of those odd dwellings on the ground floor, the bottom half underground and the top half above the street level. The daylight from the windows was meager, and she always had to keep the electric lights on in the living room. Because of the damp air, mold grew amid peeling paint on the walls. The kitchen had barely enough space for one person to cook. The bathroom had a shower without a bathtub. Roaches infested the kitchen. However, the rent was affordable.

"I could have stayed at your place," she said. "But you wanted to sleep here for a change."

"It's all right." He shrugged. "This is kinda cozy."

She laughed. "Don't be silly. Politeness isn't your strong suit. This place is rotten."

"After breakfast, we should make love again." He winked, munching a piece of bacon.

"Lucky you," she said. "You don't have to work, because you can support yourself by the income from your family estate. You live in a luxurious condo next to Lincoln Center. You have a Porsche for joy rides. You can go on vacation to Europe. Life is good for you."

"Yeah, fortunately." He poked a finger toward her. "You could have been just like me if you hadn't run away from your father. That's what my parents say often."

She felt a pang in her heart; their families were neighbors and made no secret of their wish that their children create a dynasty. But this was not the time for such reflections. She tapped her watch. "I have to go." She brought the dishes back to the kitchen. Then she fetched her purse and changed to her office shoes. "Are you ready?" She motioned toward the door.

He stood and grabbed her waist from behind. Kissing her on the neck, he pressed his groin into her hip. "One more time, babe."

"Get off me." She pushed him backward. "C'mon. Or do you want to stay here? I'll let you, but I must go." She hurried to the door and stepped out. He followed. As she climbed up the steel stairs to the ground level, she heard him grumbling.

"Sorry," she said. "Get more sleep at your apartment, OK?"

She and Bruce had both gone to Yale and studied opera. There they dated. For graduate school, she had come to New York City and he had gone to Boston. After graduation, they had met again in Manhattan and resumed dating. In the beginning he had kept quiet about her frugal lifestyle. Little by little, though, he'd seemed to grow disappointed with her. The final turnaround had occurred the past summer, after Henry broke up with Irene. Stephanie guessed that Bruce was now growing closer to Irene, who appeared financially well off. He seemed to keep the relationship with her just for sex. She thought of Glenn, whom she had started seeing as a reaction to Bruce's cheating. But now she felt trapped between two men. If she left Bruce completely now, at least she could deal with only one man. Deep down, however, she still longed for Bruce.

◖◗ ◖◗

Stephanie returned home feeling dejected. It was only eleven o'clock in the morning. Since her neighbors were all away at work, the apartment was still. She sank into a chair at the dining table. She leaned back and looked blankly at the room, which was as cluttered as she had left it a few hours before. The breakfast dishes still beckoned from the sink. She was not normally self-pitying, but today she couldn't help it. She began weeping. *What am I going to do?*

She had been working as a Microsoft Office Specialist for the Social Workers Association of New York, a small nonprofit organization. This morning she had been called in by the personnel manager, who told her that they could no longer afford to keep her. Although their work was well respected, the funding had been sluggish for some years, and they had been forced to impose a series of budget cuts to survive. Any nonessential jobs had to be eliminated, including hers. The manager offered a month's salary as severance pay. She had to clear her desk immediately.

In addition to this job, she sang at a synagogue on the Upper East Side. Plus, she moonlighted at the Café Momus. Those jobs provided her with barely enough to cover her living expenses and the costs of music lessons. She hoped that she could work more hours at the restaurant for the time being. But she urgently needed to find another job. She groaned at the grim prospect of an exhausting search.

The telephone rang. She let her answering machine respond. The caller was the leader of a string quartet, the one she had invited to perform at the opening of Michelle's group show. The leader left a message, informing her that all was ready for the coming Saturday. The call brought Stephanie back to reality. The opening was in five days. Last week Henry had told her that John had proposed a consented divorce in response to Michelle's legal action. Since then John had been sleeping on a couch in their studio. He wished that their group would perform at the opening nonetheless. Stephanie agreed it was best to leave the private matter to the couple; she hoped that they would reconcile somehow. The performance would have to go on.

For the Dolci Quattro, she served as the business liaison, coordinating musical events like this between the group and the event organizer. Now she had to make sure that the singers would be well prepared. She e-mailed the group to remind them of the opening of the Graces this Saturday with a summary of key issues, such as the call time, the dress code, and the program of arias and a quartet.

The moment she pressed Send, the fact of her layoff hit her again. She sighed, grumbling that life wasn't fair. She called Père Momus at the restaurant. He agreed that she could work at the bistro from eleven to four Monday to Friday, plus on Saturday and Sunday as needed. "*Merci*, Père Momus," she said. "You're a lifesaver." At least this solved her immediate need until she could find a new job.

Relieved, she went to the piano and warmed up her voice. Then she sang her aria for the Graces opening, followed by her part of the quartet. Her voice was steady, and her singing was flawless. *That's my girl*, she thought, caressing her vocal cords. She turned to the score of Leoncavallo's *La Bohème* and decided to focus on the aria "Mimi Pinson la biondinetta" ("Mimi Pinson, the little blonde") in Act I, in which Musette described her best friend Mimi to her fellow bohemians. First she read the verse with clear diction. Then she sang the melody with the words *sotto voce* in under-tempo, accompanying herself on the piano to ensure the correct pitch. Next she increased the tempo as specified in the score, measuring with a metronome. She added the expressions. She repeated the aria until all these elements flowed naturally. Now she sang the entire aria in full voice with the dynamics of expression and tempo. Her coloratura mezzo trotted like a delightful dance. The aria began portraying the zestful Musette as she had envisioned. She felt her energy coming back. Her confidence swelled. She resolved to learn the entire score in one month. *I can do it.*

⊰❦⊱

That evening Stephanie had a dinner appointment with her father at a restaurant off Fifth Avenue in the fifties. This had become their annual ritual for the past few years. Her father, Aaron Frank, was a partner in a hedge fund that managed more than fifty billion dollars in investments. His office was in the Wall Street area, and he commuted from his mansion in Westport, Connecticut. She was an only child. Her mother had loved her and her father dearly. While she was growing up, her mother had kept the family joyful. However, when she was a sophomore at Yale, her father had left her mother for a younger woman. Stephanie had known that her father traveled on business frequently. She remembered her mother's sad face during his absences—her father was her mother's life. At Yale she lived in a dorm, so she didn't know what had happened between her parents. Nevertheless her father's desertion completely surprised her. Afterward her mother had drooped like a lost soul. She called her mother frequently from her dorm, but she could not comfort her mother enough.

A few months later, Stephanie went to Miami on her spring break. One day she received a telephone call from the housekeeper in Westport, who informed her that her mother had been found dead in her bed that morning. The woman had called an ambulance, and they'd rushed her mother to a hospital, but it was too late. Stephanie got home the next day. Her mother's body still remained at the hospital, where they had determined the cause of the death was cardiac arrest. The preliminary analysis did not show any poison, sleeping pills, or dangerous chemicals in her mother, nor did the doctors see any injuries to her mother's body. But neither did they find any sign of heart disease. They debated the case without reaching a conclusion. It could have been a combination of many things, they told Stephanie, partly physical and partly mental. Her mother's heart had simply stopped beating while she was sleeping.

The evening she returned from Florida, Stephanie sat in her mother's bedroom. The bed, dressers, dressing table, mirror, and bookcases were as she remembered. On the table, bottles of nail colors and perfume stood grouped by colors and heights of the bottles, her mother's habit. The room was quiescent. She felt blank, unable to believe that her mother had passed away.

Suddenly she saw an apparition of her mother, sitting on the edge of her bed and gazing at her. Her mother wore a beautiful one-piece white dress, but her face was pale. She knew that this was her imagination. But she welcomed the apparition and felt comforted.

"Mom, why did you do it?" she asked.

"I didn't commit suicide, my dear," her mother said in a feeble voice. "I just lost my will to live. It was like a peaceful slumber. I didn't want to wake up."

"What am I going to do without you?"

"I'm sorry."

"Do you want me to get revenge on Dad?" She stared at her mother, ready for any response. "I'll be happy to do it for you."

"No, don't," her mother said. "I still love him."

"I can't believe this, Mom." She raised her voice. "He betrayed you. You should be raging at him. You ought to punish him."

"What would it solve?" Her mother sighed. "He wasn't happy with me. That's why he left us. It's my fault."

"I wish Dad could hear you. He'll pay for this. I'll make him." She burst into violent sobs.

Her mother rose, soundlessly moved closer, and hugged her. "Try to understand him. You are only nineteen. You need him."

"No, I don't." She clung to her mother, yet she felt she was holding the air. "I hate him. I'll never forgive him. I'm going to leave this house and live by myself."

"Sorry, my dear." Her mother wept, gently stroking her hair. "Be strong, and become a successful opera singer."

"Mom, I don't know if I can bear this."

"Courage, Stephanie. I'll be always watching you from above. And I look forward to the time when you sing at the Met." Her mother faded away.

Before the tears had dried on her cheeks, the funeral was over. Within three months, her father had married the younger woman. Stephanie had been her mother's girl ever since she was born, and they had been happy together wherever they went. She left her father's house and severed all communication with him, refusing any financial support from him. Since then she had lived by herself, taking odd jobs. How hard it had been, particularly during her school years. Without scholarships and student loans, she could not have graduated. She was still paying back the student loans. The hardship further aggravated her animosity toward her father.

Her father seemed dismayed by her absolute rejection of him and his new family. Many years later, when he reached sixty, he had started begging her to meet him. Perhaps his age made him vulnerable. Years of absence from her father had also softened Stephanie's never-ceasing reproach. She had agreed to meet him once a year on the condition that the place of meeting should be a modest restaurant in Manhattan.

《◎ ◎》

When she arrived at the restaurant, her father was already waiting for her at a table. He had aged since she had last seen him. He stood as tall as ever, but his head looked balder, his eyeglasses thicker, his beard grayer, and his belly rounder. He wore an impeccable three-piece dark-blue Brooks Brothers suit with a brightly patterned silk tie and a snow-white handkerchief elegantly folded into his chest pocket. In contrast, she wore the same office clothes she had put on that morning, the most presentable outfit in her closet. As she came to the table, he hugged her and gave her a warm kiss on her cheek. She accepted them but did not return the gestures. For her, this appointment was merely a social obligation to the old man. As soon as she sat, he was eager to make conversation. He complimented her on how wonderful she looked. She replied that she was surviving all right.

"Would you permit me to buy several dresses for you?" he asked, eyeing her clean but worn-out clothes.

"My dress is just fine," she cut in, but her voice cracked because she knew it was shabby.

"Ah yes, of course. Sorry," he said, realizing his mistake. By now he must have learned that any patronizing attitude would only irritate her.

A waiter came. Her father ordered a bottle of wine from a thick wine list. It was served promptly. He raised his glass, and she followed mechanically. The wine tasted superb. It must have cost a fortune, though for her father it was nothing.

"I go to my club often." He started a pep talk. "Recently I began visiting Temple Emanu-El occasionally for Friday Sabbath service. It's only a few blocks away from the Knick. There, I found I can get a glimpse of you singing."

"Really? Dad, I never thought you were a religious person."

"Neither did I." He raised his eyebrows in embarrassment and amusement, patting his forehead with his palm. "I guess I'm getting old. I feel kind of peaceful there."

"Am I going to see you wearing a yarmulke and eating kosher foods?"

They both laughed. How many years had it been since she had laughed with her father? she wondered. He seemed happy to see her laughing.

"The best part of the service is when you sing alone. Your voice is exquisite, and you sing excellently. I'm proud of you."

This convinced her that he only attended the services as a pretext for enjoying her singing. "Thanks, Dad."

The waiter came back, and her father ordered dinner for two, asking her preference. Although the entrées he ordered were among the most expensive ones on the menu, he complained to the waiter that the dishes were not good enough for his daughter.

The food was excellent, but her father apologized to her, wishing that it were better. He promised her that someday he would take her to his club. She knew that the Knickerbocker Club was renowned for its sumptuous food, in addition to the exclusiveness of its membership. But she had no interest in going there.

"How is your opera career?" her father asked. As she told him about the new opera in March, his face lit up. "That's marvelous, my dear," he said, sinking into thought. "I know a little about Puccini's *La Bohème*. It was one of your mother's favorites. We went to the Met to see it a few times before you were born."

"Did she like it?"

"Like it? She adored it." He narrowed his eyes. "It has so many beautiful arias and ensembles. She even sang some of them. You know she had a beautiful voice. I'm sure you got your voice from her."

His remark warmed her. She did not expect to hear her father say anything affectionate about her mother. Her mother had studied music in college but had not pursued it professionally. It was her mother who had taught her how to sing and play the piano. She remembered many occasions when, as a teenager, she went to the Metropolitan Opera House with her mother. Through her mother, she had developed a passion for opera. "It's nice of you to say that."

"But yours is Leoncavallo's?" he said. "I've never heard of it."

She explained the history of Leoncavallo's *La Bohème* and its current status as a neglected opera. That was why, she told him enthusiastically, this was an excellent opportunity for her to get recognized. Her father listened closely, uttering here and there, "Ah, is that so?" Then he took a deep breath.

"May I come to your opera?" he asked, as if fearful of her rejection.

In the past she had adamantly prohibited her father from coming to any of her performances. Unless he had sneaked into the concert halls without her knowledge, she believed he had never heard her sing on the stage. She was amazed that this evening he had the boldness to ask. He was really changing, she thought. "It may be boring for you."

"Absolutely not." His eyes grew moist. "I would love to hear you sing an opera."

She had not anticipated this kind of tenderness from him, considering how acridly she rebelled against him. "I don't think it's a good idea."

Visibly disappointed, he lowered his eyes and rearranged his knife and fork on the dish for no purpose. His eyeglasses slipped low on his nose. Pushing them up, he made an effort to find a new topic of conversation. They talked about trivial matters. The waiter served coffee for him, tea for her. They started eating dessert.

"When you came in here a little while ago," her father resumed, "I noticed your face looked troubled. Do you have a problem?" He appeared genuinely concerned.

It touched her. She told him about her layoff, immediately adding that it was no big deal because she could work extra hours at the French bistro. He took his checkbook from an inside pocket of his suit, scribbled, and gave her the check. "I'll be happy, my dear, if you use it."

She glanced at it. The check was made payable to her name in the amount of ten thousand dollars. Her throat contracted. How helpful this would be in her current situation. "I can't take this, Dad," she said, returning the check to him.

"I was afraid you would say that. You're a proud woman, my girl." He exhaled a deep breath. "Then let's consider it a loan. You use it now, and you'll pay me back when you can. How's that?"

She needed it desperately. She wanted it. Her arm almost moved to grab it. "No, I can't."

"Stubborn, like your mother," he muttered. "Here, take it. Please." He slid it before her on the table. It remained there.

He drank his coffee and ate his dessert. She sipped her tea. The restaurant was not crowded on a Monday evening. He had chosen a corner table in the main dining area, where only a few patrons occupied tables near them. It was a good place for a private conversation.

"Why are you still so hostile to me?" her father asked softly, breaking the silence.

This brought back all the vexation she had felt for years. Her exasperation awoke inside her like a poisonous snake. She saw the apparition of her mother's sorrowful face behind her father. "Why?" She raised her voice. "Because you killed my mother!" She spat it in one breath.

He frowned. "I didn't kill her."

"Yes, you did." She stared at him so intently that she felt her eyes blazing. "You may not have stabbed or drugged her to death. But morally you're responsible."

He swallowed. "It was a long time ago. You don't understand."

"You bet I don't," she hissed. "But I never forgot it, and I'll never forget it. Never!"

He sank, crestfallen, while she breathed hard. It took some time for him to muster his courage to speak again. "I'm sorry about your mother. I didn't know it would end up that way." He peered at his coffee cup. "I know you loved her. It pains me to see you suffer so much. I'm guilty for it. This is why I want to do something for you… to compensate, may I say?"

"Compensate?" she hollered. "I see, your conscience is bothering you. Is that it?" She shoved the check back to him. "You think your cheap money will cleanse your bloody hands? Don't count on it. I'll never take your money."

"Dear, listen."

"Don't dear me. I've been living by myself since I was nineteen. I don't need you."

"Stephanie, be reasonable." His eyes welled up. "Yes, you're right. I admit it. I've hurt you and your mother, though without intending to. I want to make up to you for the pain I caused. I'm getting old. Let me do something for you while I can. That's the only way I can apologize to your mother." He looked upward, as if he were searching for his late wife in heaven. "Your mother will rest in peace if you're happy. Let's wash away the past, and let me make amends to you. I want you to be happy."

Her heart began melting. This was the mighty Aaron Frank, who dealt tens of millions of dollars right and left every day with a snap of his fingers, frightening or cheering the entire financial market at his will. Yet how meek he was to his own daughter. He had changed. She appreciated his humility. "I'm sorry, Dad. I've been too harsh on you."

"I understand," he said, obviously relieved by the change in her tone. He adjusted his eyeglasses and leaned forward. "Look, Christmas is two months away. It's a holiday for gentile people, and it doesn't mean much to me. But it's also the time for Hanukkah. So, for the sake of holiday spirit, let's make a truce. I ask you only one thing: let me come to your opera in March. It'll be a precious present from you to me. In return, I'll do anything you ask."

Stephanie scrutinized her father and saw on his face shy yet sincere affection, which she did not remember ever seeing before. It stirred her. He was not an evil man after all, she realized. *A temporary truce,* she reflected, *that's all he wants. It makes sense in the season for peace. Just this once.* "All right," she said. "Let's have a truce." Yet she fretted nonetheless. Behind her father, she saw her mother encouraging her to go on. "Dad, you can come to my opera."

Her father blinked in disbelief. A moment later it appeared to have sunk in. "That's wonderful. Thank you," he said. "Now, tell me what you want in return."

"I want nothing," she declared.

"No, no. That's not right." He contemplated. "Ah, I got it." He grinned. "I recently saw an advertisement for a two-bedroom condo at the Ansonia on the Upper West Side. I understand many famous musicians live there. When I saw it, I thought of you. Would you like that? I'll buy it for you."

She searched his face and found that he was dead serious. It would cost several million dollars. What a contrast it would be from her apartment. "Even if you do, I can't afford to pay the monthly fees and real estate tax. Forget it."

"I'll pay the maintenance costs. No problem." He seized the opportunity. "This way, you don't have to worry about making a living, so you can concentrate on opera. I want to help your opera career. Say yes."

"No, I can't."

"That's not fair. We made a truce. You gave me a beautiful present. Let me give you this as my gift. Please. You didn't let me pay for college or grad school. Take it."

She knew his offer was simply too much to accept. But his demeanor softened her. She didn't want to torment him any longer. Still she hesitated. Her eyes caught the abandoned check on the table. "Then I'll take this." She picked up the check. "Thanks, Dad. Actually it helps me a lot right now. But remember, it's a loan. I'll return it when I earn enough, OK?" She slipped the check into her purse.

"Yes, of course. Whatever you say, that's fine." He broke into a huge smile and wiped his eyes. "This is great. You've made me the happiest man in the world this evening."

Stephanie saw her mother smiling behind her father.

Scene 5

$\mathcal{E}$arly Saturday afternoon Stephanie dressed in a chic, close-fitting black satin gown and matching black high heels. These had cost a lot, for which she had used her father's money. She felt grateful to him for the timely help. She could use this outfit for the performance in March as well. She swiveled before the mirror. The new dress showed off her tall, slender body, discreetly concealing her smooth bosom and arms. Her short brunette hair might have belonged to a handsome boy, yet it reflected a girlish charm. Her mother's keepsake, a large ruby in a platinum necklace, glittered around her slim neck. Dazzling! She smiled at her reflection. She could carry herself confidently, expecting appreciative glances as she hosted the show.

She thought of her father. His genuine wish to help had moved her in a way his previous offers had not. In the past she had always taken it that he was trying to butter her up with money, which only aggravated her. This time, she sensed his sincere affection. She may have been too harsh on him for too long. Perhaps the time had come to patch things up once for all. How happy he had appeared when she allowed him to come to her opera. She looked forward to seeing him in the concert hall.

She had already had an early lunch and warmed up her voice. She took a taxi to the gallery on Madison Avenue in the seventies. The door displayed a poster announcing "The Graces: Artwork by Three Female Artists," with photographs of the artists and their sample works. The show would run for two weeks. The gallery had two floors. The ground floor was used for regular business, showing a variety of artwork for sale, some by famous artists and others by artists of future fame. She headed for the second floor, which was reserved for the rotating shows. The three artists were already there, busily checking the final arrangements.

Michelle greeted her and introduced the other members of the Graces, pointing out their artwork at the same time. The two artists hugged her. They all wore black dresses in different styles for the occasion. Stephanie found herself amused at how each woman was as different as her artwork. Helen was the tallest, and her straight auburn hair was cut in a geometric style that echoed her abstract painting with a touch of Zen. Medium-built Sarah had curly brown hair and hazel eyes as cheerful as her watercolor florals. Michelle's Italian beauty paralleled her lyrical Impressionist landscapes, scenes of Central Park and the Hudson River. Instead of dividing the exhibition space into three blocks, one for each artist's work, the artwork was mixed: here one of Michelle's oils, next a watercolor of exquisite flowers, followed by a symbolic abstract in comparable colors. This pattern was repeated throughout the exhibition space, creating an intriguing harmony among the three genres.

Now Stephanie needed to work on the two models. Michelle pointed to a back room where the models were waiting, a gallery storage room converted for the occasion to a makeshift dressing room, with a mirror, a dressing table, and a few chairs. Both models were slim women in their late twenties with light skin and blonde hair. Stephanie presented them with the ancient Grecian dresses she had borrowed from an opera costume company. The dresses were made of white silk, almost see-through. She asked the models to wear them without any underwear. As she had anticipated, while the dresses covered the body, they revealed sensual female shapes. The models, used to posing in the nude for artists, giggled with delight. She had also brought golden sandals that tied at the ankles and olive wreaths that shone on the models' blonde hair. Lastly she asked them to apply heavy makeup: striking red lipstick, silver-blue eye shadow, and pink blush on their cheeks. She gave the models instructions on how to act while serving wine and food, as well as during the opera scenes. She coached them as they practiced.

At two o'clock the second floor was opened to the public. The string quartet group began playing Brahms, creating a sophisticated atmosphere. By half past two, the floor was crowded with art connoisseurs and the artists' friends and family members. Père Momus bustled about, making last adjustments to the food arrangements. The two models stood by him, as poised as if they had been born in their Grecian outfits. At Père Momus's cue, they started serving canapés and glasses of wine on silver trays.

Under the bright gallery lights, the models' shining drapery delicately suggested the silhouette of pink flesh underneath. As they cat-walked, smiling radiantly, their breasts and buttocks sensually bounced, and the diaphanous silk curled around their feminine bodies, reminiscent of seraphic maidens at the temple of Aphrodite. The guests couldn't resist staring at the pretty models. Stimulated by their appearance, or making excuses to get closer to them, everyone in the room took a glass and sampled the hors d'oeuvres. The models conspicuously walked close to the artwork to draw the guests' attention, a stratagem Stephanie had specified.

The three artists were fully engaged, showing and explaining their work to the guests. Suddenly a small hand bell rang at the desk near the door, indicating the first purchase of an artwork. Stephanie learned from a gallery official that someone had bought one of Michelle's landscapes. On the wall next to that work, a small red dot was posted, indicating that the work had been sold. Shortly another bell followed, and another. Each time, the gallery officials lit up with grins.

Stephanie saw Jennifer, Henry, and her coach in the crowd, all in proper concert attire. She spotted John talking to Michelle and her parents. On the surface, she could not detect any strain. It appeared that Jennifer, too, was enjoying the upbeat mood of the show, wandering with Henry to admire the artwork but avoiding talk in order to save her voice for the performance.

Sometime after three o'clock, the string quartet completed its performance. Stephanie beckoned Jennifer, Henry, John, and her coach to come to the piano for their performance. The gallery official rang the hand bell. Stephanie spoke into a microphone to call for attention. The guests stopped their conversation and gathered closer to the piano. She thanked them for their patronage and introduced the string quartet, then each member of the Graces, pointing at Michelle, Helen, and Sarah. Finally she presented the Dolci Quattro as friends of the Graces.

"We would like to sing a few arias and one quartet from well-known operas," Stephanie said. "We hope this will fire up your generous hearts, and you'll buy the works of the Graces. We would like to see every piece of artwork in this room marked with a red dot." The gallery official rang the hand bell several times, and the guests laughed. "The first aria is the 'Toreador Song' from Bizet's *Carmen*. Please welcome John Bertucci, Michelle's equally artistic husband."

The coach launched into the grandiose introduction to a baritone aria of the bullfighter, Escamillo. Stephanie presented her red scarf to John, who used it as a cape. The audience clapped noisily. He started singing, saluting people with a majestic hand motion.

"*Votre toast, je peux vous le rendre,…*" ("Your toast, I can return to you,…")

Then came the famous melody.

"*Toréador, en garde! Toréador! Toréador!*"

At this, the two models approached John, their heads lowered, holding two tall wine glasses against their foreheads as if they were bullhorns. Their dresses wafted as they moved, granting tantalizing glimpses of their lovely figures. John, while singing, used the red cape to navigate the models to his left and right. The delighted audience cried "*Olé!*" as the models passed beside him. They joined in singing the chorus part of the aria.

Then Stephanie flirted with John while singing as Frasquita, Mercédès, and Carmen.

"*L'amour!...L'amour!...L'amour!*"

Each time, John responded as the hero bullfighter.

"*L'amour!...L'amour!...L'amour!*"

With an exuberant flourish, they reached the finale.

"*Toréador! Toréador! L'amour t'attend!*" ("Toreador! Toreador! Love awaits you!")

The audience shouted bravos and clapped. John bowed and waved the red cape as the matador's triumphant gesture. The two models made deep curtsies.

Before the noise had ceased, the coach started playing the introduction of Carmen's "Habanera" in an enticing tempo. With a red rose on her right ear, Stephanie advanced toward the guests, swaying her shoulders. She began the mezzo-soprano's aria.

"*L'amour est un oiseau rebelle...*" ("Love is a rebellious bird...")

On went the song of seduction, tantalizing and teasing. She moved among the guests, playing the gypsy beauty, sometimes holding the flower between her lips, other times to her breasts, occasionally brushing a guest's face with it.

"*Si je t'aime, prends garde à toi!*" ("If I love you, watch out!")

The audience spontaneously sang the popular refrains "*prends garde à toi!*"

At the finale she held a long *fermata* on "*garde*" in *forte* before flicking "*à toi!*"

They broke into passionate applause and bravos.

While she was still bowing, the coach played in a debonair tempo the introduction of "La donna è mobile," a tenor aria from

Verdi's *Rigoletto*. Henry stepped forward, assuming the persona of the buoyant Duke of Mantua. He began with tremendous zeal.

"*La donna è mobile qual piùma al vento, muta d'accento—e di pensiero...*" ("Women are ever swaying like feathers in the wind, every moment changing their mind...")

The audience roared. The infamous aria went on. He sang as if he could make love to ten girls simultaneously, flirting about the Grecian-garbed models.

At the finale he sang the traditional cadenza, "*e di pensier!*" ending in a high B-flat, which he held seemingly forever in burning *fortissimo* until the air ran out of his lungs.

Again the room thundered with fervent bravos and applause. He bowed.

When the noise subsided, Stephanie advanced to the microphone and spoke in a mock-scolding tone. "Gentlemen, gentlemen. No, no. Love is a serious thing. You must not ridicule it."

The ladies in the room murmured their approbation while the gentlemen sniggered.

Suddenly, from the middle of the crowd, Père Momus yelled, "Oh, Carmen, you can't say that."

An outburst of laughter overtook the room. This was so unexpected that even Stephanie couldn't restrain herself from following the crowd. She let the room rumble and waited until the noise receded.

"Well, let's get serious, please," Stephanie resumed, composing herself. "The tenor who just sang was Henry Anderson." Then she ushered Jennifer before her. "Now, friends and lovers, the next piece is 'Dove sono i bei momenti' from Mozart's *Marriage of Figaro*. In this aria, Countess Almaviva recalls the early days of her marriage, when she and her husband were happy. Now that cherished memory is past, so she laments: 'Where have those moments gone, charming, sweet, and delightful? Where have those oaths of fidelity gone from that deceitful mouth? Remembrance of my happiness has not yet flown away from me. Ah, in the constancy of loving and suffering, I hope to change that ungrateful heart.' For some, this must sound familiar. Jennifer Schneider will sing one of the most beautiful soprano arias ever composed."

The coach played a C major chord in slow *arpeggio*, and Jennifer started singing the aria in *Andantino*, followed by the expert piano accompaniment. The gallery grew hushed, beatific, as if the listeners' souls were being purified.

Stephanie felt reassured by Jennifer's coloratura soprano voice, which was not only refined but also steady and strong. The *accident* had not damaged her vocal cords after all. The new opera could go on. She then caught sight of Michelle in the audience, her face twisted with pain as she appeared to conceal her emotion. John focused on Jennifer's singing, avoiding looking at Michelle. Stephanie remembered that the Dolci Quattro were supposed to talk to Michelle about the strenuous life of opera singers. So far, she had not found a time to do so.

The aria ended. A long silence ensued as the audience seemed to listen to the echo of the music in their hearts. Then gracious applause erupted. Jennifer bowed, a glaze of tears welling up in her eyes. Stephanie shot her a concerned glance as she disappeared into the temporary dressing room. But Jennifer's sadness would have to wait. Stephanie had a show to host.

"Ah, love is suffering," Stephanie whispered into the microphone.

People giggled. Jennifer reappeared, seemingly composed. Her eyes were dry. Again Stephanie felt relieved, thinking that the guests must have taken Jennifer's tears as part of the act.

"Before the last piece, I would like to make a short announcement," Stephanie declared. "The Dolci Quattro will sing principal roles in Leoncavallo's *La Bohème* in March, produced by the New York Bel Canto Opera. This is a rarely performed opera. I hope you will come to hear us." The news stirred the gallery. Some applauded, and others looked puzzled. As usual, she had to explain the difference between Leoncavallo's *La Bohème* and Puccini's.

"We would like to conclude with a quartet, 'Addio, dolce svegliare alla mattina' from Act III of Puccini's *La Bohème*," Stephanie said. "In this quartet, on a cold winter day, Mimi decides to part from Rodolfo until spring. 'Farewell to love and jealousy. But when spring comes, the sun will be our consoling companion.' Meanwhile, Musetta and Marcello quarrel. Musetta wants freedom, but Marcello is possessive. In the end, Mimi and Rodolfo agree to postpone the separation until spring arrives. One of the most heartrending quartets in all opera."

The coach played the introduction, followed by Jennifer and Henry as Mimi and Rodolfo, soon joined by John and Stephanie as Marcello and Musetta. The four haunting voices interlaced, filling the gallery.

The performance over, Stephanie could relax. She realized how much she had loved organizing the chamber music and the opera scenes, introducing the singers and arias, and choreographing the models. Judging by the jubilance of the audience, she even felt that she had a talent for it. She wondered if this was her calling. Maybe she could even help the New York Bel Canto Opera this way. She decided to discuss it with Arthur, the company's director.

People had started walking around again, and the two models mingled with the guests, serving more wine and food. As Stephanie had hoped, the performance seemed to have opened the guests' hearts and wallets. She heard several sounds of the hand bell. Red dots were evenly posted among the works of the three artists. About a quarter of the works seemed to have been sold. This was considered a great success for the opening day.

An elegant couple approached Stephanie. She recognized Mike Walton, a baritone, and his girlfriend, Vicky Allen, both of whom she had invited to the opening. Mike was tall and good-looking, with dark-brown skin and a gentle face. Vicky was medium-built with short straight hair. Stephanie hurriedly caught hold of Jennifer, Henry, and John, and introduced them.

"Guys, you were superb," Mike said.

His sonorous voice impressed Stephanie. The other Dolci Quattro must have felt the same.

"Thanks, Mike," John said. "Schaunard is an important role. We'll be counting on you."

"We'll try to set up a coaching session with you soon," Henry followed.

Mike beamed. "Sounds good."

"I'll be an opera widow for a few months," Vicky said with a grin. "But that's OK. I'm used to it."

Stephanie noticed Michelle standing nearby, her cheeks quivering. She must have overheard. Stephanie remembered again that she wanted to talk to Michelle about this very topic. But later.

"Mike, right now, you're on your own for studying your role," Stephanie said. "In January, we'll have to start studying ensembles. We'll be in touch then."

"I can't wait." Mike rubbed his hands eagerly.

Another couple accosted the group. "Hey, guys, I heard you," Bruce said with a smirk, holding Irene.

"I didn't ask you to come," Stephanie said, stupefied, blocking them.

Bruce shrugged. "Yeah, but I couldn't resist the temptation. I wanted to hear what kind of shape you're in, particularly tenor and soprano."

"Well, what do you think?" Henry asked.

"You were OK." Bruce lifted his chin.

Stephanie sensed a touch of jealousy in his voice. Henry glared at him but didn't respond.

"Jennifer, you were wonderful," Irene said, tossing her red hair across her shoulders. "I'm really honored to be your understudy." Her eyes blazed frosty.

What a bitch, Stephanie thought. Henry, too, gave Irene a sharp look. But despite her blatant insincerity, Irene's remark was still a compliment to Jennifer because she couldn't find a single flaw in Jennifer's singing to harp on. Jennifer inclined her head politely and turned away as if suddenly fascinated by one of Sarah's watercolors. Irene plastered herself against Bruce as if she had been his lover of the past ten years.

"Hey, this is a show opening," Stephanie said. "Don't be a nuisance. You'd better go."

Bruce held Irene closely, and they strolled out together hand in hand. At least they hadn't made a big scene, except for annoying the Dolci Quattro, Stephanie thought.

"What a nerve to come here," Henry said, his eyes following them to the door.

"Just ignore them," John chimed in.

Sensing the awkwardness amid the Dolci Quattro, Mike thanked them for the invitation and left with Vicky.

It was evident to Stephanie that Bruce had absolutely no regard for her. He was now Irene's man. She should sever the tie with him completely, if any were left. *Should I? I'm not so sure. What, you still can't make up your mind? You stupid girl.*

"Let's forget about Bruce and Irene," she told the others. "Our performance is over. We should enjoy ourselves. Shall we see the Graces' work?"

The Dolci Quattro leisurely walked, examining each artwork. Henry and John flanked Jennifer so she would not feel dejected. They drank water instead of wine to soothe their vocal cords after singing. They sampled savory canapés from the models. Soon they were laughing together in the spirit of a performance well done.

The opening was winding down, though many guests still wandered around. Stephanie watched as Sarah gripped Henry's arm, trying to fix him up with a pretty young woman. She overheard that the girl was the watercolor painter's younger sister, Christine. *Let them have fun.*

She also noticed Père Momus enjoying the exhibit with the keen interest common to his native French blood. He talked to each of the Graces, who listened to his remarks with respect. Among them, Stephanie observed Michelle's excited face. Now she wanted to make sure that John was all right. It couldn't have been easy for him to watch Michelle so happy. She spotted him eyeing one of Michelle's paintings.

"John, your Escamillo was great."

"It was fun," he said.

"You're honorable and brave. It must require a lot of courage."

"It's tough, but I'll get through. Thanks." He sipped water. "I'm sorry about your job. I hope you can find a new one soon."

"I hope so, too."

"By the way, did you see Richard here?"

Overhearing this, Henry joined them with a concerned look. "I saw him. I never told him about our singing at this opening, and I don't think Jennifer did either. He was with an attractive redhead."

"That's right," John chimed in. "She was talking to Helen about her abstract paintings. It struck me because both are redheads. They must know each other. So Richard's new girlfriend must have brought him here."

"Oh no," Stephanie uttered. "This'll be a disaster. We have to hide Jennifer. Quick!"

The gallery was not so large, but the crowd, although thinning, still occupied much of its interior space. After a frantic search, they found Jennifer alone near the window, gazing down at the street.

"Hi, Jennifer," Stephanie said, resting her hand on her friend's shoulder. "As usual, you sang beautifully. To be honest, I was a bit concerned about your voice. But you made a great comeback. I'm happy for you."

"Thank you," Jennifer said. Her face had lost color. Instead of acknowledging the state of her voice, her attention remained on the street. "I saw Richard. But he left when he saw me. I don't think he expected I'd be here. He was with a woman." She bit her lip. "The one I saw in his apartment."

"Try not to take it too hard," Stephanie said, gently caressing her.

Jennifer kept staring at the street in silence. Tears gleamed on her cheeks. Both John and Henry stood beside her, but seemed unable to find any words to console her. Stephanie needed to divert Jennifer's attention. She looked around the room. Only several people remained. The Graces were at the door, seeing off the guests. Gallery officials had started tidying up the room. Père Momus and his men had also begun cleaning. The two models had gone to the dressing room to change.

"Let's have dinner together," Stephanie said. "C'mon, we should celebrate our successful performance." She pulled Jennifer away from the window toward the center of the gallery, flanked by Henry and John. Jennifer reluctantly went along with her friends.

"We're going to have a good time," Stephanie said. "John, you must join us," she added. "Don't worry. I'll make sure it's all right with Michelle."

Stephanie found Michelle and told her that the Dolci Quattro were going out for dinner. Her face still flushed with excitement, Michelle said that the Graces, too, were going out to celebrate. Sensing Michelle's relief, Stephanie realized the arrangement would work out well between John and Michelle without embarrassing either. Then she thought that this might be a good opportunity.

"Michelle," she said, "I want you to know we singers struggle between our singing career and making a living. I just lost my day job, and I've got to work extra hours as a waitress in the Café Momus. It's not easy. I don't have time to enjoy anything."

Michelle's eyes darkened. "Why are you telling me this?"

"Because I'm sorry to see John working so hard. Other than singing, his entire time is devoted to earning a living. He can do this only because he is a strong man."

"Aren't you meddling in our personal affairs?"

"I don't mean to. But I want you to understand."

"OK, I'll think about it," Michelle said, then forced a smile. "The arias really brightened up the mood. Thanks a lot."

"I'm glad it went well. Congratulations on a wonderful show."

They parted. Stephanie detected two things in Michelle's countenance. Michelle did not want to spoil the success of the opening. Nor did she want to argue with Stephanie, who had helped the Graces so much. But Stephanie also felt that her words had sunk in with Michelle. She hoped that they would have a positive effect. She returned to the Dolci Quattro.

While they were discussing where to go, Père Momus cut in. "*Venez chez moi*," he said. "Since you sang excellently, it'll be on the house."

"*Merci beaucoup*," cried Stephanie, followed by Henry and John. In anticipation of good wine, delicious food, and pleasant conversation, with Stephanie leading, they danced, circling Père Momus. Stephanie urged Jennifer to join in, which she did. It was just like old times.

Now the Dolci Quattro came closer and presented their right hands forward, their palms stacked one on top of the other.

"Sing on!"

Scene 6

*O*ne week after the Graces' opening, Henry went home to Columbus, Ohio, for a memorial service observing the one-year anniversary of his father's death. His father had been a heavy smoker until his middle age but had quit smoking several years before. Three years ago, at age sixty-eight, he had been diagnosed with lung cancer and had an operation. Since then, he had been in and out of the hospital. When he was well, he had continued his work as a professor at Ohio State University, where he had taught the theory, composition, and conducting of classical music. Last year he had finally passed away. Henry's brother, George, an associate professor at the College of Medicine, OSU, had organized the memorial service at their family church. After the service they had luncheon at the university faculty club.

In the evening the family gathered in the parents' house where they had grown up. A grand piano occupied one corner of the living room. Bookcases teemed with music scores and books on classical music. The Queen Anne furniture was just how Henry remembered it. Now that the formalities were over, the family could relax. Adults sat on sofas or chairs, sipping their favorite wine or cocktail. Children played on the oriental rugs. Henry's mother was a retired high school music teacher. She received a steady stream of income from her own pension and Social Security. At age forty-one, George was content with his successful career. He took good care of his beautiful wife, Laura, and their three children at their luxurious house nearby. The children looked at home because they often spent time here. Judith, Henry's younger sister, had flown in from California. She was married to a professor of economics at Stanford University, who could not come to the service due to his teaching schedule. She held her son, still a baby. Her four-year-old daughter was timid in her grandmother's house but soon joined in playing with her cousins. Henry realized how much he missed this kind of domestic life. He might never be able to attain it as long as he continued his opera career.

"So how's your life in New York?" George asked, drinking a cold martini.

"As usual." Henry shrugged at the familiar question. "Recently I got a role in Leoncavallo's *La Bohème*. It'll be produced at the beginning of March. You should come to New York to see it."

"Leoncavallo? Not Puccini?" George's red face appeared puzzled.

Henry saw the same perplexed looks on his mother and sister. It amused him how many times he had to clarify this whenever he mentioned the opera to new people.

"Are you getting paid for it?" George came to the point.

"For this one, yes. But it's only an honorarium, a small amount."

"Are you making a living as a singer yet?"

Henry knew that his brother would ask this—he always did. And as always, he didn't have a good answer. He saw his mother and Judith waiting. He took a sip of wine. "For now I can't quit my day job."

George raised an eyebrow. "For now? You've been saying the same thing for years. At thirty-six, don't you think it's about time to settle and start a family?"

Henry frowned, irritated by George's patronizing tone, that of the older brother who never stopped worrying about his little brother's bohemian life.

"If you want," George continued, "I might be able to find a faculty position at OSU for you. This afternoon during the luncheon at the faculty club, Dad's colleagues were talking about you." George got up to pour himself another martini, then grinned at Laura and their children. "When I was thirty-six, I was already practicing cardiology and teaching here, with a wife and our first kid. Why don't you do the same? Get a teaching position here, find a nice girl, get married, have a few kids. We'd love to have you living close to the family."

If this had been a few years earlier, Henry would have violently protested, defending his opera career. Now, however, he had to concede that what his brother was saying was appealing. He thought of his friends. All the Dolci Quattro seemed stuck in the middle of the road, no matter how diligently they worked on their singing.

"When you're young," George resumed, "the bohemian life is attractive. But you can't be young forever. You're now at the age to make a decision whether to stay on the same course or change for the better." He softened his tone. "Henry, don't get me wrong. I'm not saying you must give up opera. We know opera is your love. We know you have an excellent voice. I'm merely suggesting you settle down if there's no prospect of getting into a first-tier opera company." George polished off his drink and concluded. "Think about it. If you want, I'll help you find a teaching position here. Dad was respected by his colleagues. I'm sure they would be pleased to have you."

George swept up his younger daughter and patted her shiny blonde hair.

"Daddy, look, I put a new dress on my doll," she said. "Doesn't she look pretty?"

"Yes, sweetie, she's beautiful." George gave her a loud kiss. "When are you going to have afternoon tea with your doll? Can you invite me?"

"Sure, Daddy. Next Sunday afternoon at four o'clock at the dollhouse in my room. OK?"

"Thank you, sweetie. I'll be there. I can't wait."

George released his daughter, who went back to the middle of the living room to play with her sister, brother, and cousin. Henry watched his niece's cherubic face. He yearned for this kind of innocent world with his own children.

Judith sighed as if she could see his mind. "Henry, I know your opera career means everything to you. But I think George is right. We don't want you to be too late. How many voice students graduate from music schools each year? Hundreds? But how many singers are hired by first-tier opera companies each year? Less than ten? I read an article that even Juilliard graduates give up on opera careers. One became a real estate agent, others a stockbroker, jewelry designer, pet shop owner, completely giving up music. That's sad. So while you can salvage your music career, you should. A voice faculty position at a university isn't a bad alternative to an opera singer's career. You should think about it."

Suddenly Henry came to realize that something similar must have happened to Père Momus when he had given up his acting and become the owner of a restaurant. Now Henry knew why Père Momus had been encouraging him to keep going.

Henry's mother had been listening to her sons and daughter. "It's Henry's life. We shouldn't interfere," she said. "Henry, you can take the opera scores, music sheets, and CDs from your father's study. He would be pleased if you used them. He wanted you to succeed. Try your best. I don't want you to have regrets later." She turned to her three grown children one by one, as if she had something important to say. "This is a good occasion. Your father and I spent all our money on your education. This house is the only valuable property I have now. When I die, you'll inherit it. You can divide the proceeds equally among you. But there's nothing else."

"Mom, let's talk about something else," George said.

"No, your father is gone, and you're discussing Henry's future." She faced him. "My point is, Henry, I regret that what you get as an inheritance won't be much. You'll have to continue supporting yourself financially." She exhaled. "These days, I know only children of wealthy families can afford to pursue music careers. I'm sorry to say, Henry, but you're not one of them. You ought to keep this in mind as you make your decisions."

"I understand," Henry said.

Henry felt overwhelmed by the concerns from his family. But what could he tell them? It was true that his opera career was going nowhere in Manhattan, and that at thirty-six, his time was running out. A teaching position at a university sounded almost seductive. But he was not ready to give up on opera. He thought of his father. His father had been disappointed with George because George refused to take up music. Judith, too, did not pay much attention to music. Henry was the only child who showed an interest in music. His father had believed that Henry had several gifts as a musician, like perfect pitch and remarkable sight-reading ability. He was good at the piano, too. His father had been particularly proud of his voice and told him that he could be the next Richard Tucker. His father had mailed him checks for a few hundred dollars occasionally to relieve him of the financial burdens of New York. He had cherished his father's moral support. He felt a wave of grief at the loss of his closest defender.

Last year, when his father died, Henry had naturally felt mournful, but somehow in the abstract, probably because of his youth. Now, however, a deep sadness overtook him. He wanted to go on as a professional singer, as his father had wished. But also he felt that his father might approve of the teaching position because it was still part of opera. But no—it wouldn't be the same. Opera meant singing, acting, music, poetry, art, all together on the stage. *That's what I want. That's what my father wished for me.* He uttered, "I'll think about the teaching position."

"Good. That's enough of Henry's career," his mother said. "Henry, sing something for your father." She took a moment to reflect. "How about Schubert's 'Ave Maria'? Your father was fond of it. He even wrote an article about it. Can you sing it for him?"

"Happy to," Henry replied, glad of the change of the subject. "I can sing it in Latin by heart. Can you play the piano for me?"

Nodding deeply with a smile, his mother went to one of the bookcases, found a music book, and sat at the piano. Henry rose and moved close to her. She began playing the introduction in *Molto lent*. The celestial melody rolled in double triplets like peaceful waves in a slow continuing motion. Henry sang.

> *Ave Maria,*
> *Gratia plena,*
> *Dominus tecum,*
> *Benedica tu in mulieribus,*
> *Et benedictus fructus ventris tui Jesus...*

> (Hail Mary,
> Full of grace,
> The Lord be with thee.
> Blessed art thou among women,
> And blessed is the fruit of thy womb, Jesus...)

He felt the purity of the intimate prayer, an outpouring of spiritual blessing, like incessant water coming from a pristine spring. For the Anderson family, it served as a private supplication, honoring the one who had gone and comforting those who were left behind. The children came to their parents and listened to him, some sitting on their parents' laps and others snuggling up next to them on the sofa. Judith and Laura sighed and wept. Even George looked moved as the music swelled and tears streamed down their mother's cheeks.

◦◦ ◦◦

Back in New York, Henry felt depressed for a few days, not only because of the memory of his late father but also because of his professional impasse. He tried to return to his normal life. He went to the office as usual. He had been doing this job, maintaining the company's website, for some years. By now it was routine work to support his opera aspirations. He wore an informal office suit and leather shoes. His colleagues in the IT department wore T-shirts, jeans, and sneakers. They considered Henry old-fashioned but accepted him as their friend because he was a cool opera singer.

Henry's cubicle neighbors popped in and gossiped, munching doughnuts and sipping coffee from their mugs. He gestured that he had to complete an assignment that was almost overdue. He had hoped that the hip IT culture of his office would distract him from his distress. But still he could not focus on the web pages he was maintaining. Noticing his taciturnity, his colleagues asked if anything was wrong. Once Henry explained about his late father's memorial service, they respectfully left him alone.

After work, he tried to practice but could not sing. He called the other Dolci Quattro. They comforted him, presuming that his sadness was due to the memory of his late father. He could not mention his worries about his opera career because they were all suffering the same fate. John's and Jennifer's parents were still living, so their sympathy was generic. However, since Stephanie had lost her mother a long time ago, her words were more personal.

"In my case," she said, "it was totally unexpected. One day she was alive. The next day she was gone. I was only nineteen. To make matters worse, my father had left us a few months earlier. I felt absolute loneliness."

"I'm sure you did," Henry said. "In my situation, we knew he was suffering from cancer. We expected the worst would come. But still, it's a loss I wouldn't want to face if I had a choice. It's already been one year. I thought the pain would fade as time passes. But the loss feels more real now than a year ago."

"I know what you mean."

"My father always encouraged me to go on with my opera career. Now he's gone."

"My mother, too. It's hard, Henry. But this is life."

The conversation solved nothing. But the sympathy of his close friend consoled him.

One late afternoon, Henry took a coaching session. He wanted to go over Marcello's demanding role in Act III of Leoncavallo's *La Bohème*. His coach, Victor Carré, lived in the Ansonia on Broadway in the seventies, which used to be a landmark hotel renowned for its Beaux-Arts architecture. It had once provided sumptuous apartments to legendary musicians, singers, artists, actors, and writers, including Caruso, Toscanini, and Stravinsky. Now it had been converted to luxurious condominiums.

Mr. Carré was in his late fifties, tall and slim, with an intellectual face and gray hair. He knew most of the famous operas by heart. He understood and spoke Italian, French, and German, almost as a native speaker. He coached diction of these languages and explained the meaning of the arias and recitatives. He played the piano, sight-reading the orchestra score, and sang simultaneously any singer's part. Mr. Carré also taught the interpretation of arias and how to express the quintessence of the meaning in given scenes. In addition to all this exceptional knowledge and skill, he had a pleasant personality and was supportive to singers. As such, he was esteemed by many of his students, particularly Henry.

Today, the session did not go smoothly. After half an hour, Mr. Carré stopped. With a concerned look, the longtime coach asked Henry if he was not feeling well. Henry explained his woes. The coach listened and then sighed.

"Yes, that's our problem. We love opera. But we have to make a living, too. It's not easy, I know. I'm the first one to acknowledge that." Mr. Carré pointed to a framed photograph of a father and son at a piano. "My father was a baritone and sang at the Met in the 1950s and 60s. I had a happy childhood and grew up with a passion for opera. Now, here I am." He gestured to the spacious living room with its high ceilings, elegant moldings, and bay windows. Besides a grand piano and bookcases, however, the room was nearly barren. "I'm a graduate of Juilliard. Fortunately I have my job with the Lyric Opera of Chicago as a conductor. It pays well, but usually I get only one opera per season. That's not enough to live on. So I have to travel around as a guest conductor to supplement my income. And the rest of time, I teach here. I own this condo. But I can barely afford the mortgage, maintenance, and taxes, and that's only because my wife works as an office manager. Without her income we would go bankrupt. She's a painter by profession, but she sacrifices it for our living so I can continue pursuing my music. I'm grateful to her."

Mr. Carré played a few scales on the piano for no purpose, which sounded desolate. Here was the conductor of the Lyric Opera, who enjoyed thunderous applause from audiences nationwide. Yet even he was going through the same challenges Henry had been facing. *So we musicians are all alike,* he thought.

"It's the cruel fact," Mr. Carré resumed, "that you must endure the hardship if you want to continue in opera. Only a few lucky singers can make a living by singing alone. The question is: Can you endure it? Or, put more bluntly, do you have a talent and voice that are worth abiding the suffering for? Every singer has to ask himself that question. In most cases one can't answer, simply because one doesn't know."

Mr. Carré played part of the aria Henry had been singing several minutes earlier. Henry was supposed to be studying. Where had his energy gone? He had none. *Talent, Mr. Carré asks. I don't know anymore if I have enough talent.*

"Let me be frank with you, Henry," Mr. Carré said. "You have an extraordinary instrument. It would be a pity if you gave up your career. This I can say. But is it worth bearing the hardship? That I can't answer for you. Where do you draw the line regarding standard of living? Some can take poverty, but others can't." Mr. Carré's met Henry's gaze. "This may sound cruel, but it's true. If you want luxury in your life, forget the opera career."

Mr. Carré played the piano again. Henry tried to sing the aria in his mind. But he was too disturbed to sing. *I wish I could forget about opera. Then all of my suffering would be over. But what would I do then? Without opera, I'm nothing.*

"In addition to your extraordinary instrument," Mr. Carré said, softening his voice, "your singing has a soul that touches people's heart. If you're willing to persevere, you might be able to make it to a first-tier opera company someday. But unfortunately it's not guaranteed. Are you willing to take that chance?"

Mr. Carré gave a shrug, as if he were the one who was undergoing the challenge. Given his experience, his remarks bore the weight of truth. Henry took the coach's words as bitter medicine. *Am I willing to take the chance? Or should I change direction?*

Seeing Henry's lost-child-like face, Mr. Carré played the last chord of the aria. "Let's stop the lesson now, Henry. Today is not a good day for you. I won't charge you. Go home and relax. I'll see you next week."

Usually when Henry completed a coaching session with Mr. Carré, although he was physically exhausted, he felt elated because his study had been fruitful. In the elevator down, he would smile with satisfaction while drinking water. Not today. He felt totally worn out, physically and mentally. He just leaned against the wall while the elevator descended. As he trudged toward the entrance door, he saw Bruce dashing into the lobby.

"Hey, you look like a ghost," Bruce said. "Have you decided to quit singing?"

"You wish," Henry replied. "I just had a coaching session. I'm tired, that's all."

"I know you're with Victor," Bruce said. "I'm going to have a lesson with Hugh Abelian right now. He's the best. I'm getting better and better under him. He'll help me make it to the Met." He jerked up his chin as if he could not resist looking down at Henry.

Henry ignored Bruce and left the building. He knew that Mr. Abelian was one of the most sought-after voice teachers in Manhattan. The maestro lived at the Ansonia and commanded the highest fees for his lessons, which had a reputation for being notoriously stringent—so it was considered a credential if a singer survived as his tutee. Henry did not know how Mr. Abelian was receiving Bruce. However, if Bruce was lasting under the maestro, Bruce's arrogance was not without reason. Bruce could be Henry's formidable rival, an alarming prospect.

⟨⟨◎ ◎⟩⟩

Henry returned to his apartment and flung himself on the sofa. He checked his iPhone. Nothing important. He visited his web pages and found that one of the daily net asset values of a mutual fund was corrupted. He had to fix it. But not now, he thought. He lay on his back on the sofa in the dim living room. He clenched his fists and smashed them into the cushions, but they lacked strength. He exhaled deeply, feeling that he was sinking to a bottomless abyss. He wanted to cry but controlled himself. The world appeared so despondent. Suicide was not in his character. But now he understood how Jennifer must have felt before her attempt. When he was young, the hard life had meant nothing. He had hope. Time stood on his side. He kept saying, *Someday I'll make it. Someday. Someday. Someday.* Yet that someday had never come. Now he was thirty-six. The weight of the age wore him out. *What should I do? What's the best course for me to take?* He began drowsing off. He heard a whirlpool of fragmented voices.

> George: When you're young, the bohemian
> life is attractive. But you can't be young
> forever. You're now at the age to make a
> decision whether you stay on the same
> course or change for the better.
>
> Judith: A voice faculty position at a uni-
> versity isn't a bad alternative to an opera
> singer's career. You should think about it.
>
> Mr. Carré: If you want luxury in your life,
> forget the opera career.
>
> Bruce: Have you decided to quit singing?

Henry cried out to them, *No! I want to continue my opera.* His howling declaration was, however, not strong enough to surmount the whirling speeches. Then Henry was caught by repeated flashbacks of happy lives: his confident brother with his beautiful wife and angelic children, and his content sister with her scholarly husband and two adorable children. His niece's bell-like exclamation of "Daddy" echoed in his ears. He felt a sharp sting of envy.

Henry was awakened by the telephone. A young female voice greeted him. It was Christine Moret, the younger sister of the watercolor painter, whom he had met at the opening of the Graces. She told him that she had called his number several times already. He apologized and described his recent visit to his home.

Christine talked about the time her mother passed away a few years earlier. She had been close to her mother and had mourned. "I've learned that in spite of the loss, for those who are left behind, we must live our life. I feel my mother is watching over me from inside my heart. She would be happier if I lived a positive life." Christine stopped as if she were listening to her mother. "Henry, when I was overwhelmed with grief at my mother's death, one poem comforted me. I'll read it for you." She took a moment to fetch a book. "It's Psalm 23," she said. "You might recognize it." She read it in earnestness.

> The Lord is my shepherd;
>> I shall not be in want.
> He makes me lie down in green pastures
>> and leads me beside still waters.
> He revives my soul
>> and guides me along right pathways
>> for his Name's sake.
> Though I walk through the valley of the
>> shadow of death,
> I shall fear no evil;
>> for you are with me;
>> your rod and your staff, they
>> comfort me...

Henry was surprised to hear such a spiritual poem from a young woman whom he hardly knew. He remembered that the priest had read this Psalm during his father's burial service. But listening to Christine, he found the Psalm warmer, more personal, and more direct. It irradiated in his heart something graceful, like an eternity where love united life and death in peace, overcoming sorrow. How consoling it sounded. He felt moved by both the Psalm itself and Christine's compassion to recite it for him.

"Thank you," Henry said when she completed reading. "I feel better already."

There was a moment of silence. "I'm not sure this is polite," she said. "But if you feel like it, we could have dinner together this evening. I live at Seventy-Third and Columbus. We could go to one of the restaurants around here. What do you think?"

Scene 7

*J*ennifer came out of the building on Fifth Avenue near Rockefeller Center where her law firm had an office. At dusk, the illuminations from the stores brightened the avenue. It was warm for mid-November. This evening Aunt Maggie was visiting from Florida. They were to have dinner together at home. Jennifer wanted to buy dessert but paused, trying to decide where to go. At an intersection, among several people waiting for the traffic signal, she noticed a tall figure with a handsome face and straight brown hair, wearing a flawless dark blue suit. He was carrying a brief-case she recognized—a birthday present she had bought just a few months before. *Richard.* She quickened her pace to catch up with him. She forced herself to greet him casually. When he saw her, his eyes opened wide and he uttered a strangled cry. She approached and asked him if he was meeting someone. He shook his head. The traffic signal turned green. They walked along with the crowd.

"I saw you at the Graces opening a few weeks ago," she said. "You could have said hello to me. How have you been?"

"Busy, as usual." He appeared to be studying the trendy women's fashion in a store window.

"How's your writing?"

"I haven't had time for it recently." He turned his attention to the glittering precious stones in the showcases of a jewelry store.

She could see that he was trying to find some excuse to hurry away. "Listen. Don't run off. I know you've got a new girlfriend. But you haven't forgotten I was your fiancée, have you? Don't you have the guts to face me? Be a man, Richard."

They kept walking, in silence, but at least he did not try to flee. Soon they came to the square across from Central Park in front of the Plaza Hotel. Jennifer pointed to an empty bench. He nodded. They sat. People walked by and cars passed them, while trees gave them privacy. Jennifer took a deep breath and faced him. He stared at his shoes.

"You were with your new girlfriend at the opening," she said. "Our relationship is over; I accept it. But at least you should have the courtesy to tell me why you left me."

Richard shrank. Jennifer could not tell how he was feeling. She waited.

"I can't tell you how sorry I am," he said at last. "I feel like a cheap clown. I know I loved you when I proposed marriage. Believe me."

That's easy for you to say, creep. If you think you can get away with this nonsense, you're wrong. You've got to explain better than that. She remembered how forlorn she had felt before taking the sleeping pills. "Then why did you leave me?"

"Jennifer, it hurts." Richard frowned. "Maybe I deserve the pain."

It hurts you, huh? I wonder how much. She resisted the urge to tell him that he deserved any pain he was feeling, and more. Contrary to the usual confident young executive, Richard now looked vulnerable. The traffic noise reminded her that they were in a public space. This was good, because it helped her to control her emotions.

"What I did to you was terrible," he resumed, "but I couldn't help it. I'm only thirty-five. I'll make a VP soon. Do you know what that means? I have power, money, energy. I want to enjoy life. What's wrong with that? Women, partying, dancing, drinking, dining, traveling, things like that. And sex, too, definitely—"

"I never refused your—" she interrupted but was immediately cut off.

"You don't understand. You were too busy with your opera. I tried to accept your stoic lifestyle. The consequence was I never had enough time to enjoy my life with you."

Jennifer thought of Michelle's similar complaints and could only nod. "And when were you planning to tell me this?"

Richard did not reply.

"Your new girlfriend satisfies you then?"

"Her name is Karen Grimes," Richard answered, gazing up at the brown-leafed trees. "She's a lawyer in my bank in a different department. We're busy, but we get together after work and weekends. We enjoy each other's company. Recently we went to the Bahamas. It was so relaxing."

She noticed the golden suntan on his face. A spasm pierced her gut. While she had been suffering through the agony of his affair, he had taken a tropical getaway with his new lover. *How could you do this to me?* Indignant blood shot up to her head. She wanted to scream but restrained herself. "So she is good in bed, is that it?"

Richard frowned and met her eyes. "Sorry, Jennifer, but I'm just a young healthy man. I want to enjoy the pleasures the world can offer. You must understand that."

Another long silence. She knew that as long as she pursued her music, the life Richard wanted was not one she could share. This did not mean that she disliked fun. She, too, wanted to enjoy life, but in her own subtle way, so she could maintain her agile voice. She wondered why he could not support this. He would have shown more sympathy if he loved her. She had thought that he knew how much the opera career meant to her. Apparently she had been mistaken.

"Are you going to marry her?" she asked.

"I don't know. I guess Karen doesn't know that either. But both of us are happy now. That's all that matters to us at the moment."

Indeed, as he said this, his face lit up. Seeing it, she sighed. Clearly an irreparable gulf had opened between them. She remembered the happy days when he had been passionately in love with her. Tears welled in her eyes.

"It's getting late," he mumbled. "I'd better go." He stood up, seemingly relieved that her confrontation had not ended up with public screaming, as he may have feared. "I'm sorry about this, Jennifer. Take care."

After Richard left, heading downtown on Fifth Avenue, Jennifer stood up and moved in the same direction. At the northeast corner of the Bergdorf Goodman building, she saw him struggling to escape from a small swarm of tourists who had bumped into him and turned him around. As he extracted himself from the group, his briefcase held high, a woman emerged from the store. His face brightened immediately. Jennifer froze. The woman was tall and curvy, wearing a provocative Henri Bendel miniskirt business suit. She carried a Gucci bag and two shopping bags from Bergdorf's. Richard hugged and kissed her. She leaned toward him, bending one leg in the air. Her long red-gold hair lifted in the breeze. Jennifer imagined it wet, flipping back in a towel, revealing her naked... *Stop it!*

She watched Richard and his girlfriend through a corner storefront window. On the street, it was difficult to hear their precise words. But since they were right around the corner, she was able to catch most of their conversation.

"I wanted to find an impressive outfit for your conference in Atlanta next week," the woman, Karen, said. "I bought a suit and an evening dress. Now I can play the part of your legal counsel by day and your lover by night."

Richard grinned and held her tight, as if he were showing off his gorgeous sex slave to the world. "I found out for sure that our executive VPs are going to the conference, so we'll have to have separate rooms at the hotel." He winked. "But I'll sneak into your room every night."

"Want to see what I bought in the lingerie department?" Karen asked with a flirtatious smile. "Come to my apartment. I'll show you."

Instantly he hailed taxi. He opened the door for the woman, who entered first. Before moving into the car, he squinted back and saw Jennifer watching him. He paled and his face quivered. But his mind seemed to be already full of images of Karen in lacy lingerie. He grimaced in apology to Jennifer, then sank into the car. As the cab sped away, Jennifer gaped after it like a white marble statue, pedestrians jostling her where she stood. A single thought dominated her mind: *I've lost.*

◦◦◦

Distressed, she came home to the Upper West Side. Aunt Maggie opened the door and stood aside. She had changed little since her last visit, Jennifer thought, her hair white but fashionably coifed, her posture still fit and erect. They exchanged a few words of greeting. Then Jennifer excused herself and went into the bathroom. No sooner had she closed the door than she burst into uncontrollable sobs. *Richard! You dumb jerk! Why her? That woman is straight out of Sex and the City. I loathe you both.*

Her wailing echoed in the bathroom, amplified as if from a loudspeaker. After a few minutes she heard a discreet knocking at the door. She remembered Aunt Maggie. She quieted and splashed cold water on her tear-streaked face. On the dining table in the living room, dinner was already served for two. It looked savory. Aunt Maggie must have worked hard on it.

"I'm so sorry, Auntie. On the way home I ran into Richard, and we had a talk. He's gone forever." Jennifer blew her nose into a tissue.

Then she sat at the table. "Thank you for preparing dinner. You're such a good cook. And—oh no, I've forgotten to bring dessert!"

Aunt Maggie uncorked a wine bottle and tasted it. Nodding with satisfaction, she poured the wine. Jennifer needed the drink. She took a few sips. Aunt Maggie narrowed her eyes. Then she served salad for Jennifer and poured more wine. She also served herself and started eating.

"It's good to be in New York," Aunt Maggie said lightly. "Tomorrow I'm going to visit the Museum of Modern Art. I like it much better now, after the renovation. I'll take in some concerts, too. I miss the culture New York offers. In Florida, it's not the same."

"It's wonderful when you come," Jennifer said. "You remind me why I love it here."

"I'm happy to hear it."

After salad, Aunt Maggie served a tuna steak with her own piquant sauce. It was delicious. Jennifer complimented her aunt, who inclined her head with a smile. For dessert, Aunt Maggie brought a platter of miniature éclairs and other pastries to the table. It looked decadent.

"See? No worries," she said.

Jennifer fetched a teapot and poured tea for them. Savoring the sweet dessert, she found herself telling her favorite aunt all about her breakup with Richard, though leaving out the incident with the sleeping pills. Aunt Maggie listened, sometimes nodding, other times shaking her head.

"I'm sorry you had to go through this," Aunt Maggie said. "I have a feeling there's a good chance Richard will come back to you. If he is using the new woman as a sex object, she'll use him the same way, particularly if she's an ambitious career climber. But sex is not the only thing in life. Maybe this affair will teach Richard a lesson. Then you'll see the real Richard, and you can judge whether it's worth taking him back." Aunt Maggie selected a bite-size napoleon. "When is your next performance? The beginning of March, isn't it? Perfect. You can just focus on your music and forget about him for now. Let him have his fling with his floozy."

"Auntie, be serious. This is very painful for me."

"Of course, my dear. And I shouldn't raise your hopes, because he may never return to you. But for now, banish him from your mind. Put yourself together again and prepare for the performance. That's more important."

Jennifer knew that what her aunt was saying made sense, but she still ached.

Aunt Maggie retrieved her purse and took out a business card. Her tone shifted to one of formality. "Jennifer, actually I came to New York this time on specific business that involves you. I was wondering how to broach the subject. But now the timing seems right."

Jennifer frowned. This was not like her aunt, who rarely spoke of business matters.

"I'm now seventy-five years old," Aunt Maggie began. "By the grace of God, I'm still healthy and independent. But any day my late husband might visit to take me."

"Auntie, you shouldn't talk like that."

"No, my dear, I have to be ready. Today I consulted with my lawyer. I had prepared a will a long time ago, when my husband was still alive. But I never bothered to revise it after he was gone. My lawyer and I updated it."

Jennifer recalled the death of Henry's father and recognized her aunt's intention as a sad necessity.

"Now, my dear, I want you to remember this," Aunt Maggie resumed. "When I die, you'll inherit all of my estate, which includes this apartment, a house in Florida, an investment portfolio, and a few bank accounts, less certain donations to charitable causes, at a net total of several million dollars. You know I couldn't have a child of my own. Being childless is a lonely disposition, particularly as one gets older. You've been my favorite niece since the day you were born because you resemble my mother, who loved to play the piano. I always felt you're almost my daughter. It has been a great comfort to have such a sweet, talented person as you in my life. I've been enjoying your company for years. So this is something I can do for you."

Aunt Maggie pondered. The next subject seemed delicate. Jennifer kept quiet. She wanted her aunt to say whatever she had on her mind.

"There's one condition," Aunt Maggie continued. "When I become too weak to be independent, I'd like you to take care of me. I hope this is not too much to ask. I can move back to New York. We can live together or separately. At my age, I fear that someday I'll need someone I can trust without reservation. Can you be that person and look after me?"

Aunt Maggie's eyes were wet. Jennifer felt her aunt's genuine love toward her. She remembered all the gracious things her aunt had done for her since her childhood, not only the lavish gifts her aunt had given her, but also the way her aunt had encouraged her to live her life. She began crying. Her throat contracted. She could not talk. She held her aunt's hands and nodded. That was all she could do.

"Thank you, my dear." Aunt Maggie gently squeezed Jennifer's hands. "Then may I consider we're mutually agreed on this? Don't worry, I've consulted with my brother, too. Your father has no problem as long as you agree. The only complaint he made was that I'd assumed he wouldn't be able to tend to me. I didn't mean that, I told him. We're both old. We need to be prepared for when we lose our independence. Like it or not, the time will come. He understood."

"I know why Dad said that to you, because he loves you," Jennifer answered. "But I understand you too, Auntie. Don't worry; I'll always stand behind you. You just enjoy your life and live long."

Aunt Maggie released Jennifer's hands and gave her the business card, instructing Jennifer to contact the attorney if something happened to her. The lawyer would take care of all the legal matters and advise Jennifer. She promised Aunt Maggie that she would take this responsibility seriously. Aunt Maggie sighed in relief. Then, smiling, Aunt Maggie took another chocolate pastry and ate it. Jennifer joined her.

The next day, Aunt Maggie went back to her lawyer and signed the will. After that, she spent several days enjoying museums, an opera, and concerts. When she was ready to go back to her home in Florida, she gave Jennifer a piece of advice.

"My dear, listen to me as the wisdom of age. Your career is important, and I hope you can make the opera your profession. But be sure to find a fine gentleman, marry, and have a child—or a few. This does not mean that you must give up your career. Marriage and work can thrive simultaneously if you choose them right." Aunt Maggie appeared to be dreaming of her married life years ago. Her face shone. "My late husband was descended from a wealthy old family in New England. You remember that he worked as the principal of a prep school, while I worked as a high school teacher until my retirement? He was a good man. We had a happy life. I consider myself a fortunate woman, and I want you to be able to say the same. My only regret is I didn't have a child. But this is up to the grace of God, and I was given you instead. It's the same to me now."

"Auntie, you're so old-fashioned," Jennifer said. "I like the traditional values, too. But how can I find a fine gentleman, as you call him? I thought I had one, and look what happened. I don't know if I'll ever find such a person."

"True, my dear, it's not easy, for sure. But don't give up. Someday I know you'll meet a fine gentleman. I'll pray for you."

✺ ❧

Jennifer's father, a retired State Supreme Court judge, lived with her mother in Milwaukee, enjoying their retirement life. The Schneiders also had a son, Jennifer's elder brother, who lived in the same city, working as a senior law clerk at the US District Court. He was married and had one child. Since her brother's family could take care of her parents in case of emergency, Jennifer had not worried too much about them. After the talk with Aunt Maggie, however, she felt concerned and called them.

Her parents sounded happy to hear from her. They chatted for a long time about their life. Her father's blood pressure was slightly higher than normal. Her mother had occasional pains in her joints. Other than these, they were healthy for their age. They played golf together and took bicycle rides in the neighboring parks. Her brother might be appointed an associate judge soon. His wife was pregnant with their second child. Their little boy was happy at the elementary school he had begun in the fall.

Jennifer told them of her paralegal courses at the School of Continuing and Professional Studies at New York University. The lawyers in her firm had even started giving her easy paralegal tasks as on-the-job training. Her parents were pleased because she could join the family tradition of the legal profession. She also described her singing at the Graces opening and her steady progress in the preparation for the new opera. The latter was not entirely true, but this was what she wanted her parents to believe. She briefly mentioned her breakup with Richard. Her parents did not make a fuss about it. She guessed that they had already heard it from Aunt Maggie. They must have been disappointed, because they had thought that Richard was a good match for their daughter, but they clearly wanted her to overcome the setback quickly. She appreciated their discretion.

"Maggie told me she discussed her will with you," her father said. "Poor Maggie. She must be lonely, living alone like that. I'm glad she enjoys your companionship. I hope you'll take care of her when she needs help."

"Sure, Dad, no problem," Jennifer replied.

"You'll be a rich woman when you inherit her estate."

"Heaven forbid. I prefer Auntie to live long."

"Of course. But nonetheless. Now you can do whatever you want."

"It won't change anything. I'm going to continue with opera."

"Are you sure? Is that really what you want?"

"Absolutely."

"Good, I can sense your determination. We look forward to your performance in March."

Jennifer promised to send them tickets. They exchanged warm parting words. The conversation with her parents had been no more than a quotidian chat. Yet it induced in Jennifer the feeling of family belonging. She was not alone after all. She was loved. She felt ashamed of what she had done with the sleeping pills.

She sat in a lotus position on the rug, her palms folded on her lap. Gently closing her eyes, she inhaled and exhaled slowly, concentrating on a point at the center of her forehead. Because of Aunt Maggie's apartment, she could study her singing without financial struggle. If she became a paralegal, her situation would improve further. As to the inheritance, this would not affect her lifestyle for now. But the prospect of the inheritance definitely gave her a sense of security. Without worrying about money, she could focus on her opera career.

Opera career? Where did it stand? She realized that because of the trouble with Richard, she had not practiced or taken voice lessons for the past several weeks; she'd barely sung, except for the Graces opening. She couldn't let her voice get rusty; this was a typical problem for singers, and the reason opera singers had to maintain a positive lifestyle with austere discipline. She counted. It had been more than one month since she had last taken a coaching session. She had to catch up quickly. To her relief, however, she felt stronger than before.

She remembered that Stephanie had insisted that she see a therapist after her low point. She had been putting it off. Now she felt that she could stand by herself. It would be a better use of her time, she concluded, if she focused on her singing, instead of visiting a therapist regularly. Fortunately the overdose of sleeping pills did not seem to have permanently damaged her vocal cords. However, because of it, combined with a respite from practice, her voice lacked its usual agility and vigor. At the opening, she had managed her aria reasonably well. But while singing the demanding Puccini quartet, her voice had cracked a little on the high notes. The flaw had been unnoticeable to untrained ears, but would certainly have been caught by professionals, maybe even by Irene.

Jennifer's eyes flew open. *Forget about Richard*, she told herself sternly. She had to concentrate on singing for now. Determined, she went to the piano and started studying the role of Mimi in Leoncavallo's *La Bohème*.

Scene 8

On a Friday John took an early lunch at a restaurant near Music Universe with Erica, his coworker, as he had done in the past. She was a quiet woman of about his age, pleasantly plump with brown hair and light brown eyes. She had a husband, an accountant in a clothing company in the garment district, and a two-year-old daughter. She worked at the music store a few days a week to supplement her family income. John appreciated her knowledge of music; her father was a high school music teacher, and she had sung in a church choir in her early years. She loved that John was an opera singer. He felt comfortable with her, for his family background was closer to hers than Michelle's. Today Erica wore an orange cardigan and a multicolored cotton skirt. She looked fragile but pretty. She bought spinach salad and a glass of milk. He wore blue jeans and a black sweater. He got his regular hero sandwich and a glass of cranberry juice. They sat at a table in a quiet corner.

"My daughter started walking and puts everything she can grab into her mouth," Erica said between bites of her salad. "She is so quick, and it's dangerous. I have to always keep my eyes on her."

"I guess it's part of the excitement of being a mother," he said.

"Yes, but…" She paused. "When I come to work here, I ask my sister-in-law to look after her. It's a kind of break for me." She seemed to fish for a smile, but it did not come out. "How are you doing with your wife?"

He had not told her of his divorce proceedings and decided it was easier to play a happy husband. "We don't have any children yet. We're kind of enjoying ourselves." He munched his sandwich. "But I have to spend a lot of time to earn money to live on, between auditions, rehearsals, and lessons. So occasionally Michelle complains." Seeing Erica about to ask a question, he said, "Oh no, no. She understands my situation. And I understand her frustration, too. So I try to go out with her for dinner and shopping as often as possible. Last Saturday we went to a cozy restaurant in Little Italy. We had a great time." This was not true. He felt like a liar and a failure.

Flushing, he looked away, only to see Mike, who would sing Schaunard in the Leoncavallo, appear unexpectedly. Mike explained that he had come to the store to buy some CDs and heard that John was having his break here. Although John had occasionally chatted with Mike in the past, this was the first time they had met privately. Smiling, he gave Mike a friendly high five. Mike seemed anxious to break the ice with his baritone colleague in the new opera, so John invited the singer to have lunch with him. After introducing Erica, John asked, "How are you doing on Schaunard?"

"I've sung Puccini's Schaunard many times," Mike replied. "But Leoncavallo's is new to me. I've made an interesting discovery." He took a big bite of his hamburger, washing it down with mouthful of cola. "In Act II of the Puccini, in the Café Momus scene, I blow on the trumpet, then sing, 'This D is out of tune.' It's like a short *recitativo* for just a few seconds, and my line is over." He took another bite of his hamburger. "But man, in Leoncavallo, lemme tell you, in the Act II courtyard scene I play the piano and speak—not sing, mind you—the same line, 'This D is out of tune' in slightly different Italian, and then sing an aria, 'The influence of blue on the arts,' with the chorus and orchestra accompanying me." He gulped his cola. "Whew! This aria is so cooool. I can show off my voice and agility to the world. I like Leoncavallo's version much better." He grinned, his dark face shining.

"Way to go, buddy," John said, lightly punching Mike's thick chest.

Erica laughed. She seemed to be enjoying the shoptalk. But when she finished her salad, she headed back to Music Universe, saying that she should give the guys some private time. John and Mike munched their few remaining french fries, licking their fingers.

"I've got a potential problem." Mike lowered his voice. "My girlfriend, Vicky—you saw her at the opening—she isn't happy, because I have to spend too much time studying this new opera." His face sank.

Oh boy, here we go again, John thought, holding a catsup-coated fry. "But she said, 'It's OK. I'm used to it.'"

"Yeah, she says that in front of other people. But when we're alone, she complains, complains, endless. Geez." Mike rolled his eyes.

John wondered if he should tell Mike about Michelle. He didn't want Mike to suffer the same fate he was facing. But before he could speak, Mike leaned closer.

"I gotta tell you this," he said. "I had arranged to take a vacation with Vicky for one week in March—to Cancun. I hadn't explicitly told her, but I was going to propose to her there. She sensed it and was dreaming about it. Then I was chosen for Schaunard. Unlucky me, the performance date happens to be right in the middle of the vacation week. So I had no choice but to cancel the Mexico trip. Vicky went through the roof." He took a deep breath and exhaled audibly. "I guess this kinda thing is very important to a woman. So she can't forgive me. She's threatening to leave me. I understand she's disappointed, but what can I do? I can't miss this opportunity. I have to sing."

Now John felt compelled to tell Mike of his pending divorce, though as casually as possible. Mike dropped his jaw. "You'd better try to spend more time with Vicky before it's too late," he concluded. Mike nodded and sighed.

"It's not easy to study a new opera while going through a divorce," John said.

"How can you manage?" Mike widened his big eyes, shaking his head. "If Vicky left me, I'm sure I would break down."

"C'mon, man," John said. "No matter what, you can't stop singing. She'll be proud of you—you'll see."

John had hoped to cheer Mike up. Judging by his colleague's dejected expression, though, he knew he had not succeeded. He wasn't even sure he could get through this crisis himself.

《❦ ❧》

John left Music Universe early. That evening Michelle had invited the other Graces to celebrate the successful run of their show. Since Michelle hadn't informed them of her divorce filing, he thought that he should be at home. Besides, he wanted to help her host the evening. First he went to his parents' home in Brooklyn. He had asked his mother to make her famous seafood salad for the occasion. She handed him a large plastic container, suggesting he add a little wine vinegar, olive oil, and ground pepper just before he served it, to revive the freshness. He nodded, tucking some money into his mother's grocery jar. His father appeared.

"So how's your singing?" he asked. The same question whenever he met his son.

"Hi, Pa, I'm getting ready," John answered.

"Good. We can't wait. Where will it be?"

"At the Italian Cultural Society on the Upper East Side."

"Really? I've been a member of the Society for a long time."

"I'd almost forgotten," John replied. "So you know the concert hall there."

"You're going to sing there?" His father's face lit up. "The members of the Society are all descendants of Italian immigrants like us. They love opera. But don't underestimate 'em. One thing they never tolerate is bad singing. They'll boo you if you do a lousy job. Oh, yeah, I've heard noisy boos many times. So study hard and sing well."

As he was saying "I will," John noticed that his father looked pale. This concerned him because his father had always been a healthy man. His father laughed it off. He was feeling short of breath lately, he admitted, but it was probably just a little cold that would go away any day. He urged John to concentrate on his music. John left his parents' home. A sense of guilt stung him. He still hadn't told them about the divorce. Someday he would have to, but not now, not yet. Michelle might change her mind.

◄◊ ◊►

Back in Manhattan, John bought various kinds of cheese and two bottles of wine, plus a large bouquet of colorful flowers. At their apartment, he found Michelle in an apron in the kitchen. The smell of roast beef rose from the oven. He put the food and bouquet on the kitchen counter. She looked up. She was flushed, probably from the heat from the oven. Or was it? Could it be his gifts? He noticed her surveying his face. Finding that he was calm, she sighed.

"Thanks, John. The flowers are gorgeous." She headed to the living room and returned with two vases. "The bouquet is so big, I can divide it in two." She poured water into the vases, arranged the flowers, and set them on the side tables in the living room.

He moved the seafood salad into a large bowl, then followed his mother's instructions and tossed it with a salad spoon and fork. The aroma of shrimp, calamari, octopus, and lobster grew tantalizing. Then he arranged the cheeses on two plates and brought the appetizers to the dining table. He felt awkward. Since the evening when they had discussed their divorce case, he had not heard anything more from her lawyer. Could she have put the process on hold? But he had been sleeping in the studio. They had only spoken occasionally on harmless topics. He realized he had no idea how to behave toward his wife.

"Michelle, I'll greet your friends," he said. "But after that, if you want, I'll stay in the studio. This evening is for your group."

She gave a queasy smile and shrugged as if at a loss for words.

"I'll play the good husband before the Graces," he added. "I wouldn't embarrass you."

"Thanks," she said timidly, avoiding eye contact with him.

At half past six, Helen and Sarah arrived with a bottle of wine and a dessert. Michelle hugged them. John politely shook their hands, taking their coats. Helen wore an ivory crewneck lace-knit top with matching pants, and Sarah had dressed in a ruffled olive blouse and a floral-print skirt. Michelle had changed to a chic mauve V-neck dress. The elegance of the Graces delighted him. He thought that Michelle was still the most beautiful among the three. He was going to lose her; the thought tormented him. He fudged a welcoming smile for the guests.

Since this was their first visit, Michelle gave them a tour of the apartment. He trailed after them. The two artists were particularly impressed with the large studio, crowded with an easel, paintbrushes, paint tubes, coffee cans for solvents, and canvas stretchers in various sizes leaning against the walls. A faint smell of turpentine oil wafted in the room.

"This is great," Helen said. "You're so lucky to have this kind of space in Manhattan."

"Look at these windows!" Sarah said, pointing to the evening view. "I can easily imagine Michelle painting the scenes of the Hudson River from here." She saw the piano and stroked a few keys. "Ah, the painter and the opera singer. You're an ideal couple."

Sarah's comment raised murmurs of approbation from Helen. John eyed Michelle, who brushed past him, guiding her guests to the living room. *If only they knew*, he thought.

He remained in the studio. This was a good opportunity to let them enjoy their dinner without him. He no longer needed to play a sweet husband. What a relief. He heard Michelle showing the guests other rooms. Soon they seemed to have settled in the living room. He started studying the opera score for Rodolfo's role. Sarah popped into the studio and said that the party would not start without the host. He felt compelled to follow her to the living room, where he shunned Michelle's eyes. Helen giggled, shaking her empty wine glass. Apologizing to them, he opened a bottle and poured wine into the glasses. Michelle proposed a toast.

The women gave delighted cries. "To the successful show of the Graces!"

John, too, raised his glass to them. "Congratulations!"

"Thank you, John," Helen said. "The singing was wonderful."

"My pleasure. But I was only part of it. The other Dolci Quattro were excellent."

"That's true. Stephanie was really a good organizer. The two models were hilarious."

Prompted by Helen's remark, the women started a jolly conversation. Each time he rose to leave, someone asked for more wine. Michelle invited the guests to take food from the table, and John provided each artist with a plate, knife, fork, and napkin. He urged them to try the seafood salad. "It's an essential item for an Italian party—and it's low-calorie, too."

The artists nibbled and complimented Michelle, who waved them off, her mouth full. John had to rescue her, explaining that his mother had made it, so they were eating a very typical homemade Italian dish. They each took a second helping.

"By the way," Michelle said, "I understand that Père Momus bought a piece by each of us. He's displaying them in his restaurant."

"That's terrific," Helen said, tossing her straight auburn hair. "I was impressed with his comments on my work. He was like a professional critic. Who is this Père Momus? It's not his real name, is it?"

"You tell them, John," Michelle called. "You know him well."

John stopped at the doorway, where he had been hoping to make a discreet exit. Coming back to the living room, he told them about Père Momus and his legend. He reminded them that the restaurant had catered the food for the opening and that Stephanie worked there.

"I've worked there, too, when I've needed extra money."

"I see," Helen said. "He's always helping artists. That's so generous of him, and so needed. Since Christmas is coming, maybe we could do something nice for him."

"Great idea!" Michelle and Sarah said simultaneously.

John suggested they should let Stephanie coordinate whatever they planned, because she was good at this kind of thing. Helen volunteered to liaise with her from the Graces.

Michelle brought the savory roast beef to the dining table. John sliced it and served the artists. By now he felt comfortable enough to stay and eat. As the women ate and drank, they started describing the difficulties of their lives. Sarah was the first. Her hazel eyes became clouded. She lived in Manhattan with her younger sister, Christine. Their apartment was a one-bedroom. The rent was so outrageous that this was all they could afford. But it was impossible to live by painting alone. She taught at the Art Students League of New York. Without sharing the rent and expenses with Christine, she could not afford to live in Manhattan.

Helen nodded wearily. She lived in Long Island City. There the rent was reasonable for a two-bedroom apartment, which she shared with her boyfriend, a sculptor. They also used their second bedroom as a studio; and she too had to supplement her income by teaching, at the School of Visual Art. Hearing the artists describe their hardships, John felt comforted. He was not alone.

Helen asked Michelle how she could manage such a large apartment. Michelle explained, but her tone was rather humble. The two artists enviously exclaimed how blessed Michelle was. She thanked them quietly. John felt alarmed, not only because the subject matter had grown gloomy for the other two artists, but also because it seemed too personal for Michelle.

"Sorry, ladies," he said. "Yes, it's hard to live in New York City and pursue our passion for art and music. But let's talk of more cheerful topics. I understand many pieces of your artwork were sold during the show. That's remarkable. I hope you'll soon enjoy not only artistic success, but also financial success."

The Graces laughed as if his comments had tickled their vanity. This seemed the right time for dessert. He headed for the kitchen and returned with pots of tea and coffee, with milk and slices of lemon. Sarah opened the box of dessert they had brought, a large chocolate cake, beautifully garnished. He served slices on fancy dessert plates. Helen joked that she would gain ten pounds. The three artists giggled. He, too, laughed, enjoying the cake.

"By the way," Sarah said, "here's a bit of gossip. My sister Christine met Henry at the opening. They're now dating. What kind of person is he? I remember he sang 'La donna è mobile.' He looked like a playboy."

John laughed at the comment, and at Michelle's gesture, he told Sarah, "Henry is no playboy. He's the steadiest person among the Dolci Quattro. In that aria he was acting as the Duke, who is a cynical cad in the opera *Rigoletto*. In reality, Henry is a respectable man and an excellent tenor."

"I'm happy to hear it," Sarah said. "I don't mean to show a big sister's concern, but Christine is still young and sentimental. I don't want her to get hurt."

"As far as Henry is concerned, you don't have to worry. Michelle, don't you agree?"

"Yes, I've known him for a long time," Michelle said. "He's kind, responsible, emotionally stable."

"Well, this is reassuring. Thanks," Sarah said.

"That reminds me of a question." John turned to Helen. "Who was that tall, redheaded woman who came to the opening? She was with a tall, good-looking man."

"Tight clothes, spike heels, bedroom hair?"

John nodded.

Helen made a face. "That was Karen Grimes, a lawyer at a bank. She buys my paintings and gives them to whomever she deems useful for her career advancement. I shouldn't complain because I appreciate her patronage, but I don't consider her a friend. She's not really anyone's friend—more just an ambitious social climber."

John described what had happened between Richard and Jennifer.

"I'm so sorry for Jennifer," Helen said. "But Richard should be careful with Karen because the moment she finds him no longer useful, she'll dump him."

"I know Richard only through Jennifer," he said with a shrug. "Since he broke up with her, his affair is none of my business. I just hope Jennifer will heal and move on. It's hard to sing when your heart is broken. It's ruined many singers' careers."

Michelle shot him a stricken look, but the others did not notice. They ate the cake and drank their coffee or tea. He stood, relieved that the dinner party was going better than he had expected. Perhaps now he could retire to the studio.

"John, it's entertainment time," Sarah said. "Would you sing something for us?"

The two artists cheered. To him, the request did not seem unreasonable. He did not want to spoil the evening. He asked if they had a request.

"Something enjoyable, please," Helen said.

Sarah giggled. "Like a love song?"

He gave it a moment's thought. "Baritones usually play villains in opera, so love songs aren't typical for us. But we often play funny characters, too. So I'll sing Figaro's aria 'Largo al factotum' from Rossini's *The Barber of Seville.*"

He went to the studio, closed the door, and warmed up his voice. He chose a CD from the Opera without Words series, on which an orchestra plays arias to accompany singers. He opened the door and directed the speakers to the living room, increasing the volume. The CD began playing the animated introduction of the aria in *Allegro vivace.* It set an elated mood. Remaining in the studio, he sang the behind-the-scene refrains, *La la le ra...la la le ra...la ran la le la...la ran la la.* When the introduction was over, he hastened to the living room. He hailed the Graces, sweeping his arm in a grand motion. Then, assuming the character of the man-of-all-trades barber, he sang the aria in a frantic tempo.

> *Largo al factotum della città, largo! La ran la la ran la la ran la la.*
>
> *Presto a bottega, chè l'alba è già, presto! La la ran la la ran la le ra la.*

> (Make room for the factotum of the city.
> La ran la la ran la la ran la la.
>
> Rushing to my shop, for it's dawn already.
> La la ran la la ran la le ra la.)

His sonorous voice rumbled through the living room. The women cracked up. The song went on. Figaro can do anything for his patrons. Everyone wants him. He is the happiest man. While singing, John popped up his eyes, squinted, and twisted his cheeks. "*Figaro, Figaro, Figaro...*" He exaggerated his voice here and there like hiccups. "*Figaro qua, Figaro là, Figaro qua, Figaro là...*" The artists kept belly-laughing. At the finale, he sprinted the refrain "*della città*" as fast as he could, and held the last "cit-" on the high G for a long time before making a slight *portamento* to come down to C to conclude with "-tà!"

Fierce clapping and high-pitched bravos showered from the women. John bowed. The women exclaimed, "Incredible" and "Hilarious." Helen and Sarah toasted him, and Michelle joined them. He returned the toast by raising his glass of water.

About ten o'clock, the Graces called it an evening. Before leaving, Helen and Sarah made a consensus comment. "Michelle, you have a beautiful studio here, your life is stable, and you have a lovely husband. You're the most fortunate person among us. We envy you." As the two left, he saw Michelle struggling to smile at them, seemingly concealing her pain.

He helped Michelle tidy up. As she put the leftovers in plastic containers, he rinsed the dishes and placed them in the dishwasher. Leaving the rest to her, he cleaned up the dining table and side tables in the living room. Finally she started the dishwasher. They sat at the dining table. He felt comfortably exhausted. Michelle looked the same. She pensively smiled at him.

"Thank you for helping me and being such good company. I really appreciate it."

"You're welcome."

Having said that, he felt fidgety again. While her friends were here, he had been able to pretend things were normal and even enjoy himself. Now that they had left, he felt lost. Michelle was quiet, but her face looked satisfied. She poured the leftover wine into two glasses and gave one to him. "You must be tired. Have some."

He sipped the wine. Michelle avoided his gaze, though she appeared happy. He felt content, too. At least he had done his duty as a husband before her friends. He wondered how Michelle had taken her friends' reaction to her life here, himself included. Worn down by the strain of her muteness, he pushed away from the table and downed the rest of wine. "Well, then, good night."

She nodded. "Good night."

◖◗

John was awakened by movements in the bed. At first he did not know what was happening. Soon he realized that Michelle had come into the studio and slipped under the blanket. She pressed against his back without a word, hugging him from behind. He felt her body through her thin nightdress. He pretended to be sleeping, relishing the familiar shape of her body, which was redolent with her perfume. Her warmth comforted him. He wondered how long it had been since he had slept with her in the same bed.

Several minutes passed in silence. He was now half asleep. Was Michelle awake? He felt her steady breathing. He rolled to face her. In doing so, his hand inadvertently touched her naked hip. Her nightdress was curled up under the blanket. *Oh God*, he groaned inwardly.

He still loved her. Her curvy body reminded him of their passionate lovemaking during the early days of their marriage. His heart started beating hard. His body heated up. He wanted her. But he remembered their pending divorce. What would be the legal implications if he made love to her now? Was it good or bad for her or for him? He had no idea. He didn't care.

He gently kissed her lips. How sweet it was. She didn't resist. Instead, she embraced him. He repeated the kiss on her lips and then all over her face. In his mind, he asked, *Why don't you stop me? Are you sure you don't mind?* Her eyes were closed. In the dim light, he thought she had a peaceful smile. He wanted to share the pleasure with her. He no longer wanted to control himself. A fury of passion swept over him.

Oh, my Michelle, I don't want to lose you. I don't want to get divorced. I want you to remain my wife. I want you to have our baby. I'm yours. You're mine. Take in my thrust. Feel me. We're one. Come. Deeper. More. Let's stay together. Let's keep going.

He consummated. She uttered a subdued moan. The waves of pleasure reverberated between them, so he felt. He collapsed on the bed, lying beside her. In addition to his own heavy breathing, he heard her heavy but steady breath. She remained silent. Yet she held his arm tenderly. Her face shone with love.

The next morning, he awoke late. Michelle was not in his bed, but her aura still remained. He remembered what had happened. It was not a dream.

ACT II

Scene 1

*C*risp November air had enveloped Manhattan. Fallen leaves skittered over the streets, avenues, squares, and parks. The opera season was in full swing at the Metropolitan Opera and other theaters. Stephanie had just finished her work at the Café Momus and had changed into the same outfit she had worn to meet her father a few weeks ago. She paused to check her reflection in the window of an apartment building off Amsterdam Avenue in the eighties: presentable. At five o'clock she was to see Arthur DeSoto, the artistic director of the New York Bel Canto Opera Company. Since her audition several months before, she had attended a few meetings here with other singers. She took an elevator to the third floor.

Arthur opened the door to his apartment and let her in. He was a tall and slightly stocky man in his early forties with an intelligent face, dark brown eyes, and a straight nose. His curly black hair was parted in the middle and flopped on his high forehead. He used the living room as a rehearsal room. A grand piano occupied one corner. Several music stands surrounded the piano, as if a rehearsal had just finished. Two sofas lined a wall where additional folding chairs were stacked. He guided her into his office, once a bedroom. Close to the window stood a large desk covered with papers, file folders, a telephone, and a PC. Behind his desk, bookcases stocked music scores, CDs, a CD player, and a printer. Several opera costumes, wigs, and props lay scattered on the sofa and floor. He invited her to sit in front of his desk as he took a chair.

Stephanie knew that Arthur lived with his wife, Claudia, and a child in a larger apartment, several floors up in the same building. He used his old one-bedroom for his opera company's business. Claudia came from a wealthy family. She taught piano to children. Otherwise, she was a homemaker. Her parents lavished largess on their son-in-law's opera productions.

"How is your study on the other *La Bohème*?" Arthur asked.

Stephanie laughed. "Is that what you call it?"

She'd been working hard and was pleased to tell him she knew Musette's entire role by now. She had found it more challenging than Puccini's. She liked her aria in Act II, "Da quel suon soavemente," which was so light-hearted and sweet. She also liked her aria "Addio" in Act III, which was very demanding for the mezzo-soprano. Arthur nodded with a grin, then asked if she had questions about the opera.

"Actually, I've come about a personal matter." She described the entertainment session she had produced for the opening of the Graces, including how enthusiastically the audience had reacted. "I came to realize that this may be my vocation. It would be wonderful if I could help your company in this capacity."

She feared that she might have sounded too audacious, as she observed him pondering in silence. Her heart sped up. She blotted her palms on her skirt.

Arthur met her apprehension with a smile. "It's curious that you would suggest this right at this time," he said. "There's no way you could have known, but until recently the company had a general manager who did all kinds of coordination for our productions— like getting choristers, arranging rehearsal schedules, scouting for rehearsal places, finding accompanists, hiring an orchestra, and other administrative tasks. Everything but finances, which I handle myself. It's a lot of work, and she just quit two weeks ago because I couldn't pay her enough." Arthur eyed her hopefully. "So—if you want this sort of work, the job is yours. But I'm afraid I can't pay you much."

Stephanie sat up in surprise. "I didn't come here to ask for work," she said, "and the last thing I expected was a job offer! The payment is secondary for me. I do need a salary, yes, but what I really want to know is whether work like this suits me—whether it's another calling, in addition to being a mezzo-soprano. I still consider myself an opera singer, of course."

"How about this?" said Arthur, inclining his head. "I need a group of choristers for the coming performance of the other *La Bohème*. The chorus rehearsals must start the first week of December, so that's only three weeks away. But because this person has quit, I haven't gotten any choristers yet. It's making me really anxious. Can you get them for me?"

She asked how many he needed. He listed his requirements: at least fifteen sopranos, twelve altos, eight tenors, and eight baritones. They had to be opera choristers, not regular choral singers, because each chorister had to have an operatic voice. They would be volunteers—no pay. The chorus rehearsals would be on Thursday evenings, starting in December, with a Christmas break of two weeks. All rehearsals would take place at the Italian Cultural Society. He searched among piles of papers on his desk, found a list, and gave it to her. It had the names of the choristers he had used in the last performance. Some might be available.

Stephanie found him down-to-earth, business-oriented, and no-nonsense, which she liked. "I have a few contacts who know good choristers around here. I think I can handle it."

"Good," he said. "Let's see how it goes. If you do well and if you like it, then I'll give you other tasks. There are plenty of things to do as the general manager. As to the payment, let's say for now it'll be an honorarium. But if you do more, I'll increase it. Do you think that's fair?"

"It sounds excellent. I won't disappoint you."

He went on to describe the financial challenges of a small opera company like his. He had been trying to get an ongoing sponsorship from the Italian Cultural Society. If they agreed, they would pay the costs of opera production. Then he could pay singers in residence and the general manager.

"We want all of our productions to be of the highest quality," he concluded. "But for this 'Other *La Bohème*' it's doubly important, because it could ensure the future of our company—and believe me, we'll have a knowledgeable audience."

Thrilled, Stephanie promised to do her best.

◆◆◆

A job offer! Stephanie gave a little skip as she emerged from the apartment building. She had thought that at best Arthur might ask her to do some kind of public relations work on a voluntary basis. How fortunate she was. She couldn't wait to tell someone. She called Jennifer on her cell phone. Jennifer invited her for supper, warning her that it would be nothing fancy. Stephanie readily accepted. Visiting Jennifer served two purposes: first, to talk about her new job with the opera company; and second, to check on how Jennifer was faring these days. Stephanie had been concerned that her friend had not yet seen a therapist, in spite of her repeated advice. She bought two small cakes at a bakery. From there it was only several blocks to Jennifer's apartment. At the door they hugged. Stephanie was pleasantly surprised to see her friend looked healthy and energetic. Jennifer seemed to have finally gotten her life under control.

Jennifer explained about her aunt's visit a few weeks before, and their openhearted talk. As far as she was concerned, she declared, her relationship with Richard was a thing of the past. She was studying Mimi's role very hard, and her voice had recovered its strength, she reported happily.

They settled at the dining table, where Jennifer served salad in a big bowl. As they ate, Stephanie briefed Jennifer on her meeting with Arthur.

"General manager?" Jennifer exclaimed. "That's marvelous. I'm really happy for you."

Jennifer went to the kitchen and came back with two plates of spaghetti and meatballs. After dinner they ate the custard cakes Stephanie had brought.

"By the way," Jennifer said in a more serious tone, "I got a call from Michelle. She wants to meet me and discuss something personal."

"Probably it's about John and their divorce," Stephanie said.

Jennifer nodded. "I thought so too, but we're not supposed to know about it. What should I do?"

"Listen to her and give her your wise counsel."

This reminded Stephanie of a recent call from John. He had asked her to come up with some Christmas event for Père Momus at his restaurant. The Graces wanted to be part of the event to show their appreciation to him. "What do you think?" she asked Jennifer.

After taking a few sips of tea, Jennifer said, "How about caroling? The Graces can help decorate a Christmas tree and the interior of the café. You can bring singers from Broadway and let them sing the carols. Maybe we could sing a few as well. It'll be fun, and will draw people into the café."

"That's a splendid idea. I'll arrange that. But first I have to find choristers for Arthur."

❧ ❧

Back in her apartment, Stephanie called Henry and John and left messages, informing them about her new job. Then she called her contacts who knew good choristers with an operatic voice. As always, she had to emphasize that the opera was Leoncavallo's *La*

Bohème, not Puccini's. They promised to get back to her. Next, she called the choristers on Arthur's list. Some agreed immediately. But many could not make it because of their prior engagements or their holiday commitments. This made her task more challenging than she had thought.

She spent the next several days busily talking to choristers on the telephone and recruiting the required number. The other Dolci Quattro recommended a few people they knew, which also helped her. She continued her hours at the Café Momus and her singing job at the synagogue. In addition, she had to study the role of Musette. In less than two weeks, though, overcoming the challenge, she managed to secure the forty-three choristers Arthur had requested, plus several more.

Arthur seemed impressed with her organizing skills and diligence. He gave her the name of the chorus master, Kate Haynes, and asked Stephanie to set up the first rehearsal with the choristers on the first Thursday of December, in one week. He also asked her to make photocopies of the chorus part of the opera, saying that she could use a copy machine in his office. Additionally, he suggested that she prepare a rehearsal schedule, as well as attendance sheets. All of these tasks normally fell to the general manager of an opera company. It was tedious work, but she tackled it all cheerfully, glad that she had talked to Arthur and he had given her a chance.

On the first Thursday of December, the rehearsal was to begin at seven o'clock. Stephanie went early to the Italian Cultural Society, off Fifth Avenue in the eighties. The midsize concert hall occupied the third floor of the building, seating some eight hundred people. The hall was used for concerts, exhibitions, and meetings. The stage was a decent size, allowing for about eighty members of an orchestra and chorus. The interior was decorated with chandeliers and light-colored wallpaper in red and cream, reminiscent of La Scala, though more modest.

She moved a desk and a chair near the entrance. At a quarter to seven, choristers started arriving. She checked their names on the attendance sheet and gave them the music and the rehearsal schedule. Forty-five people showed up. This was a good turnout for the first day of rehearsal. Kate swept through the door, almost trotting, as if to compensate for her petite figure. Although Stephanie had talked to her over the telephone, this was their first meeting. They hugged each other. Kate sat at the piano on the stage as Stephanie stood beside the piano. At her signal, the choristers took their seats in the audience, grouped in first soprano, second soprano, alto, first tenor, second tenor, baritone, and bass sections. She surveyed them with satisfaction—a varied collection of ages, colorations, and body shapes that would do nicely as bohemian Parisians. She greeted everyone and ran through the rehearsal schedule, leading up to the performance on the first Saturday of March.

Next she took a whistle and blew it. A sharp, high-pitched sound shrieked in the hall. Several women covered their ears. She told them that while she was the general manager, she was also a mezzo-soprano and would sing Musette in this performance. She did not want to ruin her voice. So if there was any disorder during the rehearsal, she would blow her whistle instead of yelling. She hoped that she would not have to do this many times. She asked them to maintain professional discipline during the rehearsals. The choristers nodded obediently.

Then she distributed a two-page document. "I presume you're all familiar with Puccini's *La Bohème*. This is the synopsis of Leoncavallo's version. Actually both Leoncavallo's *La Bohème* and Puccini's are based on the novel *Scènes de la vie de Bohème* written by Henri Murger. Music scholars consider Leoncavallo's opera closer to the original novel."

She looked around the hall. The choristers took up four or five front rows on the audience floor. They were intently watching her. She was certain that none of them had ever heard of Leoncavallo's *La Bohème*.

"You'll recognize the characters," she told them. "Act I starts with the Christmas Eve scene at the Café Momus in Paris in 1837. Schaunard, a musician, is expecting his friends to come celebrate. Soon they arrive: the poet Rodolfo; the painter Marcello; the philosopher Colline; joined by the laundress Eufemia, who is Schaunard's mistress; the flower girl Mimi, who is Rodolfo's mistress; and the seamstress Musette, who is Mimi's friend. They have a jolly time. Marcello falls in love with Musette."

She sipped water from a bottle. The choristers waited expectantly.

"Act II is a scene in a courtyard of an apartment building. Since Marcello started living in Musette's apartment, her patron, a wealthy banker, stopped paying the rent for her. Now she has been evicted, and all her furniture has been piled near a fountain in the courtyard. She comes home with Marcello and finds out. But they have invited their bohemian friends for a party—and so they have their carefree party in the courtyard. In the meantime, Viscount Paolo tries to persuade Mimi to leave her meager existence and come to him for a luxurious life. Although she still loves Rodolfo, in the end Mimi yields to the Viscount."

She asked if they were with her so far. The choristers responded simultaneously with "Yes," "Interesting," or "What happens next?"

"Act III opens in Marcello's attic. The frugal life continues for Marcello and his friends. Schaunard has broken with Eufemia. While Musette still loves Marcello, she is tired of poverty, so she decides to leave him and return to the banker. Marcello rages. Mimi comes back and expresses her desire to reconcile with Rodolfo. But he refuses her. Musette and Mimi leave. This act features many dramatic arias and tense ensemble scenes—as you'll soon hear. It will be breathtaking." She saw several choristers taking notes on their scores.

"Act IV takes place in Rodolfo's attic on Christmas Eve, one year after Act I. Rodolfo, Marcello, and Schaunard have their meager Christmas meal, remembering the happy days they spent with Mimi, Musette, and Eufemia. Suddenly Mimi appears. She has been abandoned by the Viscount, became sick, and was hospitalized. But since she has no money, the hospital prematurely discharged her. Her illness has worsened, and she is dying. Musette visits. Seeing Mimi dying, she removes her jewels and asks her friends to pawn them to pay for a doctor and medicine. Mimi and Rodolfo reconcile. But it's too late. As you all know from Puccini's version, Mimi dies."

The choristers exhaled deep breaths, which stirred the hall.

"It's a moving story, isn't it?" Stephanie said. "In spite of the general similarity in the theme of the bohemian life and Mimi's death at the end, you'll find the story of Leoncavallo's *La Bohème* is very different from Puccini's. I can tell you this because I've sung Musetta in Puccini's version many times."

The eyes of many choristers lit up, especially the sopranos. Stephanie felt that she was an opera star.

"How are they different?" an alto called out.

"For one thing," Stephanie answered, "Leoncavallo treats the main characters—Mimi, Musette, Marcello, Rodolfo, and Schaunard—equally. Puccini's opera is dominated by Mimi and Rodolfo, and some scenes don't make sense. For example, Puccini doesn't make it clear why Mimi and Rodolfo separate and how the relationship between Musetta and Marcello is broken, whereas the audience can follow these issues better in Leoncavallo's version. Also, in Leoncavallo's opera, Eufemia and Viscount Paolo play important roles, while there are no such characters in Puccini's version. In addition, in Puccini's Act I, Rodolfo meets Mimi and they fall in love, and Act II is the scene at the Café Momus on Christmas Eve. Leoncavallo's version opens with the Christmas Eve scene at the Café Momus, and Mimi is already Rodolfo's mistress. Then in Puccini's opera, in Act IV Colline appears and sings his famous aria. But in Leoncavallo's version, Colline never appears in Act IV. Lastly, in Leoncavallo's, Marcello is sung by a tenor, and Rodolfo by a baritone. In Puccini's, the voices are reversed."

She paused for a ripple of conversation amongst the choristers, then held up her palms for silence. "So I think it's an excellent idea to present Leoncavallo's *La Bohème* to the New York public, not as a challenger to Puccini's, but as a peer. The audience can compare the two operas and appreciate the differences."

The choristers seemed to understand the novel intent of this performance. Many said, "That's good," or "I agree."

"You may have noticed that it's quite cumbersome to keep saying Leoncavallo's *La Bohème* and Puccini's *La Bohème*. So for convenience, we simply call Leoncavallo's version 'the other *La Bohème*.'"

The choristers laughed.

"As to the chorus, you'll sing only in Act II. You're the friends of the opera's main characters, and you're also bohemians. You're penniless, but you rejoice in the life of young artists. I'm sure you'll feel right in character and enjoy your singing." She smiled at the choristers' appreciative chuckles. "This leads to tonight's rehearsal. One of the main chorus pieces is 'Song of the *Bohème*.' Sometimes this is called 'Anthem of the Bohemian Life.' It's a strenuous piece, but it's one of the brightest spots of the entire opera. Here you can show off how good you are. Let's sing it."

By now, she felt she had won their respect. They silently awaited her next instruction. She introduced Kate Haynes as their chorus master, who would coach them for this piece. Kate immediately suggested the choristers warm up. They straightened their posture. Kate played scales on the piano. The choristers eagerly vocalized, as if they wanted to impress Stephanie and Kate. Their strong voices pervaded the hall. The air grew warm from their excitement.

"Open to page 221 of your music, please," Kate said, her brown eyes gleaming. "This is the beginning of 'Song of the *Bohème*.' You're the bohemians, celebrating your youth, love, and art. This piece goes fast and jubilantly, like this." Kate played the piano in full tempo *marziale deciso* for the first several bars. As her hands, shoulders, head, and hair wobbled, the jovial anthem resounded from the grand piano. As if electrified by it, the choristers prepared themselves to sing. Kate interrupted. "But for now, let's sight-sing in under-tempo.

You don't have to sing loudly while you're learning the music." Kate played the piano slowly from the beginning of the chorus piece. The choristers started singing.

> *Dei vent' anni fra l'ebbrezza l'avvenir,*
> *l'avvenire un sogno, un sogno appare.*
> *Vola, vola, via la giovinezza.*
> *Vogliam, vogliam vivre ed amare.*

> (In the drunkenness of the age of twenty,
> the future appears a dream.
> Youth flees, flees away.
> We wish, wish to live and love.)

Now that the rehearsal had begun, Stephanie relaxed. She stood beside the choristers for a while. They sang lightly, attending to the melody and rhythm. Even so, she felt that they had good operatic voices. She moved behind the choristers. She was about to sit down to rest when she recognized Arthur, standing near the entrance to the hall. She hastily walked to him.

"You're an excellent organizer," he said with a broad smile. "This is a good turnout. And the rehearsal started smoothly. I'm pleased."

She blushed. She thought that this was quite a compliment, given that Arthur was a venerated opera conductor. "What do you think of their voices?"

"Good. Regular choral singers may have blending voices, but they don't project. So we'd need more than one hundred for a satisfactory performance. That's not the case for opera. Listening to the warm-up, I'm sure when these forty-five sing in full voice, they'll be as good as soloists. That's what I want. You've recruited the right singers."

His remark caressed her. She felt she was going to melt. She wanted to introduce him to the chorus. She was about to, and had turned back to the stage when he stopped her.

"Oh no, Stephanie. This evening I'm not supposed to be here. But I couldn't resist hearing what kind of choristers I've got. So I sneaked in without telling you."

"Pretty sly," she said. "But since you're here, please let me. They'll be happy to see you."

He gave up his objection. She ushered him to the stage. When Kate paused, Stephanie formally introduced Maestro Arthur DeSoto as the artistic director of the company. The choristers warmly applauded. She caught some women's eyes open wide at his good looks.

He thanked them for coming this evening. "Actually, it was Leoncavallo who proposed to Puccini that they jointly compose *La Bohème*. But Puccini composed it independently, using some ideas that Leoncavallo had suggested. Puccini's opera premiered in 1896. About one year later, Leoncavallo's version was first performed. Unfortunately, after that it was forgotten, because Puccini's had received world attention. The American premiere of Leoncavallo's version wasn't until 1977, in New York. Since then this version has been performed only a few times. That's why I want to present this opera in a highly professional way."

Stephanie had known of the initial intent of a cooperative composition by the two composers. But hearing the background from Arthur, she felt it unfair that Leoncavallo's version had been so neglected for so long. She joined in with the choristers as they cheered at the prospect of participating in such a fascinating endeavor.

Arthur returned a big grin. "For now, Kate will coach you. I'll meet you again in mid-January, a few weeks before the rehearsals with soloists start. Tonight I shouldn't disturb you too much. Kate, please carry on."

The choristers applauded again. Arthur waved and walked toward the exit. Stephanie accompanied him. At the door, he faced her directly.

"Thank you, Stephanie. You did a great job."

She took a deep breath. She felt exhausted, but also exhilarated. Raising her arms upward in triumph, almost jumping up, she said in her mind, *I did it!*

Scene 2

A week had passed since Henry received a letter from George. His brother had enclosed a vacancy announcement for a full-time faculty position at the School of Music, Ohio State University. George had urged him to apply. The position title was assistant professor. The duties were to teach voice students and to produce opera for the school. The required qualifications were a master's degree in music and diversified experience in opera performances with prominent opera companies. The salary was modest, but it would be adequate to live on in Ohio, taking into account the generous benefits the university offered. The application deadline was the end of February. He had been giving the opportunity serious thought. If he applied, he believed he would have a good chance of getting the position even without George's influence or his late father's.

A few days ago, he had called George and thanked him for the information. George seemed pleased that Henry was considering it and repeated his usual opinions about Henry's lifestyle. Yesterday he had received a call from Judith in California, suggesting he take the job. Right after his sister's call, his mother called him from Ohio. Unlike George and Judith, however, his mother stressed her wish for his happiness in his professional life as well as his personal life. He appreciated them for their candid concerns. His preference was to continue his opera career. But now he had an irresistibly tempting option.

He thought of Christine, whom he had dated a few times since her call several weeks ago. He liked her innocent character. He imagined his life in Ohio with her as his beautiful wife amid a sweet home, a few children, and a university faculty position. An alluring vision. Then he shook his head. He felt embarrassed even imagining such a silly illusion. He barely knew her.

Tonight he was to meet her again, for dinner in Greenwich Village, after which they would go to a Friday night reading at a poetry café. This was her idea because she liked poetry and wrote it herself. He had never been to such a café but thought it sounded like fun. When he found the Italian restaurant she had suggested, she was already waiting for him. She told him that her week had been hectic because she had to do all the clerical work for her boss, a senior copywriter at her ad agency, although she was an assistant copywriter. He asked if she liked her job.

"I don't know whether I'll want a copywriting career in the long run, or even if I can survive on Madison Avenue," she said, caressing her shoulder-length blonde hair. "But I would be satisfied as long as the job is related to literature. I don't mean ad copy is literature, but it's a job of word composition. It's close to poetry in a sense."

"That's good," he said. "You're still too young to limit your career prospects."

"I'm not too young. I'm twenty-nine. Soon I'm going to be thirty. That'll be the end of the world." She squeezed her eyebrows in pretense of despair.

"I felt the same way. But to my relief, I found there's life after thirty." He laughed as he saw her laughing. The idea of the voice faculty position flashed in his mind.

They ordered glasses of red wine, then toasted.

"How is your singing, Henry?"

"It's going well. I've learned the entire part of Marcello."

She clapped her hands. "You've come a long way."

He realized that she had been keeping track of his progress.

He had to be more specific. He could now sing all of his demanding arias, which were many. He particularly liked two. One was "O Musette, o gioconda sorridente!" ("Oh Musette, oh radiant smile!") in Act I, which Marcello sang to declare his love for Musette. The other was "Testa adorata" ("Adored head") in Act III, which he sang in despair of losing her. Of the two, the latter was the more dramatic. It ended with weeping, one of the most emotional scenes of the opera. To demonstrate it, Henry groaned loud, covering his face with both his palms. His chest contracted and swelled violently. She cracked up. Her long, light-beige dress swayed. He liked the way she laughed.

The waitress came again. They ordered salad and the day's special, sautéed red snapper.

"Henry, I'm curious," said Christine. "How do you study an opera of two to three hours? I just can't imagine how you do it. There's so much to learn."

"First I study by myself with the piano at home," he explained. "Then I work with my coach, Mr. Carré, who plays the piano for the orchestra part, and I sing to his accompaniment. Arias are relatively easy because they're sung alone. But for ensembles, like duets, trios, and quartets, Mr. Carré sings my counterparts while I sing my part. It helps me a lot. I usually see him once a week, but recently twice or even three times while I'm preparing for a new opera."

"Maybe sometime I could come with you to the coach?" Her eyes widened, as if she could not wait to hear him sing.

He shrugged. "It may be boring for you. Sometimes I make mistakes, like singing wrong notes or wrong rhythms, or missing a cue to enter. Then we go over the same section to correct these errors—sometimes several times." He saw her squeezing her lips. He hastily added, "But if you want, I could bring you to a dress rehearsal. All the soloists, choristers, and orchestra members participate to polish the opera for the real performance. We usually do this one day before the performance. Would you like to come?"

"Yes, if it's not too troublesome for you," she said, her face perking up.

Troublesome? More like paradise. He could not remember ever having dated a non-singer this interested in his music. He promised her. She cheered.

Food was served, but he declined more wine, noting that for singers, vocal cords were their instruments, which they had to look after with tender loving care.

"What kind of care?" asked Christine.

"Again, very boring," Henry replied. "Constant vocalizing, adequate physical exercise, sound sleep, and a healthy mental state. Absolutely no smoking, no heavy drinking, and no loud talking. And it's out of the question to attend noisy parties."

She shook her head. "You sound like an ascetic monk in a monastery."

"In a sense, we are."

Henry munched for a while. Then he told her a legend about Beniamino Gigli, a famous Italian tenor. On days before his performances, Gigli would go to a restaurant with his wife. He never uttered a word to save his voice. When the waiter asked him what he wanted, he wrote his choices on the napkin, and his wife would convey it to the waiter.

"Really?" Christine looked dubious, as if she might not put up with such behavior herself.

He waved his fork. "This may be too extreme. But it illustrates how sensitively we need to take care of our voices. Also, singers need to stay mentally stable." He went on to recount the tragedy of Maria Callas, the renowned dramatic soprano. For years she was a mistress of Aristotle Onassis. She loved him with all her heart. But he terminated their relationship to marry Jacqueline Kennedy. After that, even though she performed for several years, the quality of her singing grew dismal. She essentially died of a broken heart. She was only fifty-three.

"I didn't know Maria Callas was Onassis's mistress before he married Jackie," Christine said, her eyes welling up.

"Yes, it's a sad love story. My point is that opera singers cannot afford to go through the rough emotional ups and downs caused by unsteady personal relationships. So I'm not the kind of guy who goes after many women."

"I'm glad," she said, nodding and sighing.

He thought that her voice held a tone of genuine relief. "In addition," he continued, "just as instrumentalists bring their instruments for periodic maintenance, I still see my voice teacher at least once a month."

At this, she cocked her head. He had to explain the difference between a voice teacher and a coach. The voice teacher specialized in developing the voice as an instrument. It was hard to find a good voice teacher. His had been his mentor at the Manhattan School of Music, one of the voice teachers most in demand. On the other hand, the coach focused on perfecting the singer's performance of specific music.

"If you have to maintain such an ascetic life," Christine said casually, "it must be hard to be a wife of an opera singer." She picked at her plate.

"I don't know about that," he replied, trying to hide his hurt. "Many opera singers are happily married." This was not really true, he thought. What about John, who was going through a painful divorce right now? And Jennifer, whose fiancé wanted to have more fun? But Henry wanted to present Christine a positive image of opera singers—of himself. And she appeared pleased by his answer.

He tilted his head to the edge of the single spicy-smelling chrysanthemum that adorned their corner table. The shell-pink petals perfectly matched her tempting lips. *How like this flower she is*, he thought. *Delicate and intricate, velvety and piquant.* Again, he imagined a secure life with a faculty position in Ohio.

⋘ ⋙

Henry and Christine strolled leisurely toward the café. The stores and restaurants in the Village were already decorated for Christmas, illuminating the old-fashioned streets. Jazz musicians were playing merrymaking music. An old woman, clad in gypsy attire with several colorful bracelets in her arms, was reading the palm of a giggling young female client. Christine clung to Henry's arm as they shuffled amid the Friday evening crowd.

The café was in the basement of a small restaurant. Dim light glinted in the room, which was cramped with small tables and chairs. At the far end, a small stage held a table, a lectern, and a microphone, lit by a pale spotlight. They had arrived during an intermission. They settled at a table in the middle and ordered a glass of red wine. As Henry's eyes adjusted to the low light, the details of the interior became clear. Rough paint covered the walls without much decoration. Raw pipes and electrical wires snaked around bald industrial lamps on the ceiling. Patrons of all ages filled the space. Most were dressed casually in T-shirts, sweaters, blue jeans, and sneakers. No men wore ties except Henry. Some had long hair, and a few had ponytails.

Christine mentioned that she was taking a poetry workshop at The New School, where her classmates looked like the people here, typical poets and writers. Henry agreed. This was the Village, home of writers, poets, and artists. They always appeared bohemian—hip and a little scruffy. He was glad they were not allowed to smoke in the café. He noticed a signup sheet on the wall and asked if Christine had read her poems here. She told him no. She liked to read in the workshop, because the critiques from her teacher and classmates were helpful, but she could not expect that here because this reading was for enjoyment.

The spotlight at the microphone brightened up. A middle-aged woman in a black sweater and black pants came to the stage. "I'd like to read three poems. The first one is titled 'Seagull.' I wrote this when I spent my vacation in Cape May last summer." She cleared her throat, then began reading in a firm voice with no ostentation.

> Fly, fly, a lone seagull,
> Through billows,
> Into the sky,
> Above the sun,
> Conquer the summer.

Henry had occasionally read poems of traditional masters, but he was unfamiliar with contemporary poetry. He had no idea whether the poem being read was good or bad. He raised an eyebrow at Christine, who threw him a ho-hum look. He liked the poem, though, because he thought it had the rhythm of life. When the poet finished reading, loud applause echoed through the café.

"Not bad," Christine muttered.

"Just not bad?" Henry said. "I thought it was good. But you're the better judge."

Another woman came to the stage. She was young, dressed in a red sweater, jeans, and a white beret. "I'm still a beginner, but I'm crazy about poetry. I want to read two poems. The first one is titled 'Ode to Love.' I wrote it for my boyfriend." She looked to one corner of the café. A young man waved his hand at her. The patrons giggled. The woman recited in a high trembling voice. As if synchronized with it, the pieces of paper she held quivered.

What a poem, Henry thought. Almost every line squeaked the word *love*. Christine explained in a low voice that this was called a list poem, in which the subject was repeatedly listed in varying forms. The audience liked it, laughing whenever the poet pronounced *love*, which was too often. Someone yelled to her boyfriend, "Hey, you're a lucky guy, eh?" The boyfriend stood and bowed. The audience roared. He then blew a kiss toward the stage to his girlfriend, who returned a big smile. Henry winked at Christine. She shook her head, pursing her lips.

Next a well-dressed man in his early thirties rose and spoke into the microphone. "I recently lost my girlfriend. She simply disappeared. I miss her very much. So I wrote this poem. It's titled 'Come Back.' I hope she'll hear this poem and come back to me."

I stroll in our park.
Sun beams your smile.
Breeze whispers your song.
Roses waft your scent.
Yet our bench is empty.
Leaves fade, birds sigh.
Lonesome is our path of iris.

On the sand at our pond,

Thrice I scribe your name.

Friendly applause came from the audience. A patron suggested that he place this poem as a personal ad in the *New York Times*. The poet acknowledged the excellent idea and said that he would do so. A total of seven people read before another intermission.

"This is a typical evening," Christine said. "Most poems are mediocre. Some are OK, though." She moved her face closer to Henry. "Sometimes a *prima donna* reads. Talk about attitude! Like, 'I'm a poetess, I'm beautiful, look at me,' her nose up high. But her poetry is all stupid. It makes me sick. Thank goodness she wasn't here this evening."

He grinned, wishing to see and hear such a poetess. It would be like a comic opera.

"But I don't want to be too critical," she added. "People here all love poetry and want to share their poems with others—and it takes courage to read your work to strangers. I'm glad you're enjoying it."

He noticed that several couples in the café were holding hands or leaning shoulder to shoulder. He hesitantly moved one of his hands closer to hers on the table. His hand touched hers. He felt a kind of electric shock and pulled his hand back. She just smiled. To camouflage his embarrassment, he excused himself and checked his iPhone, explaining to her that this was part of his job. No duty-call messages. He displayed his web pages on the screen. Then he showed her several digital photos of himself in opera costumes. He took a picture of her and flashed it on the sliding screen. She looked pretty. While operating his gadget, he had to get closer to her. Their heads and hands almost touched. He even felt her warm breath on his cheek and ear. It made him happy. He sipped more wine and cleared his throat.

"Who are your favorite poets?" he asked.

"I like Emily Dickinson and Christina Rossetti," she replied without any hesitation. "They were born in the same year and are considered the two greatest female poets of the nineteenth century. In general, I think Dickinson's poems are withdrawn. Rossetti's are more positive. So depending on my mood, I prefer one on one day, the other the next day."

He knew Emily Dickinson, but not Christina Rossetti. Christine explained. Her father had been a famous Italian scholar in exile in London. So she was born in London and wrote her poems in English. Her brother, Dante Gabriel Rossetti, was a well-known Pre-Raphaelite painter, and also a poet. Christine liked Christina Rossetti not because they shared the same name, but because the voice of her poems was superb. He asked her to recommend some of Rossetti's poems so he could check his anthology. She named three: "When I am dead, my dearest," "Remember," and "Sleeping at last." He thought they sounded rather sad.

"In a way," she said, "but they are all idyllic." She recited the first one in a dreamy voice.

> When I am dead, my dearest,
> Sing no sad songs for me;
> Plant thou no roses at my head,
> Nor shady cypress tree:
> Be the green grass above me

With showers and dewdrops wet;

And if thou wilt, remember,

And, if thou wilt, forget…

What a sweet melody it sounded. Henry felt moved not only by the poem itself, but the way she recited. How lyrically did the word *sing* resonate? *Did she select this poem especially for me as a singer? Is she thinking of me?* "It's beautiful, Christine."

"I'm glad you like it. On the surface it may sound sad, but it touches my heart."

He nodded as he saw her face flush. *Is it because she is moved by the poem? Is it because she is happy to be with me?* "Christine, what do you want to do in your life?" he asked.

"I'd like to write poetry," she answered, as if she had been expecting this inquiry. "Of course these days, nobody can live only by writing poetry, except for a very few gifted poets. So I hope I can work at a literary job to make a living." She narrowed her eyes. "I want to increase my portfolio of poems, and someday I want to have them published. That's my dream."

"I'm sure you'll have your poetry published soon." He wanted to encourage her to write. How wonderful it would be to live with her and to listen to her poems. He imagined asking his composer friend to write a song based on one of her poems and singing it to her. It would be a sweet life together, a poet and an opera singer. He had not felt this kind of sentiment for a long time. He felt intoxicated. "Someday I hope you'll read your poems for me," he whispered.

"I'd love to."

They left the café at about ten o'clock and took a taxi to Columbus Circle. From there they walked on Central Park West to the north. As Christine lived at 73rd Street and Columbus Avenue, they would have some fourteen blocks to stroll. Street lamps and trees lined the avenue. The trees were decorated with twinkling lights for Christmas. The air was misty in the December evening. Christine leaned into Henry, holding his left arm, resting her head lightly on his shoulder. He felt her body warmth through their overcoats. A faint floral aroma wafted from her hair. He enjoyed the slow walk in silence. He felt that she, too, was enjoying his companionship.

She confided that she wished to invite him to her apartment for a nightcap. But she shared her apartment with her elder sister Sarah. Their apartment was a one-bedroom, and their living room was crowded with Sarah's painting tools and equipment.

"Does she know you're seeing me?" he asked.

"Yes, but she doesn't object. That's unusual, because she always wants to be a big sister."

"Oh, so I have your big sister's approval?"

"I think she trusts you because she heard good things about you from Michelle and John."

"That's nice to know."

They walked on in companionable silence. Cars and taxis passed them, brightening the sidewalk. Then the area grew dim and peaceful again. Christine promised to invite him for dinner soon, claiming that she was a good cook. She hoped that she could find an evening when Sarah would be out.

"I don't mind if she's there," he said. "She's a pleasant person."

"But I'm not a child, as Sarah still thinks I am."

"I guess she's just protective."

"I know. But sometimes it's annoying. I'm entitled to be independent."

He could not stop the warm feeling swelling up in his heart. He wanted to spend his life with her. He wanted to make her smile. *But what can I offer her? I can offer my love, but I cannot offer luxury.* The idea of the voice faculty position flashed back to him again. *Should I apply for the post? I don't know. I still can't give up my dream. Can't I spend my life with her as an opera singer? That would be ideal. She can pursue poetry writing. I'll encourage her. We might not be rich. But we would be happy together.*

He stopped and turned to face her. Her blue eyes shone. He thought how beautiful she was. He kissed her…a delicious kiss. They held their embrace. The mist surrounded them.

Scene 3

*J*ennifer had invited Michelle to a Thursday evening service for prayer and meditation at her church on Central Park West in the seventies. After the service, she thought, they could talk in the church library. Although she did not go to church every Sunday, she attended as much as her schedule allowed, usually at least once a month. Her father was of German descent and a Lutheran, while her mother was of Scottish descent and a Presbyterian. She felt comfortable with both denominations. She had chosen this Lutheran church because it was an intimate Gothic building with fine music and choir. Several students from the Juilliard School also attended, so she had good company. She selected a pew in the middle of the church. Only a few dozen people had come, most of whom she knew by sight. She greeted them.

At six o'clock the minister lit the vesper candle, and the service began with a short Bach piece played by a string quartet. Soon afterward Michelle slid into the pew next to Jennifer. As the final notes died away, the priest said a prayer attributed to St. Francis.

> Lord, make us instruments of your peace.
> Where there is hatred, let us sow love; where
> there is injury, pardon; where there is discord,
> union; where there is doubt, faith; where there
> is despair, hope; where there is darkness, light;
> where there is sadness, joy. Grant that we may
> not so much seek to be consoled as to console;
> to be understood as to understand; to be loved
> as to love. For it is in giving that we receive; it
> is in pardoning that we are pardoned; and it is
> in dying that we are born to eternal life. Amen.

A silence followed for the meditation. This cycle of music, prayer, and meditation was repeated. The congregation members sometimes participated in singing the hymns and reading the prayers. Jennifer liked the service because she always felt her heart cleansed.

Afterward, she escorted Michelle to the hushed privacy of the library adjoining the narthex. They settled at an empty table. She had not seen Michelle since the opening of the Graces. Michelle wore a smart business suit, but in spite of her neatness, she looked befuddled.

"I've never been to a service like this," Michelle said. "It's really soothing."

Jennifer nodded. "Every time I come, I feel my heart filled with peace."

"Well then, would you hear my confession?" Michelle listlessly laughed.

Jennifer was pleased that Michelle was not in a state of despair. It was better to keep the conversation light. She told Michelle to feel free to discuss anything as long as she wanted.

"I'm so confused," Michelle began, taking a deep breath. "I don't know what I should do. I need an impartial opinion. You're a thoughtful person, Jennifer. Hear me out."

Michelle talked about her unhappiness with her marriage to John and her divorce filing. But she had realized that her difficulty was rather typical among artists and musicians. Her Graces friends had told her that she was better off than most artists in New York City in terms of her financial situation and personal life. They praised John highly for his devotion to her, in spite of his challenging life as an opera singer. So she was having second thoughts.

Jennifer was amazed by the similarity between Michelle and Richard. When Michelle completed her story, she wiped her eyes with her handkerchief and blew her nose. "It must have been difficult for you. I've never been married. But I understand your pain because I just went through a similar experience." Then she described her confrontation with Richard, why he had broken their long engagement, and his new relationship with the female lawyer. "It was excruciating. When I saw his betrayal, I actually took sleeping pills. I didn't mean to kill myself. But I didn't know what I was doing. Stephanie and Henry rescued me."

"Oh, Jennifer," Michelle gasped. "John told me your engagement was broken. But I didn't know you attempted suicide. I'm sorry. It must have been so dreadful."

"I call it an accident. But yes, I was completely depressed. It's been hard, but finally I feel I've regained control of my life. Most days, anyway." She paused. "Michelle, Richard abandoned me because I didn't have much time to be with him. Now he's enjoying a shallow life with this woman. If that's what he wants, I'm disappointed. I thought he was better than that as a person. I'm sorry to say it, but it seems to me you're trying to do the same from a woman's point of view. Is that really what you want?"

Michelle's face twisted in pain.

"I've known John for a long time, perhaps longer than you," Jennifer went on. "He was born to be an opera singer. Nothing will stop him. He divides his time between opera, earning a living, and you. He has no time to fool around. Yes, unfortunately this will hamper your married life a little. But do you really want a husband without substance, just to have dinner with and stroll with? He'll be just like Richard. Sooner or later he'll find excuses to have affairs with other women. Many men are like that. Do you know the torment of adultery by a person you love? You'll suffer like hell. And you'll always compare every new man to John."

Michelle paled.

"I know John loves you dearly," Jennifer said, giving a sage nod. "Once he breaks through his initial difficulty and finds a stable job in a first-tier opera company, I'm sure he'll spend much more time with you. Don't you want to help him achieve his dream? Isn't life with John better than life with someone like Richard? Would you trade John's love for a few trips to the Bahamas?" She stopped. She wanted Michelle to compare two potential patterns of life. Maybe she would realize how special John was.

After a long silence, Michelle said, "I must say you sound reasonable. I can't find any fault in what you've said. I feel like a stupid woman. What should I do?"

"If I may say so, nothing is wrong in your marriage. John is a hardworking and loving husband. Right now he is going through a rough time. Someday he'll make it. Until then, can you be patient and supportive to him? Once he breaks through, you'll have a comfortable married life with him. If you love him, this won't be so hard." She heard Michelle's deep sigh. "I may sound like I'm preaching. But I can tell you this because this is exactly what I wanted Richard to do for me. But he didn't have the patience, because his love wasn't strong enough for me. I don't want this to happen between you and John." She saw Michelle's face recovering some color.

"I feel better now," Michelle said. "At least I wasn't wrong in having second thoughts about the divorce. I do love John—this is why I miss him so. I want to ponder what you've said."

"Good. Think about it. But before we go, I want to read something for you." Jennifer fetched a Bible from one of bookshelves. She found the page she wanted. "This is from 1 Corinthians. It's a famous passage often quoted during weddings." She recited.

> Love is patient; love is kind; love is not envi-
> ous or boastful or arrogant or rude. It does
> not insist on its own way; it is not irritable or
> resentful; it does not rejoice in wrongdoing,

but rejoices in the truth. It bears all things,
believes all things, hopes all things, endures
all things.

As Jennifer closed the Bible, she saw Michelle's eyes had welled up.

"It's beautiful," Michelle said. "I remember this was read during our wedding. It was the happiest day of my life. John and I were so full of love and hope. What happened to that? What's wrong with me? I need to think." She slowly stood. "I'm really glad I talked to you. Thank you very much." She dabbed her eyes.

Jennifer hugged Michelle. She felt as if Michelle were her sister. "Call me anytime when you want to talk. I want you and John to be happy—whatever the future holds. I'll pray for both of you."

⟪◎ ◎⟫

Jennifer walked back to her apartment on West End Avenue in the eighties. After the meditation service and the discussion with Michelle, she felt peaceful. She hoped that Michelle and John would reconcile. At her apartment building, as she walked up the steps to the entrance door, a man accosted her, gripping her arm. She swerved her head toward him and froze. It was Richard. He looked nervous and clumsy in an untidy business suit and coat. He smiled faintly.

"What are you doing here?" she snarled, jerking away.

"I came to say I'm sorry," he said, his voice coarse. "I was wrong."

"You creep! How dare you talk like that after sleeping with that woman?" Indignant blood gushed to her head. She could not keep her voice from rising. "I want nothing to do with you anymore. Leave me alone." Her hands trembled as she tried to find her key.

"I deserve your wrath," he said, moving between her and the door. "I have no excuse. But I need to talk to you. Can you spare a few minutes?"

"Absolutely not. We're finished. Go away. Let me open the door, or I'll scream."

One of the residents came down and opened the door from the inside. The person went out, greeting her. Jennifer returned a casual smile. Then, taking the opportunity, she slipped inside the building and shut the door behind her, hearing the lock snap into place. She stared at Richard through the door glass. He made a desperate attempt to open the door. He gazed at her with despondent puppy eyes. She looked at him coldly for several seconds. He attempted a final appeal to her to open the door. As nothing came from her, he nodded weakly, sighed, slowly turned, and shuffled away.

What a difference. When Jennifer had seen him several weeks before, he had been a confident corporate executive in an impeccable suit, happy with his trophy redhead. What had happened to him since then? She struggled to decide whether or not she should hear him out. The last time she had seen him, he had not wanted to talk to her. Now at least he wanted to talk. It would not hurt as long as she maintained her stern composure. She promised not to compromise herself out of pity for him. She opened the door and caught up with him.

"Richard, what's the matter?" she said. "You're sorry, huh? That's easy to say."

"Yes, I know. Even so, I wanted to say it, facing you."

She heard sincerity in his voice, which mitigated her anger a little. They walked together along West End Avenue toward the south. It was dark. Warm lights came from the windows of the apartment buildings on both sides of the avenue. Several people were walking along the sidewalk. But it was quiet. Jennifer and Richard had privacy.

She raised an eyebrow. "The woman lawyer dumped you?"

She could see his face flush even in the dim light. He began explaining. He and Karen had gone to Atlanta for a conference. They were supposed to have hot evenings together after the business during the day. Instead, she slept with one of the most powerful senior VPs in their bank. Since then she had been his mistress. He was married and had children. But she didn't care. She wanted to be promoted. Then, just to get rid of Richard, the senior VP fired him, accusing him of mishandling currency trades, resulting in the loss of millions of dollars. Now he was out of a job.

"Whatever you enjoyed with that woman—sex, drinking, partying—" she said, "she is now doing with the senior VP. What kind of sexual positions did she like with you? Can you see her naked on top of the naked senior VP?"

"That treacherous bitch," he spat, his face twisting in disgust. He clenched his fists so intensely that his knuckles turned white.

Jennifer had intended her remark as a strong insult, laced with payback. Even so, his anger was not directed at her, but at his latest ex-girlfriend. "That's exactly how I felt when you left me for her," she said. "That treacherous SOB."

Richard groaned. "Yes, I deserve your contempt. I was just plain stupid. She played me, and she cost me my job, my reputation—and you. The angrier I felt toward her, the more betrayed, the better I understood what I'd done to you. Now I can feel your pain as my pain."

Finally Richard was making sense. This was the man she had known before that woman came into his life. She took a deep breath, exhaling cold December air. "She just used you until a better man came along—another stepping stone."

"Precisely. And for that, I abandoned you. How foolish I was. I'm so ashamed."

Jennifer had regained her calm to some degree, although she still felt irate. Just as her aunt had predicted, Richard had learned his lesson in a hard way, and he had gotten the punishment he deserved, she thought. But this would change nothing. Their relationship was over. "Do you know I took sleeping pills the night I saw that woman in your apartment?" she asked. "I could have lost my life, or my voice . . ." She trailed off.

"Yes, Henry told me. I'm so sorry."

She took in a sharp breath. "So you knew. Yet you refused to tell me why you dropped me, and you went through the relationship with that woman. I hope it was worth it." She looked sharply into his eyes, remembering the excruciation she had suffered.

"The hell with that bitch," Richard snapped. "I don't know why I was so blind. I wish I could erase every minute I spent with her." He bit his lip hard, as if it would wipe out the worst part of his memory. Then he shook his head in resignation. "I know what has been done cannot be undone. I caused you great pain. It's unforgivable. I take full responsibility. If there is anything I can do for you, I'll do it without any hesitation."

They walked for a while in silence. She realized that although he showed a consistent absence of anger toward her, he was also consumed with the pain of betrayal and loss. He was still too self-involved to attract her again. Whatever she had once felt for him, he had killed it. She felt the same detachment toward him that she would feel for a pitiful stranger.

"Since I was fired, I'm looking for a job," he continued. "I hope I can find one soon. But right now the economy seems to have topped out, so the banks aren't hiring. In the meantime, I'm running through my savings. I may have to sell my apartment because I can't afford the high maintenance and the mortgage payments. As you can see, my life is falling apart. But this is the problem I created. I have to sort it out by myself." He bent his head. His voice became penitent. "I don't mention this to burden you. But I wanted you to know that I'm reaping what I've sown, and confessing to you is my way of apologizing to you."

They continued walking the avenue. She wondered how much longer she should walk with him. At least he didn't seem to expect her to take him in and fix his pain.

"I asked you to forgive me," he went on. "But I'm not really expecting your forgiveness after I treated you so despicably. I say it because now I know you better as a genuinely trustful person who deserves tender love from an honorable man. Not me. I'm unworthy of you."

His words moved her. She was able to see in him the man she had loved a long time ago. She stopped walking. "Richard," she said, "it took all this time for me to regain myself. I'm all right now—at least I'm starting to heal. So will you. I'm busy preparing for the opera. It'll be performed at the beginning of March. Don't disturb me. I need to be able to concentrate so I can sing. There is absolutely no way we can reconcile. You hear? Today, this was so unexpected, and I was completely unprepared to see you. That's the only reason I'm talking to you. I don't want to see you or hear from you again. We're finished. Done. Is that clear?"

He nodded. She felt that at least he had been honorable enough to come and confess his guilt. The happy days with him flashed back to her, softening her attitude with nostalgia. Immediately, she dismissed her weakness. Then she turned toward her apartment and walked swiftly away without looking back. She heard his voice from behind.

"Thank you, Jennifer. Thank you for listening to me."

⊰⊱

Back in her apartment, Jennifer had a quick supper. Then she went to the piano to go over the second half of Act III of the other *La Bohème*. This was the scene in which Mimi comes back to Rodolfo, asking him to take her back. Rodolfo rages at her for having fled to Viscount Paolo. He refuses her plea. Jennifer saw the bitter irony. In the opera, she was singing the role of Mimi. But an hour before, she had undergone a complete role reversal in reality. She thought that she should be able to sing the scene well because she understood the conflicting emotions in both Mimi and Rodolfo. But the image of Richard imploring her bobbed up in her mind. She could not concentrate. Finally she gave up the practice session.

She turned the TV on and flipped channels. Not a single program interested her. She switched the TV off and made a pot of tea. She poured it into a cup and added some honey. She sipped the tea for a while. But her mind was still agitated. She sat in the lotus position, her palms on her lap. She closed her eyes and breathed slowly in and out. Richard's face. Richard's voice. She gave up the meditation.

She fetched her laptop and checked e-mail. While going through the inbox, she came up with a strange one. The sender's address was "Darkforce13." The message was simple but ominous: "Dark force is increasing. It will strike you soon. Your days are numbered." That was all. Nothing to identify the sender. She thought that she might have received it by accident. She trashed it immediately. As time passed, however, it increasingly troubled her. She wondered if someone might have sent it to her with malicious intent. Richard? She didn't think so, because if it had been him, he would not have appeared before her tonight. Besides, he had been sincere; so it couldn't have been him. Then who else? And most of all, why? She hoped that this was the first time and the last she would receive such a threatening e-mail.

She pulled Willa Cather's *The Song of the Lark* from the bookcase. She read the chapters where Thea Kronborg, then a voice student and a piano accompanist for her teacher, became engaged to Fred Ottenburg, a wealthy young gentleman, only to find out that he was already married, although his marriage had been estranged for many years. *How stoically Thea dealt with that situation.* Jennifer thought that she had to be as tough as Thea.

She wanted to talk to someone. She called Aunt Maggie in Florida, who was in a good mood. Jennifer conjectured that her aunt had had a few glasses of wine at dinner. They gossiped innocuously.

"Auntie, you usually come to New York around Christmastime," Jennifer said in an intentionally cheerful voice. "When are you coming this year?"

"I've been thinking, my dear. Since your opera is in the beginning of March, I want to visit New York for that, instead of the usual December visit. Would that cause you any problem?"

"Oh no. I was just wondering so I could make a plan for Christmas."

"Hmm, did you find a new boyfriend?"

"Oh, Auntie, I'm too busy with the opera. I don't have time for that kind of thing."

"Just teasing." Then her aunt changed to a more serious tone. "When you called me, I sensed some distress in your voice. Are you sad? I guess Richard came back to you."

"How did you know?" Jennifer asked, surprised by her aunt's clairvoyance. "Yes, he came to me and apologized. But I rejected him." She described her encounter with him. "There is no way we can reconcile. I told him so. But still, I'm shaken." Her voice was trembling.

"That's natural, my dear," Aunt Maggie said. "But keep a distance from him for now. It's only good if you let him struggle. Let him sort out his life. The more he suffers, the wiser he'll become. There's nothing you can or should do for him now. Just leave him alone. That's best for both of you. In the meantime, Jennifer, you have your opera to perform."

There was no bitterness in her aunt's voice, which convinced her that her aunt was right. "Auntie, you make me feel strong."

They chatted for another several minutes. When Jennifer hung up the telephone, she went straight to the piano. The energy had come back to her. No time for self-pity.

For a change, she wanted to sing something lighthearted. She opened the score to Mimi's aria "Musette svaria sulla bocca viva" ("Musette purrs on her lively lips") in Act I, in which Mimi introduces her best friend Musette to her bohemian friends. The aria was the first soprano aria of the entire opera, so it served to establish the mood of the opera, as well as to make the first impression of the soprano. Therefore it was important for her to sing it perfectly. She had already studied the aria with her coach. This evening she wanted to review and enjoy. She played the introduction on the piano in *sostenuto*. She then sang *colla massima eleganza*.

The aria streamed friskily like a waltz: Musette loves to sing; she loves to fall in love. Jennifer's coloratura voice scurried on the sixteenth notes with precise agility. She sang a high G and A with vigor and ease. She pumped her diaphragm in time with the changing tempo. She sang with full expression, trusting the strength of her vocal cords. She wanted to emphasize Mimi's sisterly love for Musette. She could do it all. She forgot everything else.

The singing made her happy. This was the pleasure of being an opera singer. Her gift was her life.

Scene 4

*J*ohn took his lunch break with Erica again. Since she was married, he felt somehow less guarded. She, too, seemed to feel comfortable with him as a married man. It had become their custom to spend breaks together, though not too often. They went to his regular restaurant near Music Universe. She looked happy in her peach snap-front sweater and plum-colored slacks.

"Yesterday, my husband bought a Christmas tree, quite big for our apartment," she said, eating her habitual spinach salad. "The smell is so good. My daughter got all excited. We spent a whole afternoon decorating it."

"That reminds me," John said, wrangling his usual hero sandwich. "I'm going to get one this weekend. Michelle likes a Christmas tree because it's festive." He remembered that last year he had been so busy he had not even bothered to buy a tree, despite Michelle's protest. This year, since the divorce was on the table, he was sure that he wouldn't make the same mistake.

"We got our tree early this season because we're planning a Christmas vacation to Disney World in Florida," Erica resumed. "I think my daughter is too young to enjoy the theme park, but she insists that she has to see Snow White, Mickey Mouse—and Cinda-*wella*." She imitated her toddler's little voice.

John grinned. "Sounds like fun. We're also planning a vacation, after my opera in March." He hated his lies and his cowardice. *Why don't you just tell her the truth?* he asked himself. *She might give you advice from a woman's point of view. But I can't; I have my pride.*

Then he received a frenzied call from his mother on his cell phone.

《◎ ◎》

Pa, hang on. Don't give up. Not now. You have to hear my performance.

John was on his way to Brooklyn. The subway had never felt so slow. At three o'clock in the afternoon, the train was not crowded. But the cars appeared to linger at each station and move along the track at a snail's pace. He drummed his thighs with his fingers. The hospital was located at the southeast edge of Prospect Park. He got out at Parkside Avenue, in sight of the building. He ran. At the reception desk, he announced himself as the son of a patient in the ICU. In no time he found his mother anxiously sitting on a sofa, twisting a handkerchief in her hands.

Seeing John, his mother's face lit up momentarily, then fell as if she were crushed. She told him that his father was on medication and sleeping. She started weeping. He sat beside her and took her hands, caressing them. In a halting voice she told him that after lunch, his father had gone out to take a short walk around their house. This was routine for him. Several minutes later he came back. His face was ghostly white. He was covering his left chest with both his arms. He barely made it into the living room and collapsed on the sofa. He complained of pain and discomfort in his chest. His breath was short, and he was sweating. Then he lost consciousness.

"I was terrified," his mother said, wiping her tears.

Responding to her call, paramedics arrived quickly and resuscitated his father. Then they let her ride with him in the ambulance. When they arrived at the hospital, according to the paramedics, his father's heart had stopped beating. Doctors applied electrical shocks to his heart. It worked, and his heartbeats resumed. His mother sobbed again. John patted her shoulder gently.

A doctor came by with nurses. "Mrs. Bertucci, don't worry," the doctor said with professional confidence. "Your husband will be all right. You called the ambulance right away, and the paramedics came quickly. That was good. Otherwise it could have been a difficult case."

John's mother thanked the doctor. John introduced himself.

"We've done all we could," the doctor said. "We'll keep him here for a few days for observation. Then he can go home."

John thanked the doctor. His mother crossed herself. The doctor nodded with a grin. A moment later, however, turning serious, the doctor informed John that this was a small hospital. They were not equipped for major heart surgery. Once his father came home, the doctor suggested that he make an appointment with a larger hospital, like the one at New York University, to have a comprehensive examination of his heart. Most likely he would require bypass surgery.

"Oh, Santa Maria," John's mother cried, covering her face with her hands.

"That bad?" John said.

"Relax," the doctor said. "Heart bypass surgery is common these days. It's not the end of the world. The most important thing is to see a good doctor with expertise in cardiac surgery."

"Understood," John said dubiously. The sound of heart surgery of any kind disturbed him.

The doctor asked if John and his mother wanted to see the patient. John nodded firmly. His mother gripped his arm. The doctor led them into the ICU, where his father lay calmly in bed, hooked up to beeping machines. An IV was connected to his left arm, and an oxygen tube affixed to his nose. He was pale but sleeping peacefully. This was the first time John had been inside an ICU. He felt a little frightened. He watched his father's heartbeat pattern on the electrocardiogram. The doctor checked the monitoring devices and took his patient's pulse. Nurses adjusted the IV and the oxygen tube. They consulted each other. Then the doctor spoke reassuringly to John and his mother.

"Mr. Bertucci is stable. There is nothing you can do for him now. You should go home and rest. Tomorrow you can come back when he's awake."

John accompanied his mother home and stayed there overnight. He called Michelle and explained the situation. She was relieved to hear the fortunate outcome. John also called Henry. Since Henry's brother was a cardiologist, John asked him to ask his brother for advice.

A few days later John's father came home. In addition to taking the prescribed medication, the doctor had advised him to get good long sleeps, do regular exercise, eat less fatty meats, less pasta, more vegetables, more seafood, drink less alcohol, and take one tablet of baby aspirin every day. John's mother followed the doctor's advice on food, and his father practiced the rest of the doctor's suggestions. The retired subway engineer resumed his daily routine with these slight alterations. John went back to his parents' house after work each day and stayed overnight until it seemed safe to return to his apartment with Michelle.

◦◦ ◦◦

John kept in constant communication with Henry. Fortunately George had a close friend who was a renowned cardiac surgeon at the School of Medicine at New York University. His name was Dr. Silverman. Both George and Dr. Silverman had spent their residencies at the Mayo Clinic in Minnesota, one of the most prestigious medical institutions in the world for heart treatments. According to George, Dr. Silverman was "a genius" at cardiac surgery. George arranged a comprehensive heart examination with Dr. Silverman for John's father and, if required, bypass surgery at NYU Hospital. After the examination, Dr. Silverman advised John's father to have a double bypass, promising him that the surgery would make his heart as tough as a steel pump. The Bertucci family decided to follow the doctor's advice.

In the middle of December, John's father had the surgery with Dr. Silverman. While it took a few hours, due to the excellent doctor, his competent staff, and cutting-edge equipment, everything went flawlessly. Throughout the surgery, John stayed with his mother. She prayed the rosary, clinging to the cross and beads. Back home that evening, John reported to Michelle that the surgery had been a success. It was only a matter of time until his father completely recovered.

"I'm happy to hear it," Michelle said. "When are you going back to the hospital?"

"Every day until Pa goes home. The visiting hours end at five o'clock, so I'll go during my lunch break. Since Ma will be there every day, I don't have to stay for a long time."

"I have to work tomorrow and Friday, but if you're going to visit on Saturday, I'll go with you."

He regarded her face. She seemed calm and full of sympathy. However, the idea flashed in his mind: *We are getting divorced.* He had not mentioned the divorce to his parents yet. And this certainly was not the time. "Are you sure you don't mind?"

"When I had the gathering of the Graces, you were good company to my friends. I appreciated it very much. I want to do the same for you."

"Thank you. Your presence will mean a lot to my parents."

Then he reminded her that one week from Saturday would be the day of Christmas caroling at the Café Momus. Stephanie had managed to assemble many singers and actors who volunteered to sing. Michelle told him that Helen and Stephanie had been discuss-ing this issue constantly. Père Momus insisted on buying a Christmas tree, as he had always done. The Graces were to decorate the tree and the interior of the restaurant the Friday before. Michelle was paint-ing something cheerful to post on the walls. Helen and Sarah were also doing their parts. Michelle seemed excited. John was pleased to have a casual conversation with her. He thought that this was the kind of domestic life between wife and husband she wanted—and he liked it too.

"Sounds good," he said. "According to Stephanie's plan, the Dolci Quattro and the Graces are going to have dinner on Saturday evening. You and I will have to be there."

"I heard Sarah's younger sister Christine and Henry are pas-sionately in love," she said, "so she'll join us as well. The dinner is going to be fun. I'm looking forward to it."

"Me too." He smiled at her. Then he thought of their pending divorce. *What about us?*

⟪◎ ◎⟫

On Saturday, John and Michelle visited the NYU Hospital. He had bought a bouquet of seasonal flowers, and she carried it. He wore a suit, and she a fashionable dark brown dress and a pair of suede boots in matching dark brown that set off her brunette hair and brown eyes. When they entered the room, John's mother broke into a huge smile. Michelle seemed startled by the sight of the monitoring devices and the smells of disinfectant. His mother's joy seemed to mitigate her alarm. She hugged her mother-in-law and presented the bouquet.

"Thank you, honey. It's pretty, and you look beautiful like these flowers."

Mrs. Bertucci turned to Mr. Bertucci, who was sitting up in bed, supported by a pillow at his back. Three days after the surgery, he still had an IV in his left arm but no longer had an oxygen tube in his nose. His face had recovered some color, and he was able to speak.

"What a pleasant surprise to see you, Michelle," he said. "You look as lovely as ever."

He opened his arms as she drew close to his bed. She gave him a gentle hug while he patted her back softly with his right hand.

"I'm glad you look well," she said.

"At my age," he replied, "a heart attack can be expected. It scared my wife like hell. But I'm all right. I can't die now. That was what I kept saying when I got the chest pains. I have to hear John's opera in March."

"Pa, you scared me, too," John said. "Tell us how you feel today."

"I feel fine. I can't move too quickly yet, because if I do, my chest feels tight. But as long as I move slowly, I can walk around. I even enjoy the food at this hospital. It's better than the other hospital." He laughed.

"Yes," Mrs. Bertucci said, "the doctor said he is recovering faster than average patients in the same situation. He should be able to go home early next week."

John asked his father how he liked Dr. Silverman. His father praised the doctor and asked John to thank Henry and his brother.

Then his father gave John a sharp look, as if he had remembered the most important thing in the world.

"How is your singing, son?" his father asked.

"I'm practicing very hard. I've learned the entire part of Rodolfo. So far I'm studying with my coach. But in February the rehearsals will start with the other soloists and the chorus. I'll be ready by then."

"Son, go for it. I won't miss your performance. I'm thinking of bringing your grandpa's portrait to the concert. Don't laugh! I want my papa to listen to you sing. He would be a severe critic because he knew many Italian operas by heart." He turned to Michelle. "He taught opera in Napoli." He turned back to John. "So you'd better be good."

"Pa, trust me. I'll sing like Caruso in a baritone voice. I hope Grandpa will approve."

"Excellent, my boy." His father nodded repeatedly with satisfaction.

After the initial excitement of the visit, their conversation turned innocuous for a while. John noticed that his father was watching Michelle with perplexed interest.

When there was a pause in the chatting, Mr. Bertucci said, "Michelle, you look different today. I've been thinking what it is. Come closer to me. Let me take a good look at you." He gazed at Michelle as she obediently faced him. "Young woman, you're bloom-ing. Look at you. You're shining with life. John, you're a lucky man to have a beautiful wife like her."

John felt a pang in his stomach, a sign of his guilt. Someday he would have to reveal their divorce plans. He saw Michelle, too, trying to hide her own distress by shyly looking at the floor.

"Yes, you're beautiful," his mother chimed in.

Michelle smiled faintly at her parents-in-law. An awkward silence fell. She looked down at the floor again. John's parents' eyes met, as if they had said something immodest. John deliberately changed the conversation to a safer subject. They resumed chatting. Mr. and Mrs. Bertucci looked content to spend a comfortable afternoon with their son and daughter-in-law. Soon after John and Michelle took their leave with repeated well-wishes to his father.

"Michelle, come to our home more often," his mother said, walking with them to the elevator. "Let's cook together. I'll pass my secret recipes to you."

"I will, Mother," Michelle said, hugging her mother-in-law. "You're too kind."

◀◎ ◎▶

Outside, the sun was already setting on the December afternoon. John and Michelle walked west on 34th Street. The traffic was light. Few pedestrians scurried on the sidewalk.

"Thank you very much, Michelle," John said. "My parents were so happy to see you."

"You're welcome," she replied.

They continued walking quietly. He thought that with the weather being mild, they could walk to Penn Station and take the subway back to their apartment. Soon he noticed that she was dabbing her eyes. She slowed her pace and looked into his face. "You have lovely parents."

"We're close to each other—like a traditional Italian family. Pa's heart attack has been scary. But I think it made us even closer."

They walked in silence again.

"My friends compliment you," she said. "And your friends praise you."

"Oh? That's nice to hear."

More silence. The street was now dark, except for occasional flashing headlights and the reflection of lights from stores on the sidewalk. Michele stopped walking and sobbed. "John, I'm so ashamed. I have to confess, I don't know what to do."

"Sorry?" John said, dumbfounded. "What are you talking about?"

"About our divorce," she said. "I know I initiated it. But I may have been wrong. I'm having second thoughts. What am I looking for by the divorce? I just don't know any more." Even though they were on a public sidewalk, she leaned against him and hugged him, sobbing.

He caressed her back. "You know I don't want to lose you. But I'm the one who failed to make you happy. It's my fault. You have no need to apologize."

"You're so honorable, and I'm so wretched."

"Don't talk like that. I pushed you into a corner. I'm the one to blame. But please don't give me false hope, either. Take time to decide what you want." John remembered their dreamy lovemaking after the party with the Graces. Why they had done it, he didn't know. How it would affect their divorce, he didn't know either. All he knew was that he still loved her.

Except for that incident, they were still sleeping separately in their apartment. He thought of asking her to salvage their marriage. But he reconsidered because it was she who had to make the decision as to whether she would pursue the divorce action or drop it. All he could do was wait. He sighed and held her. Then he kissed her on her lips. It was a devout kiss. To his delight, she kissed him back.

Scene 5

Stephanie arrived at the Café Momus. Outside the front door, she saw Helen in her jeans and sweater on a ladder, hanging brass decorations above the lintel: two old-fashioned golden trumpets crossing in an X and two golden bells above the trumpets, as if they were rhythmically tolling. Helen climbed down and looked up with satisfaction. They went inside. This year, Christmas day being a Thursday, they had chosen the Friday one week prior to do their Christmas decorating. At about four o'clock in the afternoon, the restaurant was virtually empty. Other members of the Graces were busily working. On the walls, Sarah was arranging paper snowflakes in various sizes and watercolors of snow-covered evergreens. Michelle was hanging several small oil-painted cardboard canvases of sleighs with reindeer, horses, and dogs. Helen pointed to her abstract painting, reminiscent of a quaint landscape of a snow-topped church in New England.

In the center of the restaurant stood a towering Christmas tree with a big silver star at the top. Helen started decorating the tree, soon joined by Michelle and Sarah. Stephanie, too, pitched in. Cotton snow covered the branches, which were hung with golden and silver balls. When all was completed, she plugged in the electrical cord. Bright lights flickered, and the tree full of ornaments majestically sparkled. They all applauded and sang.

> Deck the hall with boughs of holly,
> Fa la la la la, la la la la.

The kitchen door opened, and Père Momus appeared. "*C'est magnifique*," he said. "Ladies, you did a splendid job." He came close to the tree and studied it from top to bottom. Then he examined each painting on the walls. Stephanie invited him to see Helen's work at the entrance door outside. All went out and looked up. The trumpets and bells were shining as if they were making merry music. They cheered. Back inside the café, Père Momus was all grins. He chortled like Santa himself when he saw the Graces' artworks that he had purchased from the show: each now bore a holly wreath or garland of pine in addition to their frames.

◖◔ ◑◗

The following day, Stephanie sang in the morning service at the synagogue. Then she worked the lunch shift at Café Momus, her regular Saturday schedule. After three the crowd thinned. She relaxed until six off-duty waiters and waitresses showed up. They wore casual clothes with something red, like mufflers or gloves. She gave each of them a red Santa hat and a booklet of Christmas carols. They were to sing outside the restaurant, *a cappella* in four parts. Being singers and actors at Broadway theaters, they were eager to show off their harmonizing skills.

At five o'clock, they started singing familiar carols. Stephanie saw the red Santa hats rhythmically bouncing as they sang. The weather being mild, many people gathered around the restaurant and listened to the music. They noticed the golden trumpets and bells at the top of the entrance door, which seemed to frame the caroling. Between songs, the carolers invited people to try the restaurant. "Please, c'mon in. Food is excellent. Desserts are heavenly." The caroling was repeated at six and seven o'clock. Stephanie occasionally watched the singers from inside the café. They were competent enough to be left to themselves. Some people outside, after listening to the carols, decided to come in to have dinner. Business was booming.

At a quarter to eight, Stephanie stopped working and changed to her formal black attire. When she came out of the changing room, she saw Jennifer, Henry, Christine, John, Mike, Vicky, the Graces, Kate, Arthur, and his wife, Claudia. All were in chic dresses or dark suits for dinner, with something red in their outfits, mingling and talking near the large table reserved for them. Stephanie had heard from John that his father was recovering well. He looked in good spirits.It had been several weeks since she had started working as the general manager of the New York Bel Canto Opera. She found

Arthur to be a bright conductor and a dignified gentleman. She had been feeling the awakening of affection toward him and had been desperately trying to suppress it. She thought that such a feeling would be unprofessional. Above all, he was married. But she couldn't help it.

At eight o'clock, the carolers, now numbering ten, started singing Christmas songs inside the restaurant, this time accompanied by Kate on the piano. Their brisk singing created a celebratory air in the restaurant, which was by now packed. All patrons appeared to be enjoying the food and the music. When the caroling was over, Stephanie spoke into a microphone near the piano, welcoming the patrons. She asked them to give carolers a big hand. "They are off-duty waiters and waitresses at this restaurant. When they are not here, they work in Broadway theaters as singers and actors, or are at least trying to get there."

The patrons laughed and applauded.

Stephanie said, "Père Momus has been very generous in hiring them, which has helped them financially. So in return, they wanted to do something for him. They are singing here this evening as volunteers."

"Thank you, Père Momus," the carolers shouted. "*Merci! Merci!*"

Père Momus stood at the entrance to the kitchen. He fondly threw kisses to the carolers.

"Père Momus has been also a patron to a group of female artists, called the Graces," Stephanie resumed. "In return, the Graces volunteered to decorate this restaurant for Christmas. You can see their artworks and efforts." She pointed them out.

The patrons looked around and murmured in admiration.

"Thank you, Père Momus," the Graces said in unison.

Père Momus beamed and blew more kisses.

"Père Momus has been also good to four opera singers, called the Dolci Quattro," Stephanie continued. "In return, this evening we would like to sing arias from Leoncavallo's *La Bohème*, which the New York Bel Canto Opera will perform at the beginning of March. We will play the major roles in it." She pointed to Arthur. "This evening we have the honor of the presence of Maestro Arthur DeSoto, the artistic director of the opera company."

The patrons looked at Arthur and applauded. Arthur lowered his head courteously, his dark curls bouncing. Stephanie had to force herself not to stare at her handsome boss.

"For us," she said, "this is a practice run. I hope the maestro will approve."

Arthur waved his hands amicably to her. The patrons giggled. She introduced the evening's accompanist, Kate, who took a bow.

"First," Stephanie said, "Jennifer Schneider will sing a soprano aria from Act I. In this aria, Mimi introduces her dear friend Musette to her bohemian friends. Then I will sing a mezzo-soprano aria from the same act, in which Musette praises how adorable her dear friend Mimi is."

Stephanie stepped back. Jennifer came close to the piano and bowed. She took Stephanie by the hands as if they were best friends, Mimi and Musette. Kate played an introduction of one bar in an elegant waltz tempo. Jennifer started singing in a bell-like coloratura soprano voice, introducing Musette as a lovely young girl, fond of singing and dancing, a little flirtatious, but passionate for love. Jennifer ended the aria with a dramatic climax, "*L'amor!*"

The patrons started applauding, but Kate immediately began playing the end of the scene prior to Musette's aria. Stephanie commenced singing right away in a smooth mezzo-soprano voice, depicting Mimi as a graceful young blonde, a little fragile, but everyone's favorite, who loves singing, her gown, and her *cuffia*, or bonnet. She completed her singing with a swinging finale, "*La cuffia di Mimi Pinson!*"

The patrons applauded. Jennifer and Stephanie took deep bows and hugged each other. Stephanie sneaked a look at Arthur. He was clapping heartily.

"Next," Stephanie spoke into the microphone, "Henry Anderson will sing a tenor aria, "Io non ho che una povera stanzetta" ("I have but a poor small room") from Act II. In this aria, Marcello tells Musette how much he cherishes her love although he is only a poor painter."

Henry came to the piano. Kate played a B-flat major chord in *arpeggio*. Henry began singing in *andantino cantabile*. His glorious tenor voice billowed in the ears of the listeners. After showing off his brilliant high B-flat by holding it dramatically, he gradually ended his aria with a passionate pledge of love. As the piano accompaniment descended, Stephanie advanced and sank into Henry's arms, singing, "*Mio buon Marcello!*"

The patrons shouted "Bravo!" Stephanie noticed that Christine was clapping like a mad girl, sometimes licking her lips. She appeared dreamy, as if she herself had been singing Musette's line for Henry.

"Next," Stephanie said into the microphone, "John Bertucci will sing a baritone aria "L'immenso testro" ("The immense treasure") from Act II. In this aria, Rodolfo comically yet proudly explains to his friends how he sold his poem that day for thirty francs, which is a great amount of money for a poor poet."

John moved to the piano as Kate played the introduction. He began singing in his sonorous baritone voice with subtle passion, projecting a poet's pride and joy at successfully selling his wares. Stephanie saw Michelle absorbed in listening to him with pride. This was different from the way she had looked at the Graces' opening. Stephanie wondered whether they had reunited. When John finished, warm applause came from the patrons. He took a bow.

"The opera will be performed on the first Saturday of March at the Italian Cultural Society," Stephanie said into the microphone. "There are flyers on the counter at the bar. Please take one and come to the opera." One of the carolers went to the bar, took a batch of flyers, and walked around to the tables, distributing them. "Next," Stephanie said, "we would like to sing a Christmas song, 'O Holy Night.' For this, Maestro DeSoto will conduct."

Arthur stood next to the piano. The carolers with red Santa hats gathered behind the Dolci Quattro. Mike also joined in. At Arthur's cue, Kate started playing in triplets in E-flat major. The carolers sang the first verse in four parts.

> O holy night! The stars are brightly shining,
> It is the night of the dear Savior's birth...

The second verse was sung by the opera singers in four parts without carolers. For this, Henry sang the soprano part and Jennifer sang the tenor part, while Stephanie and John with Mike sang alto and bass, respectively, as usual. At the repetition of the end, Henry sang "O holy night, O night divine!" splendidly holding a high B-flat. Arthur skillfully guided Henry and the accompanist to come back to the normal tempo. The third verse was sung by all. This time, Jennifer sang soprano and Henry sang tenor. Although the carolers sang in full voice, the voices of the five opera singers stood out, virtually making the carolers mere background. Here, Arthur showed his conducting power, commanding about fifteen voices and the piano to produce the music as pure oneness. At the end, while the soprano carolers sang the regular soprano line, Jennifer sang "O holy night" with a soaring high B-flat that resounded in the restaurant.

The patrons shouted "Bravo" and burst into applause.

"We would like to conclude with 'Silent Night,'" Stephanie said. "At the last verse, please join us in singing."

Arthur gave a cue, and Kate played the last four bars. The carolers started singing.

> Silent night! Holy night!
> All is calm, all is bright.

The second verse was sung by the opera singers. Then the carolers and the opera singers started singing the third verse. Arthur turned to face the patrons and gestured for them to join in. Following Arthur's hands, they started singing. The waiters and waitresses also joined. Père Momus, too, sang. The entire restaurant echoed with song. Bright lights on the Christmas tree blinked as if in tune with the music. The song ended with a hush, a moment of reverence. Arthur applauded the patrons. In return, they gave him a long ovation. Arthur took a bow, then gestured to the opera singers, Kate, and the carolers, who bowed.

"Merry Christmas!" the carolers yelled.

Prompted by their merriment, everyone greeted everyone else.

"Happy Holidays!"

"Merry Christmas!"

The opera singers, Arthur, and Kate returned to their table. Everybody spontaneously sat where they liked. Arthur sat with Claudia. Christine never left Henry's side. John and Michelle sat together. Kate settled next to Jennifer, which Stephanie had asked her to do to keep Jennifer comfortable, as she had been distressed by some mysterious recent e-mail threats, notwithstanding her residual woe about Richard. Mike and Vicky were together, sitting next to John. Sarah sat close to Michelle. Helen sat with her boyfriend. Stephanie was pleased to find that the seat next to Arthur was provided for her, perhaps as the general manager of his company.

This was the first time she had seen Arthur's wife. Claudia appeared a refined woman, probably in her late thirties. Her dark hair, dark eyes, and fine complexion suggested a northern Italian descent. She wore a black evening dress with a string of pearls around her slender neck. She was beautiful but modest. It was apparent that she was proud of her handsome conductor husband. He must be a sort of trophy husband, Stephanie thought. Otherwise, her wealthy parents would not have helped Arthur financially so much.

The friends at the table ordered wine, appetizers, and main dishes. As usual, Stephanie coordinated between her friends and the waiter. When wine was served, they toasted. "To the Dolci Quattro!" "To Arthur and the New York Bel Canto Opera!" "To the Graces!"

"To Père Momus!" "Merry Christmas!" The toasts seemed never to cease. The artists talked cheerfully. The five opera singers were careful not to talk too loudly, protecting their vocal cords. Stephanie saw Christine noticing the opera singers' caution and giving Henry a concerned look.

"You guys did a good job," Arthur told the Dolci Quattro. "I can see you've been studying your parts well. As far as these arias are concerned, I don't have anything to correct. You're doing just fine." He sipped wine.

"Yes, you all sang excellently," Mike said. "I can't wait to sing with you."

"Mike, I'm glad you're here," Arthur said. "You'll be a fine peer to the Dolci Quattro."

"Thank you, Maestro." Mike grinned. "I'm honored to sing in your company."

The main dishes were served. Since it was rather late, the friends started eating with good appetites, talking happily about the food and complimenting the chef.

Sarah asked who had prepared the flyer. Stephanie said that as the general manager, it was her job to coordinate with a professional graphic designer who specialized in concert posters. Sarah proposed that the Graces could help the company on future flyers. Helen suggested that Michelle would be the best artist for opera posters.

Michelle said, "Arthur, if you give me the name of the opera you're going to produce next and a few scenes that represent it, I could come up with a couple of illustrations in oils or acrylics."

"Sounds good," Arthur said. "Stephanie, please coordinate with Michelle next time."

"This is fantastic," Stephanie said. "I know Michelle is good. But the other Graces may also be able to contribute, depending on the nature of the opera. Sarah for watercolor and Helen for abstract. Then the Graces will be novel collaborators with the New York Bel Canto Opera."

"Yes, let's try," Arthur said. "I need any creative assistance I can get from talented artists." He patted Stephanie's shoulder. "My trusted general manager will coordinate with you."

How sweet Arthur's words sounded. Stephanie felt her shoulder burning. She wanted to purr like a kitten.

"Fabulous," the Graces cried.

"But sorry, folks, I can't pay you much." Arthur chuckled.

The artists moaned in pretense of disappointment. The friends laughed. Noticing the empty wine bottles, Stephanie ordered more wine. The friends went back to eating and drinking. Jolly chatting resumed.

Arthur spoke into Stephanie's ear in a low voice, asking if she had told her friends about the encore performances. She shook her head, because it was not definite yet. Arthur nodded. Stephanie was pleased that Arthur didn't mind discussing business matters with her here in confidence, even next to his wife. She looked at Claudia and met her eyes. Claudia gracefully smiled at Stephanie. His wife, too, seemed to consider Stephanie her husband's trusted general manager, nothing more, nothing less. Stephanie whispered to him that if he made the announcement now, they would be thrilled. Arthur took a spoon and gently rang the wine glass a few times. The friends at the table stopped talking and looked up.

"I have an announcement to make," Arthur said. "I wasn't sure in the beginning. But Stephanie has been working hard on this, and thanks to her, it's almost a sure thing. So I want to share the good news with you."

Everyone at the table stared at Arthur, holding their breath. He explained that their coming performance was getting a lot of attention in the opera community in New York because Leoncavallo's *La Bohème* was so rarely performed. The *New York Times*, the *Wall Street Journal*, and *New York Magazine* had all agreed to send their opera critics to their performance. Most of all, ticket sales were going extremely well, almost selling out the house. So he was considering encore performances the two Saturdays following their initial performance.

"Bravo," John shouted. He stopped immediately so as not to hurt his vocal cords. Instead, he banged the table several times with his palms. The friends hooted and clapped. Arthur waved his palms, gesturing them to calm down. He continued his explanation. Stephanie had negotiated with relevant parties. The Italian Cultural Society had no problem on the two additional Saturdays, as long as they could fill the hall. Since the members of the orchestra were all pickups, they wanted more business. Stephanie asked the soloists for their schedules. They were available. The chorus wouldn't be a problem, because they would like the idea of encores. The stagehands, lighting technicians, and sound technicians were available. So it seemed to Arthur that all was clear. Again everyone applauded.

"Right on!" said John, wildly waving both his hands. "That means more money."

"John, please!" Michelle patted his shoulder to restrain him, while laughing.

The friends roared. Stephanie was glad to see Michelle talking to John as if they were an affectionate husband and wife of many years.

"So guys," Arthur said, "you must condition yourselves to be physically fit for three performances. Since you have one week between each performance, I'm sure you can manage it."

This was obviously welcome news to everyone. Jennifer said that her entire family was coming to the opera—her aunt, her parents, her brother, his wife, and their son. Henry, too, listed his mother, his brother, his wife, their children, his sister, her husband, and their kids. Stephanie observed Christine eyeing Henry nervously, as if she had been asked to meet her in-laws for the first time. John announced that his parents were impatient for the show. Michelle said that her parents were coming, too. Stephanie saw John looking back to Michelle in surprise. But she saw no tension between them. With grins, they turned back to their friends, who were charmed by the couple's affection.

"I'm now arranging a revision of the flyer to add these two new dates," Stephanie said.

"When the new flyer comes out," Christine said, "would you give me several of them? I'll post them in the Poetry Club and poetry reading cafés. Poets love *La Bohème*, but I don't think they know of the existence of the other *La Bohème*. They'll be intrigued."

"Sure," Stephanie said. "Let's do some promotion. We need all the help we can get."

"I've got an idea." Michelle looked at Arthur. "I'll assign a painting project to my students at the Rudolf Steiner School. The subject will be opera. I'll encourage them to go see opera and paint their impressions from it. Then I'll casually mention this opera. The Italian Cultural Society is located less than ten blocks from the school. They can get their parents to take them to the performances."

Arthur said, "Super," smiling broadly.

Sarah and Helen likewise asked for the flyers so they could post them at their schools.

Stephanie said, "Let's try to sell out the house for all three performances."

Noisy assents showered from the friends.

As they completed their main courses, waiters and waitresses cleared the table. Père Momus emerged, smiling paternally. "Ladies and gentlemen, *merci beaucoup* for dining in my restaurant. Also, thank you for the Christmas decorations and singing. This evening, business has been extraordinary. I'm overjoyed. So dessert is on the house. Enjoy, *s'il vous plaît.*"

The friends hurrahed. Dessert, coffee, and tea were promptly served. They resumed their animated conversation. Stephanie looked around the table. As usual, John was making hilarious jokes with both his hands in motion, which cracked up the ladies, their faces turning up to the ceiling with open mouths. Even Jennifer was laughing. Henry, the unofficial photographer of the Dolci Quattro, was taking pictures with his bulky professional Nikon and showing them off. Mike and Vicky seemed happy to be included in the company, joining in the banter. Vicky's attractive dark face shone as she spoke with her neighbors. When she laughed, her high-pitched voice shrieked out. Yet she seemed to avoid eye contact with Mike. He, too, was throwing jokes to his neighbors, but occasionally he squinted anxiously at his girlfriend. Stephanie noticed that John gave them a concerned glance from time to time.

As the evening wound down, Stephanie proposed a battle cry of the Dolci Quattro. They gathered in a circle before their friends. They presented their right hands forward, their palms stacked one on top of the other.

"Sing on!"

The Dolci Quattro laughed amid cheers from their friends.

"Stephanie, you have such a lovely group of friends," said Claudia, leaning behind her husband, when Stephanie returned to her seat.

"I'm glad you're enjoying our company," Stephanie replied.

"And thank you for helping Arthur. The general manager's job is not easy. But observing you, I must say you're a natural. No wonder you have Arthur's full trust." Claudia had a pretty soprano voice. As she bent toward Stephanie, her dark hair brushed her ivory forehead.

"Thank you," Stephanie said. "I like the job."

"It's been Arthur's dream to establish the New York Bel Canto Opera as a respectable opera company in New York City." Claudia caressed Arthur's palm with her hand. A wedding band and a diamond ring shone on her slender finger. "Please keep up your good work." Her dark brown eyes glistened.

"I'll do my best to help Arthur."

Arthur smiled at both Claudia and Stephanie. Stephanie felt defeated. Claudia appeared to be an ideal wife for Arthur. Nevertheless, she couldn't help her swelling affection—and pangs of jealousy as well. In fact, her heart felt as full as the glass of red wine on the table before her—and as fragile.

On this evening, Stephanie reflected, she had experienced a perfect Café Momus scene in reality: joyful Christmas singing and dining amid singers, musicians, artists, poet, and actors. They'd even sung arias from the other *La Bohème*. Yet the night had lacked one thing: Marcello hadn't fallen in love with Musette. Suddenly she realized that the scene had ended with an unexpected twist. She had fallen in love with Arthur.

Scene 6

few days before Christmas, Henry received an e-mail from Stephanie. As the general manager, she had notified all soloists, understudies, and choristers that as soon as February arrived, they would have extremely busy days ahead. She advised them to refrain from excessive partying and drinking during the holidays. Attached was a rigorous rehearsal schedule. In essence, soloists had January to themselves. Starting in February, they had two rehearsals every week until the dress rehearsal, two days before the first performance. To this, Henry had to add his private sessions with Mr. Carré every Saturday. He felt overwhelmed just reading the list. Practically all of February was completely booked up with rehearsals and coaching sessions, followed by the three Saturday performances in March. Plus, he had to work on weekdays, except for the days of rehearsals with the orchestra and the dress rehearsal, which he would have to take off. Stephanie was right, he thought. A war of willpower was about to begin. There would be absolutely no time to loosen up during the holidays.

Christine and Sarah were to spend Christmas with their father and stepmother in New Orleans, as had been their tradition. They would be away for two weeks, until after New Year's Day. In truth, he felt relieved, because the holiday season was always filled with temptations, which he needed to avoid this year. He simply could not afford to begin a physical relationship with Christine, given the inevitable emotional consequences. The intoxication of a new love was every bit as distracting as the torment of a breakup.

But now that he did not have to worry about her, and in spite of the prospect of the dense rehearsal schedule, he suddenly felt empty. As people busied themselves shopping for gifts, writing cards, decorating trees, and partying, he thought how lonely his Christmas would be this year. He knew that many people committed suicide around Christmastime. Then the image of Jennifer flashed in his mind. He did not want her to feel this way. Never again. Also he was bothered by her recent complaints of threatening e-mails. He wanted to check her laptop for any information he could glean. He called Stephanie and asked her plans for the holiday. She had none, except for working at the Café Momus.

"This year," she said calmly, "Christmas and Hanukkah will be just ordinary days for me. The opera has the highest priority. By now you've seen the rehearsal schedule. Plus, like you, I have my private coaching sessions. I also have the general manager's job. On top of that, I have my work at the Café Momus and my singing job at my synagogue. I don't know how I'll manage—but I know we all will. We have to."

That was exactly how he felt. So he had good company. He mentioned his concern for Jennifer. Stephanie was worried, too.

"I've got an idea," he said. "I'm expecting a Christmas bonus. I know John will be singing at his church and has holiday plans with Michelle, but what if the rest of us have Christmas dinner together—you, Jennifer, and me? I'll buy what you tell me and you girls do the cooking. What do you think?"

"That's a deal," Stephanie cried. "Let me speak to Jennifer."

Jennifer had decided to sing in the Christmas Eve service at her church. Therefore, they all agreed that Henry and Stephanie would attend the six o'clock service, after which they would have dinner at Jennifer's place. To avoid the hassle of cooking, they would buy take-out appetizers and entrées from Café Momus. Stephanie would bring dessert, and Henry the wine.

⊰⊙ ⊙⊱

On Christmas Eve, Henry found Stephanie already sitting in a pew at the middle of the church. She said that she had come directly from the Café Momus. Reflecting the character of the Lutheran denomination, the church was simple and stern, but gracefully decorated for the occasion. The music was building up the mood for a joyful service. Henry looked back. At the rear of the church, on the second floor, he saw a chorus and a small chamber orchestra consisting of strings, brasses, and timpani. Henry spotted Jennifer singing there, wearing a choir robe of red and white. She appeared to be enjoying herself.

Promptly at six o'clock the bells tolled. The pastor and torchbearers entered from the sacristy. The torchbearers lit the people's candles. Then the pastor solemnly announced the birth of Jesus. The congregation responded with cheers of joy. A children's procession moved from the rear of the church to the altar, carrying crèche figurines, led by an angelic young girl in a white dress, wearing a candle wreath on her head. All sang "Oh, Come, All Ye Faithful." The service proceeded with prayers and scripture recitations, and the choir sang hymns, psalms, and Christmas songs, accompanied by the organ and the chamber orchestra. From time to time, Henry looked back as he recognized Jennifer's strong soprano voice projecting through the church.

At one of these moments, he noticed a man sitting in the last row of pews, dressed decently for the service, his hair smartly combed. It was Richard. Henry froze, considering his options. Then he discretely left the pew. When he reached the last row, he gestured for Richard to come out. Richard tried to hide, but it was too late. He had no choice but to follow Henry outside the church. After closing the door, Henry glared at Richard.

"What are you doing here?" he asked.

Richard extended his hand. Instead of shaking Richard's hand, Henry hit the church door with his fist and repeated the question. Richard recoiled. "I came to the service, hoping to hear Jennifer sing."

"I don't want you to come near Jennifer," Henry said. "She went through hell because of you and has just regained her balance. She has the opera to perform. This opera could make her career. It's only two months away. She doesn't need another emotional trauma. Upheaval with you could ruin her life. You've come close to doing that once already."

Richard did not argue back. "I understand," he simply said, nodding. "I just wanted to hear her beautiful soprano. I miss her very much. I didn't think she would see me because she would be up in the choir as usual. But you're right. It was insensitive of me to appear here."

Henry wanted to yell at Richard. But there was something in his countenance that neutralized Henry's anger. Richard did not appear arrogant or aggressive; he seemed sincere.

"I'll go now," Richard told him. "It was nice to see you."

Richard extended his hand again. Henry refused it a second time. Richard's shoulders slumped, but with no further protest he walked away. Henry stayed outside for a few minutes to cool off. After making sure that Richard was not coming back, he returned to his pew.

"Why did you leave?" Stephanie whispered.

"Richard was here," Henry muttered back.

She stared at him, her eyes bewildered. "Oh, that's horrible."

"I asked him to leave. He's gone now."

"That's good. Do you think Jennifer saw him?"

"No. But let's not mention this to her, OK?"

"Of course." Stephanie bit her lip.

After the service, he and Stephanie waited for Jennifer at the entrance. Soon she came out, her eyes shining. She asked if they enjoyed the service. He acknowledged that he had. It was a little different from the Episcopal service he was familiar with. The candle wreath on the young girl's head was beautiful. Stephanie inclined her head.

"I recognized your voice from the rest of the choir," she said. "It's as strong as ever."

"Thank you," Jennifer said, beaming. "By the way, Henry, in the middle of the service, I saw you leaving the pew. What happened?"

Stephanie shot him an anxious look.

"I swallowed the wrong way," he said in haste. "I had to go out and cough loudly. It was kind of embarrassing. I'm fine now. Oh, there's a cab." He hailed a ride.

（◎ ◎）

Back at Jennifer's apartment, Henry found a small plastic Christmas tree on the coffee table in front of the sofa. On the bookcase she had fastidiously arranged several Christmas cards. He guessed that Jennifer had hastily tidied up her living room. Otherwise, he thought, it would have been a miserable Christmas Eve for her. The dining table had already been set for three. The women had assembled a lovely salad and now they bustled in the kitchen, warming the food.

Taking this opportunity, Henry examined Jennifer's laptop. In her inbox, sure enough, he saw an unopened e-mail from Darkforce13. She had been getting one every day now. With her permission, he opened it. He gasped, as, instead of a message, a color image popped up, showing a voodoo doll with sharp needles piercing at its eyes, vocal cords, heart, and womb, covered with blood all over. He immediately trashed it. Then he added Darkforce13 to the

Block Sender list in her e-mail options, ensuring any new e-mails from Darkforce13 would be erased before appearing in her inbox. Finally he started a full virus scan, recommending she run her anti-virus program at least once a week, for this kind of e-mail often came with a malicious virus attached or embedded. He told Jennifer that he deleted the nasty e-mail, without disclosing the nature of the e-mail.

"I wish I could do more," he added, "but I can only trace the origin of the e-mail to the service provider. Unless it's required by the police or FBI as part of a criminal investigation, service providers won't release the identities of their customers to protect their privacy. All you can do is block a specific sender—like I've done. But if this person changes to another name, you'll need to block that one, too. You know how?"

Jennifer nodded.

Henry frowned. "I don't like to speculate without any proof; but I wouldn't be surprised if this turns out to be Irene, trying to intimidate you. She'd do anything to knock you off your game so she can take over your part. But you won't let that happen, right?"

Jennifer shook her head firmly.

"Good. Just maintain your positive attitude and don't be let this kind of harassment get to you. This person is a vicious coward."

"You've said it!" echoed Stephanie. "Let's eat!"

The three friends sat at the dining table. Jennifer wore a black two-button jacket and a matching skirt, setting off her blonde hair, green eyes, and fine white skin. Stephanie wore a navy-blue V-neck one-piece dress. With her short brunette hair and hazel eyes, she looked as vivacious as ever. Henry felt happy to be dining with his ladyfriends of such beauty. He uncorked the wine. They toasted.

"Merry Christmas!"

The appetizer was a sampler of different kinds of charcuterie that Père Momus personally chose for them. The chardonnay was excellent. One bottle for three would not hurt, the friends wistfully concluded. They slowly sipped the wine.

"Henry, how are you doing with Christine?" Stephanie asked with a wink.

"She and Sarah went to New Orleans to spend Christmas with their parents," Henry said.Stephanie persisted that he must have been disappointed. He did not feel so, he said, because she would be back on the Monday after New Year, and they would visit the Poetry Club on Tuesday to post the flyer for their performance. After that they would go to a few poetry reading cafés and post flyers there.

Stephanie scooped up the last appetizer on the plate. Then she poked her fork toward him. "Actually, I meant *personally* with Christine—not your appointment book." The two women giggled.

Henry blushed; they'd caught him being evasive. "I love her very much," he admitted. "But I don't want to get involved physically with her now, if that's what you want to know. At least not until the opera is over."

"A tenor can handle that easily, can't you?" Stephanie hummed. "*La donna è mobile.*"

Jennifer trilled with laughter.

Henry shrugged. "I want to know her more."

"Sorry, I was pulling your leg," Stephanie said. "Seriously, I'm glad you feel that way."

"Yes, that's the right attitude," Jennifer chimed in. "This is no time for intense emotional changes, even when they are happy ones."

Jennifer served the salad. The dressing was her own recipe, she told them. It punched up the taste of the greens, Henry thought. He was now in the mood for a counterattack. "So, Stephanie, how are you doing with Arthur?"

"We're busy," Stephanie replied. "Too many things to do in too little time."

"I meant *personally*, Stephanie." He faked clearing his throat, enjoying the revenge.

Her cheeks turned pink. "What do you mean? Our relationship is strictly business. Besides, he's married. You saw Claudia the other day. She's gorgeous."

"Don't be embarrassed," he said soberly. "We know."

"What do you know?"

"Never mind, darling." Jennifer rescued her. "He's just teasing you."

"Well then, let me tell you this," Stephanie added. "I'd love to have a wealthy sugar daddy like Mimi and Musette had. You know, expensive dresses, Tiffany jewelry, fancy restaurants, an apartment on Fifth Avenue, a chauffeured Rolls-Royce…sounds nice, huh?"

Henry frowned. "You can't be serious."

Stephanie stuck out her tongue at him. Jennifer laughed, seemingly at ease that both her friends were apparently joking. She carried in the entrée, which was duck confit. For a moment the three friends concentrated on the main dish, enjoying the tender flavor.

"I meant to ask you," Henry said in a more serious tone. He explained about the vacancy for the voice faculty position at Ohio

State University. The deadline was the end of February. He had not applied yet. He asked what they would do.

"For some people," Stephanie immediately replied, "that kind of job is ideal. But not for me. I'll keep trying to be an opera singer. Also, I've got the general manager's job now. I can't let Arthur down. Besides, if I decide to teach, I can always do it later, even when I'm old."

"In my case," Jennifer said, "my aunt is my benefactor, so I can keep doing what I'm doing now—pursuing what I love. So I wouldn't apply."

"And I'm sure John wouldn't even think about it," Stephanie added. "He is a born opera singer, and he'll remain so, no matter how much he has to endure."

"You two make me feel strong," Henry said. "It's hard to get into a top-tier opera company. I often feel discouraged. But at the bottom of my heart, I know I want to keep trying." He nodded firmly. "So be it. We four will continue what we're doing now."

"That means you're not going to apply?" Stephanie asked.

"I have two months to think about it. Most likely I won't. I would rather stick with you two and John. Remember our pledge?"

Stephanie raised an eyebrow. "Does Christine know about this?"

"No, I haven't told her yet, because it's for me to decide first." He visualized himself with Christine and their family in Ohio. Probably that life was not right for him. He felt the pain of not attaining it. But this evening he felt strong enough to endure that pain, recalling the pledge of the Dolci Quattro and the other members who had never changed their minds.

He poured the last of the wine for his friends. It was Christmas Eve. They should have a night off to relax. He wished they could have two more bottles. But his friends were content with the wine they had. No carousing this year. Dessert was a Christmas cake with a frosting Santa and a candle on top. The three friends sang "Silent Night." It was a simple mesh of soprano, mezzo-soprano, and tenor in unison, because John, the baritone, was absent. Henry was pleased to see Jennifer so lively. As they completed the singing, Stephanie blew the candle out.

"I've been thinking," he said, savoring a piece of sweet cake. "Since I got the bonus, I'm planning a special session with my coach. I'd like to invite you two, John, and Mike. We can go through Act III together. The act is loaded with heavy arias and ensembles, but the cast is only the five of us. If we have a two-hour session, we can accomplish so much."

"That's generous of you," Jennifer said. "You're right. It would be extremely helpful."

"But it will cost you a fortune," Stephanie said, exhaling.

Henry shook his head. "Not really. I've already discussed this with Mr. Carré. He says a double rate will be fine with him for five singers—so I can manage. Don't worry."

Jennifer rose to get another pot of tea. She glanced out the window. "Look, it's snowing!"

They went to the window together and gazed outside. The snow was lightly falling. The street and trees were dusted white. Children were making a snowman on the sidewalk. Dogs jumped around them, wagging their tails. But the snow absorbed the sounds, rendering the scene still and dreamy. A few snowflakes rested on the window glass. Spontaneously the three friends sang "White Christmas." When the singing was over, Jennifer faced him and Stephanie, her eyes moist.

"Thank you, my dearest friends," she said. "I know what you're doing for me. Don't worry. I feel strong enough. I'm determined to sing the opera."

"We know you can do it," Stephanie said.

"We're with you," he echoed.

"I promise I won't let you down," Jennifer said firmly. "It'll be our best performance."

ACT III

Scene 1

A New Year had arrived. This could be a pivotal year for Henry; he felt it in his bones. His New Year's resolution was none other than to perform the other *La Bohème* to perfection. He hoped that all of the Dolci Quattro would have breakthroughs this year.

After work on Tuesday he took the subway to Spring Street. When he came up to the ground level, Christine was already waiting for him. Catching sight of him, she waved her hand high. She wore a bone-white coat, white wool hat, muffler, thin black leather gloves, and tall boots, perfect for the cold weather. She looked charming. Henry's heart raced. He realized how much he had missed her. Christine hugged and kissed him. He relished the softness of her body through her coat. The kiss was irresistibly sweet. When their initial excitement had waned, she held his arm and guided him toward a building just a dozen yards away.

The Poetry Club, on the second floor of the building, consisted of a few offices, a conference room, an exhibition room, and a library. At the entrance to the library hung a large bulletin board posted with many announcements: poetry writing workshops, poetry reading events, new publications, editorial services, and printing services. Christine had to move a few announcements on the board to make a space for the opera flyer. Then she posted it carefully with pins she had brought. She and Henry took a few steps back and admired it. The flyer shone, inviting the poets to the opera.

"Voilà!" Christine said.

Henry's mood soured instantly as a man came from the library. He could hardly believe his eyes. It was Richard, wearing jeans, a flannel shirt, and sneakers. He greeted Henry and explained that he was a member of the Poetry Club and came here often. Christine enthusiastically handed Richard a flyer.

"I see you know Henry," she said, "so of course you'll want to come."

Henry frowned, then asked her to give him a few minutes so he could talk to Richard privately. She inclined her head and went into the library. Henry and Richard moved to the vacant chairs next to the elevator bank.

"You seem surprised to see me here," Richard said. "I guess you want to know what's happening with me. Jennifer might have told you. I was fired from the bank."

"Yes, I heard," Henry said. "To be honest, I don't have much sympathy for you."

Richard gave a simple nod. "I was just plain stupid. But when I think of that Senior VP and that bitch—the ambition, the politics, the treachery—I'm glad I'm out of it." He gazed at the floor. He went on to explain that he'd sold his co-op apartment on Park Avenue and bought a decent studio apartment in the Village. With the net proceeds, his savings, and his investment portfolio, he estimated that he could live for about two years without getting a new job if he maintained a modest lifestyle. So he had decided to write fiction on a full-time basis.

"That's a big change," Henry said, still skeptical.

"It is," Richard said, meeting Henry's eyes. "But I always wanted to be a professional fiction writer. Now I can pursue it. I'm going to take a novel-writing workshop, a poetry writing workshop, and a playwriting workshop in the spring semester at New York University. It begins in a few weeks. In the meantime, I'm reading novels and poetry. I'm enjoying it immensely. Jennifer always used to encourage my writing; now I understand her own passion for music better. It's important that we use our gifts."

Henry had to agree. "Does Jennifer know about this?"

"Yes," Richard answered. "I sent her a Christmas card with a brief note. I mailed it the day before Christmas Eve, because I was busy moving and settling into my new apartment. The mail delivery around then can be slow, but it must have reached her by now."

Henry recalled that on Christmas Eve, she did not seem to have read it.

"As you said at the church, I won't try to see her until her performance is over." Richard sighed. "I'm more aware of my position with Jennifer than you might think. Believe it or not, I, too, want her to have a brilliant performance."

Christine came to check on them, looking a bit anxious. Henry hastily said that he would be with her in a few minutes. She went back into the library.

"I just started scribbling a novel," Richard said, rubbing his palms. "It's kind of a confession of my misdeed and stupidity. The idea has been growing day by day in my mind. I'm at the stage where I have to spit it out on paper. Otherwise I'll go crazy. So I'm writing. I feel like I'm obsessed." He spoke with passion.

"I can't believe it," Henry said. "You've completely changed. I'm happy to see it." He recalled the Richard he'd known in the early days of his engagement to Jennifer. Richard now was like Richard then. Therefore, Henry thought, it was entirely possible that his transformation was genuine.

Richard stood and extended his hand to Henry, who could not refuse it this time. They shook a little awkwardly. Henry noticed the flyer in Richard's hand.

"One more thing," he said in a friendlier tone. "I guess you want to come to the opera. I won't stop you. But do me a favor. There're three performances, as you can see in the flyer. If you want, come to the last performance, and don't show your face to Jennifer until it's over. Be discreet and sensitive. Understand?"

"Henry, I appreciate your suggestion," Richard said. "I'll do that. Don't worry. I want Jennifer to sing her best. So long."

Richard waved to Henry and took the elevator downstairs.

◖◗

Originally Henry and Christine had expected that they would spend only a few minutes at the Poetry Club, just long enough to post the flyer. But because of their encounter with Richard, they were running behind schedule. They hastily took a taxi to visit two poetry-reading cafés, one in the East Village and the other in the West Village. As the latter was the café they had visited weeks before, they decided to have dinner at the small restaurant above it. The restaurant specialized in Mediterranean cuisine. Henry and Christine ordered an appetizer and the entrée with salad. He stayed away from wine.

Christine asked about the man they had met at the Poetry Club. Henry told her the gist of the story, but Christine did not seem convinced that Richard was the kind of man who would abandon his fiancée. Henry didn't want to violate Jennifer's privacy, or even Richard's, so he merely asked Christine not to mention the encounter around Jennifer. She assured him she would pretend that she knew nothing about Richard.

The restaurant was half full and quiet. Soft Greek music came from the speakers. Raising glasses of water, Henry and Christine toasted in late celebration.

"Merry Christmas and a Happy New Year!"

He searched a shopping bag he had brought. He took out three gift-wrapped boxes. "These are my Christmas presents for you."

Christine's face lit up. She opened the gifts: a bottle of Chanel No. 5, a pair of white mink earmuffs, and a colorful silk scarf. She leaned over and kissed him. In turn, she gave him three boxes: a CD of Caruso recordings, a digital metronome with a pitch-maker function, and a thick wool muffler. He kissed her joyfully. She smiled. What an adorable smile that was. He realized how much he loved her. The waiter brought the appetizer.

"So, tell me about your trip home," Henry said. "I want to know about your family."

According to Christine, the Moret family was descended from French settlers in Louisiana who had owned a plantation. But as plantations became things of the past, the family sold their property and moved to New Orleans. There they founded an architecture company, which specialized in restoring the quaint mansions commonly found in the Garden District. Her father ran the firm. Her mother had been a high school teacher of the French language and literature. In her spare time, she had written poetry. To Christine's distress, however, her mother had passed away a few years earlier. Her father remarried a year ago.

Sarah had inherited her characteristics from her father and studied art at the Parsons School of Design in New York, while Christine, more like her late mother, had studied French at Tulane University in New Orleans. Sarah continued living in New York after graduation to try to make it in the art world. Soon after, Christine moved to New York to work for an ad agency as an assistant copywriter. Sarah was now considering returning to graduate school to study landscape architecture so she could work with her father. She had a boyfriend, who was a director of a theater group and a playwright. If their relationship grew permanent, she would stay in New York. Otherwise, she would go back to graduate school and eventually to New Orleans. If Sarah left New York, Christine could not afford to live alone in Manhattan. But she had no desire to leave New York as long as Henry lived here.

"I was glad to see my father and my stepmother in good shape—physically, mentally," Christine concluded. "Other than that, I don't have much to tell you about what we did in New Orleans because it was routine for us."

By now the waiter had served the entrée. Henry did not remember the name of the Mediterranean fish. But it tasted good. They ate quietly for a while.

"Henry, actually I wanted to spend Christmas with you," she said abruptly. "But Sarah forced me to come with her. My big sister ruined my Christmas with you." She pierced a piece of fish with her fork.

"She didn't want you to break your annual tradition," Henry said, hoping to console her.

"You're not upset with me, are you?" She looked into his eyes, like a little girl afraid of her father's scolding.

"Why would I be?"

"Instead of flying to New Orleans, I could have come to your apartment to decorate for Christmas. This would have been the only way to spend our Christmas together, Henry, because I can't invite you to my apartment. I mean, there, Sarah would be watching us every minute. At your place, I could have made a nice dinner for you—cold caviar, champagne, a roast goose. It would have been lovely." She pouted.

"That would have been wonderful," he said. "But please, don't be so hard on your sister."

"I wanted to be with you." She shrugged, maintaining her pout.

They returned to the entrée. Henry imagined Christine alone in his apartment. A romantic Christmas and a delightful feast. After that, they would have made love. Definitely.

Hey, you've got a gorgeous woman here, who never wants to leave New York as long as you live here. She is dying to come to your apartment and would be thrilled if you carried her to your bed. Why don't you do that? Aren't you a tenor? Jussi Björling had a reputation for maintaining several mistresses, yet he sang glorious opera. You can do that, too, can't you? Oooh, yes, certainly I can. She has cute breasts. What joy will it be to undress her. I want to see her naked in my bed. Let the passion sweep us away.

But, no, I can't do that.

No? Are you sure? Unbelievable. You just don't have the guts to sleep with her. Bah! You really are dull. You can't blame Irene for leaving you.

No, damn it! Not now, you idiot! I have to prepare for the opera.

"Henry?"

Henry was envisioning life with Christine in Ohio as he had done a hundred times already. A beautiful wife, a cozy house, a few kids, a stable job at the university . . . this still remained an attractive option. What had happened to his determination when he'd discussed the teaching position with Stephanie and Jennifer two weeks earlier? This evening, however, so close to Christine, he remembered his niece's angelic cry of "Daddy." He craved that domestic happiness.

"Anything wrong?" Christine asked in a trembling voice.

Henry came to himself, embarrassed. He looked up, only to find tears streaming down her cheeks. "Oh, I'm so sorry. I was thinking of something else."

"You're not with me." She wept, her face turning pink. "I knew you were upset."

"No, please, Christine." Henry extended his hand and caressed her palm. "I apologize. Actually I was thinking of you."

"Me? How?"

"Christine, I have strong feelings for you. More than you can imagine. But I need to wait until after the opera to let loose. I'd have been too tempted by a romantic Christmas with you. So it actually worked out well. I'm not upset about Christmas at all, believe me."

Christine nodded in silence, dabbing her eyes. He explained how he and Stephanie had spent Christmas Eve with Jennifer to keep her company, showing Christine his iPhone photo of the two smiling women at the window of Jennifer's apartment. He mentioned the unexpected presence of Richard at the church prior to their dinner. So it was shocking to him, he said truthfully, to meet Richard again today. Christine listened, sighing here and there. When Henry finished the story, she gazed at him.

"I envy Jennifer," she said, "because she has such caring friends as you and Stephanie."

"So much for that," he declared, wanting to cheer her up. "Are you free Thursday afternoon? I'm going to have a coaching session with the Dolci Quattro and Mike at my coach's studio. We're going to sing the entire Act III. Do you want to come?"

"Can I?" She instantly perked up. "What time would it be?"

"It'll last for two hours, starting at five o'clock."

"I'll make up some excuse after four."

"But I have to ask you a favor," he said cautiously. "In Act III, I have many passages of heavy singing, and a two-hour session will be taxing for me. So after the session, I'll have to go home to rest my voice. I won't be able to take you to dinner, though I wish I could."

"Don't worry," she said. "You can go home directly. I won't bother you. I swear."

"Thank you. My coach lives in the Ansonia, close to your apartment. I'll meet you there."

"This is exciting. I wanted to come to your coaching session, remember? Now I'm going to see what it's really like. I can't wait."

Her high-pitched squeal made Henry happy.

So she is truly interested in my singing. Maybe I don't have to take that teaching job in Ohio. Maybe I can pursue my opera career while building the relationship with her. I'm not completely out of luck.

Scene 2

*J*ennifer breezed into the heated lobby of the Ansonia, where the other Dolci Quattro and Mike were already waiting, holding their winter coats and hats. *You can always tell the opera singers,* she thought, amused. *Once we've warmed up our voices, we all keep our mufflers wrapped around our necks, even indoors.* Soon Christine arrived. Starry-eyed, she hugged and kissed Henry, barely noticing the others. Jennifer didn't think she'd ever seen Henry look so happy either. *Oh boy,* she thought, *they're head over heels in love.* Henry led the group to Mr. Carré's apartment on the twelfth floor. He introduced the opera singers and their roles. As for Christine, he presented her as his friend and an aspiring poet. Mr. Carré shook their hands amicably.

The eminent coach went to the piano and sat. For Jennifer this was the first time to have a session with him. His scholarly face and gray hair reminded her of Johannes Brahms without a beard. The singers gathered around the piano, facing him. They arranged their music scores on stands, putting their bottles of water on the floor. Christine settled on a sofa. The five singers exercised for a few minutes to stretch and loosen up their bodies, particularly their necks, chests, and abdomens. When they finished, they sipped water.

Mr. Carré introduced himself as a conductor at the Lyric Opera of Chicago. A few years before, the Lyric Opera had produced Leoncavallo's *La Bohème*, which he had conducted. So he knew the opera well. Act III took about thirty minutes. He suggested that first they go over four duets: Mimi and Musette, Musette and Marcello, Mimi and Rodolfo, and Schaunard and Marcello. Then they would run through the entire act. This should take about two hours.

Mr. Carré played scales while the singers vocalized. Their voices trembled the air of the studio like a mixture of animals roaring and birds twittering, at low F and G by John and Mike, high B-flat, B, and C by Henry and Stephanie, and high C, D, and E by Jennifer. She felt pleased that her instrument was in its best condition. She saw Christine's eyes open wide, seemingly impressed.

"Now," the coach said, flipping the music score, "let's go over the duet of Mimi and Musette. Why don't you read the words? Just the words without the rhythm. Mimi, go ahead."

Henry, John, and Mike withdrew to the sofa and chairs. Jennifer sipped some water and read, trying to use her best Italian diction.

"*No, la miseria non mi fa paura;…*" ("No, the misery does not frighten me;…")

"Very good," the coach said when she finished. "Next, Musette."

Stephanie cleared her throat and began reading her part.

"*Fuggi! Mimi! Pari è il tuo fato al mio!*" ("Flee! Mimi! Your fate is like mine!")

"Excellent, both of you." Mr. Carré nodded. "Here Mimi wants to come back to Rodolfo. But Musette urges Mimi to go away, just as she is fleeing now from Marcello. She reminds Mimi of the harshness of poverty and her comfortable life with Viscount Paolo. Mimi loves Rodolfo, and Musette loves Marcello, yet they know they can't live without food and clothes. The tempo is *sostenuto cantabile,* and the orchestra accompanies you beautifully. So try to be expressive."

The coach started playing the piano. Then Jennifer began singing Mimi, followed by Stephanie as Musette. This was the first time Jennifer and Stephanie had sung with Mr. Carré. Also, this was the first time they had sung this duet together. Jennifer thought they were singing timidly, their voices stiff. At the finale of the duet, they sang their parts simultaneously.

"*Oh! Lasciami obliar nel sogno mio…*" ("Oh! Leave me to forget in my dream…")

"*Mimi, pari è il tuo fato al mio!*" ("Mimi, your fate is the same as mine!")

The coach played the piano until both singers finished, but then abruptly stopped.

"Here you're not exactly together," the coach said, but in a positive tone.

"Sorry." Jennifer felt embarrassed and saw Stephanie flush as well.

"Don't be sorry," the coach said mildly. "This is part of learning."

Jennifer sipped water, anticipating some suggestions from him.

"Mimi," the coach continued, "you expressed your emotion well. But because of that, you slowed down here too much. That's why Musette couldn't follow you. You were not wrong, though. You see the accent marks on Mimi's line and the orchestra? I personally like a slowing with the big accents here to dramatize the emotion. But it'll be up to the conductor. You'll have to watch him carefully. Today we'll slow down a little, but not too much. As you can see, it's *forte*. So I'll play the piano with a big gesture. Try to follow me together. All right?"

Jennifer and Stephanie assented. This time at the finale, they closely watched the coach's movements and sang each note precisely together.

"That's the idea," the coach said, grinning. "Let's go over it again from the top, shall we?"

They repeated the duet. Jennifer felt bolder as her coloratura soprano voice rolled. She heard Stephanie singing more confidently as well in her smooth mezzo-soprano voice. Jennifer again felt an irony because she was singing Richard's mind. She understood the emotion. At the finale, both Jennifer and Stephanie melded perfectly together.

"Brava!" The friends applauded.

"Well done," the coach said. Then he turned to Christine. "How is our lady poet feeling?"

"Fantastic," Christine exclaimed. "I felt my eardrums physically vibrating. The duet was beautiful. I almost cried."

"Ah, don't spoil your friends," Mr. Carré said sternly, but with a warm tone. "They need to polish their singing. Too much praise isn't going to do them any good."

"Ooohhh," the five singers playfully moaned. All laughed.

Mr. Carré flipped the score forward, eyeing Christine. "I suppose you want to hear Henry sing. The next duet is by Musette and Marcello." He inclined his head to Henry.

Henry came to the piano. Jennifer withdrew to the sofa. As she sipped water, she felt good because she had been able to sing the duet to Mr. Carré's satisfaction. Stephanie gave her a wink.

"Let's read the words without rhythm," the coach said. "Marcello, go ahead."

Henry cleared his throat and read.

"*Sei proprio tu che hai scritto ciò?*" ("Was it really you who wrote this?")

"Good. Now, Musette."

Stephanie began reading her line.

"*Son io!*" ("It was I!")

"Pretty good, both of you," the coach said. "In this duet, Marcello confronts Musette and asks if she wrote this farewell letter. Musette admits it. He rages. She expresses her love and her grief over leaving. He still loves her and tries to persuade her not to go. But she has made up her mind. Note that the same theme is repeated in Musette's line, beginning at the bottom of page 345, '*So che tutt'ora,...*' ('I know that every time,...'), and Marcello's line, beginning at the top of page 349, '*Tu m'ami ancora!*' ('You love me still!'). You are sharing the same emotion. This ensemble is heartbreaking—so sing with passion. OK?"

The coach played, and Henry began singing Marcello in his bright tenor voice, soon joined by Stephanie as Musette in her ravishing mezzo-soprano. Henry's expression of rage was breathtaking, particularly at the burning high A and B-flat. Jennifer saw Christine completely stirred up, ogling Henry as if seeing a stranger. Stephanie sang the theme so sweetly, expressing her agony at leaving. After her line Henry sang the same theme in a manly tone, appealing to Musette not to leave. At the finale, both sang high A brilliantly, holding it for a long time. This was immediately followed by Marcello's rage and Musette's despair simultaneously at high G.

"*Va! Va via!*" ("Go! Leave!")

"*Ah! Sei vil!*" ("Ah! You are cruel!")

The coach played the final chord. "Excellent, both of you." He patted his music stand.

Christine clapped wildly. Jennifer, too, applauded with the other friends.

"The lady poet got excited," Mr. Carré joked.

Christine blushed. *Poor lovebird*, Jennifer thought.

"Since Musette and Marcello have a lot of heavy singing in this act, I won't repeat this duet," the coach told them. "You did fine. Rest your voices."

They nodded, sipping water.

"Let's move on to the duet of Mimi and Rodolfo." The coach did not waste time.

Jennifer advanced to the piano with John, as Stephanie and Henry retreated to the sofa. Jennifer saw Christine leaning toward Henry and holding his arm, dewy-eyed and love-struck. Christine's blonde hair and blue eyes matched Henry's light brown hair and hazel eyes. She thought they looked like lovers of several years.

"Let's read the words without the rhythm," the coach said. "Mimi, go on."

Jennifer looked back at her score and began reading her line. "*Rodolfo! Non lo credere…*" ("Rodolfo! Don't believe him…")

"Good. Now, Rodolfo."

John read his line.

"*Ah! Grazie! Troppo onore, Viscontessa!*" ("Ah! Thank you! Too much an honor, Viscountess!")

"All right." Mr. Carré smoothed the page of the score. "Here Mimi finally faces Rodolfo. She declares her love for him, but he coldly refuses her as the mistress of Viscount Paolo. He announces that their relationship is long over. He returns to his room, lamenting that what he sees now is a ghost of the past. She implores him to take her back. Is this clear?"

Jennifer and John nodded. They sang skillfully without any mistakes. But Jennifer reflected that the duet seemed to lack some emotional depth.

"Not bad," the coach said when they finished.

Jennifer sipped water and caught her breath. John did the same.

"Rodolfo," the coach said to John, "this is one of those operatic scenes where a baritone makes lady listeners cry. Your singing must be focused—intense, but subtle. Be cool, and do not be overly emotional. How bravely you conceal your emotion paradoxically makes your singing even more emotional to the audience."

"I understand what you're saying," John replied. "I'll try."

"As for Mimi," the coach said, "this scene is your last chance to come back to your lover. But you're coldly refused. Unlike Rodolfo, you're a woman. You should show your emotion openly. It's not easy. If you really cry, you can't sing. So you sing as if you were weeping."

Jennifer breathed deeply, determined to attempt what Mr. Carré instructed. Feeling bolder, she began, once more imagining herself as Richard, beseeching Rodolfo (/Jennifer) to take her (Mimi/Richard) back. At the end of her plea, John began singing in a masculine baritone voice, cold and unmoving. Jennifer felt John's singing like her own resentful response to Richard. John's seemingly unemotional tone intensified the chillness of his refusal. As John sang his last line, Jennifer sang her outcry, almost bawling Rodolfo's name twice. She sobbed. The duet was over.

"Bravo," the coach murmured, holding the last chord. "My compliments, both of you. This time your singing had real power and depth. Not many singers can sing this way."

The friends applauded. Jennifer sipped water, content with her achievement. She saw the same expression in John.

"In your school," the coach said, "you must have taken an acting class. Do you remember an exercise called the emotional recall? In the exercise you recall your emotional experience in the past, and you reflect that emotion onto your ensuing soliloquy or act. What you just did now was exactly that. I don't need to know your personal life. Your singing reflects the depth of life. That's all that matters. Good job."

Jennifer thought of Richard. She also thought of John's pain with Michelle.

Mr. Carré said to Christine, "Sorry, you're too young to understand the cruelties of life."

"No," Christine said, dabbing at her eyes. "But I'm crying anyway, because this duet was so moving, and their singing had a spiritual depth."

"Ah, she is a true poet," Mr. Carré said, eyeing at Henry. "She has the sensitivity to understand the delicacy of life."

Jennifer gave Henry a teasing grin. She saw Stephanie doing the same.

"OK. Let's sing the opening scene between Schaunard and Marcello," the coach said.

Jennifer returned to the sofa and John to a chair. Mike and Henry came to the piano. Mr. Carré repeated the same process: reading the verses; interpretation of the scene; a first run-through; corrections and suggestions; another run-through.

For Jennifer, this was the first time to hear Mike sing opera. He had a big, deep baritone voice, which rumbled through the studio. He accurately phrased his lines, sometimes somber and at other times comical. Jennifer thought that, like her, his first try was rather stiff. His dark forehead soon glistened with sweat. The second time, though, he sounded more relaxed. The transition of two voices was natural and precise between Schaunard and Marcello.

"Uh huh. You got it," the coach said when they finished. "How do you feel?"

Both Mike and Henry said that they got the idea, and they gulped water. They went back to the sofa and chair. Jennifer again saw Christine pull Henry close to her and kiss him. While the singers were resting, Mr. Carré gave suggestions to each of them.

"All right," Mr. Carré said, turning the pages backward. "Let's do the full act. In this act, the introduction is brief. I may stop here and there to correct errors or to fine-tune your interaction. Once the run-through is over, and if time permits, we can try the entire act again, this time without interruption. OK? Here we go."

Jennifer walked out of the Ansonia along with her friends. Her body was still hot from singing. They had completed the run-through of Act III twice. The wintry air was cold, but she felt it rather soothing. "I'm exhausted," she said, pulling her muffler around her throat.

This triggered mumblings from her friends, who were also arranging their coats and mufflers to protect their vocal cords.

"You were all great and sounded as though you could sing forever," Christine said.

"I wish," said Henry, wrapping an arm around her. "My voice is so tired, I can't talk."

"C'mon, guys. Cheer up," John said. "We had a really productive rehearsal."

"It's true." Stephanie hopped from one foot to the other. "For me, Act III is a killer. Now I feel much more secure."

"Thank you, all, for inviting me," Mike said. His handsome dark face was still glistening with sweat. A faint steam rose from his frizzed short hair. He was beaming. "This rehearsal really broke the ice for me. I feel I'm now part of your group."

"Mike, it was great to sing with you." Henry clapped a hand on his back. "We know you're of one of Arthur's best baritones. You sang excellently. We'll get along well."

"Appreciated. It makes me feel proud." Mike shook Henry's hand.

A group of people rushed to the Ansonia from the street. Jennifer took in a sharp breath. They were Bruce, Irene, Glenn, and another woman and man.

"We meet again," Bruce said to Henry. "Did you have a session with Carré?"

"Yes, we went over Act III," Henry answered.

"We're going to rehearse Act I together with Abelian—so we'll be ready." Bruce sneered.

Jennifer did not know the other two singers. They must have been the understudies for Musette and Rodolfo. So they, too, were studying hard. She saw Stephanie awkwardly look between Bruce and Glenn. Then she caught sight of Irene, glaring at her like a sharp icicle.

"Well, so long, guys." Bruce motioned the others to follow him into the building.

"Bruce is now a ringleader of understudies, eh?" Henry said.

"I hate hostility between primaries and understudies," Stephanie said, clearly speaking as the company's general manager. "We must be supportive of each other."

"I agree," Henry replied. "But what can we do when Bruce behaves like that?"

"I'll talk to him," Stephanie said.

Jennifer recognized an unmistakable rivalry in Irene. The best defense was to be prepared for Mimi in perfect shape. "I'm heading home to rest."

The others said the same, except John, who had to go back to Music Universe, as he needed money, he mumbled.

"I guess you want to have dinner with Henry," Jennifer said to Christine. "Enjoy."

"Oh no." Christine disengaged her arm from Henry's. "We've agreed that after the rehearsal he would go home right away. Now I understand why. I can't believe you can stand that kind of strenuous exertion for two hours. Henry, please go home. You need a rest."

"Good girl," John said. "I wish my Michelle were that understanding."

"Oh, John, you can't mean that," said Christine.

"Oops." John covered his mouth. "Yeah, I didn't mean that. Don't tell Michelle, OK?"

All laughed.

"I, too, wish my Vicky were like you, Christine," Mike said, giving her an envious look.

"Not going well, huh?" John said to Mike.

"Getting worse," Mike said in low voice.

This was the first time Jennifer had heard of Mike's trouble with Vicky. She sighed. Why did all singers have to suffer this kind of relationship misery? She hoped Mike's relationship would survive.

Back in her apartment Jennifer collapsed on the sofa, exhausted but satisfied. Her voice was strong, her singing had agility, and her interpretation had Mr. Carré's approval. This was real.

She remembered Richard's Christmas card, which she had received a few days before. She fetched it and read it again. He mentioned that he now had a new apartment and had decided to work on his novel full time. Wishing her Merry Christmas, a Happy New Year, and a successful opera performance, Richard signed off with *Love.* When she had read it the first time, she had felt furious and shoved his card back into the envelope. To her surprise, however, she realized that her anger had now disappeared. She was glad for the change in his life. Writing was what he had always wanted to do.

This was the Richard she had loved. She shook her head. But their romance was finished; and this was all right. She did not feel lonely.

Then she opened a letter she had received in her mailbox that day. She gasped, as she found inside a crushed roach. No message. She felt a wave of nausea. She checked the envelope again. While the sender's name and address were missing, it was correctly addressed to her in machine-printed characters, presumably to conceal the hand-writing—a carefully planned deed. Who would do such an abomina-ble thing? Presumably it had come from Darkforce13, whose e-mails had ceased coming since Henry had blocked them. Now this. Clearly someone was targeting her to perturb her mental state. But why? And who? Irene's chilling glare less than an hour before flashed in her mind. Was Irene really so petty? So—so wicked? A portentous prospect unnerved her. What else might she do? Then she ordered herself to cast it from her mind. She had no proof. *Besides, Henry is right,* she thought. *I cannot let this harassment throw me. I must be strong.*

The following week, while Jennifer was working at her office, she received a call from Michelle, who wanted to see her urgently. She did not say anything about the subject matter. Jennifer sug-gested that Michelle come to her apartment that evening. After supper Michelle arrived. No sooner had Jennifer closed the door than Michelle began crying loudly, leaning on Jennifer. She caressed Michelle's back, then guided her to the sofa. Michelle sank down and covered her flushed face with a handkerchief, which became sodden. Her dark hair was fluffy.

"I want to die," Michelle wailed.

"Calm down, Michelle," Jennifer said. "What happened?"

"I'm pregnant," Michelle burst out.

Jennifer was astounded. Michelle continued to wail like a madwoman.

"That's a blessing." Jennifer ventured. "Does John know?"

Michelle shook her head. "We're getting divorced."

"You are? I thought you were reconsidering."

"I want a new life. This ruins it." Michelle gave in to another frenzy of weeping.

When Michelle quieted, she explained the situation. She had missed her period in December. Since this kind of thing was not unusual, she had ignored it. She missed it again in January. She did a pregnancy test using an over-the-counter kit. It showed positive. This morning she had visited her gynecologist, who confirmed the pregnancy. She asked for a termination. The doctor said that he did not perform the procedure in his office. If she really wanted one, he would refer her to a colleague, who did it at a well-reputed hospital. But he recommended a cooling period of at least two weeks. Until then, he counseled her not to do anything one way or the other. She could go to a women's clinic and have it done. But that scared her. She was stuck.

Jennifer sighed. She thought that Michelle had been leaning toward reconciliation with John. However, she guessed that deep down Michelle still had a desire to be free, to meet new men, and hopefully to find a new husband and an easier lifestyle. That opportunity would be forever closed once she had a baby with John. So, Jennifer concluded, Michelle was panicking.

"I've never been pregnant," she said. "It must be emotionally so stressful. I'm sorry for that. But this is a deeply personal decision. The choice is yours."

Michelle kept silent, still weeping.

"If you want, you can have a termination. You can finalize the divorce. You'll be free. All right. Then what? The problem will still remain. There's no guarantee you could find a better man than John. Remember our talk in the church?"

Michelle nodded. Her face had lost color.

"If you want to take that risk, you go ahead. But John deserves to know."

Michelle trembled. "One moment I feel I should do it, the next I don't want to."

"The doctor is right," Jennifer said. "You need to cool off. Don't make any decision for two weeks. Think about it. Let's discuss it again in two weeks."

"It's driving me crazy. I can't stay in this situation for another two weeks."

"I think the cooling period is the best idea."

"I suppose." Michelle exhaled deeply.

"I'm hesitant to say this, Michelle. I'm not suggesting you do this. But can't you think about it more positively? A baby will give you joy. The baby will be part of John. You wouldn't feel lonely. I'm sure John would rejoice to have a baby. A child will create a bond between you and him, so your marriage will become more intimate. Of course, the baby will give him an extra financial burden. But knowing him, he will be determined to overcome the challenging situation. He loves you, so he'll love your baby, too."

Michelle frowned. "I-I don't know."

"Again, I'm not asking you to do what I say," Jennifer went on. "But I want you to think of the other side, too. It could be wonderful, if you can believe in John."

"I don't know. I don't know. I don't know."

In the end, Jennifer secured a promise from Michelle that she would ponder for two weeks without taking any action. Michelle made Jennifer swear not to tell anyone. They agreed to meet again in two weeks.

Scene 3

On Saturday, John's coach had rescheduled his usual session, so he was working a few extra hours at Music Universe. After the holiday season, business was slow but the shelves were a mess. As John was straightening the disorder, Mike showed up, looking distressed. He walked beside John, appearing to check CDs as if he were a customer.

"Yesterday, I had a big argument with Vicky," he said, pretending to read the label of a CD. His voice sounded hoarse. "My voice teacher's appointment schedule is awfully tight. Yesterday he had an unexpected opening, and I took it. I had to cancel a dinner out with Vicky. She got mad." His face sank. "I remembered Christine's loyal support for Henry. So I asked Vicky—nicely, though—to be patient. But she said she was fed up. Why can't she be more understanding, like Christine?" Mike bit his thick lip.

"You've got the same problem as mine." John tapped the CD stand. "That's why Michelle filed for divorce."

"We ain't married. So the worst thing to happen would be she leaves. That's a real possibility now." Mike sighed. "Sometimes I think of quitting opera. Maybe I should go into a retail business, something related to classical music and opera. I wouldn't be happy, because I'm an opera singer, one hundred percent. But that way at least I could be with her."

"Then to you, Vicky has more priority than opera?"

"Both are equally important." Mike compared two CDs. "I don't want to be in a situation where I have to make a choice, one way or another. I can't."

"Then you have to mellow her out." John faintly grinned. "What are you doing here? Go home and take her out to a nice dinner. A few glasses of wine. Then back home, make love to her. Sex talks, you know." He winked.

"C'mon, buddy," Mike gently punched John's side. "Be serious."

"I'm not joking. In my situation, I simply couldn't find time to spend with Michelle. That's what's I'm saying. Before it's too late, do something."

Mike squinted at John. "I have to study Schaunard."

"I know." John sighed.

Mike left, his shoulders dropped low. He was a big, athletic man. Today he looked smaller. John regretted that he could not offer Mike more useful advice. But what could he have said? If he had known ways to make Michelle happy, he would have tried them himself.

Customers scarcely visited the store that day. At five o'clock the manager let John go. Erica invited him for supper at her apartment. Under normal circumstances, he would have turned down her invitation. He would have gone home to be with Michelle, even though they didn't talk too much these days. But the conversation with Mike had depressed him. He needed some time to lighten up his mind. Since he had already taken breaks with Erica many times, he thought it would be pleasant to spend time with her, her husband, and their daughter. He might learn something new about married life.

To his surprise, her apartment was a decent studio in the district of Hell's Kitchen on the Midtown West Side. The interior was simple and clean, with little furniture. He noticed books and CDs of opera. Out of politeness he did not ask where her family members were. She changed to a comfortable pink cashmere cardigan and olive wool skirt. This evening her face had a lively color. She served takeout gourmet food, which she had bought on the way home. She served wine, too, but he declined, explaining that he needed to protect his voice. After supper they relaxed on the sofa.

"I have to apologize, John," she said. "I've been lying to you. I'm actually divorced. I live on alimony and work at Music Universe a few days a week to supplement my income." She spoke calmly but with a sad expression.

John couldn't have been more surprised. "I never doubted you were happily married," he said.

"Two-year old daughter and a family vacation at Disney World—I made it all up." She gave a bitter laugh.

"But you looked like a mother who loved your daughter." He gazed at her in wonder.

"So how is your divorce going?" Erica asked.

"What?" John felt like a thunderbolt had struck his body. "How did you know?"

"Don't be embarrassed. I was there when you received the summons at Music Universe. That was exactly how my divorce got started, so immediately I knew. Since then I've been watching you. You hid it from the others. Not me. Are you sure you don't want wine?"

"I shouldn't. But I'll have one glass."

She poured, and he gulped it, then collapsed back on the sofa cushions. She had known all this time of his pretense as a happily married man. He felt his cheeks burning. He wanted to hide under the sofa.

"We all have our vanity," she said. "I couldn't tell you the truth, either."

"How did it go in your case?" he asked.

Erica told him she had been married for three years—happily, or at least so she thought. Her ex had enjoyed working in the garment district, where many pretty women worked. Then he met a younger woman and slept with her. He wanted to get rid of Erica so he could marry her. There was a complication in the settlement. It took two years to settle. She warned John that his case might drag on that long.

"Two years?" John groaned. "I wouldn't have the patience."

"Yes, it's hell. You have my sympathy." She sipped her wine. "But finally it was over. That was one year ago."

"What's it like being divorced?"

"Wounded," she said, swirling the glass. "Lonely."

"I'm going to be like that," he said.

"Sad." She started sobbing.

He gently stroked her back. She leaned on him. He smelled her perfume in her hair.

"Why does your wife want a divorce?" she asked. "Does she have a lover?"

"I don't think so."

John took the wine bottle and poured some for her and him. He drank. He explained his situation. She listened, sipping wine.

"You're too busy with your singing and earning money for a living. For that she wants to divorce you?" She shook her head. "She's selfish, no?"

This was the first time he had spoken about his divorce with someone other than his Dolci Quattro friends. Erica had said plainly what he had been desperately trying to suppress. He found her an unexpected ally. It was gratifying. He felt like he was going to melt.

"Maybe," he said. "But I didn't want to fight. So I proposed a consented divorce."

"No!" She put both her hands on his shoulders and looked into his eyes. "John, you should contest. Marriage is a commitment. If she wants a divorce for that trivial reason, let her pay for it. You can draw a lot of money out of her. It's only fair." She took his hand and rubbed it. "I'm saying this from my experience, because that's exactly how I felt."

Here was a woman who spoke her mind—and his mind, too. Things he had never wanted to admit. He had not been entirely wrong. Her words echoed his aggravation of the past three months. How comforting it was.

"But it's my fault, too," he said. "It's true I can't spend much time with her."

"You're so honorable."

She moved closer to him. He felt her soft breast through her sweater. She kissed him on his cheek. "That was my first kiss to a man since my divorce." She giggled.

John did not know what to do. He was afraid that they were moving in a dangerous direction. But her empathy touched him. She had gone through the same emotional rollercoaster. He could share the torment with her. "Haven't you dated other men?"

"Yes, a few times. But somehow I wasn't up to it. I guess I still feel burned."

"You're young and attractive. You should meet new people."

She shook her head, then buried her face into his chest and started crying. He embraced her and patted her back. Their thighs touched.

"I like you, John," she said. "I knew you were special ever since I started working there."

"I didn't know why you looked so sad. Now I know."

"We're alike."

She kissed him on his mouth. Her tongue hungrily searched his. Her hand guided his to her breasts. He caressed her. She moaned, pushing her body even tighter against him. Her breaths grew shorter. Her heartbeats quickened, he could feel. He continued caressing her. Strangely he did not feel guilty. *Yes, we are alike. Abandoned or being thrown out.*

"I haven't slept with a man for more than three years." She wrapped her hands around him and whispered. "You can have me if you want."

"I'm married." He didn't care.

"To be divorced, though." She clung to him. "We can lick our wounds together."

⟪◉ ◎⟫

Sunday morning John's father was rushed back to the NYU Hospital. His heartbeat had become irregular and intermittent. The medication kept him alive. On Monday, Dr. Silverman performed another double bypass surgery. This time a pacemaker was implanted. According to the doctor, one month before, John's father had not been fit enough to take a quadruple bypass. So the doctor performed only a double bypass. The case turned out to be more serious than the doctor had initially thought. John shuttled among the hospital, his parents' house, Music Universe, his coach's studio, and his apartment. In addition to his father, he was also concerned for his mother, who he feared might suffer a heart attack of her own. At night he stayed in Brooklyn with her. Fortunately the surgery seemed to have stabilized his father's condition for now. But the prospects were still far from secure.

John had been raised a Catholic, like most Italians. But since his adolescent years, his faith had been nominal. In his adult life he frequently went to church as a paid singer, not as a practitioner. Nonetheless, he felt his father's rehospitalization as a punishment for his misdeed. He remembered that in Italy, even thuggish taxi drivers crossed themselves whenever they drove past a church. He felt the same fear.

No matter how comforting the lovemaking with Erica had been, no matter how understandable the circumstance, no matter how forgivable the two wounded should be, the fact remained that it was an act of adultery. His minimal faith did not send him to a formal confession before a priest and a subsequent absolution. Still, he confessed directly to the nameless and asked for forgiveness. Erica's sad face flashed in his mind. He did not blame her. It had happened so naturally. He could not blame himself either. But he expressed his contrition. Then he asked the nameless for two things: that his father's life be spared, and to let him sing his opera success-fully. These two were inseparable. If he had to be punished, he would endure the divorce. So he prayed.

His father's condition worsened. Dr. Silverman was against further surgery; he'd already done what he could, and the patient was too weak. For now, medication and rest were the most effec-tive treatment. As a precaution, however, the doctor advised John to inform his relatives of the situation so they could visit his father in case he did not survive. John felt like he had been hit in the head by a steel bar. His mother shrieked in despair. With trembling hands, she prayed the rosary. Every day she visited the hospital and sat beside her husband until visiting hours were over.

He asked Michelle to accompany him to the hospital one day soon. Her visit would mean a lot to his father. She did not say much, except to express her sympathy. He wondered why she was so dis-tant these days. She seldom spoke to him. He could not recall any instances when he might have offended her. Could she know about

Erica? No, because her detached attitude had begun weeks before his misdeed with Erica. Whatever Michelle's demeanor meant, he missed her. As he contemplated the possibility of losing his father, he longed for his lost wife.

On the afternoon they visited the hospital, Michelle wore a black velvet skirt and a matching velvet shirt with a red floral print. John loved her in that outfit. In the ICU room, his father lay on his back. He was awake. How ghastly he looked in his white hospital gown, his face and body skin dark purple, his eyes sunken, his cheeks retracted. He must have lost dozens of pounds. He could not move well. He could not speak well either. With the IV and oxygen tube, he looked pathetic. John told his father that Michelle had come to say hello. Mr. Bertucci tried to rise, but his face twisted in pain. His wife rushed beside him and helped him lie down on the bed. Her tear-stricken eyes were surrounded by dark rings. Wrinkles on her face had increased tenfold. Her hair had turned whiter, seemingly overnight.

"Michelle, good to see you," Mr. Bertucci managed. His voice was weak and hoarse. "You look beautiful as usual." He coughed feebly. "My son has a lot of flaws. But would you look after him for this ol' man's sake?"

Michelle inclined her head, gazing at her father-in-law without a word.

"Son, how's your singing?" Mr. Bertucci asked, turning to John.

"Pa, I've already told you," John said. "I had a great rehearsal last week." He recounted his upbeat rehearsal with five cast members under Mr. Carré. "In a few weeks rehearsals with soloists will start. Then with the chorus, and then with the orchestra. February will fly by. Then the performances. Three times. You hear? Three times. You must get ready for it."

"Dear, it's true," Mrs. Bertucci said. "The opera is only one month away. I had your best suit dry-cleaned. I also polished the portrait of your papa. You'll go to the Society Hall in style."

"Son, I know I'm dying." Mr. Bertucci exhaled and coughed.

"Pa, you're not," John exclaimed. "Dr. Silverman said you're doing well. He assured me you'd be able to attend my performance."

"Dear, John is right," Mrs. Bertucci said. "You mustn't talk like that. Tomorrow your old subway friends are coming. I had to warn them—no beer for now. You know what? They said, 'No, no, of course not,' all polite. I'm afraid they might sneak beer in here."

John laughed aloud. In his mind he wept. Mr. Bertucci shook his head on the pillow in a slow motion. His wife turned her face away and blotted her eyes with her handkerchief.

"Son, I can't make it to your opera," Mr. Bertucci said. He coughed again. "I've asked your mother to carry my photo and your grandpa's portrait to the concert."

"No, no, Pa. That won't be necessary," John replied. "You're coming in person."

"We may have had a lot of arguments," his father continued. "But I've been proud of you. You're our hope for restoring our family legacy of opera. My only regret is I can't come to your performance. I'll listen to you from above with your grandpa."

Mrs. Bertucci started wailing. John felt a lump in his throat, which prevented him from saying anything. He remembered his confession and prayer. He again asked the nameless to spare his father's life. *At least until my performance. Please.*

Michelle had been sullen. Suddenly she walked to the bed. "Father, you must get well soon," she said timidly, "because I'm pregnant."

Mr. Bertucci looked elated but not surprised. Mrs. Bertucci turned to Michelle, her mouth wide open. John, too, was flabbergasted. The three stared at Michelle.

"I'm pregnant with John's child," Michelle said again, this time in a firmer voice.

The other three still could not speak.

"The baby will arrive in August," Michelle said. "You must see your grandchild."

Mr. Bertucci's eyes crinkled into a huge smile. "Baby?"

"Yes, father." Michelle touched her abdomen lightly with her hands.

"Oh, *Dio*! Congratulations, Michelle!" Mr. Bertucci cheered.

"Ah, Santa Maria," Mrs. Bertucci crossed herself. "This is a blessing."

"I'm going to be a grandfather."

"I'll be a grandma."

I'm going to be a father? John stood frozen, then dropped into a chair, his mind racing. *What's happening here? Is this real?*

"Wonderful," Mrs. Bertucci was saying. "I have to start preparing the baby clothes. Michelle, I'll help you." She wiped her eyes.

Mr. Bertucci kissed Michelle on her cheek. Mrs. Bertucci, too, hugged and kissed her daughter-in-law. Both times, Michelle received them obediently. John noticed that his father was pondering, trying to recall something. Suddenly, his father slapped his thighs with his hands.

"Aha, I was right," he said. "What did I tell you in the hospital last December? Remember? I knew you were different then."

John remembered it well. Had Michelle known all this time?

"I can see it again," Mr. Bertucci continued. "Michelle, you're shining with life."

"Yes, you're beautiful." Mrs. Bertucci said, fondly gazing at her daughter-in-law, her eyes welled up. "I can see the mother in you."

John wondered whether Michelle was saying this only to cheer up his father. There was no reason to believe it. Was there? He remembered their dreamy lovemaking that November night. Could that be it? Erica's lonely face reappeared. *We can lick our wounds together.*

John came to himself. He remembered that he was before his father in the hospital. He went along with Michelle's words. "Pa, lie back and rest," he said, assisting his father to settle in the bed again. "Now you've got another reason to get back to your feet quickly."

"Yes, dear, you must get well soon," Mrs. Bertucci said.

"Michelle, I thank you," Mr. Bertucci said. "Your ol' man will fight to survive. This is the first time I've felt like it since I was brought here. I want to see my grandchild."

A lively color had come back to his skin. His face was now peaceful and beaming. Mrs. Bertucci said grace. Michelle left the room. John hastily saluted his parents and followed her.

"Michelle, thank you," he said. "It was nice of you to say that. They're so happy."

She ran to the elevator. John watched the numbers descended to the lobby, dumfounded.

Two days later, the retired subway engineer passed away.

Scene 4

*S*tephanie had spent the past few days in a frenzy. Along with Jennifer and Henry, she helped John get through the traumatic days following his father's passing. Two days before, they had attended Mr. Bertucci's funeral at his family church near his home. Many Metropolitan Transit Authority employees, retired and active, paid their last respects to their beloved colleague. Appearing drawn, John had stood with his mother. Stephanie noticed that Michelle was keeping a respectful distance from the Bertucci family and the Dolci Quattro. She could not figure out why. Since then, Stephanie had spoken to John by phone a few times. He said his mother seemed to be adjusting amid lots of support, and so was he. As the general manager, she felt relieved, because John had one month to regain himself in time to sing the opera.

Stephanie lay in her bed. Glenn would stay over tonight. He was one of the gifted opera singers who had graduated from the Manhattan School of Music on a full scholarship. His father ran a small general store in a working class neighborhood of New Jersey. How Glenn had become so talented an opera singer, she did not know. He was proud to have landed the understudy role of Schaunard. He came to bed from the bathroom. His waist was wrapped with a bath towel. Like a typical baritone, he was stocky and of medium height. His dark brown hair was tidily combed. His skin was reddish, and he had a bushy thick chest. He slid into the bed.

They briefly made love, after which he rolled over and lay on his side next to her. To her disappointment, this was his monotonous routine. She could count the mold spots on the ceiling. She thought that the ceiling needed fresh paint; for that matter the entire apartment could use it.

"Hey, what are you thinking?" Glenn asked.

"Oh, nothing," she said lightly.

"I always feel at home here. You've got a cozy apartment. If you want, I can move in here and share the rent. It would help both of us."

"I'll think about it."

She turned on her side, her back to him. She remembered that the rehearsals with soloists would start in less than two weeks. She had to make sure that all logistics were in order. She asked Glenn if he could leave her alone tonight. He did not answer. She repeated her request.

"You mean I should go home?"

"Would you mind?"

"Hey, you're not upset, are you?"

"No, I'm just worried about work tomorrow."

"I like you. So I'll let you sleep alone."

He got up, put his clothes on, and left, slamming the door. Tears ran down her cheeks. *Why do men and women have to have sex? I hate sex.* That was not true. With Bruce, she had enjoyed it. Now he had Irene. He still occasionally called her, presumably for sex. She refused him. She thought of Arthur. Probably he was making love to Claudia now. She wished she were Claudia. It would be beautiful. She fantasized about Arthur making love to her, being inundated by his kisses. Her body heated up.

◄◙ ◙►

Usually Stephanie let herself into the office at nine o'clock and worked until eleven before leaving for the Café Momus. As was his custom, Arthur came down around half past ten, unless he had an early lesson with a student. This morning she arrived late. It was almost ten o'clock. She wore a combination of well-washed-out blue jeans and a lavender sweater, both of which she had acquired from used clothing stores. The studio was empty. Arthur was already in his office, having a meeting. She saw he wore a dark blue business suit and a matching tie, so the meeting had to be important. Six people sat in front of his desk. As she entered his office, they turned to greet her. Stephanie yelped, "Dad, what are you doing here?"

Her father shrank, as if trying to hide. There was not enough space for him to escape. Looking resigned, he sat up. As usual, he wore an impeccable three-piece business suit. He appeared in a good mood, except for the embarrassment of being caught by his daughter. "Do you work here?"

"Mr. Frank, Stephanie is your daughter?" Arthur exclaimed. "I can't believe this."

Arthur introduced Stephanie as the general manager to the well-dressed people before him: Mr. Umberto Zappia, the chairman of the Italian Cultural Society; His Excellency, Mr. Sergio Biondi, an Italian ambassador to the United Nations; Mrs. Lotti, a patron of opera; Mr. Salvatore Giordano, Claudia's father; Claudia; and Mr. Aaron Frank.

Stephanie's father stood hastily, gathering his coat and hat. He stopped at the door between Arthur's office and the studio. "I'll leave the rest to Umberto. I have to go," he said. "Stephanie, you look well. Nice to see you." He bowed to the others. "Good day, ladies and gentlemen." He quickly walked through the studio and left.

An odd silence enveloped the people in the room. They gazed at Stephanie. Mr. Zappia, in his mid-seventies, appeared to be a wealthy patriarch, with white hair and white mustache. Ambassador Biondi indeed looked a distinguished career diplomat with a gray beard. Mrs. Lotti, a graceful grandmother, wore a silk blouse and a large necklace. Mr. Giordano, probably in his late fifties, seemed an energetic corporate executive. Claudia was as beautiful as ever in her peach cashmere dress. Stephanie felt embarrassed in her shabby clothes.

"Now I began to see why Aaron wanted this project," the chairman said.

"What project, may I ask?" Stephanie said. "What's my dad up to?"

"Don't be alarmed, Ms. Frank," the chairman replied. "It's all good for the company."

"Yes, Stephanie, I'm thrilled by the offer," Arthur said. "Mr. Zappia, please explain to Stephanie. As our general manager she should know about the project."

Stephanie took the chair her father had occupied. The chairman briefed her. Aaron Frank had proposed to establish an endowment fund for the Italian Cultural Society to support the New York Bel Canto Opera as the opera company in residence. According to the plan, the company would produce one opera per year in the concert version at Carnegie Hall. Using the income from the endowment, the Society would compensate the company for the production cost. The revenues from the ticket sales would be shared equally by the Society and the company. In addition, the company would produce showcase concerts in the Society Hall twice a year, presenting opera arias and scenes. For this, again, the Society would pay all expenses to the company, and the revenues from the ticket sales would be divided equally by the two.

As the seed money, Mr. Frank had donated five million dollars to the Society on the condition that the Society would raise a matching amount, because less than ten million dollars would not be effective for the purpose. Mr. Zappia, to be a role model for others, had put down five hundred thousand dollars. Mr. Giordano, a member of the Society, had agreed to donate two hundred thousand dollars. Mrs. Lotti, a friend of the Giordanos and another member of the Society, had pledged one hundred thousand dollars. Mr. Zappia assured Arthur that the Society itself would be able to come up with at least two million dollars. Ambassador Biondi, an honorary member of the Society, was trying to get a grant from the Italian government. The ambassador apologized that the amount might be modest. Mr. Zappia pointed out that the grant would give legitimacy and prestige to the endowment, which would only help with additional fundraising efforts. So the funding appeared to be promising.

The proposal was subject to formal approval at the annual meeting of the Society in April. However, since the members of the Society were opera lovers by heritage, approval was expected with near certainty as long as the funding was secure, according to the chairman.

"Stephanie, can you see how generous this offer is?" Arthur said, tapping his desk. "It would cover all expenses for the production of operas and showcases. The company's share of the ticket revenues can be used to administer the company for the rest of the year."

Stephanie's eyes welled up. "Sorry," she said. She wiped her eyes with both her hands. "Yes, it's wonderful. Thank you, ladies and gentlemen."

"You should be thanking your father," the chairman said. "It was his idea. He is a bighearted benefactor. We've been discussing this for some time. Things are moving quickly in a positive direction, even though the project involves a lot of money."

"Yes, Stephanie, please thank him on my behalf, too," Arthur said. "I didn't know you were related. It's a small world."

Stephanie could not utter a word.

"I should be going," the chairman said. "I want to call several potential donors. The more money, the better." A wide grin lit his aristocratic face. "Arthur, you take care of opera. We'll take care of the finances." He took Stephanie's hand and kissed it with grace. "My pleasure to meet you, Ms. Frank."

Ambassador Biondi, Mrs. Lotti, and Mr. Giordano greeted Stephanie with warm civility. Arthur and Claudia went to the studio to see off the guests. Stephanie remained in her chair. It was obvious that her father was initiating this project to help her opera career, all without telling her. Probably he was afraid of her rejection. But he also just wanted to make her happy, and probably never thought she would find out. In her mind, she thanked him for his kind thought. He was a good man and a good father. Why had she been so hostile toward him? Now she understood why her mother had loved him so much—and, at last, why her mother did not want Stephanie to take revenge on her behalf. Everybody had their weaknesses. Including her father. And herself, too. She'd stoked her anger for long enough. She felt that now she was the one who was being unreasonable. *I'm sorry, Dad.*

Her mother appeared. Instead of her usual sad face, she looked happy today.

"Mom, what should I do?" Stephanie asked.

"Just talk to him as your father," her mother answered. "That's all he wants."

Stephanie sobbed. She hugged her mother. She felt like mist in the air. Her mother stroked her head softly.

"I've been too hard on him," Stephanie said.

"Yes, but he understands that," her mother replied gently.

"What should I talk about?"

"Anything. Your opera, your friends, mundane things about your life, joke, gossip. He would love to hear this from you. Then things will follow naturally."

"That's not so difficult."

"No, you can do it."

Stephanie looked up and saw Claudia's anxious face. Arthur was behind her. Stephanie apologized for her embarrassing reaction to the unexpected encounter. She said she was glad that her father was doing this for them. However, she expressed her concern that this might cause a conflict of interest on her part. She was a mezzo-soprano who sang opera, as well as the general manager of the company. If her father lavished his money on the company, it might appear that he was buying up the company to promote his daughter. So she would have to make up her mind: either ask her father to withdraw his project or resign from both the mezzo-soprano's role and the general manager's position in the company. An impossible choice. Furthermore, if she resigned from the company, most likely her father would cancel his project. A deathtrap.

Arthur vehemently dismissed her concern. She had been hired by the company for both positions months before her father initiated his project. Besides, Arthur added, this kind of patronage was common in the opera world. For example, he knew a female opera conductor whose husband spent millions of dollars so she could keep running her opera company. In a sense, Arthur himself was in a similar situation, because Claudia's father contributed a significant amount of money to the company so Arthur could produce opera. Arthur's arguments seemed reasonable, which persuaded Stephanie that she could and should stay in the company. Arthur and Claudia appeared to rest at ease.

"I'm grateful to your father," Claudia said, sitting next to Stephanie. "He is such a nice gentleman. This'll put the New York Bel Canto Opera into the limelight."

"Not yet, not yet," Arthur replied, clasping his hands behind his head and leaning back in his chair. "In my business, fundraising is the most tiresome task. But with this endowment, we'll be free of our financial burdens. We can concentrate on opera-making."

"I can see that," Stephanie said. "Our future is opening up."

"Opera performance at Carnegie Hall will be great," he went on. "Not only that, these showcase concerts will provide young singers with the opportunity to perform in public. And the grant from the Italian government might give us international exposure." He gestured to the wall where a poster of their coming performance was posted. "If this plan becomes official, I could hire several singers in residence, like the Dolci Quattro and Mike. I can pay them more than an honorarium." Seeing Stephanie's excitement, he waved for her to let him finish. "And I can formally appoint you as the general manager with a regular salary."

"Right on!" Stephanie cried. "Now you're talking."

They all laughed.

"This is all because of your father," Claudia said. "My father has been helping the company financially as best as he could. But your father's financial power is much greater than my father's. Stephanie, I'm really grateful to you." Claudia hugged Stephanie and kissed her on the cheek. "I'll invite you for dinner soon."

"Thank you," Stephanie said. "You're too kind."

Stephanie was pleased that while her father's first objective was to help her, he was also aiding the opera company. Arthur's gratitude might be expected. But she would not have predicted such genuine magnanimity from Claudia, who did not seem to have the slightest bit of suspicion. Stephanie remembered her fantasy the night before and flushed.

"I have one more surprise for you," Arthur said. "Actually, this is for all the Dolci Quattro." He handed her a letter. "I received this yesterday."

She noticed the distinctive letterhead. "The Lyric Opera of Chicago?" she shrieked.

"Read it." He jerked his chin forward, urging her.

She read the letter hurriedly, her hands shaking a little.

Dear Mr. DeSoto:

We are writing to invite your artists to apply for the following positions for the fully staged production of Leoncavallo's *La Bohème* in the season after the next.

Ms. Jennifer Schneider:	Mimi
Ms. Stephanie Frank:	Musette
Mr. Henry Anderson:	Marcello
Mr. John Bertucci:	Rodolfo

We extend this invitation at the recommendation of Mr. Victor Carré, the conductor of the Lyric Opera of Chicago.

The letter further described the logistics of application. The deadline was the end of February. The letter was jointly signed by Walter Reihwald, Associate Artistic Administrator, and Nancy Welsh, Casting Coordinator. Stephanie read it again and looked at Arthur, speechless.

"What do you think?" he asked, grinning.

"Fantastic!" That was all she could say. Her heart was pounding. She could hear the beats.

"I called Mr. Carré and asked if he knew anything about this. He told me he did indeed recommend the singers to them. But he insists the letter has nothing to do with him. He strongly encourages you all to apply. And of course, so do I."

Stephanie promised that she would speak to the others, and they would take immediate action. Claudia congratulated her with a big hug. Stephanie politely accepted it. She felt reprehensible, but deep down her feelings toward Arthur only heated up.

◖◗

After Stephanie came home, she called the Café Momus and informed them that she would be late because an emergency had come up with the company. Then, using the conference-call feature, she reached the other Dolci Quattro and informed them of the invitation from the Lyric Opera of Chicago. The news set them on fire. She heard them shouting cheers. After impassioned exchanges, they agreed to send in their applications together.

For opera singers, auditions were one of their most common activities. They had readily at hand their résumés, audition CDs, references, and copies of reviews of their past performances. All they had to do was to update the information to reflect their current status. They were to make a note in their application that a new CD, containing their singing of Leoncavallo's *La Bohème* with the New York Bel Canto Opera, would be sent as soon as the performance was over in the middle of March. They were going to bring their completed applications and attachments to the first rehearsal with the soloists. Stephanie would take care of the rest.

One task was over. This was easy. She took a deep breath. The next one was a challenge. She wanted to call her father at his office. This was the first time she had ever done such a thing. She mustered her courage and picked up the phone. Her mother appeared again. She wrapped her arms around Stephanie on the sofa. Her father was in. He sounded surprised by her call. But hearing her thanking him for his initiative, he sighed with relief.

"I never thought you would be there," he said.

"I never thought you would," she replied.

They laughed. She relaxed. This was a good start. Her mother tapped her shoulder. Stephanie described Arthur's excitement and his vision if the project was formally approved by the Society. It would help not only the company, but also the singers and the general manager. Thus she would doubly benefit. She realized that her voice had stirred up.

"Pleased to hear that, Stephanie," her father said. "Don't worry about their funding. If they can't come up with enough money, I can pay another five million. That's not the problem. But I thought they should be part of the project. If they provide their own money, they will be more serious about running the project."

"I agree, Dad," she said. "They should be responsible for their project. The best way is to let them invest their money in it."

"Precisely. You've got a good business sense, Stephanie. No wonder you're the general manager. But you didn't tell me about it when we met last October."

"I got the job right after that."

"I see. Do you like it?"

"A lot of work. But I like it. I think I have a gift for it."

"Good."

She was glad that the conversation was proceeding as she had hoped. Her mother rested her head on Stephanie's shoulder. Stephanie asked her father if he had known Mr. Zappia long. He replied that Umberto was a member of the Knickerbocker Club. When he'd heard her opera would be at the Italian Cultural Society, he remembered that Umberto was the chairman there. So at the Knick, he had proposed this idea.

"Claudia told me he is an opera fanatic," she said. "He adores your idea."

"I've figured that out. As soon as I proposed the project, he grabbed it. I'm glad he's making concrete progress. Maybe we can have dinner with him at the Knick."

"OK, but that'll have to be after the performance."

"Fair enough."

She hesitated momentarily. Her mother poked her side gently, signaling her to go on.

"Hey, Dad, if you want, you can bring your wife, son, and daughter to the opera."

Silence.

"You mean it?" His voice sounded cautious.

Her mother tapped on her to continue.

"Yes, I mean it. It's about time for me to meet your family."

"They'll be happy to hear you sing. Afterward, can they meet you for the first time?"

"That'll be nice."

"I hope your mother would approve of this." His voice cracked.

Her mother kissed her cheek.

"I'm sure she would," Stephanie said.

She heard her father crying.

Scene 5

enry had dinner with Christine in the East Village on
Friday evening. Afterward they went to a nearby theater
to see a play called *Sisters*. The show was the first of four previews
before the formal opening. The director wanted to gauge reactions
to the script, actors, setting, and the direction. The author and director, Charles Reilly, was Sarah's boyfriend. Christine and Henry met
Sarah, who led them to good seats. Henry was familiar with opera
stages, but he had not been to a play for a long time. The theater was
in an old converted warehouse. In the center, the stage was set as
a trendy New York apartment with a sofa, bookcases, and an open
kitchen. The audience sat encircling the stage, as if they were guests
in the apartment.

The one-act play was about two sisters sharing the same apartment, each of whom was going through a difficult time with her

boyfriend, tormenting each other with envy and jealousy. Both sisters ended up with broken relationships. They embraced and comforted each other. At least they were sisters and still friends. The audience gave a standing ovation.

As the guests started leaving, Sarah brought Christine and Henry to Charles, who was a tall man in his early forties with straight brown hair, brown eyes, and a high forehead. Sarah introduced Henry as an opera singer.

"So you're familiar with the stage then," Charles said. "How did we do?"

"Excellent," Henry replied. "You wrote and directed it?"

"Yes. I think the audience reacted well. But I feel the climax needs more build-up. I have to revise the script a little."

As Henry was surveying the stage, Charles explained his challenge. In a traditional stage setup, the director could use the space and directions of stage right, stage left, downstage, and upstage. But in a theater-in-the-round, he had had to try many different ways to locate the props and position the actors. Henry commented that the play had looked quite natural. Charles smiled broadly, then waved to the four actors. They approached, followed by a man. Henry held his breath. It was Richard. He shook Henry's hand as the actors greeted Sarah and Christine.

Richard explained that Charles was the instructor of a playwriting course he was taking at NYU. He introduced his new girlfriend, Nicole, who had played the younger sister. Nicole, a slender woman in her early thirties, wore heavy stage makeup but was dressed in casual blue jeans and a white turtleneck sweater, which happened to be her costume for the play. Charles suggested that

Richard take an acting class. It would be helpful for him as a fiction writer to improve his skills in character building and emotional expression. Richard seemed interested. The actors talked about how they study, analyze, and express an assigned character from a script. Christine told Henry that Richard was in the poetry workshop she was taking at NYU.

"Yes." Richard turned back to them. "I'm enjoying that, too."

"I like your work," Christine said to Richard.

"Thanks, I'm flattered. I consider myself intermediate as far as poetry is concerned. My main focus is literary fiction. I'm taking a novel-writing workshop, too."

"How is your play coming?" Charles asked Richard. "The last draft was terrific. In two weeks we'll workshop your next submission in class. Right?"

"It's coming along," Richard said. "Your play gave me new energy. It'll be ready."

Henry was astonished to see the new Richard enjoying such a variety of writing styles. He seemed to be seriously pursuing a literary career. *Why did you treat Jennifer so wickedly? Damn you, Richard.* When he looked up, he was embarrassed to see Richard gazing at him.

"I know what you're thinking," Richard said. "I was plain stupid. But if I hadn't gone through that, I wouldn't be like this now. I'm not going to mess up my life this time."

"So you have a new girlfriend," Henry said. "What about Jennifer?"

"How can I go back to her after what I've done? I'm sure she'll find a deserving man." Richard sighed. "A few weeks ago Charles hooked me up with Nicole. She is studying scriptwriting and acting. She and I have a passion for literature. We're getting along all right."

Henry felt abashed by his own silliness. He had thought that he might help Richard get back together with Jennifer. That seemed no longer necessary.

◖◗

The evening after the play, Christine invited Henry for dinner at her apartment. Sarah had gone to the theater again to help Charles. Henry had told Christine that rehearsals with soloists would begin during the coming week. He would be drawn into the hectic schedule. She wanted to have a pleasant evening with him before it started, so he could concentrate on the rehearsals and subsequent performances. She had expressed her concern over his voice and promised that she would do all the talking. He could just enjoy the food and wine. She would be all right with it because she was getting used to being with an opera singer.

This was the first time he had come to her place. A large drafting table with a swing-arm lamp and chair occupied a corner of the living room, presumably Sarah's working place. He noted all kinds of art supplies—collections of brushes, watercolor paper of various sizes, and watercolor tubes. The opposite corner held a dining table and chairs. In the middle sat a sofa and a coffee table. Sarah's work hung on the walls, both in frames and without. Bookcases were full of poetry, suggesting the presence of Christine. A small fragment of cast-iron fence with a rosette pattern hung on the wall. It held a vase, in which a few roses were arranged. Christine explained that Sarah brought it from a mansion that their father's company had renovated in the New Orleans Garden District. It gave the apartment an air of a quaint French garden.

Henry had worn a dark-blue suit with a red tie. Christine matched his elegance in a deep-red wool dress. Her blue eyes shone in contrast. A small pearl earring peeked out from her blonde hair, and a thin gold necklace hung from her slender neck. He recognized the fragrance of Chanel No. 5. Her charm delighted him more than ever.

The dining table was lit by two candles in silver candlesticks. A Chopin piano concerto came from a CD player. Dinner consisted of smoked salmon, salad, roast veal, and red wine. Christine was a good cook, as she had claimed. The medium-rare veal, with its irresistible aroma, was prepared just how he liked it. The French wine livened up the tenderness of the veal. She played the hostess role graciously, making pleasant conversation. Whenever he spoke, she put her forefinger to her lips, signing not to talk too much. Henry thought that she was learning quickly to be a good companion to him. As a joke, he composed and sent a text message to himself on his iPhone. He showed it to her in silence. "May I have another glass of wine?"

She burst into laughter. "A veritable Gigli." She filled his glass immediately.

For dessert and tea, they sat on the sofa. The CD player was now playing Brahms's violin concerto. They listened to the music. Since they had dated many times already, a pause in conversation like this did not create any awkwardness. Instead, it increased their intimacy. As the music entered the second movement, she leaned against him, resting her head on his shoulder. He felt as if the purity of the harmony between the violin and the orchestra drew them ever closer.

"You want to hear another poet?" she asked when the concerto was over.

"Yes, by all means. Who else do you like beside Christina Rossetti and Emily Dickinson?"

She fetched a book from a bookcase and opened to one of the earmarked pages. She explained, "Anne Bradstreet is considered the first female poet in America, born more than two hundred years before Rossetti and Dickinson. She isn't very popular, but is admired in literary circles. Recently I'm attracted to her poetry because her voice is full of love, particularly when she writes about her family life with her husband and children. I'll read one of her typical poems for you. It's titled 'To My Dear and Loving Husband.'" She recited in a solemn voice.

> If ever two were one, then surely we.
> If ever man were loved by wife, then thee;
> If ever wife was happy in a man,
> Compare with me, ye women, if you can.
> I prize thy love more than whole mines of gold,
> Or all the riches that the East doth hold.
> My love is such that rivers cannot quench,
> Nor ought but love from thee, give recompense.
> Thy love is such I can no way repay,
> The heavens reward thee manifold, I pray.
> Then while we live, in love let's so persevere
> That when we live no more, we may live ever.

The poem conveyed its forthright adoration as if Christine were revealing her heart to Henry in all her honesty and sincerity. He felt honored by it. A natural next step for him would be to propose marriage. He was ready, except for the ever-present issue: *Can I be with her while I continue my opera career?* He remembered the coaching session with Mr. Carré that Christine attended. From her excitement during the session, he thought, she could be an understanding partner to an opera singer. The poem further confirmed it.

"That was so beautiful," he said. "Her husband must have been a happy man."

"He was the governor of the Massachusetts Bay colony and a good family man, too."

"I'm sure, if his wife could write this kind of poem."

"She didn't only write about her husband, but also about her children and even her grandchildren. These poems are full of wifely and motherly affection." She softly placed the book on the table. "From our generation's point of view, this poem may sound too old-fashioned. But I like it, because even though women of our time enjoy our professional work and independence, the relationship between a woman and a man should be like this poem. There is no difference between Anne Bradstreet's time and our own." She spoke these words firmly.

He nodded. He thought that he would respect her as an independent woman and a poet.

"I wish I could find a matching poem to this one. But I'm no poet." He pondered. He tapped his thigh. "I've got it. I think this'll be the best reply to your poem. It's a nocturne of Norina and Ernesto in Act III of Donizetti's *Don Pasquale*. This is actually a duet by these two lovers. Here they affirm their love to each other. The words of both the soprano and tenor parts are the same, and the melodies of the two parts are similar. The verse means:

> "Once more tell me you love me,
> tell me that you are mine only;
> when you tenderly call my name
> life elates me.

> "Your voice so dear
> reassures the oppressed heart:
> I am safe when you are nearby,
> I tremble when you are far away."

Then he sang the nocturne in *sotto voce*.

> *Tornami a dir che m'ami,*
> *dimmi che mia tu sei;*
> *quandro tuo ben mi chiami*
> *la vita addoppi in me.*

> *La voce tua sì cara*
> *rinfranca il core oppresso:*
> *sicro a te dapresso,*
> *tremo lontan da te.*

Even though it was without accompaniment, his lyric voice resonated as if accompanied by a symphony orchestra under a bright moon. Christine listened to the sweet melody with dreamy eyes, as if she were reciting the same verse back to him. He forgot that he was singing a nocturne composed by someone else. He was expressing himself to her, his passion undisguised. At the finale, he took time to sing three triples "*da—te—, da—*" and held the last "*te*" at high A for a long time, like the sound of a flute.

Henry kneeled before Christine. This was not planned. He was surprised at himself. But the nocturne had opened his heart and convinced him that the time had come.

"Christine, I love you very much."

She blushed, but calmly took in his words.

"I love you, too, Henry, from the bottom of my heart."

He clasped her hands in his.

"I would like to spend the rest of my life with you. Will you marry me?"

"Oh, Henry, yes!" Christine threw her arms around his shoulders and kissed him. "My mind has been made up for a long time. You're the only person I've ever loved this way. I'm not a perfect woman. But I'll do everything to be a good wife to you."

"You know what happened between John and Michelle and between Jennifer and Richard. An opera singer is not an easy spouse. But I'll do my best to build a sweet home with you."

"You'll find only support from me for your opera career."

"Actually," Henry said with a sigh, "my brother and sister are urging me to apply for a voice faculty position at Ohio State University. That's where my late father taught and my brother currently teaches. It's a stable job with an adequate salary. If I take the job and go there with you, we'll be able to enjoy a comfortable life. But I've decided not to apply. I want to be an opera singer. This means—I'm sorry, Christine—I cannot provide you with a luxurious life."

Christine laughed. "Don't you know what I want for my life? Not money. I want to write poetry, so I don't expect riches. Of course I'd like us to maintain a decent standard of living. But above all I want a peaceful life with a husband and children. That life will inspire me to write poetry like Anne Bradstreet. Other poets might disagree with me, but this is what I feel about myself." Her face shone with a writer's pride.

Henry inclined his head gravely. "You give me courage to go through all the challenges ahead. In turn, I'd like to help you to keep writing poetry. I hope you'll publish your chapbook someday soon. It's not only good for you, but also stimulating to me as a singer."

"It's difficult to find a man who appreciates poetry. I'm fortunate you do."

He looked at her with a gentle smile. She smiled back, her face radiant.

"So, do you think we can live together," he said, "for better for worse, for richer for poorer, in sickness and in health?"

"With your help," she said, "yes, I do."

"I'll cherish you and honor you."

"I'll do the same."

"Until we are parted by death?"

"No, we'll live together even after death because our flesh and soul will be one."

"Even better."

"Oh, Henry, I've loved you since the first time I saw you. I'll love you forever."

"You've made me a happy man." He kissed her hands.

"I'm so happy. Come close to me."

⟪◎ ◎⟫

After that evening Christine moved into Henry's apartment. She wrote a poem to celebrate the occasion. He read it and was immersed in it, because she captured exactly what he felt for their future. This was a splendid beginning. He sent an e-mail to the Dolci Quattro, Mike, Arthur, the Graces, Mr. Carré, Père Momus, and his family members, announcing their engagement. He attached the poem and a digital photo of the smiling couple.

Intermezzo

By a brook in the woods,
We will build a timber cottage,
Crystal windows all the sides,
Water cadence rippling.

When you are in despair,
Come to me.
I will share you my refuge,
For hard frost melts away.

When you are in joy,
Come to me.
I will share you my happiness,
For sunflower follows sunshine.

Seasons go by everlasting.
We will cherish our cabin,
You in me, I in you,
One flesh, one soul.

Scene 6

On Sunday evening Jennifer invited Michelle for dessert at her apartment. She had not heard anything from Michelle since they had last spoken three weeks before. The funeral of John's father seemed to have put her quandary regarding the pregnancy up in the air. John was still staying with his mother in Brooklyn at night.

Jennifer thought Michelle looked calm and artistic in a casual black wool tunic and leggings. She sat with her legs curled beneath her, her brown eyes introspective. They ate chocolate tarts and drank tea.

"I have a feeling John is sleeping with another woman," Michelle said abruptly.

"What?" Jennifer thought that Michelle was joking, but her face was serious. "I'm sure it's just your imagination."

Michelle stirred her tea and gazed at the swirling liquid. She recounted that she had called his mother a few times in Brooklyn. He wasn't there. She had called Music Universe. They told her that he had left a long time ago. This had happened several times already. Jennifer reminded her that he might have gone to a coaching session or rehearsal at his church.

Michelle shook her head. "No; I know his schedule." She paused. "If he's sleeping with someone else, will it help my divorce?"

"Good lord, Michelle. You mustn't talk like that."

"I didn't know how filing for divorce would affect our relationship."

What did you think, that it would bring you closer to John, you dimwitted girl? Jennifer thought. But she said, "I know it hurt John deeply. And now, losing his father, too. Can you imagine what kind of grief he is feeling? He's always been loyal to you, and I think it would be completely out of character for him to cheat. But even someone as devoted as John could be driven to do something extreme under such circumstances."

Michelle sighed. "So I suppose sleeping with another woman is a real possibility."

"Whose fault is that?" Jennifer saw Michelle quivering. "Sorry. I didn't mean to criticize you. I just wanted you to consider John's point of view."

"Our marriage wasn't so bad to begin with," Michelle said, her voice shaky. "My divorce filing completely messed up our relationship. Now he's sleeping with another woman, and I'm stuck with this." Michelle pressed her abdomen.

Although Jennifer considered Michelle a close friend only few years younger than her, she thought that Michelle's idea of marriage had been no more than a girlhood fantasy. Her admission this evening was the first sign of her maturing as a woman. Maybe there was still hope for reconciliation between Michelle and John.

"I checked out PlanB at a pharmacy," Michelle went on. "It works only within seventy-two hours of unprotected sex. It's not for me. Mifeprex works only within eight weeks of pregnancy, and I'm already two months. So a surgical procedure is the only way left for me now."

"It's good these choices are available to women. But they do sound dreadful."

"Sometimes I feel like thrusting a knife into my belly and cleaving this thing into bits." Michelle glared at her abdomen, punching it with her fists.

"Horrible! Stop, stop!" Jennifer exclaimed. "I don't want to hear you talk like that!"

Michelle clasped both hands over her face, sobbing. Jennifer now understood the psychology of a woman in despair over an unwanted pregnancy—a woman who would do anything, anything at all, to get rid of it, even though the act might kill her. She prayed Michelle would never do anything self-destructive; but Jennifer was no stranger to despair, having recently acted thoughtlessly herself. What could be done? The ideal solution would be for Michelle and John to reconcile and keep the baby. But as it stood, they seemed far apart.

"Have you told John yet?' she asked gently.

The Other La Bohème

Michelle nodded. "I announced I was pregnant when John and I visited his father at the hospital. But John believed I only said it to please his father before he died. John's been staying with his mother, so I haven't had a chance to tell him it's true."

"You mean you hadn't told him before that?" Jennifer said. "Oh, Michelle, you must tell him plainly again. Please. I'm sure he'll be delighted."

"But he doesn't come back to our apartment," Michelle wailed. "I still haven't decided whether to keep it. What if he's fallen for someone else? I can't raise a child alone. And time is passing so quickly." She started crying again.

What a mess, Jennifer thought. But she didn't want Michelle to do anything drastic; certainly not before she talked with her husband. Probably they should stop the conversation. The day after tomorrow, rehearsals with the soloists would start. She proposed that Michelle come to the rehearsal to see for herself how opera singers worked. "I'll ask John to invite you." Michelle did not object. They called it a night. Jennifer again made Michelle promise not to take any action without talking to her. Michelle agreed.

◖◗

Jennifer stepped out from Vanderbilt Hall on Washington Square South into a mild night. She had just finished her paralegal class at NYU. She started walking toward the subway station at West 4th Street and Sixth Avenue. Although it was ten o'clock, many people were still hanging around Washington Square. Some were

280

walking their dogs. A few were playing chess. The sounds of a guitar wafted from the east side of the park.

She heard fast footsteps approaching her and turned at the familiar voice calling her name. She saw Richard with a pretty woman. He wore casual clothes and an overcoat, but looked tidy and respectable, his face thoughtful. She wanted to veer off, but since he was with a woman, she felt safe. He reached her first and extended his hand. She fretted for a moment but shook his hand, thanking him cordially for his Christmas card.

"You look wonderful," he murmured.

The woman caught up with him and held his arm. She wore a belted wool coat and a fuzzy turtleneck sweater with blue jeans. Her long blonde hair swayed about her in the breeze. She did not have any makeup on. Her large brown eyes had an irresistible charm, and she clearly knew it. Richard faltered, then introduced his friend, Nicole, as an actress and a scriptwriter. Nicole reached out her hand. Jennifer countered politely. She felt Nicole's gaze at both her and Richard, as if curious about what kind of relationship they had had. Jennifer assumed that he had not told Nicole of their engagement and breakup. If he had, she would have slapped his face. He introduced Jennifer as an opera singer.

"Then you know well about the stage," Nicole said, with a clear diction that suggested she was trained as a professional actress.

"You have a beautiful voice," Jennifer said.

"Thanks." Nicole beamed. "Some compliment, when it comes from an opera singer."

"I presume," Richard cut in, "you were at your paralegal class. How is it going?"

"It's tough, especially after my regular work. Four-hour sessions," Jennifer said. "Thank God it's only once a week. I can barely manage. What are you doing here?"

He explained that he was taking a poetry-writing workshop at NYU. He needed to expand his appreciation of literature in order to write fiction more seriously. This evening after class he'd been doing some research at the library for a class assignment to present a poet who had influenced the students most. Nicole had helped him. He looked happy.

"That sounds fun. Who is the poet you chose?"

"Until I went to the library, I had had no idea. But after browsing through several anthologies, I decided on Robert Burns. His poems are so musical."

She inclined her head in approval. Her less-guarded conversation seemed to please him.

"Do you know Christine, Henry's girlfriend? She's in the same class," Richard said. "Boy, she writes so well. She is a born poet with an ardent voice. I really like her work."

Jennifer remembered the times she and Richard had talked of novels and poetry. Then he had been a literary gentleman and a competent bank manager. She missed that time.

"I'm glad you're back into your literary life," she told him.

Richard said that he was working on a novel while taking three workshops. He went on to describe the play Nicole was in. "It was a good experience for me to see how a play script is put into action by the director and actors." He chatted on about the playwriting class.

How much he has changed, Jennifer thought. Then she realized that he had not changed. He had only returned to the former self she had loved. The only difference was that now he was no longer a bank manager. And he had a new girlfriend.

"By the way," Richard went on, "in the theater last Friday, I saw Henry and Christine. It's a small world. I can see Christine is really in love with Henry."

"So is Henry with her." Her voice cracked. "They just got engaged."

A fleeting frown creased Richard's brow. "Really? I'll have to congratulate them."

What about our engagement? Jennifer shouted in her mind. This was enough. She did not want to get into their past. The sight of Nicole disturbed her, too. She took her leave and pivoted toward the subway station. Immediately she halted and turned back.

"Richard," she said, "I wish you hadn't called after me this evening. Why did you stop me? Did you want to show off Nicole? Are you enjoying sex with her now? Does she know about that red-haired lawyer? Don't toy with me anymore." She raised her right hand but held it in the air, glaring at him. "I want to slap your face, you bastard," she blasted, "but I won't do it for our old times' sake. But I hope this is the last time I ever see you. From now on, just leave me alone."

Richard paled. Nicole hid behind him. Jennifer turned back to the station and ran.

The subway station was crowded even at this late hour. A pop musician was singing, accompanying himself on a small electronic piano. Amid the crowd, Jennifer saw a young woman of her height in a black coat and boots. The woman wore a black wool hat, blonde hair appearing from its edges. Christine. Jennifer felt flushed and short of breath and would have turned away, but it was too late. Christine had spotted her and was smiling at Jennifer as she approached.

Jennifer had time to catch her breath as Christine described the poetry workshop she had just attended at NYU. Jennifer responded that she had run into a mutual acquaintance, Richard, who was in the same workshop and had mentioned seeing her at Sarah's play with Henry. "And congratulations on your engagement!" she added.

Jennifer had been so upset with Richard. But the presence of Christine mitigated her aggravation, as the young woman's face was shining, full of love.

"Thank you," she said. "It happened so fast, I still can't believe it. I've been moving my things from the old apartment. It'll take another a few weeks."

"I like your poem Henry sent."

"That came out so naturally, I didn't have to think. All I needed was to write it down."

"Richard told me that you're a gifted poet."

"He's very kind," Christine said. "But Richard is very good, too. He has already presented a few of his poems in class." She searched her bag and dug out a folder of papers. "This is his poem we work-shopped this evening. It's beautiful."

Christine handed it to Jennifer. She read it cautiously. The poem was titled "*De Profundis,*" and it proclaimed in a dolorous tone an apologia for his misconduct without explicitly saying what it had been or against whom it had been committed. For her it was obvious, and she understood what he was trying to say. The poem concluded:

It is not a question
of forgiveness.
I carry this stain
to the end of my journey.

Jennifer sighed, as if all the air were escaping from her lungs. Her legs trembling, she barely managed to keep standing. Her eyes welled up. Thanking her for it, Jennifer returned the paper to Christine, who slid it back in her folder, gazing at Jennifer in a sympathetic manner.

"Can you hear his inner voice crying out?" Christine said. "His expertise may be in prose. But in poetry, his voice has such intensity and depth. I can feel it."

"He would be proud to hear you say so," Jennifer said, turning away to swipe her tears on her leather glove.

"Sarah's boyfriend told me that he workshopped a scene of Richard's play manuscript in his class. He said it was very good, too. I haven't read any of his novels or scripts. But he seems to be a really talented writer."

"Maybe so. This evening he was with his girlfriend. That'll give him more inspiration." The train rumbled into the station before Christine could push her to further sarcasm, or sadness, or happiness for him, or any other emotion connected to Richard.

Back at her apartment, Jennifer examined a letter that had come with the daily mail. Like the ones she had been receiving weekly, it was correctly addressed to her with a typed label, but bore no return address. She consigned it to the wastebasket without opening it. While she was at it, she fetched Richard's Christmas card, tore it to pieces, and threw them into the wastebasket as well. She wished she could do the same to the entire memory of Richard in her head.

I refuse to be intimidated, discouraged, or distracted, she told herself. She made sure that her application to the Lyric Opera of Chicago was ready for the next day. Now she needed a good night's sleep.

But she felt stupid. Richard had found a new girlfriend. Even after that redhead. She had thought of it countless times already. *Why does his presence still hurt so much? Do I want him back? Silly girl. Forget it. Tomorrow the rehearsals will begin. I mustn't think of anything else.*

The telephone rang. She answered it, but there was no response. She held it a few seconds, fearing it was her unknown e-mailer and letter-writer. As she was about to hang up, she heard a sob, followed by an almost inaudible: "Jennifer."

"Aunt Maggie?"

This was uncharacteristic of her aunt, who was usually a fit and clear-headed woman. In her trembling voice, Aunt Maggie told her story. One week ago, she'd been informed that one of her best friends in Florida was in a coma in a hospital. Aunt Maggie had known that her friend had been suffering from colon cancer, but had not thought it was that serious. She'd visited the hospital, but her friend never regained consciousness and had died a few days ago. Today was her funeral. The service was beautiful, but afterward she'd grown depressed. She had always thought that she was too healthy to worry. This incident made her realize that this kind of thing could strike her at any time. It scared the hell out of her. She did not want to live alone anymore. She broke into heavy sobs again. Jennifer could not do much, other than let her weep for several seconds.

"Auntie, I'm so sorry to hear that," Jennifer said. "But don't you have other friends there?"

"Yes, but she was the closest and the same age. That's why it hit me so hard."

"I'm sure it did. Do you want me to come to Florida?"

"No, I'm going to come to New York. Would you mind?"

"Of course not. Come, Auntie. Stay here as long as you want. I've been concerned about you living alone. But you always laughed about it, saying you were in perfect health. Maybe it's time to think about a change in your lifestyle?"

"That's exactly what I'm thinking. When I come to New York, I'll look for an apartment."

Jennifer took the next day off. The night before had been too stressful, between the paralegal class, the encounter with Richard, the anonymous harassment, and the call from Aunt Maggie. Tonight she was to have her first rehearsal with the other soloists. She needed a good rest. She got up late, took a shower, and had brunch. After exercising and warming up, she went over Acts III and IV, which they were to rehearse that evening. Her voice was vigorous, and she managed to sing to her satisfaction the arias and ensembles, which required physical power in Act III and emotional concentration in Act IV.

After that she sat in the lotus position and meditated. Her mind was peaceful. Then she took out Willa Cather's *The Song of the Lark* and read Part VI, subtitled "Kronborg," which was the climax of the novel. At age twenty, Thea Kronborg left the United States for Germany. Four years later she made a debut in Dresden as Elisabeth in Wagner's *Tannhäuser*. A few years later she debuted as Elsa in *Lohengrin* at the Metropolitan Opera House in New York. One evening, while she was having dinner with her friends, her management called and asked her if she could sing Sieglinde in *Die Walküre* because the soprano had become sick during Act I. Within minutes she was in a cab to the Met. She had only studied the role without ever performing it. No rehearsal yet, either. But she sang brilliantly from Act II onward before the appreciative audience. Her fame exploded like a shooting star. The four successive Friday evenings, she performed Wagner's entire Ring Cycle: *Das Rheingold, Die Walküre, Siegfried,* and *Die Götterdämmerrung*. This time she sang Sieglinde in *Die Walküre* as part of the regular cast, not a stand-in. To her spirited yet gracious singing, the audience responded in "almost savage" applause. It was Thea's triumph.

As she read, Jennifer felt a dazzling admiration for Thea, who was completely in control of both her opera career and her personal life. She recognized that Thea was a fictional character; but like Thea, Jennifer wanted to be brave and bold, prudent yet passionate. She would add to the list *com*passionate. She felt she had a willing desire, as well as responsibility, to look after her aunt. Similarly she felt protective toward Michelle.

When I was desolate, Stephanie and Henry consoled me. I'm no longer a weak woman. I don't need Richard anymore. I can stand by myself. Now it's my turn to do something for others. This I can do and should do while I pursue my opera career.

Jennifer felt she was being transformed into a new woman.

So help me, Thea, please.

Scene 7

*J*ohn mourned his father's death more than any other loss he had encountered in his life. He had anticipated his father's presence at the upcoming concert, where he would prove himself to be the heir to their family opera legacy, as had been his father's lifelong wish. Now, instead, the concert would be an homage to his father and his grandfather. It loomed only one month away. He pledged himself to show his best singing ever. His mother was going to bring the portraits of his father and grandfather to the concert. *Pa and Grandpa, watch over me as I sing.*

His father's death had closed one chapter of John's life and opened a new one. He now had a responsibility as the head of the Bertucci family. Although he was temporarily staying with his mother in Brooklyn, he thought that he should return to her house permanently and take care of her. All he had to bring back from

Michelle's apartment were his piano, music scores, CDs, and clothes. He would not have to pay rent. His mother had some income from her husband's pension and Social Security. He could contribute his earnings to the new household.

As for Michelle's announcement of her pregnancy, he realized she hadn't been lying. On one hand he knew that it was his child; on the other hand, he didn't want to believe it could be so. He suspected that she was having affairs with other men; she had admitted she had been seeing them. That was why she wanted a divorce, he convinced himself. He suggested to his mother that the pregnancy was Michelle's act of compassion before his father's death—that she was not really pregnant. His mother was persuaded that this was the case, for she knew that Michelle was a warm-hearted daughter-in-law. She was disappointed but soon forgot about it.

He continued his relationship with Erica. Love was not the right word to describe his feeling toward her. Comfort sounded more like it. She seemed to feel the same way. The two wounded souls could console each other. That was what they needed, and that was what they could offer each other. Through such simple yet warm closeness, over time, he thought, love might grow between the two. Erica worked at Music Universe a few days a week, but when she was off he went to her apartment for lunch, and they made love. She adamantly asked him not to spend the night at her place. She also advised him not to mention their liaison to Michelle until the divorce was finalized. He agreed, because Erica was more experienced in divorce proceedings. Otherwise, he spent his days as before, between work, coaching sessions, and rehearsals. He planned in his mind that someday soon he would bring Erica to his mother's house, and introduce each other.

One day before the first rehearsal with the soloists, he received a call from Jennifer, asking him to invite Michelle to the rehearsal. At first he faltered. He now had Erica. He wanted the divorce to be concluded soon. Then he remembered his joke to Christine about how understanding she was toward Henry. He realized that although Michelle had attended his concerts and operas, she had never seen what it took to get there. He thought that it would do no harm, so he called Michelle and suggested it. She accepted without any question.

⟪◎ ◎⟫

John arrived at the Italian Cultural Society after work and went up to the third floor. Stephanie, Jennifer, Henry, Mike, and Kate were already there. He congratulated Henry on his engagement to Christine. Henry's happy face reminded him of his own engagement to Michelle. He had been happy like Henry. How long ago was it? Not so long. And what a mess he was drawn into at the moment. Stephanie collected the applications to the Lyric Opera of Chicago, carefully inserting them into a large envelope. They all wished each other good luck.

John spotted Michelle at the door and went to her. She wore a conservative business suit and looked like a dignified young female teacher. He felt proud of her.

"So this is the place you rehearse," Michelle said, looking around. "It's very big."

He had sung here a few times before. "This is actually a concert hall," he told her. "It may be too big for soloists only. But when we have soloists, chorus, and orchestra all together, this is a good place for the rehearsals."

He ushered her to the front. His friends were all pleased to see her with him. Jennifer hugged her. Soon Arthur and Claudia arrived. Arthur greeted all with enthusiasm, full of energy. They settled in for the rehearsal, taking off their coats and coming up to the stage with their music scores. The singers did quick exercises. Kate sat at the piano and Arthur secured a music stand close by. The singers stood, facing Arthur. Michelle and Claudia sat in the audience side by side with a draft libretto Stephanie had given them so they could follow the story of the opera. Claudia wore a turquoise and olive print dress, looking classy and elegant as usual. John noticed that Stephanie was staring at her.

Stephanie turned to the singers. "Acts III and IV require only five soloists: Mimi, Musette, Marcello, Rodolfo, and Schaunard. We know each other already, so let's skip the formalities. Kate, would you warm us up, please?" Kate played scales and the singers vocalized. When the five were ready, Stephanie said, "Maestro, now we're all yours."

"Thank you," Arthur said, addressing the singers. "As you saw in the schedule, I would like to rehearse each act backward from Act IV to Act I. So today we'll go over Acts IV and III. The day after tomorrow, Act II with chorus, and next week Act I. This way, you'll first learn how the opera ends. Then, as we move backward, you'll learn how to build up each act toward that end."

The singers assented because this was not an unusual strategy for preparing an opera.

"There is another reason why I want to rehearse backward," Arthur went on. "Acts IV and III require only five soloists; so the rehearsal will be relatively easy to control. Act II involves eight major soloists, a few minor soloists, and two choruses. That'll make the rehearsal more complex. Act I involves nine soloists, who all sing the finale in ensemble. I like to accelerate the rehearsals gradually from easy to challenging. I hope you'll all help me to maintain a professional order in the rehearsals."

The singers assured Arthur of their cooperation.

"Good. Let's go over Act IV, shall we?"

The singers opened their scores to the first page of the act.

"Act IV takes place at Rodolfo's garret on Christmas Eve, one year after Act I," Arthur explained. "There isn't much dramatic singing in this final act, except for Rodolfo's aria at the beginning. This is because the artists have lost their lovers and they are broke. They are depressed and hungry. Mimi appears, but she is dying. So they can't sing *dramatically*." He let the singers laugh. "However, your singing narrates the scene leading to Mimi's death. So you must have emotional intensity in your singing, culminating in the tragic finale." Arthur checked his wristwatch. "The entire Act IV takes about twenty minutes. There is not much ensemble. So let's just run through it. Are you ready?"

Arthur gave a cue, and Kate played the piano for the orchestra part of Act IV, taking the tempo from Arthur's hand movement. After a short introduction, John started singing his aria.

"*Scuoti, o vento, fra i sibili,...*" ("Shake, oh wind, between your hissings,...")

John had studied this aria repeatedly with his coach because it was Rodolfo's most important and longest aria in the opera. He wanted to show off his voice. He concentrated with his full energy, singing from memory. His masculine baritone reverberated through the hall. In the aria Rodolfo reads his poem. He has no lover, nor money. All he has is a passion for poetry. He is proud of it. But he is also tired of his miserable life. Death may be a solace that he might welcome. John thought that he would feel this way if he were divorced from Michelle. Or would he? He now had Erica. He saw Michelle absorbed in his aria and following the libretto. He wondered if she understood his feeling. He also wondered if she knew about Erica. He banished these thoughts immediately as he concentrated on his singing. He reached the climax. His focused high G pierced the hall. He sang the subsequent concluding words with a strong accent on each note and held the last one, E-flat, in a smooth full voice for a long time, until Arthur snapped his baton for John to cut off. Before John was to move onto the next phase, Arthur abruptly raised his right hand. Kate interrupted the piano accompaniment.

"Bravo." Arthur gave his kudos.

The other singers applauded. John saw Michelle clapping. Claudia was cheering, too.

"John, I can see you studied this aria well," Arthur said. "Your singing had the emotion to express Rodolfo's melancholy state of mind. Your voice was focused like a sharpshooter, so it projected far out. This is what we need here, because the aria establishes the mood for the final act, and the audience will be drawn into the scene. An excellent start." He clapped his palms together and shook them near his chest in appreciation and encouragement.

"Thank you," John said, sipping water, very pleased. He stool a look at Michelle and found her smiling. He felt good.

"OK, let's move on. Right after the aria. Rodolfo, '*Chi è la?*' ('Who is there?') and Marcello, '*Son io*' ('It's me'). Kate, from the second bar at the bottom. Ready? Go."

Following Arthur's cue, Kate played. John came in, immediately followed by Henry. The tale unfolded as the rehearsal advanced. Rodolfo, Marcello, and Schaunard have their poor Christmas Eve meal in the shabby, cold garret. Mimi comes, but at the verge of death. Musette arrives and tries to help Mimi. But none of them can do much. Mimi is now happy because Rodolfo has taken her back. Mimi recalls the Christmas Eve one year before. How happy they were then. Rodolfo sobs. Mimi dies. Kate played several bars of the finale in *fortissimo*.

There was a long silence. Then warm applause came from the audience. John looked at Michelle. She was clapping, her eyes filled with tears.

"Excellent," Arthur said, wiping sweat off his forehead with his handkerchief.

Kate cheered. Claudia, too. The singers breathed easily now, sipping water.

"This was the first time for you to sing together," Arthur said. "So understandably, some entries were tentative and insecure. We need a little polishing here and there. But overall, for the first run-through it was pretty good. Thank you, all of you."

John felt pleased. The other singers seemed content, too. "Pretty good" was high praise coming from Arthur.

"Now let's move on to Act III," Arthur said.

◀◉ ◉▶

John emerged from the Italian Cultural Society with the others. He wrapped himself in his coat, hat, muffler, and gloves. He helped Michelle to bundle herself up, too. "That was a great rehearsal," he said, stretching his arms skyward.

Stephanie and Arthur remained in the hall to discuss some business matters. Kate complimented everyone on how splendidly they had sung. Jennifer chimed in that they had done well. John added that it had been an excellent idea to go over Act III a few weeks before with Henry's coach. He repeated his thanks to Henry.

"Michelle, I'm really glad you came," Jennifer said. "Give us your impression."

"This was my first time at one of John's rehearsals," Michelle answered. "I never realized before how exhausting it is both physically and mentally. Three hours of singing with total concentration. You must be worn out. You have a lot of discipline to go through this."

"Yes, it's not easy," Jennifer said. "That's why we have such an ascetic lifestyle. Not that we like it, but it's a necessity. Otherwise, we couldn't do it."

"People always think a tenor is a playboy, chasing around pretty girls," Henry said. "But actually I maintain a very quiet life."

"Does Christine believe that?" John asked.

Henry chuckled. "I hope so."

All laughed.

"I'm spending a lot of time preparing for Schaunard," Mike said. "But lately Vicky has been threatening to leave me. Yesterday she packed her suitcase and was about to go. I begged her on my knees not to leave. I promised to make space in my schedule for her. Fortunately she changed her mind. But I don't know how long I can go on like this." He sighed. "What the heck. I'm not going to give up Schaunard." He bit his thick lower lip.

John shot a glance at Michelle, who stared at her shoes.

"I'm sorry to hear she's so hard on you," Jennifer said.

Mike shrugged. "Are you in a similar situation?"

"One way or another, we're all alike," Jennifer answered.

"I'm glad I'm not only the one," Mike said, his dark face grim. "Tell you the truth, I love Vicky very much. If she leaves me, I don't know how I'll survive. I don't want to break down, particularly now. I'm just hoping she'll hang in there with me."

"Buddy, you must sing," John said, trying to give Mike a high-five to which he failed to respond. John deplored that his colleague's situation had not improved. But what could he say? He was in the same boat. Besides, Michelle was listening.

"Courage, Mike, all right?" Jennifer said.

Mike nodded but appeared unconvinced. An awkward silence ensued. John saw Michelle's face had turned sad. Jennifer held Michelle by the waist and comforted her. Suddenly he felt chilly. He told them that he and Michelle would get a taxi and go home because she had school early tomorrow. He hailed two taxis. He and she got into one, and the rest into the other.

"My voice is tired," John said. "I can't talk too much. Don't think I'm neglecting you."

"I understand," she said. "Don't worry. Rest your voice."

John was pleasantly surprised by her reaction. The taxi drove north on Madison Avenue till 110th Street and turned to the West Side. It was already after half past ten. Inside the taxi their silence persisted. He studied Michelle. Even though she had been just an observer, she, too, seemed tired from the rehearsal, particularly after working all day. Because of that, perhaps, she appeared pensive. He believed that she now had a better understanding of how demanding his rehearsals were. Mike's comments had emphasized the typical troubles of opera singers. It had been a good idea to bring her to the rehearsal after all. He remembered her tears at the end of Act IV. He couldn't tell, though, what she was feeling about their estranged married life. Would she still leave him for a life of ease, as Mimi had chosen the Viscount Paolo? And if so, would she, too, live to regret it? He recalled Michelle's distant attitude for the past few weeks. He didn't understand what it meant. And now he had a new problem.

What should I do with Erica if Michelle withdraws her divorce action? If I return to Michelle now, it'll break Erica's heart. So maybe it would be best if Michelle presses the divorce—even if it breaks my heart. I'm ready to accept it.

≪◦ ◦≫

The Graces had been coordinating an art project with Stephanie for the concert. The idea was to hang their artwork from the ceiling as the background behind the chorus on the stage. If Arthur liked

their work for this concert, they hoped he would ask them to contribute to the New York Bel Canto Opera on a regular basis. At their
apartment, Michelle showed John her work. The canvas, four by five
feet, dominated a large part of a studio wall. It had only an outline
and underpainting in acrylics. It suggested a snow-covered café from
the outside in the evening. Inside patrons were enjoying food, drink,
and conversation under golden light. John commented he thought it
reflected an air of the Café Momus. Michelle appeared pleased.

They sat at the dining table in the living room. Michelle
made tea. He had not slept there for more than two weeks. When
he needed something, he'd come home during the daytime to avoid
her, so he had not seen her since his father's funeral. He still thought
that she was a beautiful woman. Certainly prettier and more refined
than Erica.

Unwieldy stillness enveloped them. Michelle sipped her tea
in muteness. He felt the thick air unbearable. He swallowed his tea,
which he felt had no taste. He sensed they were both waiting for their
unavoidable showdown. He mustered all his guts.

"Are you really pregnant?" he began.

Michelle did not answer. He repeated the question.

"Yes, I am," she said flatly, unafraid to meet his eyes. "My doctor told me so."

"Who is the father?"

"You, of course!" she shot back, scowling.

That sounded so beautiful. He felt a rush of joy. She was going
to bear a child for him. He felt immediately grateful to her—ecstatic.
The mother, the father, and the child—how happy their lives would
be. He imagined himself pushing a baby stroller, in which the baby

was smiling, and she walking along with them, holding his hand. He saw himself feeding the baby a bottle, following her instructions. He feared his heart might burst with elation. He wanted to hug her and shower kisses upon her. But no, not so fast.

"You were dating other men. You acknowledged that. Can you prove the baby is mine?" This wasn't what he wanted to say. How mean to say such a thing.

"I never slept with another man," she said, her eyes narrowing in anger. "I'm two months pregnant. We made love that November night. That was it."

John tried to convince himself that didn't prove he was the father. But deep down, he knew that dreamy November night had been the night of conception. It was his child. He would have been overjoyed, if only she had not filed for divorce. He clasped his palms on the table. "What are you going to do about it?"

"I don't know." She gazed at him. "Are you happy with the news, or don't you care?"

That was a good question. "I don't know. It would depend on your reaction." He bit his lips.

"Do you still love me?"

This was a dagger. He frowned and sat back in his chair. He didn't have a good answer. Erica's image appeared to him. It took several seconds before he became ready to speak again. "What kind of question is that? You initiated the divorce." This was true. He felt hot blood racing through his head.

"I thought you would say that. I'm thinking of terminating the pregnancy."

A bombshell. He never expected Michelle would consider that. He grasped his head with both his hands. *You can't do that. It's my baby, too. I want my baby. You really want to terminate? I won't allow it. No, never!* The sudden reversal from joy to rage and crushing disappointment was so extreme that he couldn't speak.

"As we stand now, it's pointless to have the baby," she said in chillness of conviction.

She was right. He pressed his lips into a tight line, but couldn't respond.

"What other choice do I have?" Her eyes began blazing.

"I don't know," he finally answered. "All I can say is the whole thing started when you filed for divorce. You have to bear the consequences." He looked up at the ceiling and pondered. "What's the purpose of the termination, may I ask?"

"To be free," she replied instantly, as if her mind had been made up for a long time.

"I see. You want the divorce to be concluded."

"If I'm not pregnant, there'll be one less problem. That's for sure." She glared down at her abdomen, twisting her hands on the table.

This was it. He was forced to the edge of a cliff. "Go ahead. Terminate it, and ask your lawyer to conclude the divorce." He had jumped off the cliff. "But in that case, I'll contest. I'll bring that fact to the court. Let's see how the judge will take the matter into consideration." His voice sounded menacing, although he didn't intend so.

"Oh, John, don't get angry. I didn't know what I was doing." For the first time, fear appeared on her face; her forehead creased and her eyes darkened.

"When you started the divorce action, I sympathized with you because I felt I was responsible for your unhappiness. I wanted you to go through the process as painlessly as possible. That's why I offered you a consented divorce, even though I didn't want the divorce at all. Now I feel you're just selfish. Why should I yield to a spoiled kid like you?" He never thought of saying the last two sentences. He wished he could retract them.

"Are you sleeping with another woman?" Her eyes flashed.

This time, it was he who couldn't answer. She repeated the question. Her woman's instinct must have sensed it. He felt there was no way to retreat. He was already tumbling down from the top of the precipice.

"Yes," he declared.

"Oh, God." Tears quickly filled her eyes.

"I had no reason to do this. You created the situation for me. Blame yourself."

"John, you're breaking my heart." She burst into sobs.

"Do you know how I felt when I received the summons for divorce? You broke *my* heart." He wanted to bawl. Was it out of self-pity or anger? Maybe both.

"I love you," Michelle wailed. "Don't you want our baby?"

"What a question. You wanted to get rid of it, didn't you? Besides, I'm sure I'm not the father. You brat!" He couldn't believe these words had leaped out of him.

It was too late. She shuddered. "John, it's your baby."

"I don't believe you." He didn't mean it. He said in his mind, *I believe you.*

"Do you still love me?"

He saw her miserable face, tear-stricken and desperate. He felt he was falling into an abyss, deeper and deeper. The air was gushing beside him. Nothing could stop his plunge.

"Want to know? I'll tell you. I don't love you anymore. It's over." He slammed the table with his fists. He started shouting. "Over! Over! Over! Finished!" *This isn't true. I still love you.*

She came to him and tried to hug him. "John, I'm sorry."

"No, no, no." He pushed her back. "Finished! It's over!" He pointed his trembling finger at her. "Now I want the divorce. You hear? I want the divorce. I'll fight to the end." He didn't know what he was saying.

He rushed to the studio. Her shriek battered his ears.

"John, forgive me, please!"

⟪◎ ◎⟫

John paced the studio. He had not intended to behave so cruelly. But his frustration of the past three months had exploded. He tramped back and forth countless times until his legs quaked. Then he lay on the convertible bed. He breathed heavily. He felt as if he had smashed at the bottom of the precipice. An image of Michelle's dejected face appeared. Even after all his words to her, he knew he still loved her. But he felt he had lost her forever. Her image was replaced by Erica's. What was he to do with Erica? Her image was replaced by Michelle's. Erica's face. Michelle's. Finally both images were swallowed into a mist.

He was awakened by a movement. He put the light on and saw Michelle standing in her nightgown. Her face was cadaverous. She was covering her abdomen with both hands.

"What's wrong?" he said.

"I'm in pain," she said.

"Where?"

"Here." She looked down at her abdomen. "It's excruciating. I'm bleeding, too."

She sank on the floor. Her face contorted.

He called 911.

The ambulance brought her to New York–Presbyterian Hospital at Columbia University.

She survived, but the baby was lost.

ACT IV

Scene 1

*F*our weeks had passed since the first rehearsal with the soloists. Stephanie and her friends grieved over Michelle's miscarriage and her subsequent separation from John, who had returned to his mother's house in Brooklyn. He had confessed all that had happened between him and Michelle, and between him and Erica. With his father's death, he was suffering a triple misfortune. But he seemed resolute to sing the opera. He never missed a rehearsal.

Henry's calm temper had been an anchor to the Dolci Quattro. Stephanie was happy to observe his radiance after his engagement to Christine. She also noticed how Jennifer had changed. Jennifer was no longer the fragile woman she used to be. She was now looking after her aunt, who was preparing to move from Florida into a two-bedroom condominium apartment she had recently purchased, several blocks from Jennifer's apartment. Jennifer informed the

Dolci Quattro that Nicole had dumped Richard. But she was determined to keep her distance from him. She was also spending a bit of time with Michelle, comforting her friend, and quietly mediating between her and John. As time passed, Stephanie learned that John had stopped seeing Erica and that John and Michelle had started talking again. It would take a long time to heal the estranged marriage. But they appeared to have begun working it out. Jennifer's discreet devotion to them was bearing fruit. Stephanie admired Jennifer's transformation.

As for herself, Stephanie was glad that she and her father were getting along well these days. Although it made her nervous, she was looking forward to meeting his family after the concert. The past strain between them had been washed away as they focused on forgiveness and reunion. About Arthur, however, she felt conflicted. She knew well that he was married and that Claudia was a sweet wife. She had no right to disturb their marriage. Nevertheless, she could not suppress her deepening attraction to him. She had kept her intimate relationship with Glenn, but due to the intense rehearsal schedule, they had been spending nights together less frequently.

In the meantime, Bruce had been calling her often lately. He would ask how she was doing with the opera, or if she wanted a nice wool sweater he found at Saks Fifth Avenue. He even suggested they get back together. Her heart warmed up. Although he might be a spoiled, rich kid, she had known him for a long time as a good man in his heart. These days probably he had been pushing himself too hard to surpass Henry, which may have driven him to behave so aggressively. Once the performance was over, he might return to a caring man. She would be happy with him again. Then she would be able to work together with Arthur in a perfect business partnership. She could become a close friend to Claudia, too. That would be ideal. But only if Bruce broke with Irene.

◆◆◆

For four weeks the rehearsals had proceeded in an orderly manner, which pleased Stephanie as the general manager. The soloists had gone through Acts I, III, and IV with the piano. The chorus had sung Act II with the soloists and the piano. The orchestra had played the entire opera alone. Last Tuesday, the soloists had sung Acts I, III, and IV with the orchestra. This afternoon, Thursday, the soloists, chorus, and orchestra were to go over Act II together. The understudies would also attend rehearsals from this week onward.

Stephanie barely managed to position everybody on the crowded stage, which held a podium for the conductor at the down-stage center, several soloists in the front line, a thirty-piece orchestra in the middle, and the fifty-member chorus at the upstage. Now the place looked like a real, midsize concert hall, at least on the stage. Stephanie saw the understudies in the audience, clustered around Bruce and Irene. Claudia also sat there to show her support for Arthur.

Ready to begin the rehearsal, Stephanie realized that Mike had not shown up yet. She asked Glenn to sing Schaunard until Mike arrived. Glenn eagerly jumped up to the stage. He winked at her as he took the chair for Mike. She blinked her eyes a few times and looked the other way. She took her place and nodded to the maestro on the podium.

Arthur opened the music score, held his baton aloft, and addressed all on the stage.

"As a warm-up, let's sing from 'Song of the *Bohème*.' For the orchestra, sixteen bars before the rehearsal number thirty-four. Chorus, show us all you've got." He surveyed all performers. "Are you ready? Go."

So the rehearsal had begun. The latter half of Act II involved two choruses: one for the apartment tenants upstairs and the other for the bohemian friends downstairs in the courtyard, in addition to several soloists and the orchestra. This created occasional chaotic moments, requiring corrections and repeats. Arthur navigated the company with a cool temperament.

More than half an hour later, Mike arrived. Stephanie observed that he was limping. He had a bandage on the right side of his head, and his face appeared swollen. Carrying the music inconveniently in his left hand, he mounted the stage as the rehearsal continued. At the end of the scene, Arthur raised both hands to halt the rehearsal. Mike apologized for being late and said that he had had an accident. Choristers uttered concerned murmurs. Arthur asked if he could sing.

"Definitely." Mike staggered to Glenn's place and nodded politely.

Glenn withdrew from the stage, snapping his score from the music stand. Mike put his music on the stand in a clumsy manner, seemingly protecting his right arm. Stephanie saw all understudies cheering Glenn as he returned to the audience.

"All right," Arthur said. "Let's go over the finale again. For the orchestra, from seventeen bars before the rehearsal number fifty-three. Schaunard's line '*Ahi! fiera scadenza del quindici april!*' ('Ah! merciless expiration date of April fifteenth!')"

Kate immediately told the soloists and the choristers the page number of the chorus score, which was different from the orchestra score. They found the indicated page of their music.

"Mike, are you ready?" Arthur eyed him closely.

Mike flipped the score furiously. "Here it is. I'm ready."

"Oboe, give him C," Arthur said. The oboist played a C. "OK, from the pickup. '*Ahi!*'"

Arthur gave the cue, and Mike started singing Schaunard's line, soon joined by the chorus of the tenants upstairs, and later followed by the chorus of the bohemians downstairs. Musette, Marcello, and Rodolfo sang their parts. Stephanie immediately knew that Mike was not up to singing. His voice was weak, and his singing was tentative, lacking vigor. By contrast, the two choruses sang the finale exchange of fighting yells enthusiastically, as if they were at war. Mike barely managed to complete his part.

Arthur threw him a sharp look. Mike mumbled the excuse that he had not been warmed up. He was now fine, he claimed. To give him another chance, Arthur said that he would run through the entire Act II from the beginning. He pointed to the tenor who would sing Durand. The tenor eagerly stood up, clutching his score. The business coordinator of the orchestra stepped in and suggested a fifteen-minute break. Since this was a union regulation, Arthur had to comply. Stephanie announced the break, and people dispersed from the stage. Some went to the restrooms, while other sat in the audience and sipped water or ate snacks.

Stephanie brought Mike to a corner, along with the Dolci Quattro. Mike explained that two days before, after the rehearsal, he had gone back to his apartment. Vicky was not there. Her belongings were gone, too. He found her note on the table. It said that she was leaving and asked him not to search for her. He had a sleepless night. Yesterday he hadn't gone to work, staying home and waiting for her. Not even a telephone call. As evening came he was convinced that she had really left him. The humiliation he felt was unbearable. He went out and stopped at a pub, where he drank too much. When he came out he could barely walk straight. He stumbled off the sidewalk and ran into a car. He'd hit it hard with his whole right side, starting with his head. Fortunately, since the car was moving slowly to find a parking space, his injury was not fatal.

The Dolci Quattro murmured sighs. Stephanie examined his face. His right eye was swollen, hidden by his dark complexion. The bandage on his head was crusted with desiccated blood. He twisted his face in pain whenever he moved his right hand. Since Glenn appeared eager to snap up Schaunard's role, she asked if Mike was going to withdraw. Mike shook his head again. He would try his best. He dried his eyes with the back of his good hand.

Stephanie checked her watch. They returned to the stage. The concertmaster gave a sign, and the orchestra members retuned their instruments. Arthur tapped his baton on the lectern.

"OK. From the beginning of Act II," he said, looking at the orchestra. "The tempo is *andantino mosso*. Watch my baton. Are you ready?"

At Arthur's cue, the orchestra began the introduction of Act II, soon followed by Durand. Then Stephanie and Henry took the lead as Musette and Marcello, joined next by Mike as Schaunard. John came in as Rodolfo, followed by Jennifer as Mimi and a baritone as Viscount Paolo. There were many singing exchanges among them. All sang well but one. It was obvious that Mike was in terrible shape and was struggling to sing. Stephanie felt pity for the poor, floundering baritone.

Mike appeared to concede his failure. Even before they reached "Song of the *Bohème*," he weakly waved his hand to Glenn to cover him. Glenn hopped onto the stage and picked up the role of Schaunard as soon as Mike ceased singing. Mike dragged his feet as he left the stage to sit in the audience. The rehearsal continued without interruption.

Act II was a lively act with few quiet moments. All of the performers required deep concentration. Arthur conducted busily. The run-though took more than an hour, with some corrections and repeats. When they finished, it was about five o'clock.

"Excellent," Arthur said, wiping his forehead with a towel. "Thank you all. See you one week from today for the dress rehearsal. We're getting close."

"Just in case, chorus," Stephanie called. "Dress rehearsal doesn't mean you have to wear the concert attire. Come with your regular clothes."

"We know that," one of choristers yelled.

The choristers chattered and laughed as they dispersed from the stage.

Arthur came down from the podium and addressed the soloists. "You've worked hard for the past four weeks. After this, you have one week until the dress rehearsal. I intentionally arranged the rehearsal schedule this way. Rest your voices, and get ready physically and mentally for the dress rehearsal and the three performances. I'll see you then."

Everyone left the stage. When Stephanie came down, she saw Mike crying. She signaled the other Dolci Quattro to join her. As they surrounded Mike, Bruce and Irene sidled over.

"Glenn did a great job," Bruce said. "Like him, I'm ready for Marcello." He inclined his head at Henry. Stephanie detected a hint of envy.

"Jennifer, as usual, you were gorgeous," Irene said, exaggerating the word *gorgeous*. "I'm sure you won't need me." She gave Jennifer a sweet smile. Stephanie imagined behind her reddened lips Irene wore little pointy fangs.

"Stop, guys," Stephanie said, cutting between them and the primary singers. "As I've told you before, I don't want any rivalry in this company. The understudies are supposed to be supportive to the primaries."

"That's exactly what we're doing," Bruce said with a grin. "Take it easy, Henry. I'll cover you anytime." Then he softened his tone. "Seriously, Henry, I wish you good luck." He extended his hand with a smile to Henry, who dubiously shook it.

"I'm absolutely certain Jennifer will give an outstanding performance. My best wishes, OK?" Irene said, winking at Jennifer.

"Guys, you should go," Stephanie said tightly.

They left. Stephanie saw Henry watching them coldly as they exited the hall. She exhaled. While she recognized the familiar menace in Irene, she sensed a little difference in Bruce. His hawkishness was somehow mellowing. Not completely yet, but she could certainly detect the trend. She could not fathom what might have triggered this change in him.

"Mike," Stephanie said, "you heard it from Arthur. One week from today is the dress rehearsal. Two days later, the first performance. You can't quit now."

Mike wept bitterly without a word. Tears gleamed on his dark face.

"As I've been saying to you," John said, "we go through this kind of difficulty. But we try to overcome our pain, and we sing. It's not easy. But this is our life."

"I know, but I can't help it," Mike blurted, shaking his head. "Without Vicky, I can't sing. We've lived happily together for five years. Now this. You don't understand how much it hurts. I just can't take it." He sobbed aloud, his big athletic body swelling and contracting violently.

"Mike, look at me," John said. "You know I'm in the midst of a divorce. The situation is worse than you may think. Recently my wife lost our baby, we were separated, and my father died. Believe me, I *do* know how much it hurts. But I'm still singing."

"Me, too," Jennifer chimed in. "A few months ago my fiancé broke our engagement. He's had fun with two girlfriends already after me. But I'm still singing."

Henry added, "I've been under pressure from my family to quit my life here and take a stable teaching job. But I've decided to continue my opera career. Don't think you're alone."

"And I've had to make peace with my father," Stephanie said. "Until recently we had barely spoken for years because I blamed him for my mother's death."

"Really?" Mike clumsily rubbed his wet eyes with his palm as he gazed back and forth at the Dolci Quattro one by one. "That's intense. I feel I'm a damn fool."

"Don't say that," John said. "It's a natural reaction. But try to overcome your grief if you want Schaunard's role. It would be a pity if you lose it to Glenn. This is your chance for some real recognition. So fight and sing."

◖◉ ◎◗

The performance was only one week away. Stephanie made sure all publicity activities were in order: newspaper and radio advertisements, invitations to critics, and more. Then she checked the box office at the Society. Ticket sales were going extremely well. Since the Society Hall was a midsize venue, this was not like selling out Carnegie Hall. But for a second-tier opera company like theirs, the brisk early sales could be considered excellent. She reported to Arthur, who hugged her in childlike delight.

Arthur briefed her on the progress of the endowment at the Italian Cultural Society. Mr. Zappia had managed to squeeze two million dollars from its operational budget. The donations and pledges were pouring in, totaling about one and a half million. Pleased, her father had donated an additional two million, bringing the total to exceed ten million dollars. Ambassador Biondi had managed to persuade the Italian government to authorize a generous grant to the endowment, so the formal approval of the endowment at the Society's annual meeting appeared a certainty. This was all because of her father, Arthur said. He kissed her cheek. She felt grateful to her father. He was closely following up his initiative to help her opera career. Because of it, Arthur seemed to be opening up his heart. His attitude toward her was growing more personal.

Stephanie and Arthur were pleased to find that the Italian mission to the United Nations had bought many tickets and was distributing them among the UN's diplomatic circles. At the same time, the French mission appeared eager to promote the fact that a French writer had written the original novel, based on which two Italians had composed two versions of the opera *La Bohème*. The French mission had also purchased many tickets and was giving them away.

On the Sunday prior to the first performance, Stephanie checked the Arts and Leisure section of the *New York Times*. It showed the announcement of Leoncavallo's *La Bohème* by the New York Bel Canto Opera with the three performance dates. She called Jennifer.

"Have you seen our ad in the *Times*?"

"Yes, doesn't it look magnificent?" Jennifer said.

"Next Saturday," Stephanie cried. "It's really coming."

"I'm ready."

"I'm glad you are. Me, too. This general manager thing kept me really busy, but somehow it made me more alert than ever. So I'm in my best condition now." She changed her tone. "How is the harassment?"

"The nasty e-mails have stopped since Henry's intervention. But the anonymous letters are out of my control. A few days ago I received another one. I don't open them, but this one smelled like it contained the droppings of a mouse or something. Just disgusting. I've gotten three of so far. They really unnerve me. I don't know how long I can stand this before I call the police or something."

"Hang on, sweetie. If you show signs of strain now, it'll only encourage the sender, and she'll send more to break you down once for all. You must be tough, OK?"

"I know. I'm trying. And I know who you mean by 'she.' But we mustn't accuse her without evidence. Otherwise, she could sue me for slander or something."

"I understand," Stephanie said. "I loathe this kind of ploy. But somehow, whoever is doing this must be stopped." She reminded herself that she had to maintain her impartiality as the general manager. Irene was not guilty unless proven otherwise.

"The other thing that concerns me is Mike," Jennifer said. "Last Thursday he was really in dreadful shape. I think John is the best person to speak to him. Both are baritones, and John understands Mike's pain. Mike seems a strong man. What he needs now is our moral support."

"You're right. Let me call John and ask him to check on Mike."

《◎ ◎》

On the day of the dress rehearsal, Stephanie arrived at the Society Hall half an hour early. She had two things to check before the rehearsal. The first was the subtitle projection system. Since the opera was not well known, Arthur had insisted that English subtitles be provided to the audience. The technicians informed her that the system was set to go. The second thing was the Graces' artwork. The art objects had been raised on steel cables and hung from the grids atop the fly loft above the stage, covering the back wall. Stephanie went to the last row of the audience and found Arthur and Claudia there, also observing the stage. At the top of the proscenium arch, a horizontal screen was secured.

"The screen is less distracting than I thought," Arthur said, pointing. "Watch. Some test messages will appear."

A message flashed on the screen from the left corner and streamed to the right: "Welcome, ladies and gentlemen. This is a test. Can you read me? The English subtitle of the libretto will appear here..." The words were clear even from the last row, and the moderate speed of the word movement would allow the audience to read the content.

"That'll do," Arthur said. He gave a thumbs-up to the technicians.

"It's easy to see," she said. "The audience will appreciate it."

Now Stephanie paid attention to the artwork. Flying at upstage-right was Michelle's acrylic painting of the Café Momus exterior in an Impressionist style; at the left hung Helen's abstract painting of the garret interior. Sarah's watercolor snowflakes, stars, and moon glowed over and between the two paintings. The Graces surrounded Stephanie, Arthur, and Claudia. John stood next to Michelle. They did not appear quite an intimate couple yet, as he kept one step distant from her. But at least they were together. Helen asked what they thought.

"Cool," Stephanie said. "They certainly create an ambience of *La Bohème*."

Arthur and Claudia complimented them, too. The Graces whooped in joy. An idea sparked in Stephanie's head. The art objects looked captivating as they were, under the general stage lights. On top of that, she thought, in Acts I and II, Michelle's Café Momus painting could be highlighted by spotlights; in Acts III and IV, Helen's garret painting; and Sarah's snowflakes, stars, and moon would sparkle as the spotlights moved. This would add visual variety to the static concert setting. The Graces welcomed the idea.

Stephanie and Arthur returned to the stage. She gave instructions to the lighting technicians for the art objects. The spotlighting would be tested during the run-through. The Graces and Claudia settled in the audience seats. Stephanie saw Jennifer hugging Michelle. They were very close these days. As Jennifer left for the stage, John gently waved to his wife. Stephanie saw Michelle's mouth forming, "Good luck." He grinned at her and took his place onstage. Henry arrived, ushering Christine. She was gazing around the hall, her eyes wide open and her mouth forming a pretty "O". This must have been her first time to come to a dress rehearsal or to see her sister's artwork in place. She greeted the artists and sat next to Michelle.

As before, the understudies clustered around Bruce and Irene in the audience. Stephanie noticed Glenn nervously scanning the hall. Soon Mike arrived. He was still limping, but he looked much livelier. Stephanie was pleased; he must have been heartened by John's talk. Mike cheerfully greeted the soloists and climbed up to the stage. Glenn bit his lip and clenched his fist on his lap.

At Stephanie's sign, all orchestra members, soloists, and choristers took their seats on the stage. She thanked everyone for their hard work during the past weeks. Then she inclined her head to the maestro. Arthur climbed up to the podium.

"The entire opera takes about two hours and fifteen minutes," he said, "and today we have four hours, including two fifteen-minute breaks. First I'd like to go over Act II from 'Song of the *Bohème*' to the end of the act, which is the most chaotic part of the opera. Then we'll run through the opera from the beginning to the end. As I expect some corrections and repeats, this'll take care of three hours and thirty minutes. We cannot waste any time. Bear with me. All right?"

On Arthur's cue, the orchestra played and the chorus sang with enthusiasm, following Arthur's decisive baton movements. The rehearsal was trouble-free for about fifteen minutes, until Schaunard's aria "L'influenza del blue sulle arti" ("The influence of blue on the arts"). After the low D unison by the orchestra, Kate played the low C-sharp and D together on the piano, which created a strange sound, followed by a scale. Arthur gave a cue to Mike.

"*Oh! Questo Re sempre falso!*" ("Oh, this D is simply out of tune!") Mike spoke comically as Schaunard.

Some choristers laughed, because the piano really sounded out of tune. Kate went on. After the pristine piano introduction, Mike started singing Schaunard's aria.

"*Alza l'occhio celeste la bella al ciel turchino*" ("The beautiful maiden lifts her light blue eyes to the deep blue sky").

Mike sang flawlessly. His romantic aria about blue was complemented by the chorus, singing "*Azzurra*" ("Azure") and "*Turchin*" ("Deep blue") in thirty-second notes. Arthur raised both hands. All stopped and looked at him.

"Schaunard is singing very well. Thank you, Mike." Arthur grinned at him.

Stephanie saw Mike brighten. He cocked his head toward John and chuckled. John threw a big thumbs-up. Glenn was staring at his lap, his lips tightly pursed.

"Chorus." Arthur frowned. "You're sliding here. That spoils the aria. I've explained this part to you before. This aria is supposed to be a parody of Rossini's Bel Canto style. I want thirty-second notes detached, like Azzuuuu, uuuu, uuuurra…Turchiiii, iiii, iiiin." Arthur spat the detached sounds like a machine gun, demonstrating what he wanted. "Many of Rossini's operas are like this. You may have heard this kind of singing by coloratura sopranos and lyric tenors. It's not easy for a baritone to do this. But Mike did excellently. Like him, try to exaggerate the detaching, and don't slide. No 'h' sound either, like 'huhuhuhu' or 'hihihihi.' Don't do that, or you'll sound like a bunch of amateurs."

The choristers laughed. Some practiced "Azzuuuu, uuuu, uuuurra…Turchiiii, iiii, iiiin," forcefully disconnecting the thirty-second notes. The orchestra members giggled.

"All right. Let's try again. From one bar before Schaunard's aria."

Arthur beat the baton in a slow tempo of two. After the piano scale, Mike began. His strong voice projected through the hall. With confidence, agility, and concentration, he sang his aria beautifully in Bel Canto style. This time, the chorus sang their part to Arthur's satisfaction. The chaotic section of Act II was completed. All soloists, choristers, and orchestra members seemed to feel more secure.

"Let's do the run-through," Arthur said, turning the pages of the score to the beginning.

At his cue, the run-through began. Murmurs came from the audience. Stephanie looked back. Three spotlights were highlighting Michelle's painting. It accented the stage background. She faced back to the audience and gave an "OK" sign. The Graces returned their waving in joy.

So the dress rehearsal went on.

Suddenly, during the first break after Act I, Stephanie heard the cry of a woman backstage, followed by a few dull noises. Everybody turned their heads toward the direction of the cry and froze. Stephanie rushed over, joined by a few stagehands. Their footsteps bustled noisily. They found Jennifer on the floor, moaning in pain under a fallen followspot, a movable lighting fixture used to follow a moving performer. Stephanie, with help from the stagehands, brought the followspot upright. The light had struck Jennifer's right leg. Stephanie saw somebody scurrying away behind a curtain. Or was it just a draft curling the fabric? Jennifer leaned on Stephanie and got up, her face distorting in pain. Her leg was not bleeding, but it was bruised. She also seemed to have twisted her left arm in the fall. It was bruised, too. In addition to the physical pain, Jennifer's face also showed a deep fear, presumably that this mishap would put her out of commission for the performance. But also, Stephanie thought, Jennifer might be feeling terrified that someone would intentionally sabotage her this way. Was someone out to actually hurt her friend?

Stephanie asked Jennifer if she'd seen anyone pushing the followspot. Jennifer shook her head. She had been returning to the stage from the ladies' room through the backstage. Then out of blue the light had fallen on her. Fortunately the followspot was not a heavy piece of equipment, and it was simply standing on the backstage floor. If it had been heavy equipment, or if it had dropped from above, it would have seriously impaired her. *Poor Jennifer,* Stephanie thought.

Losing Richard, the malicious e-mails, the harassment letters, and now this—how much could one woman take? Jennifer was putting up a fierce fight; but Stephanie knew she still remained fragile.

Stephanie blew her whistle several times, which shrieked in the concert hall. She asked people to return to their posts immediately. Soloists, orchestra members, and choristers came back to their seats on the stage, while understudies, the Graces, and other friends sat in the audience. Stephanie explained what had happened. A loud commotion erupted.

Arthur hurried to Jennifer, followed by Stephanie, Henry, and John.

"How do you feel?" Arthur asked. "Can you sing?"

"My leg and arm really hurt," Jennifer replied weakly. "I'm not sure I can. I don't want to push myself too hard and damage my vocal cords."

"I'm sorry for this, but glad that at least you're not seriously injured. Otherwise, it would have been a disaster. I don't want to lose my Mimi." Arthur gently patted Jennifer's shoulder. "Maybe you should rest for a while."

Henry and John, too, expressed their concern, agreeing to Arthur's suggestion.

Stephanie faced the people on the stage and said, "Did any of you do this by accident?" She turned to the audience. "Did anyone see someone pushing the followspot?" She turned back to the people on the stage. "Has anyone observed anything suspicious?" She faced the audience again. "I thought I saw someone running away. Come forward. Don't be a coward."

No response.

She observed Irene in the audience; she appeared nonchalant, as if the incident did not concern her a bit. She was studying the score, or pretending to. In contrast, next to her, Bruce was intently— and sympathetically—watching Jennifer, sometimes shaking his head. He even eyed Stephanie a few times as if he wanted to tell her something.

"If no one comes forward," she went on, "we will have to interrupt the rehearsal and investigate the incident."

Silence.

"Oh no," Arthur muttered, coming back to the podium. "We don't have that kind of time," he announced. "This is our dress rehearsal, the only chance we get." He paused. "Maybe we can interrupt the rehearsal, investigate the incident, resume the rehearsal, and pay the overtime to the orchestra."

Immediately some orchestra members objected, saying that they had another commitment right after this rehearsal. Since this was a unionized freelance orchestra, Arthur seemed to have no choice but to complete the rehearsal as originally scheduled. He anxiously looked at his wristwatch. The break time was already over. He had to resume the rehearsal one way or the other. In resignation he gestured Irene to come to the stage.

Irene quickly skipped up to the stage. Standing before Jennifer, she said, "Are you all right? I hope you'll get well soon."

Could Irene have tried to injure Jennifer so she could sing Mimi? Stephanie felt suspicious, but couldn't read anything from Irene's expression other than her predictable pleasure at getting a change to sing.

The clock was ticking. Arthur spoke kindly. "Jennifer, please go to the audience and rest. Let Irene sing Mimi for now. When you regain the strength to sing, please let me know."

Irene advanced with a triumphant smile, but Jennifer remained seated. Then she cocked her face and stared at Irene, an intense glowering. Irene immediately looked down at the floor, though she remained standing in defiance, just a step from Jennifer. Everyone's eyes froze on the primary Mimi and her understudy. Stephanie feared a physical fight would break out between them. She imagined chairs and music stands flying, like in a bar brawl. Surely she would defend Jennifer and throw a good punch at Irene. *Enough of your attitude, you bitch!* If only she could prove Irene had done it. Unfortunately that was not the case. She had to maintain her impartiality as the general manager, an impossible task. She helplessly watched the two Mimis, as their silent confrontation continued—until Michelle rushed from the audience onto the stage and cut between Jennifer and Irene.

Michelle stood facing Irene, holding her hands wide behind her as if protecting Jennifer. Irene backed off a step. Glaring fiercely at Irene, Michelle slapped her face with full force. The noise was so loud that Stephanie thought everyone in the hall must have heard it.

"You bitch! Stop this nonsense!" Michelle yelled. "I saw you ducking behind the curtain a moment after Jennifer fell. I was coming back from the ladies' room through the backstage. I didn't know what it meant at the time, but now I understand. You pushed the spotlight, didn't you? Be honest."

The onlookers erupted in shrieks and gasps as Jennifer's eye widened.

Irene's cheeks turned visibly red, but she composed herself. "I don't know what you're talking about." She gestured toward the audience. "Did anyone see me push the followspot?" No response. She sneered at Michelle. "See? There are no witnesses. Even *you* didn't see it."

"I can't take this anymore!" Bruce leaped up from his seat in the audience and bounded to the stage, where he stood next to Michelle. "I know Irene did it, because she told me so," he announced firmly, pointing his finger at her.

A loud commotion of voices and shouts filled the hall.

"You traitor!" Irene brayed, balling her fist to strike Bruce's face.

Bruce intercepted her punch and gripped her wrist. "I don't care, you brat!" he said, his voice low. "Are you in high school? Sending malicious e-mails and disgusting letters to Jennifer—and now this. Shame on you!" He wagged his finger like an angry parent. "This is not professional."

Arthur approached Irene, his lips a tight white line, and stared at her sternly. "Did you do it?"

Irene looked down at the floor, pursing her lips.

Arthur repeated his question. Irene made no response. "Out!" yelled Arthur. He motioned to the exit. "You're fired! Get out of here immediately!"

Stephanie felt stunned, as clearly did everyone else, to hear such strong words from Arthur. She doubted anyone present had heard him so much as raise his voice in anger. Irene emitted a furious squeak, ran from the stage, and disappeared through the exit door.

A long silence permeated the hall. Jennifer wept silently.

"I'm so sorry, Jennifer." Bruce broke the heavy quiet. "I should have come forward much sooner. Irene's little tricks were so childish that I thought she would get bored and stop. I never dreamed she was capable of actually hurting anyone. Please forgive me."

"I'm glad she got what she deserved," Michelle said, pronouncing "she" contemptuously, as if it were not worth mentioning the name.

"Thank you, Bruce and Michelle," said Jennifer, faintly smiling at them.

John joined Michelle and patted her shoulder with affection and pride. Stephanie, too, admired Michelle's courage for coming forward. She was also happy for Bruce. This was the Bruce she had known for a long time—until he had begun dating *her*.

"Whew!" Arthur exclaimed. "I've never experienced this kind of she-devil act." He wiped his forehead with his palm. He looked at his watch. "Oh my God, we must resume the rehearsal." He pondered for a moment. "All right, I'll sing Mimi's part. This way, we can move on."

Jennifer spoke calmly, "I'll do it, if you don't mind if I sing sitting down. I'm not really injured—but my arm and leg hurt. I may not be able to sing in full voice, but at least you can continue the rehearsal. Let's not waste our time. Please resume."

"Are you sure?" Arthur asked.

"Yes," Jennifer replied firmly.

"I really appreciate it. Singing in a sitting position isn't really a problem at all. Let's do it."

The choristers applauded Jennifer as Arthur returned to the podium. Michelle and Bruce went back to the audience. Jennifer faced Arthur, straightening her posture on her chair.

"Folks," Arthur said, turning to all the performers, "we've lost some precious time. We need to catch up. Bear with me, OK?" He took his baton. "The opening of Act II."

The rehearsal resumed. Shaken, Jennifer bravely sang, even though her musical execution was not her best. Stephanie watched her carefully for signs of fatigue, but she seemed determined to sing on.

Now that the crisis was over, Stephanie needed to turn her attention to her own singing. Serving as the general manager was one thing, but she also had to perform her role. The opera was a daunting challenge. Musette had intensive arias and ensembles in first three acts. Even the last act required an emotional focus. She recalled Mr. Carré's advice: Maintain your stamina evenly. That was exactly what she did. Because of that, she survived the first two acts.

During the second break after Act II, Stephanie, Henry, John, Michelle, and Mike surrounded Jennifer, who assured them that she could handle the rest. They praised her courage.

Bruce returned to apologize to Jennifer again. He also asked forgiveness of Henry for the insolence he had shown. Stephanie nodded her approval as Jennifer and Henry appeared moved by his humble repentance. Bruce offered his hand for peace, and Jennifer and Henry shook it thoughtfully. John and Michelle, too, shook his hand.

Lastly he turned to Stephanie and begged her pardon for his desertion to Irene. Stephanie felt her heart warm, and she too shook his hand. A little awkward remained, but at least this appeared to her as the beginning of a reconciliation between Bruce and the Dolci Quattro and their friends. She felt a joyous energy arising inside her.

The rehearsal moved on to Act III, the most demanding act for Musette. Stephanie sang her heartbreaking showcase aria "Addio" ("Farewell") with total concentration.

"*Marcello mio, non stare ad aspettarmi! Esco, ne so se ritornar potrò.*" ("My Marcello, do not keep waiting for me. I am going out. I do not know if I can return.")

She finished, satisfied that her mezzo-soprano voice had projected well and her singing held grace and passion, expressing her torment at leaving her lover. After this aria, she sang a duet with Mimi, then another with Marcello, both of which she had studied with Mr. Carré and the Dolci Quattro. She felt secure and upbeat, enjoying being Musette, in spite of the tragic scene. She saw Arthur smiling at her as she sang, which energized her further.

❦

"Thank you all. We had a good dress rehearsal. See you on Saturday," Arthur said as he concluded the rehearsal. Then he turned to Mimi. "Thank you again, Jennifer. You've saved us from a disaster. How do you feel?"

"I'm fine," she answered, sipping water.

"Super. Now go home and have a good rest."

Choristers applauded again.

Stephanie spoke about the logistics on Saturday, such as the call time, dress code, makeshift dressing rooms, and waiting rooms. The chorus would be on the stage from the beginning. In Act I they would just listen, and in Act II they would sing. Then there would be an intermission of fifteen minutes, during which the chairs for the chorus would be removed from the stage. In Acts III and IV, soloists and orchestra would perform. By ten o'clock, the opera should be over.

Stephanie also reported on the ticket sales. The first performance was nearly sold out, but there were still many empty seats left for the second and third performances. She asked choristers to invite their friends and family members.

Arthur turned to the audience and asked how the subtitles and spotlights had looked. The understudies, the Graces, Christine, and Claudia all responded enthusiastically. Arthur nodded in satisfaction. Then he faced Bruce and his comrades.

"Understudies," he said, "thanks for your patience. You never know when your time will come. Last week we had a situation. Today it was close. Something like that could happen anytime. During the performances, you won't have to be here. But be on call and stay alert."

"You can count on us," Bruce shouted, but in a friendly tone.

The other understudies chorused their agreement. Particularly Glenn waved fiercely.

Stephanie thanked all on the stage for their cooperation and dismissed them. They dispersed, sighing and chattering in relief after the four-hour rehearsal.

She went down to the audience, where she found Mike talking to the other Dolci Quattro. Michelle stood next to John, and Christine with Henry. Mike assured Stephanie that he was back to normal as far as his singing was concerned. By the time of the real performance, he should have much more physical strength. All congratulated him. Then their concern turned to Jennifer. She admitted that her arm and leg still hurt. Otherwise, she was all right. For the concert she was going to wear a long-sleeved gown, so the bruises would not be noticeable.

"I'll escort you home," Michelle said. "I want to make sure you safely arrive there."

"That's a good idea," John said. "I'll go with you."

"Thank you both," Jennifer replied. "You're very kind."

Forgetting about her bruises, Jennifer seemed to be pleased that Michelle and John were doing something together of their own accord. Stephanie, too, gave them approving nods, thinking that it was an excellent idea, not only for Jennifer, but also for Michelle and John.

"I'll join you," Henry said. "I want to check your mailbox and the inbox on your computer—though no harmful letters should be waiting for you." Christine held Henry's waist, resolute to go with him.

"Thank you, Henry," Jennifer said. Then she faced all the friends. "And I appreciate your concerns. Tonight I'll take a long, hot bath and massage the bruised muscles. I have two full days to recover. I should be fine by the performance." Her tone brightened. "It's been a long road. But we're finally here!"

"Can you believe it?" said Henry. "I grew up as a professional opera singer while I studied this opera. I feel more matured." He held Christine, who rested her head on his shoulder.

"I barely got through," John said, and grimaced at Michelle, who nodded.

"I learned how to be a professional opera singer," Mike added.

"We've done all we could," Stephanie said. "Now rest well, and I'll see you on Saturday." Then she held up a hand. "But wait! Before you go, we need our battle cry. Mike, watch. Someday we hope you'll join us."

The Dolci Quattro gathered in a circle. They presented their right hands forward, their palms stacked one on top of the other.

"Sing on!"

Stephanie felt reassured and secure. She saw the other Dolci Quattro appearing to feel the same. Mike grinned as if longing for the day he would join the group. Gathering their belongings, they walked to the exit. She returned to the stage, where Arthur was talking to the concertmaster and the business coordinator of the orchestra. Claudia stood next to him.

"Is Jennifer all right?" Arthur asked as Stephanie approached.

"She seems to be managing," she said. "They're going to escort her home."

"Good," Arthur said. "This really scared me. Let's hope for the best." He paused. "Just in case, I'll find another understudy for Mimi. I know a soprano who has already sung this role."

Stephanie thanked him.

The concertmaster and the business coordinator shook Arthur's hand.

"Yes, we're all set," Arthur said. "We'll see how the performance will go."

Stephanie nodded. "We shall see indeed."

She gazed around the hall, which was empty now except for them. Although exhausted after the four-hour dress rehearsal, she felt an indescribable excitement. The performance would begin in two days.

At last.

Scene 2

$\mathcal{T}$he day of the first performance was unceremoni-
ously disrupted.

Stephanie had taken the day off from the Café Momus and
from singing in the morning service at her synagogue. She stayed
in bed longer than usual. Well rested, she had a late breakfast and
studied Musette's lines for the last time. After lunch she did physical
exercises, then took a shower. She felt full of energy and in her best
condition. She cheerfully answered the phone when it rang. Mike was
calling from Cancun, Mexico. His voice was agitated on top of the
blurred noise of international call. She listened to his long narration.

Vicky had been depressed by their separation. To cheer herself
up, she'd taken a vacation in Cancun. She had flown there from New
York without a hotel reservation, presuming that she would find
accommodation easily, as it was off-season. At Cancun International

Airport, she was mugged. Stolen were all her valuables and identification, including cash, credit cards, passport, driver's license, and return air ticket. She reported the theft to the police. They expressed their sympathy, but since she did not have a hotel reservation or any identification, they were a little skeptical of her story. Nonetheless, since she was American, they offered to let her stay at the police station as a guest if she wished. She took their offer, for she did not want to sleep on a street in a foreign country. She had called Mike, who talked to the officers. After a long discussion, the police suggested he come there to vouch for her in person. It pained him to realize that their Cancun vacation, which he had cancelled, had represented such a sentimental dream to her. He felt obliged to go there to take her home. On Friday morning, he had flown to Cancun. She was released. But he would have to stay there until she received a new passport from the United States Consulate General. There was no possibility he could be in New York today.

For an opera singer, not showing up for a performance was a cardinal sin, unless the cause was illness or a force majeure. Mike's case would be considered personal. His career would be over. This was the harsh reality of the opera world. Mike told Stephanie that he was well aware of the situation he was in. He had weighed the choice between his performance and Vicky and chosen her. He just couldn't leave her in the police station, even though her stay was voluntary. He had no regret, he said. Stephanie wished Mike a safe return with Vicky.

She called Arthur and explained the situation. He groaned. He asked her to contact Glenn.

"Bingo!" Glenn shouted at the news. "Hey, babe, you hit a jackpot for me."

"This isn't my doing," she answered, slightly put off by his comment. "Do you think you can manage?"

"I had a hunch," he said. "So yesterday I worked with my coach and sang Schaunard for the entire opera. Today I've been reviewing the score. All I need now is a good warm-up."

"I'm glad you're up to it. Do you have the tail and the white tie?"

"Yeah, they're right here. I wouldn't miss this opportunity." He paused for a breath. She could hear him inhaling and exhaling. "Tell you the truth, if this were a fully staged version of the opera, I would be scared, because I would have to sing entirely from my memory. But fortunately this is a concert version. I can use the score. So don't worry, I can handle it."

Stephanie reported back to Arthur. At least the worst had been avoided, it seemed. But there still remained a risk. Hopefully Glenn would sing satisfactorily. The telephone clanged again. Her heart sprang. She feared that something might have happened to Glenn. He couldn't sing after all? That would be a catastrophe. She cautiously answered the phone. It was Bruce. She sighed in relief. He sounded like he was in a good mood. He chatted for a while, then paused.

"What's the matter?" she asked.

"Oh, nothing," he replied quietly. "I just wanted to wish you good luck. Once the performances are over, I'd like to take you to dinner. We have a lot to talk about. I miss you."

His warm tone touched her. "Thanks for exposing Irene. I'm really proud of you. Those nasty tricks of hers caused Jennifer a lot of additional pain during a tough time in her life—and that last one, she may have been seriously hurt."

"I know. I realized that it was more important to me to be a good friend to the Dolci Quattro than to cover for Irene. I want you to know that I broke it off with her immediately and haven't seen her since. I heard she left town."

This was all good news, particularly on the first performance day. Stephanie felt this would bring her good luck, as Bruce wished. But it was not the time for a sentimental talk.

After an early supper, she vocalized for half an hour and sang the most challenging parts of her arias and ensembles, taking care not to over-sing. After that, she quickly changed into her concert attire and took a cab to the Italian Cultural Society.

❧ ❧

Stephanie found the concert hall already prepared for the performance. The podium and music stand stood solemnly at downstage center. Surrounding them, chairs and music stands were neatly arrayed in several rows for soloists and orchestra members. Upstage, the chairs for the chorus looked a little cramped, but were arranged with as much space as possible. The art objects were flying where they had been at the dress rehearsal. The subtitle screen remained secure at the top of the proscenium arch.

She checked the fifth floor. The chorus members were arriving gradually. Some were just chatting, and others were changing clothes. On the fourth floor she went to the room assigned to the conductor. She found Arthur, already in his formal tailcoat with a white tie, accompanied by Claudia and Mr. Zappia. Claudia was dressed in a wine-colored evening gown set off by an exquisite emerald necklace that glinted against her slender white neck. Mr. Zappia wore an evening jacket with a black bowtie. With his white hair and mustache, he looked like a Roman aristocrat. The chairman's eyes lit up at the sight of Stephanie. Last time he had seen her, she had been clad in blue jeans and a sweater from used clothing stores. This evening, in her concert dress, she must have looked more like the daughter of a billionaire. He kissed her hand with utmost respect. He informed her, his face beaming, that the hall had been sold out this evening. Arthur hugged Stephanie. Her heart soared.

"Stephanie, you look beautiful," Claudia said. "I wish you the best of luck with Musette." Her voice held no trace of cynicism, jealousy, or enmity.

Acknowledging Claudia, Stephanie withdrew to the makeshift dressing room in the library assigned to the female soloists. Jennifer was already there, wearing a black formal dress with a shimmering pearl necklace and matching earrings. Her green eyes shone.

"You look absolutely fabulous," Stephanie said in whisper to save her voice.

She reported the sold-out house. Jennifer clapped her hands, saving her voice as well.

"How are your arm and leg?" Stephanie asked.

"They don't hurt anymore," Jennifer said. "I'm in a good shape."

Stephanie informed her that Arthur had secured another understudy for Mimi in case, so Jennifer shouldn't push herself too hard to sing the role. But Jennifer seemed all right.

Next Stephanie visited the conference room assigned to male soloists. She found all in their tailcoats and white ties. They were vocalizing. She let them know about the sold-out concert, to which they responded with high thumbs-ups.

"Schaunard is ready," Glenn said, beaming. "Don't worry. I won't let you down."

"Marcello can sing anytime," Henry whispered.

"Rodolfo is also in *primo* condition," said John. "I've dedicated this concert to my pa and grandpa. I feel their presence."

She talked about Mike. They regretted the situation and sympathized with him. But there was nothing they could do for him. He would have to rebuild his reputation from scratch. In the meantime, they had their concert to worry about—particularly the switch-over to the understudy.

"We'll be counting on you," she said, facing Glenn.

"I'll do my best," he promised.

He smiled affectionately at her. She faltered and left quickly to check on the orchestra members, most of whom had arrived. She stopped at Arthur's room and reported that Glenn was well prepared and that Jennifer was in a good condition. The last-moment disaster had been averted.

Responding to the ten-minute call, the chorus members started moving onto the stage in an orderly line, coordinated by their leaders. The orchestra members also streamed onto the stage. Stephanie asked all soloists for Act I to come to the third floor and stand by.

At half past seven, Stephanie signaled the stage manager to dim the lights in the hall. The audience side went dark, while the

Yorker Keith

stage became brighter. People's rustling and chatting subsided. After the entry of the concertmaster, the orchestra members tuned their instruments. The entire hall grew hushed. Stephanie announced to the audience that due to an emergency, this evening Schaunard would be sung by Glenn McKenzie instead of Mike Walton. She signaled the soloists to come on stage. Men first, in the order of Barbemuche, Un Becero, Gaudenzio, Colline, Schaunard, Rodolfo, and Marcello. Then the ladies took their places: Mimi, Musette, and Eufemia. The audience welcomed them with friendly applause. Stephanie felt the stage lights too glaring until her eyes adjusted. Then she felt a wave of satisfaction. Every seat in the audience was occupied.

Arthur made his entrance. Warm applause again filled the hall. He shook the concertmaster's hand, then went to the podium and took a deep bow, facing the audience. As he raised his upper body, he gazed across the hall from right to left, smiling at the sight of the sold-out house. He turned to face the orchestra and lifted his baton. Profound stillness fell upon the hall.

Arthur nodded to the soloists and gave a signal to Gaudenzio, who stood up. Arthur turned to the orchestra to make sure that they were ready. He raised his right hand with the baton while gesturing the light and swift mood with his left hand. He took a deep breath and gave the cue. The orchestra started playing the introduction in *andante mosso*.

So began the other *La Bohème*.

◖◗

On the following Tuesday morning, Stephanie bought the *New York Times* on the way to the Café Momus. In the changing room of the restaurant, she nervously perused the concert review portion of the newspaper. There it was.

> The Other *La Bohème*
> The Italian Cultural Society Hall
> By William Tumbrel
>
> For most opera lovers, *La Bohème* is synonymous with Puccini, whereas Ruggiero Leoncavallo's *La Bohème,* which is based on the same novel as Puccini's, has been long forgotten. Since the New York premiere of the latter in 1977, the opera has been rarely performed. Therefore, it was refreshingly enjoyable to hear the revival of this neglected work by the gifted young conductor Arthur DeSoto, leading the New York Bel Canto Opera in a concert version last Saturday.
>
> Stellar performances were heard from soprano Jennifer Schneider (Mimi), mezzo-soprano Stephanie Frank (Musette), tenor Henry Anderson (Marcello), and baritone John Bertucci (Rodolfo), each of whom sang superbly. Schaunard was sung by baritone

Glenn McKenzie, an understudy, who covered an emergency situation.

Mr. DeSoto provided a sensitive, intelligent, spirited interpretation of Leoncavallo's score. The small but refined pickup orchestra and supporting soloists did their best to sustain the high vocal standard lavishly displayed by the principal soloists. The chorus, loyal followers of Mr. DeSoto, contributed no small part to the polished performance. The English subtitles helped the audience to follow the opera. Artwork flying over the stage complemented the music.

The challenging nature of an event such as this may be further restricted by budget constraints, particularly for a second-tier opera company like Mr. DeSoto's. There were ten soloists, three of whom sang double roles, with a thirty-piece orchestra and a fifty-member chorus. However, the risk Mr. DeSoto took was handsomely rewarded by the presence of an appreciative audience in a sold-out house.

Nonetheless, my only complaint is the frugal production. Considering the caliber of the conductor and the soloists, it would have been only just had the concert been presented more generously—for example, with an eighty-piece orchestra and a one-hundred-member

chorus at a larger venue like Carnegie Hall. It is
a pity that such a talented company as the New
York Bel Canto Opera has to struggle financially. I understand that the Italian Cultural
Society is trying to establish an endowment to
support the company as the opera company
in residence. I am sure that New York would
deeply appreciate such a move.

The performance will be repeated on the
next two Saturdays.

Thrilled, Stephanie waved the paper at Père Momus, who read
the review aloud to his lunch customers. She asked him to excuse her
for an hour so she could e-mail the review to all involved in the company. She hurried to the office. Arthur had already read the review,
of course. They embraced in joy. Since Bill Tumbrel was reputed to
be a merciless opera critic, this review was the best they could expect
from him. She sent the review to all participants and asked them to
forward it to everyone they knew, inviting them to the remaining
two performances. She also asked the company's webmaster to post
it on the New York Bel Canto website. Arthur wrote his own letter
of appreciation and e-mailed it with the attachment to the officials
of the Italian Cultural Society, Mr. Frank, and Ambassador Biondi.

A few days later the *Wall Street Journal* and the *New York
Post* ran their reviews, which also praised the professional quality of
the performance. Stephanie heard WQXR, the sole classical station
in the New York metropolitan region, announcing the intriguing

performance of the other *La Bohème* and giving away the complimentary tickets she had sent.

The added publicity seemed to generate more interest among opera lovers. According to the box office, Stephanie was informed, ticket sales were picking up. The second performance was quickly filling, and the last performance was nearly sold out.

The following Saturday the house was about ninety percent full. Since this was the second performance, everyone felt more relaxed. The performance went as well as the first, Stephanie thought.

《◎ ◎》

By the day of the final performance, *New York Magazine* had featured a rave review, which seemed to tickle the curiosity of those who might not otherwise be operagoers. According to the box office, the house was sold out, but in order to meet popular demand, standing room tickets had been issued, and they were selling well even on the day of the performance.

Stephanie had worn the same dress to the previous two performances, the one she had worn to the Graces opening. For the final performance, she wanted something different. Using more money from her father's gift, she had bought a long velvet gown in a champagne color. She slipped it on and swept her hair into an elegant chignon. Then she added a platinum necklace with a large glittering ruby and matching earrings, once her mother's.

Lately, since she had been preoccupied with the rehearsals as both a singer and the general manager, she had not had time to think of her mother. The necklace brought back her memory. Stephanie longed for her mother to be at the concert this evening. *Mom, I'll dedicate this concert to you. I'll sing at my best ever. Listen to me from above.*

The final performance began flawlessly. The soloists and choristers had had a week to rest. They sang confidently in their richest voices, Stephanie thought. While singing, she felt the opera proceeding quickly.

Act I presented an explosion of merriment on Christmas Eve at the Café Momus. Act II continued the celebration of the young bohemians' love and joy, yet foreshadowed a change with Mimi's reluctant desertion. In Act III the mood darkened, as Rodolfo and Schaunard had lost their lovers. Marcello was to lose Musette, too. Mimi returned only to be rejected by Rodolfo. Fervent and tormenting exchanges among principal soloists swelled the air of the hall. By Act IV, one short year after Act I, all love was lost. What a change. What misery. At the end of the opera, Jennifer moaned Mimi's dying words, "*Natale! Natale!*" ("Christmas! Christmas!") while the orchestra played its part in quintuple *piano*. Then Arthur raised his baton high and gave the cue with full force, triggering the orchestra to play the majestic finale of the tragedy in *fortissimo*.

So ended the other *La Bohème*.

There was a deep silence in the hall. Stephanie heard actual sobbing, not from the audience, but from the stage. She saw John weeping openly, while gazing at the portraits of his father and his grandfather, which his mother held high at her chest in the center middle row of the audience, where she had sat for every performance. Jennifer was also looking intensely at Aunt Maggie and her family, while Henry was gazing at Christine and his family.

Then applause came gradually like a tsunami in slow motion, climaxing in overwhelming cheers. All the patrons stood and clapped furiously, shouting their kudos.

"Bravo!"

"Bravo!"

"Bravissimo!"

Arthur turned to the audience and took several deep bows. He extended his hands to the soloists, who bowed as well. Stephanie felt numb…then ecstatic.

Several patrons rushed to the front and presented fragrant bouquets to the female soloists. Jennifer and Stephanie received them graciously. Among the patrons Stephanie saw her father. He leaned to the stage and offered her an exquisite bouquet, repeating, "Wonderful! Wonderful!" She accepted it with a grateful smile and nod, tears streaming down her cheeks.

Arthur gestured to the orchestra members to stand. They took a bow. The applause continued. Arthur signaled the soloists to retreat offstage, then followed. As soon as he reached the offstage wing, Stephanie hugged him passionately. The other soloists did the same or firmly shook Arthur's hand. Then they congratulated themselves.

"We made it!"

"We did it!"

The applause and shouts from the audience had not stopped. Stephanie suggested all soloists appear on the stage again. They took another bow. Arthur returned and bowed, then clasped his hands before him in gratitude to the audience. The jubilant standing ovation seemed never to fade away.

Finale

*T*he Dolci Quattro entered the second floor lobby for the reception. A mob of exuberant family members, friends, and patrons rushed to them, applauding, congratulating, saluting, hugging, kissing, shaking hands, and patting shoulders. Snapping party favors were fired toward them, sending merry noises, colorful tapes, and confetti in the air. They were showered with rose petals of red, pink, yellow, and white. Countless wine glasses were raised in toast to their talents, as they were half-blinded by incessant camera flashes, as if they were celebrities.

In the midst of the euphoric chaos, the Dolci Quattro observed each member mingling among their family and friends.

They saw Jennifer embrace Aunt Maggie, her parents, and her brother's family. Richard coyly presented her with a stunning bunch of flowers. With a smile she accepted it like a tribute from an old friend whose offense had been forgiven.

They saw Stephanie receive the blessings of her stepmother and half-siblings, introduced by her father. A warm air of reunion enveloped the new family. She occasionally looked up with a longing stare, probably reporting on her triumph to her mother. Bruce presented her with a small but elegant bouquet. Receiving it with a smile, she embraced him. Her father ushered Bruce to meet his family.

They saw Henry introduce Christine to his mother and the families of his brother and his sister. Christine, her face flushed, appeared happy to be welcomed. George seemed to have approved Henry's opera career. Henry's mother and Judith were clearly proud of his singing.

They saw John kiss his mother, who was still clutching the portraits of his father and grandfather. He kissed the portraits, too, as his mother soaked yet another white lace handkerchief with tears. Michelle stood beside him, gently holding his arm.

They threw their arms around Arthur, whose face shone in pride and joy. They hugged Claudia, who returned them a graceful smile.

They took in the congratulations from Mike and Vicky, who were now engaged. They thought that Mike had made a right decision. They wanted to help him rebuild his opera career.

They beamed at the compliments from Père Momus, the Graces, and Kate.

They felt honored to receive congratulations from Ambassador Biondi. They were surrounded by dozens of diplomats from Italian, French, and other missions. They felt as if they were enjoying international fame.

They heard from Mr. Zappia that the Executive Board of the Italian Cultural Society had approved the establishment of the endowment. Since the annual meeting of the Society usually followed the Executive Board's recommendations, the formal approval of the endowment in the annual meeting was all but a done deal. The New York Bel Canto Opera would be the Society's opera company in residence, and the Dolci Quattro would be the company's singers in residence.

They had shared the burdens of life together since they had formed the Dolci Quattro years earlier. Now they felt their bond growing closer than ever.

Once the initial excitement waned, they reflected. Yes, they had achieved a grand milestone in their professional opera careers. However, their personal lives still remained challenging. They had endured their hardships because they placed the opera as their highest priority. This did not mean that their private lives were less important. No, they were inseparable from the opera singers' pursuits. So the battle was not yet over.

This evening, however, they wanted to relish their success. *Just this evening. Let us celebrate. We deserve that, don't we?* They toasted each other with glasses of water. How delicious it tasted.

Mr. Carré approached them and introduced two representatives from the Lyric Opera of Chicago: Mr. Walter Reihwald, Associate Artistic Administrator, and Ms. Nancy Welsh, Casting Coordinator. After greetings, Mr. Reihwald announced that Jennifer, Stephanie, Henry, and John had been awarded the roles of Mimi, Musette, Marcello, and Rodolfo, respectively, as they had applied for Leoncavallo's *La Bohème*. It would be a fully staged opera, conducted by the maestro Victor Carré in December of next year. The representatives congratulated them.

The Dolci Quattro stared at the representatives, completely mute. According to Mr. Carré, by the end of last week, Mr. Reihwald and Ms. Welsh had completed their initial evaluation of the Dolci Quattro's applications. The two had also read the reviews of the performance. Mr. Carré had invited them to New York this evening as part of the final evaluation. They had made the decision on the spot. Mr. Carré, grinning at the Dolci Quattro as if they were his favorite pupils, reiterated that in December of next year, they would be performing the fully staged version of the other *La Bohème* under his baton with the full orchestra and the full chorus of the Lyric Opera of Chicago at the Civic Opera House in Chicago.

It finally sank in. The Dolci Quattro erupted into jubilee. They hugged each other and jumped around. Mr. Carré fondly beckoned them to calm down. They shook the hands of Mr. Reihwald, Ms. Welsh, and Mr. Carré.

What an evening, the Dolci Quattro thought. *What a turn of events. Our aspiration has finally borne fruit, marking the rise of the Dolci Quattro. From now on the world will be watching us. More than that, the universe will be listening to us. Do we not see the glowing spotlights upon us? Do we not hear the thundering bravos? Look at that crowd, shouting their tribute to us. This is not a dream anymore. We are going to do it. December, next year.*

The Dolci Quattro saw, in the gleaming lights of the crystal chandeliers on the ceiling, the Muses singing, dancing, and playing the lyre and the flute.

Rejoice. Rejoice.

Rejoice. Rejoice.

The Dolci Quattro felt fresh courage swelling inside them. They gathered in a circle. They solemnly presented their right hands forward, their palms stacked one on top of the other.

"Sing on!"

CURTAIN

Acknowledgments

The scenes of opera preparation and performance are based on the author's experience with opera companies, workshops, and private lessons. The author is grateful to all those with whom he has had occasion to sing.

The references to the music score of Ruggero Leoncavallo's *La Bohème* are from the version by Casa Musicale Sonzogno di Piero Ostali, Milan, Italy.

Quotes of Biblical passages, prayer, psalm, and marriage vows are from *The New Oxford Annotated Bible*, New Revised Standard Version, Third Edition, Oxford University Press, New York, 2001; and *The Book of Common Prayer*, Oxford University Press, New York, 1990.

About the Author

Yorker Keith lives in Manhattan, New York City. He holds an MFA in creative writing from The New School. His literary works have been recognized four times in the William Faulkner–William Wisdom Creative Writing Competition as a finalist or a semifinalist, including this novel, *The Other La Bohème*.

Opera has been his passion since his adolescent years. He has sung operas in workshops, at private lessons, and with opera companies, both in concert versions and, on many occasions, performing on stage with full costume and makeup. He has studied acting, painting, and drawing. He loves literature and reads widely. He has been living in Manhattan for many years. He knows how challenging life is for opera singers, musicians, artists, actors, writers, and poets. In this novel, *The Other La Bohème*, he has tried to portray the lives of present-day bohemians as he has lived among them. He is not only the author of this novel, but also part of it.

Praises to Yorker Keith's Debut Novel (2016)

Remembrance of Blue Roses

"A skillful tale that explores relationship nuances and redemption."
—*Kirkus Reviews*

"A gem of a novel, providing a deep and satisfying journey with flesh-and-blood characters, excellent writing that occasionally soars to memorable heights, and a fearless exploration of the complexity of falling in love with a person who, while irresistible and reciprocal, is also attached to a dear friend who deserves loyalty. Highly recommended!"
—*The Columbia Review*

"Yorker Keith's *Remembrance of Blue Roses* is a slow-burning, passionate literary novel that speaks to the romantic in all of us."
—*Chanticleer Book Reviews*

"A deftly crafted, multi-layered, compelling read from beginning to end, *Remembrance of Blue Roses* establishes novelist Yorker Keith as an extraordinarily gifted storyteller."
—*Midwest Book Review*